The WEDDING PARTY

Diane,

Enjoy!

Cheryl J. McCullough

The WEDDING PARTY

Cheryl J. McCullough

TATE PUBLISHING
AND ENTERPRISES, LLC

Published by Tate Publishing & Enterprises, LLC
127 E. Trade Center Terrace | Mustang, Oklahoma 73064 USA
1.888.361.9473 | www.tatepublishing.com

Tate Publishing is committed to excellence in the publishing industry. The company reflects the philosophy established by the founders, based on Psalm 68:11,
"The Lord gave the word and great was the company of those who published it."

Published in the United States of America
ISBN: 978-1-61862-123-8
1. Fiction / African American / General
2. Fiction / Family Life
12.01.06

ACKNOWLEDGMENTS

As always, I thank God for His love, His grace, and His mercy. I thank Him for Jesus and for salvation and everlasting life and for the promptings and the manifestations of the Holy Spirit.

To my sons, Darius and Jared. I thank God daily for trusting me to be your mother. You hold the biggest piece of my heart. Thank you for your agape love and for your support and your patience and for making me laugh. I pray that you will prosper in all things and be in health, even as your souls prosper.

To Bishop Terrell L. Murphy, my pastor and spiritual father. Thank you for who you are in my life. You have given me the keys, the courage, the desire to walk into my destiny.

To my family and friends and my family at New Birth-Charlotte Church, thank you for your love and support and your prayers.

PROLOGUE

The sanctuary of Hattiesville Community Church was a gorgeous edifice, much too beautiful for the event taking place that day. There were dozens of flowers across the front of the church. The family filed past the stunningly beautiful casket as they were preparing for the visitation. They would have to smile and greet the thousands of people who had come to pay their respects while not being able to make sense of any of it. There were sobs and outbursts as they viewed the remains of what was such a young, successful, and significant life. Their favorite praise and worship songs filled the air, and though they served to set the atmosphere, a sadness and unbelief was still very present. Nobody would question God out loud, but they all did privately, in their personal time with Him. There seemed to be no peace, no comfort, no level of understanding. A note in a card said, "God does all things well." What was well about this?

ONE

Leah Robinson looked absolutely gorgeous standing before the full-view mirror in the fitting room of Bella Maria Couture. Her size-eight figure complemented the beautiful pearl white wedding gown with the tea-length front and the waltz-length back. She had considered five other designs, finally choosing this one, and Bella Maria Valez, the shop owner and couturier, personally made it.

Kathy agreed that it was the one. "Sis, you look fabulous."

"You don't think it's too contemporary, do you?"

"I think it's perfect. Now hurry up and get out of it. You still have to choose attire for your honor attendant and the other attendants."

Maria wanted to get Leah finished before she started on the others. She would have one of the other seamstresses assist with the work on those.

"Don't forget the mother of the bride," Katherine Robinson said as she observed her two daughters. She was so happy for her older daughter. Leah had been through so much. The Robinsons were a praying family, and they all knew that only prayer had seen them through. Mrs. Robinson thought of how her husband, Bishop Lee Robinson, would feel when he gave his baby away.

Leah, her mother, sister, and future sister-in-law, Gretchen, had started making wedding plans four months before, after Grant Sturdivant, Leah's sweetie, had surprised her and proposed. The wedding was still months away, but it seemed like they had not even scratched the surface of all the details.

Grant had volunteered for the Army as soon as he had graduated from high school and decided to make it a career. His family tried to talk him out of reenlisting when the United States invaded Iraq, but he wouldn't change his mind.

"Mama, I know what I'm doing. If I don't go back, the time I've spent in the military won't account for much. The benefits are good, and I can see the world."

Again, when he proposed to Leah, his family thought he would get out. His mother prayed he would.

Grace Sturdivant was forty-one when Grant and Gretchen were born. She and her husband, Paul, had been married seventeen years and had long since given up on ever having a family. And at age twenty-seven, they were still her children and she was still overprotective.

Before the threesome left Bella Maria's, they had chosen a design in apple green for the mother of the bride and salmon pink for the attendants. They had had a full day, but Katherine Robinson felt it had been worth it. They were all ready for dinner.

"We're going to Lola's," Katherine cut in. "Call your daddy and tell him to meet us there in thirty minutes."

Lola's was a family restaurant owned by a family from the Robinsons' church. Lola was the matriarch of the family and the mother of the community. Before she passed, her family had opened Lola's for lunch only and three years later were serving breakfast, lunch, and dinner seven days a week. She would be proud of what they had done. Their latest venture was catering, and Leah planned to ask them to cater her wedding reception.

Katherine, Kathy, and Leah arrived at Lola's, greeted the people they knew, and sat down to wait on Bishop Robinson. The discussion of wedding flowers was interrupted by the sound of a child's cry. Leah turned around and looked into an unfriendly face. It was Janis Mitchell and her two-year-old daughter, Carmen. Leah hadn't seen Janis in a long time, and the memories flooded her mind.

Janis Mitchell was a teller at the bank when Leah first came in contact with her. They met when Janis handled a transaction Leah was taking care of for Grant.

"Is this the Grant Sturdivant who has a twin sister named Gretchen?"

"Yes," replied Leah. "Do you know them?"

"Yes. Gretchen and I used to work together, and she introduced me to Grant. We dated for a while. Tell him Janis Mitchell said hello."

There was something about that hello that Leah didn't like. When Leah gave Grant Janis' message, he laughed and went on to explain that what she had said was true, that they were introduced by Gretchen and had spent some nonproductive time together. Leah didn't ask many more questions because she didn't feel that the subject was worth pursuing, especially over the telephone.

Bishop Robinson finally came in, and most of the people in the restaurant knew him. He was a celebrity of sorts in the small community of Hattiesville, a suburb of Charlotte. He was the very successful pastor of the Hattiesville Community Church, which split from another local church. Sixteen years later, that congregation of three hundred was now over ten thousand and was a church outside the four walls. Politicians came to Bishop Robinson for his support and the support of his congregation. Business leaders courted his congregation, and local employers wanted his people to work for their companies.

When Leah and Grant started to make wedding plans, there wasn't much need to discuss attendants. They both knew who they wanted and, for that matter, who the other would want. Of course, Kathy would be the maid of honor. Jillian Strauss, her close friend, and Gretchen would be the bridesmaids.

Enoch Casebier, Grant's lifetime friend, would be the best man, and Clay Sturdivant, Grant's cousin, would be the head usher. Grant really wanted his father to stand with him, but Paul's situation was so uncertain. He had thanked his son for asking but said he would rather not.

Paul had been paralyzed as the result of a doctor's mistake. He walked into the hospital and came out paralyzed from the chest down. He had had a procedure done to his spine that doctors do fairly regularly, but something went terribly wrong. Paul had been in that condition for eight years. He had more good days than bad days, but every day was a struggle. He was able to use his arms and hands, but he didn't have much strength. He had no feelings below his rib cage. What he was most thankful for was that his mind was good; he could hear, see, and speak. He had embraced the scripture that stated he should be content with his circumstance.

Enoch Casebier and Grant had been friends for most of their lives. The Casebiers lived next door to Clay and his family when they were all growing up. Enoch was the proprietor of a very successful business, but not without a lot of hard work and sacrifice. Enoch wanted to go to college, but the opportunity didn't present itself. He could drive, and he made the best of it. He had driven a school bus in high school and had no trouble getting a job driving a delivery truck for an office supply company after graduation. He took a few business classes at the local community college and dreamed of owning his own business. He often remarked that his father told him, "Son, it's okay to work for the man, but God bless the child who's got his own." When Enoch's father died, Enoch stood over his grave and promised him he would have his own.

Casebier Collection started as a trash pick-up service for families outside the city limits who had to pay for trash collection. He started with a pickup truck and doing his own billing by hand. In five years, it had grown to four trash collection trucks, one recycle truck, a computer system, a website, and a full-time administrative assistant.

Enoch married Kirby Flowers three years into the business. Kirby had worked for the company that sold Casebier the computer and software package to use in the business. She had trained him on the system and had agreed to be his consultant on setting up his profiles. Eventually, she became his part-time assistant. They were inseparable from that point. He asked her to marry him after they courted for almost a year. They were married two months later.

It was Kirby's idea to investigate including recycling. The trash collection business was good, and she felt like those same customers would pay a little more to have their recyclable trash handled separately. "Recycling is fashionable," she told him, "and practical." They started by putting the recyclable trash in the back of the pickup, bringing it back to the warehouse and sorting it all out. He couldn't afford to hire another driver, so he had to drive himself. The first day on the route in the new truck, Kirby left a note on the seat that said, "God blesses the child who drives his own."

If asked to describe his marriage, Enoch would say, "Near perfect." They were in business together, but Kirby was very much his wife. She took care of him and their home, and that was the way they both wanted it. When she woke up in the morning, she knew everything was all right. Enoch worked hard—very hard. He often quoted what he had heard Bishop Robinson say many times: "Success is intentional." Enoch intended to be very successful.

TWO

He couldn't believe he was close enough to her to touch her. She was so beautiful. She had smooth, caramel-colored skin and dark-brown eyes. He had seen her in church many times, but she always managed to get away. Her hair was immaculate and her smile beautiful. And to complement it all, her twin daughters were beautiful too. Their complexion was darker, but they definitely had their mother's eyes and smile.

Standing in line at the grocery store with Grammy and Auntie Avis wasn't the time to introduce himself. But if Grammy would take one step to the right, he could touch her.

Ben awakened from his daydream to hear Grammy and Auntie Avis talking with the little girls. As they walked out of the store, following their mother, one of them said, "Bye, Minister Coffey."

Minister Benjamin Coffey had been the youth minister at Hattiesville Community Church for two years. He had come back to Hattiesville a few years after graduating from seminary in Dallas. The bishop had asked him to come back. He packed up and moved. Hattiesville was his home, but it was never his intention to return.

He knew it would be hard to go back home and hard to go back to the church where he grew up. He knew he would have to overcome his past, the stuff he and his friends had done growing up. Some of the youth were the children of his childhood friends.

Victoria Coffey and Avis Johnson were sisters who found themselves at a point in life where they needed each other. Auntie

Avis had lost her husband, and Grammy insisted she move back to Hattiesville. So Avis Johnson sold the home she and her husband lived in for thirty-five years and raised their children in and moved in with her older sister, Victoria.

Ben was glad they were under one roof, but he could only laugh at the possibility of all the things the two sisters could cook up. He loved the two old ladies, and they loved him. Grammy had done a good job raising Ben and educating him. He was the only child of her only child. Ben was born out of wedlock, and his mother had died in an automobile accident when he was only three years old. Grammy and Grandpa never considered Ben going to live with any of the other family members. Avis did manage to get him out of Hattiesville and to the city on holidays and summer vacation. After Grandpa died, Avis offered to take Ben and raise him, but Victoria wouldn't hear of it. The family thought a twelve-year-old boy was too much for the older woman, but she wouldn't hear of him leaving, and he had no intention of going.

Ben loaded the groceries in the trunk and climbed into the car. The conversation was in full swing.

"It's a sin and a shame you can't even buy toilet tissue with that food stamp card," said Victoria.

"Yes, it is," agreed Avis. "What in the world are people supposed to do?"

"Honey, you know that card has to last the whole month, and with two children to feed, I imagine it doesn't go far."

"Well, she's a pretty thang, and so are those little girls, and mannerable too. Know how to look you in the eye when they talk to you."

Ben interrupted partly because he needed an answer and partly because he just wanted the conversation to move on to something else.

"Auntie, where else do we need to stop?"

"I don't need anything else, sugar."

"What about you, Victoria?" Avis asked.

"Nothing else for me either. Benji, you are staying for dinner?" It was half a question and half a command.

"I'll be back around six. I need to get a haircut and pick up my shirts." As soon as it was out of his mouth, he regretted saying it.

"I don't know why you insist on paying somebody to wash and press your shirts when I can do that for you," Grammy said for the hundredth time. "Just a waste of money."

There was no need to respond. They had had that conversation more times than they needed to. In the same breath, Grammy asked if he wanted broccoli or squash.

"Why can't I have both?"

Belinda Stewart was the widow of Marine First Class Canady Stewart and the mother of Brittani Candice and Candy Brianna Stewart. She lost her husband in the Iraq war.

Belinda had been devastated. She still had nightmares of the day the two men in uniform came to her door to deliver the news that her beloved Canady had been killed.

There was no air in the room. Everything was going black. Her ears were ringing, and her head was hurting. Some man that she didn't know had his arm around her waist. Her legs weighed a ton. She could hear someone screaming, and it took a minute for her to realize it was her. Why were these two men in the crisp dress uniforms telling her that her husband had been killed? One of them was asking who he could call. She couldn't answer. The other one noticed her cell phone, picked it up, and started to scroll through the address book. Fortunately, she had an "ICE" —in case of emergency—entry. He pressed the button, but the phone went immediately to voice mail.

A knock at the door took the attention off Belinda for a split second. With no hesitation, Lorraine came in. She knew when she saw the two marines there that it was not good news. Belinda was hysterical and fell into Lorraine's arms. She asked the men if they were there for the reason she thought. They asked who she was, family or friend. She explained she was a friend and neighbor and that her husband was a marine commander. They officially told her that Marine Canady Stewart had been killed. They asked if she could contact family. She said she would, and Lorraine dismissed the marines. She sat and held Belinda for what seemed like hours.

Kirby had one message on her cell phone. She listened to it twice. She was afraid to return the call. It simply said the caller was marine somebody, US Marine Corps, and that she should call Belinda Stewart as soon as possible. Kirby knew she had to gather her strength, so she called Enoch first.

Kirby handed Enoch the phone. He listened to the message and sat down. Without missing a beat, he pulled Kirby into his arms and started to pray. He asked God for strength, the right words to say and to know what to do. He prayed that God would give Belinda peace. Enoch made the call.

The ringing phone startled Lorraine and Belinda. Lorraine answered and talked to Enoch. She told him what she knew and handed the phone to Belinda. He simply told Belinda that Kirby was on her way. Enoch packed Kirby a bag between hugs and wiping tears, took her to the airport, and bought a ticket to California. Kirby had made the flight to Camp Pendleton many times before. This was the first time she didn't want to go.

Kirby and Belinda were sisters in every sense of the word except biologically. They had grown up in the same foster home. Belinda went to college in North Carolina, and Kirby went to college in South Carolina. They never physically lived together again, but they were never further away than the phone. Kirby graduated, got a job with a software company, and married a great guy with his own business. Belinda got pregnant, married a great guy who was a Marine, and had two beautiful daughters.

He wanted a career in law enforcement and wanted her to finish her degree in nursing.

A few months after Canady passed, Kirby and Enoch moved Belinda and the girls to Hattiesville. For the first few months, Kirby walked with Belinda step by step. One of the major decisions they made together was for Belinda to go back to college to finish her nursing degree. Kirby put Belinda in touch with Leah Robinson, a nurse manager at a hospital in Charlotte. Leah helped Belinda negotiate the process, and Auntie K stepped in to help with the twins.

Over the two years that Belinda, Brittani, and Brianna had lived in Hattiesville, they had done a good job of acclimating into the community. Belinda was doing well in school and was a few weeks from doing the clinical part of her training. One of her instructors had recommended that she take the additional courses to become a surgical nurse. Originally, she didn't consider it, but one Sunday, Bishop Robinson's message convicted her for selling herself short, for not living up to her full potential. He had reminded the congregation that before the foundation of the world, they had agreed with God to fulfill a purpose in the Earth. Belinda knew that nursing was her calling, her ministry. She also knew that she had thrown herself into her studies to keep from dealing with the hole in her heart.

$\mathscr{T}$HREE

One of the first things discussed in orientation for the mentoring program was not to get personally involved with the mentees' parents. Clay knew better, had heard it and even said it in the few orientations he led for the agency, but he had crossed that invisible line. Clay was a confirmed bachelor, the "playa" of the group. Enoch was married and Grant was engaged, but Clay was content not being committed. Clay became involved with the Hattiesville Big Brothers program several years before. Jeremy's mother, Delia, enrolled Jeremy in the program when he was suspended from school for fighting. Delia was a single mother of two children, ten-year-old Jeremy and his six-year-old sister, Crystal.

Clay was immediately attracted to Delia. He didn't know if she was playing hard to get or if she really wasn't interested. He would pick Jeremy up from school on Thursday for dinner and usually saw him every other Saturday. Occasionally, they would see each other at other times, but that was the usual routine. Jeremy's attitude was better since he started spending time with Clay, but it was a work in progress.

One evening, Delia called Clay to ask him if he could possibly switch days the following week and take Jeremy to the barbershop on Wednesday before a school play on Thursday night. She had never asked him to do anything like take Jeremy to the barbershop, but he decided it was okay. Of course, Jeremy invited him to attend the play. He was the stage manager, and Crystal was in the choir. Clay agreed. He knew it would be good for Jeremy, and he could afford to sacrifice the time.

The third time Delia called and asked for a favor, the phone call lasted thirty minutes. Twenty-five minutes of the conversation had very little to do with Jeremy. Clay wasn't sure if he was getting mixed signals from her or if she simply needed someone to talk to. She told him about some of her frustrations as a single parent, and he suggested she come to the church and that she investigate being a part of the single parents' ministry.

Delia had not grown up in a family where church was important, so she was not sure how to respond to Clay's recommendation. She told him she would think about it. The truth was Delia had not been to church in years. When she was growing up, she would go once in a while with her childhood friends and her mother would send them to Bible school at the neighborhood church in the summer.

Her parents were good people, but they just didn't go to church. Her father had always worked two jobs, and her mother worked a part-time job, and Sunday was when they rested. With four children, there was always a lot to do. Plus, she didn't want to go to church to be judged because she was a single mother with two children by two different men. She had heard enough of that.

OUR

Leah took two more ibuprofen for her headache. That was six that day. She couldn't keep popping the pills. She knew better, and she knew the headache was more than a regular headache. It was not caused by all the reasons she was telling herself and Kathy. She knew it wasn't the twelve-hour workdays, and she knew she didn't need glasses.

Leah's headaches had started several weeks before. Then came the noise in her ears and the spots in her eyes. Miss Notice-Everything Kathy detected that something was wrong and made Leah promise to go to the doctor.

"For a person who works in health care, you sure aren't proactive about your own health."

"And for the same reason, don't you think I know what I'm doing?"

"No, 'cause your head still hurts. Leah, you need to do something about this. It's been weeks. If you don't, I'm tellin' Ma."

Leah knew she meant it, so she called Jill to see if she would get her an appointment with Dr. Strauss, Jill's dad.

"Jill Strauss. Good morning." She was glad to hear from Leah.

"Hey, Jillie. How are you?"

"Hey, Leah. What's up?"

"My headaches haven't let up, so I need to get an appointment with your dad, I guess."

"Do you want me to call him?"

"Yeah. Please. Kathy is threatening to tell my mom."

21

"I'll call you back in a few minutes."

Jillian Strauss and Leah had become friends as co-captains of the middle school cheerleading squad. Kathy would call Jill Leah's tall, blonde friend. At six feet two inches, she gave up cheerleading for basketball in high school. Jill's family had old money, and her full-time job was to spend it. She was the executive director of the Z. W. Strauss Foundation. The Strauss family was the first non-African American family to join Hattiesville Community Church. Jill wanted to join the first Sunday she attended with Miss Lola, their housekeeper, but her parents said they needed to visit again.

"Who made the rule you can't join on the first visit?" Lola asked Dr. Strauss. He didn't bother to answer her.

Jill went to college, earned a degree in business administration, came home, went to work at the foundation, and took over from her mother two years later. Her great grandfather started it to give his wife something to do. Four generations of Strauss women had managed the foundation, and four generations of Strauss men were doctors. Jill told her mother she wanted a son who could take over the foundation and a daughter to become a doctor.

"Hey, Leah. They will work you in right after lunch. Be there at two. I'll meet you there."

"You don't—"

"I'll meet you there."

Dr. Zachary Strauss Jr. and his son, Dr. Zachary "Trey" Strauss III, had a thriving practice. Dr. Zack was in family practice, and Trey was a general surgeon. Their offices were in the medical park across the street from the hospital. Leah knew them well personally and professionally. Dr. Strauss had often told Leah she could work in his office if she ever tired of the hospital hustle and bustle. Their professional admiration was mutual.

Leah's head was pounding, but it would take less time to walk across the street than get the car out of the deck and drive over.

"Ma'am, are you okay? Ma'am, let me…I need some help over here," yelled the ER security guard.

A second guard brought a wheelchair, and they rolled Leah back into the hospital.

The triage nurse recognized Leah immediately and started yelling orders. The orderlies put her on a stretcher and rolled her into an exam room. Her blood pressure was 180/110, stroke level. She was in and out of consciousness but somehow managed to signal the nurse that her head hurt.

It was unlike Leah to be late, but not unlike her to do one more thing for somebody else before leaving to do something for herself. At 2:30 p.m., Jill called the nurses' station and was told Leah had gone to lunch. No answer on the cell phone. Ten minutes later, still no answer. It would take less than ten minutes to walk over there, and Jill didn't like this.

Trey Strauss was the doctor on call but didn't expect to see his sister's best friend on the table when he walked in. He immediately started barking orders. When Trey called the office an hour later to tell his dad that he was going to admit Leah, Dr. Strauss told him that Jill was there and that they had been expecting Leah in the office. Trey told Jill to call the Robinsons and tell them to come now.

The Robinsons arrived at the hospital to find Leah in intensive care, unconscious. Trey explained that he had given her a heavy sedative so she would sleep and help her blood pressure go down. He also explained that he had called in a neurologist/ neurosurgeon for consultation.

Dr. Zack came in and shook hands with Bishop Robinson, hugged Katherine, and listened as Trey continued to explain. Bishop Robinson looked at Dr. Zack for confirmation. Trey did not take offense. He knew it wasn't personal, and he knew that if the situation was reversed, his dad would have looked to his friend, Lee, for support.

Dr. Zack confirmed what Trey said. He assured the family that he had read the chart and would follow the same procedure at this point. He told them that he knew Dr. Rajagopal, who was the best in his field.

But Dr. Zack had a few more questions. He wanted to know how long Leah had had the headache and high blood pressure. The bishop and first lady looked at each other. Kathy looked at Dr. Zack. Jill spoke up. She admitted that Leah had mentioned the headache to her weeks ago. Kathy said she pulled it out of her about a month ago. Dr. Zack and Trey looked at each other with concern on their faces. Trey spoke first and said that he wanted to check for the results of some tests he was waiting on. Jill and Kathy walked the Robinsons to the waiting room as Jill recounted the events of the day.

Kathy called Grant late that night, after she and Jill convinced the Robinsons to go home. She left a message. She didn't really know what to say to make it better. Jill and Kathy had dozed off in the waiting room. The ringing cell phone startled both of them. It was Grant.

"Hey, G." Kathy tried to sound upbeat. "I'm at the hospital. Leah is sick."

"What do you mean sick?"

"She had a really bad headache yesterday, and her bp was really high. She fainted. Heavy sedation…" Then the tears came. Kathy had not cried until that moment.

Jill could hear Grant yelling and took the phone from Kathy. "Grant, it's Jill." She told him what they knew, including that there was no diagnosis and a specialist had been called in.

"Okay. Let me figure out how I can get there."

"Wait, Grant, at least until tomorrow. Let Trey get some test results, and let the specialist take a look at her."

"You call me the minute you know anything."

"I promise I will."

Kathy reached for the phone. "I'm sorry, G. I hadn't cried, but when I said it out loud, it hit me."

"Have you called Gretchen?"

"No. I wanted you to know first. You know how dramatic Gretchen can be, and I didn't want her to upset your dad."

"Let me call her before she goes to work."

"Do you want me to call your parents?" Kathy asked.

"No. I'll handle it. Kathy, *please* call me the minute you know anything."

"I will. Pray, Grant. Please pray."

For the thirty years Lee and Katherine Robinson had been married, it was the first morning they had not prayed together before either of them did anything else. Katherine found Lee in his office in his chair, obviously praying, tears streaming down his face, the praise music going in the background. She sat down in front of him on the ottoman, took his hands, and put her head on his shoulder. He prayed out loud.

"I decree and declare complete healing and restoration and redeeming of time for Leah in the name of Jesus. Thy kingdom come, Thy will be done. Amen, amen, amen."

It was really early for Dr. Zack to be in the hospital. He didn't have a regular on-call rotation anymore. His explanation was he had "been at this too long to get up in the middle of the night." His early appearance made Jill uneasy. Trey was a few steps behind him with a very tall, absolutely gorgeous man who looked vaguely familiar.

Kathy and Jill met them before they reached the waiting area. Trey made the introductions.

"It is my pleasure to meet you, Miss Robinson, and to finally meet you, Jillie."

He and Trey laughed.

"Please, call me Kathy."

Jill realized that this was the infamous Raja. She had seen pictures and had actually spoken to him on the phone. The pictures didn't do him justice, and the accent was as beautiful as the man. Trey's specialist was very special.

Kathy and Jill started asking questions, one after the other, at the same time before anybody could answer one. Dr. Zack was finally able to get a word in and told them Dr. Raja had just gotten there and hadn't even seen Leah yet. By the time Dr. Zack told Kathy to call her parents, Gretchen, Katherine, Bishop Robinson, and Grace walked down the hall. There were more introductions, hugs, and a few tears. Grace and Katherine held hands tightly. Trey updated everybody and excused himself and the other doctors. Gretchen suggested that Kathy and Jill go home, and the bishop echoed the thought. He said it would be at least an hour before there would be any discussion.

Cerebral aneurysm. In his heart of hearts, Trey knew. Raja confirmed it. She would need immediate surgery. Raja would do the surgery. Trey would assist. Dr. Zack would observe. He knew the bishop would want him there. He would tell the Robinsons while Trey and Raja scrubbed and gave instructions to get Leah prepped.

Dr. Zack went back to the waiting area to tell everybody what he knew. He explained what an aneurysm is and what they had to do.

Gretchen's phone rang. It was Grant.

"Why hasn't somebody called me?"

"We wanted to have something to tell you. Dr. Zack just told us Leah has an aneurysm on her brain."

"Where did that come from?" Grant shouted.

"She's going to surgery right now."

"Surgery? What does that mean? Are they cutting her head? Can't they do something else?"

Gretchen started crying. "Ma, it's Grant. He's crying and screaming."

Grace took the phone and talked to Grant, and he calmed down but was adamant about coming home.

"Grant, honey, wait please. I promise to call you as soon as she's out of surgery. I promise, son. This is major surgery. Her recuperation will be long. She will need you then. The best thing for you to do now, sweetheart, is pray. Leah is going to be your wife. You need to cover her now like you were here."

"Ma, I—"

"I know, son. I've been where you are, but we're looking at weeks, maybe months, and I need you to think and make good decisions."

"Okay, Ma." His voice cracked. "May I speak to Bishop?"

"Lee, Grant wants to speak with you."

"Hello, son. Your mother is right. You don't need to come all the way here now. We'll keep you posted."

"Sir, I just don't want you to think I'm not ready to accept responsibility for Leah. I love her. I just want her to be fine."

"I understand, son, but you will have plenty of time with Leah. She is going to be fine."

"Yes, sir."

Grant didn't know what to do, but he wasn't satisfied. He hung up and called his dad.

"Hello."

"Hey, Dad."

"Hello, son."

"Did Gretchen tell you about Leah?" Grant asked his dad.

"Your mother told me."

"It's an aneurysm on her brain. I just talked to Gretchen," Grant said.

"I'm sorry, son. What's the doctor saying?"

"She has to have surgery. She's probably in surgery right now."

"I only talked to Gretchen, Ma, and Bishop. Trey Strauss and his dad and some specialist are the doctors. Dad, I don't know what to do. I feel so helpless. Leah's dad told me not to come home."

"Wait a minute, Grant. He didn't tell you that to keep you away from Leah. He knows you would have to get special permission to come home, and you know dealing with Uncle Sam would take time. It won't be easy."

"But this is an emergency. Leah is going to be my wife."

"What do you think Leah would say if she knew you were trying to come all the way from Germany?"

Grant had to laugh. He knew where his father was going. He knew Leah would have a fit and tell him that she was a big girl and could take care of herself.

"Yeah, Dad, but if the situation was reversed, she would come see about me."

$\mathscr{F}$IVE

Manavendra Rajagopal was born in India, grew up in London, and was educated in the United States. The only child of working-class parents, the expectations for Manavendra were great. He did not let his parents down, earning academic scholarships for his undergraduate studies and receiving fellowships while in medical school. Manavendra earned extra money working as an interpreter. He was fluent in Punjabi, Hindi, French, Latin, and English. Trey and Manavendra met in medical school and became friends and study partners. Using last names was the norm for those in the study group. Rajagopal was a mouthful, so it quickly became *Raja*.

Raja often told Trey that he was too privileged to appreciate his education. Trey's only defense was he would do great things with his education. He wanted his parents to be proud of him too. Trey told Raja that his grandfather had instilled in all of them a work ethic based on the words of Luke 12:48: "For everyone to whom much is given, from him much will be required." Raja seemed to be satisfied with that.

Often over meals, Trey and Raja discussed God. Trey had confessed Christ as a teenager but was what Lola called a quiet Christian—he didn't talk much about his faith. Because Raja was from a non-Christian background, Trey felt a responsibility to introduce him to Christ. Raja believed in God, but having grown up with Muslims, Hindus, and Sikhs, he considered himself a mutt. He often told Trey that he believed a little of this and a little of that. Trey knew he couldn't beat him over the head with Christianity, but he would drop nuggets as often as he could. In their second year of medical school, Trey led Raja to Christ. That was a first for Trey, and it sealed their relationship.

Later that day, it hit Trey what had happened. He called home to tell his mother, but Lola was the only one there when he called, so he told her. Lola told him that God was pleased but that he had the responsibility to "walk with that young man."

"Does he have a Bible?"

"I don't know"

"If he doesn't, you give him yours."

"Mine! I'll buy him one."

"Zachary Strauss…"

"Miss Lola, I can't give him my Bible, but I'll make sure he has one."

Walking with Raja took a turn one day that Trey didn't expect. Trey walked into the break room to find Raja on his laptop, wearing the same clothes he had left him in the evening before.

"What's up, man? Didn't I leave you in that spot? Have you been here all night?"

"Yes, actually, I have. I needed to finish this translation."

"Why are you working so much?"

Through the course of the conversation, Raja confided in Trey that he was having some financial difficulties. He was going to have to move into a less expensive apartment.

"I know someone who might be looking for a roommate. I'll let you know."

"Thank you, my friend. That will be a tremendous blessing."

Trey wasn't sure why he told Raja that because it wasn't true. But he felt compelled to help his friend, and the look of relief on his face made it all right. He had to figure out what to do to make it good.

He called home to talk to Lola but got his mother instead.

"Is Miss Lola off today?"

"She had a doctor's appointment, so I told her not to worry about coming back out here today."

"Is she all right, Mom?"

"Your dad said she's doing well—actually really well. She's staying on her diet. What are you up to looking for Lola?"

"Um…just needed a recipe and instructions on how to make her chicken broccoli casserole. I'm tired of eating out so much."

"Well, call her at home a little later."

Trey hated not telling his mother the truth, but he and Jill had always discussed things with Lola before telling their parents. Jill said Lola could discern the times and knew if they needed to go forward or go back to the drawing board. Trey wanted to know how he could help his friend, especially since he had offered to.

Lola was one of the few people who called Jill and Trey by their full names. She wasn't fond of nicknames. They never knew their maternal grandmother, but Lola often told Jill and Trey that she was her best friend. Lola had basically raised their mother, Ellen, after her mother passed. And when she married Dr. Zack, the natural progression was for her to continue to care for them and then their children. She also told them that their grandmother didn't care for nicknames either.

"Zachary, where should you be other than on this telephone?" Lola asked as she sat in her recliner, a smile on her face.

"I'm on break, Miss Lola, but I'm going to the clinic at three. How was your visit with my dad?"

"If you're asking about your dad, he was fine. If you're asking about my health, that was fine too." She laughed. "If I could just go there one time and not give them my blood, that would be fine too."

Trey went on to tell Lola about the conversation with Raja.

"That your friend from India?"

"Yes, ma'am."

"Does he have any habits you don't like, eat anything you don't want in your house, or practice any rituals you know to be wrong?"

"No, ma'am. He's a vegetarian, and I don't like debating him on the pros and cons of eating meat, but that's about it."

"Well then, I think you let him move in with you."

"With me?"

"Yes, Zachary, with you. Who's in that other bedroom? Didn't you say you can walk to the campus if you need to? He can pay half the mortgage and won't have a cost for riding the bus. That will help his finances, won't it?"

"Well, yes, but half my mortgage is probably still more than his current rent. I don't need the money, Miss Lola. I could let him stay for free."

"No, Zachary. Don't take away his pride. It ain't good to make a man feel like he can't carry his weight."

"But I don't think he can afford half."

"Then let him pay half of that. And you need to tell your mother what you're going to do. She'll square it with your father."

$\mathscr{S}$IX

Why is Kathy running that vacuum cleaner if she knows I'm trying to sleep? Why is it so cold in here? What is that strange light? I have to do something about this headache. Kathy! Kathy! Why won't she answer me?

Leah's surgery had lasted several hours. Raja was pleased with the result. He had been able to repair the aneurysm. But the next few hours would be critical. He expected her to have some memory loss and maybe even some temporary paralysis. He wanted her to stay sedated for a few hours to assure that her blood pressure didn't go up.

Leah awakened in the recovery room, but she didn't realize where she was or what had happened. She had a tube in her mouth and oxygen in her nose. It had been ten hours since the surgery. She tried to open her eyes, but she was so sleepy. Her eyes felt like they had rocks in them. Her mouth was dry. She wanted to go to the bathroom. But more than anything, her head hurt. The nurse came in to check her vital signs. Leah opened her eyes for only a few seconds. The nurse paged Trey.

Trey and Raja came in, but Leah had dozed off again. Raja checked the chart while Trey tried to wake her.

"Leah, it's Trey. You're in the hospital."

A look of panic crossed her face. Raja looked at Trey and shook his head no.

"Everything is okay. Get some sleep."

She had already closed her eyes.

Raja wasn't happy with Leah's vital signs. He wanted her blood pressure and her heart rate down more. He ordered more tests and asked to see the results of the previous tests.

He explained to Trey that twelve hours after surgery, things should look different.

It had been a while since they had updated the family. Raja needed to check in with his office, so Trey went to the waiting area. Grace was talking to Grant when Trey walked in. He took the phone and explained to Grant with everybody listening that Leah had opened her eyes for a few seconds and that Raja had ordered some additional tests. Trey was very honest with them that she had not progressed to the point they expected that many hours later.

"Trey, be honest, man. Am I going to lose Leah?"

"No, Grant. I don't think that's the case, but her recovery is going to be long and hard."

"Do you think I should come home?"

"Let's make that decision once she's fully awake and we know what her condition really is and what we're facing. We'll keep you posted."

"Mommy, phone. It's Auntie K."

"Hey, Kirby. My answering service told me it was you."

"Hey, Belinda. Did you know about Leah Robinson?"

"Yeah. They told us in class today that she had emergency surgery and probably won't be back this semester," Belinda said. "She had an aneurysm."

"I have really been praying for her. I can't imagine what her family is going through. Enoch went over this morning to check on the bishop and first lady. He said that they were doing well, all things considered. I went to noon Bible study, and we are all fasting and praying for Leah."

"I'll stand in agreement with you and get the girls to fast something too. You know how much they love Leah. I told them she was sick, and we prayed for her. I guess I should tell them the whole story."

Belinda went on to talk about Brittani and Brianna, but Kirby was not responding.

"Kirby, are you there?"

"Oh. Yeah, I'm here."

"What is it, Kirby?"

"I'm not pregnant, Belinda. I'm not pregnant."

"Did your period start, or did you take a test?"

"I took a test. How am I going to tell Enoch again that I'm not pregnant?"

"Did you tell him you missed your period?"

"No."

"Then just don't mention it. It's been long enough, Kirby. You need to go to the doctor."

"What am I going to tell Enoch?"

"The truth. What else?"

"Belinda, he wants children bad. What if I can't get pregnant? You've seen him with the twins."

"We can what-if all night, Kirby, but if you go to the doctor, then you'll know what you need to do. Plus, it might not be you. It might be him."

"Oh, don't say that! That would be worse. He would never accept that."

"He would have to. God does all things well, and if either of you are unable to have kids, then I know He has a plan. You can always adopt."

"But what if—?"

"Kirby, don't do that. You sound like somebody who doesn't know who God is. Don't overanalyze it. Like Bishop always says, 'Be intentional. Do something.' If anybody needs to adopt, it's us anyway. We didn't get adopted, but we were blessed. But we know that's not always the case."

Belinda went on.

"The point is, Kirby, you and Enoch have the resources and the space, and you can adjust your work schedule. You are perfect candidates to adopt. You know, Canady and I were going to adopt some kids, but now…" Her voice trailed off.

"Well, you can adopt some with your new husband."

"I won't ever be able to replace him, Kirby."

"It's not about replacing Canady. It's about allowing you to love and to be loved again."

"I'm not ready, Kirby," Belinda said, her voice cracking.

"How do you know you're not ready?"

"I just know. I still miss him so much. There are days when I don't want to get out of bed. The only reason I do is for the girls."

"Like you told me, it's been long enough, Belinda. You need to get some help."

Belinda went to bed that night and dreamed about Canady. It had been a while since that had happened.

Leah opened her eyes, but she couldn't move. She tried to remember what had happened. She still had a headache, but she knew this wasn't her room. The room was dimly lit, and there was a loud noise that sounded like a vacuum cleaner. Her mouth was dry. She tried to lick her lips, but something was in the way.

The nurse came in, looked at her IV, and then checked her blood pressure. It was good.

"Hi, Leah. It's Kim Horng. You're in the hospital. Relax a few minutes and I'll get Dr. Strauss." She paged Dr. Zack and Trey.

Leah tried to remember.

"Everything is okay. Get some sleep." She thought she remembered somebody saying that to her.

Dr. Strauss? Trey?

"Leah, if you can hear me, blink your eyes," the nurse said.

She blinked twice.

Kim pulled the blanket off Leah's feet. "If you feel me touching your feet, blink your eyes. Nothing. She took the socks off and tried again. Still nothing. Leah's face showed that she knew that wasn't good.

Dr. Raja came in first. Nurse Kim explained what she had done and reported Leah's vitals.

He told Leah who he was and said that Dr. Zack and Trey would be in in a moment. He took the tube out of her mouth. She licked her lips. She tried to say something, but Dr. Raja told her not to try to talk. Trey walked in, and Kim updated him quickly.

"Leah, listen to me carefully. You had to have surgery. Do you remember having a headache?"

"Yes," she whispered.

"You had a cerebral aneurysm. I called in Dr. Raja, and he repaired it."

"I know you can hear me and see me, Leah," Raja said, "but I need to know where you are otherwise."

Dr. Zack came in during Raja's assessment. When it was over, he went to tell the Robinsons and have someone call Grant.

EVEN

Ben stopped at the sub shop to get a foot-long meal, including some macadamia nut cookies. He couldn't believe his eyes. Sitting in a booth in the middle of the room were Brianna and Brittani Stewart. If they were there, their mother probably was too.

Brianna noticed him first. "Minister Coffey, we see you again."

He leaned down to hug her and her sister. From what he knew about them, Brianna was the more outgoing one.

"Which sandwich do you like best?" she asked him.

Belinda was in line, ordering their food, but she turned around to see who Brianna was talking to. Their eyes met. She smiled. He had to do something. He walked over and shook her hand.

"How are you, Mrs. Stewart?"

"I am doing well, Minister Coffey, and please, call me Belinda."

"I will, if you will call me Ben."

Brianna still wanted to know what his favorite sandwich was. He looked at Brittani and asked what she was having.

"Turkey on whole wheat," she answered.

Belinda was at the cash register and told the girls to take their seats. Ben told the cashier to include their order with his.

"Thank you, Min...thank you, Ben."

His phone was vibrating, but he didn't answer it. Brianna invited him to join them. He thanked her but said that he was on his way to meet some people.

Ben remembered the phone as soon as he got outside. It was Bishop Robinson. He should have answered it. He called back immediately.

"Good evening, sir. How are you?"

"I'm doing well, Ben. I was able to get a few hours sleep, and I'm headed back to the hospital."

"How is Leah, sir?"

"She is in intensive care, so I'll know more when I get there."

"What can I do to serve you, Bishop?"

"That's why I called. I want you to deliver the message on Sunday."

"Yes, sir."

The bishop and Ben talked a few minutes more, and then Ben pulled in at his townhouse. The people he was meeting were Enoch and Clay for their Friday night Xbox tournament.

He had plenty of time before they got there, but he couldn't stay at the sub shop and eat with Belinda and the girls. He wasn't sure why. He wasn't shy around women, and the girls made it easy to have something to talk about. Maybe he would mention it to Enoch and Clay. Maybe he wouldn't.

Jeremy's basketball team had a playoff game on Saturday morning. Clay told him he would come. He was spending a lot of time with Jeremy and Delia—too much time with Delia. One night they stayed on the phone all night. One night they sat in her living room all night. One morning he had to sneak out of her bedroom before Crystal and Jeremy awakened.

Clay was way over the top, way too involved. He suggested to Delia that she ask that Jeremy get another Big Brother, but she didn't agree. She didn't think Jeremy would understand, or so she said.

Delia had said dozens of times recently that she didn't want to be in another relationship that didn't have a future. She wasn't sure this one did, and some days she wanted out. But she liked the way Clay made her feel mentally and physically. It was getting harder and harder to hide the relationship from Crystal and Jeremy.

Clay liked Delia, but he wasn't sure he wanted a ready-made family. It was fun spending time with Jeremy and Crystal, but he knew that was not what he wanted every day. Making sure to check Jeremy's report card and planning outings for them was all a part of the job, but he didn't want to be responsible for always setting a good example and for always being available to a family. Clay preferred doing Clay. That's why he was looking forward to his evening with Ben and Enoch.

When they played at Enoch's house, Kirby always prepared healthy snacks, but when they played at Clay's or Ben's, it was usually pizza and ginger ale for Ben and Enoch and cherry soda for Clay.

At the moment, Enoch was the reigning champion. But he was a little distracted that night. He had found the negative pregnancy test. Kirby had not told him she was taking the test. Maybe she wanted to surprise him and, since it was negative, decided not to mention it. That wasn't what distracted him. He was becoming more concerned about why she wasn't pregnant. They had been trying for over a year. Maybe he was putting too much pressure on her. They had often said that they would adopt at least one child, but they also wanted at least one of their own. Being a good mother was critical to Kirby because she never knew her biological mother. Growing up in foster care gave Kirby a different perspective on motherhood.

IGHT

Raja held the phone, and Grant listened attentively.

"Leah is awake."

A collective hallelujah went through the room.

"She can hear and see, and she squeezed my hand. She does not, however, have any movement or feeling in her lower extremities."

"Is she paralyzed?" Grant asked, holding his breath.

"She has temporary paralysis, and that is not unusual in this situation. The next forty-eight hours are critical."

Jill felt guilty for the way she was looking at Raja. Everything about him impressed her: his intellect, his professionalism, his accent. Her best friend had just had brain surgery, and she was smitten by the surgeon. She snapped back to reality when he handed her phone back. The phone smelled like his cologne.

"Jill, may I speak to my mom?" Grant asked.

Jill handed the phone to Grace.

"Ma, please go see her and call me back. See if she can talk to me. I need to hear her voice."

"I'll do what I can, Grant. I promise. The family is praying. Can you stay on the line a few more minutes?"

Bishop Robinson prayed a prayer of praise and thanksgiving and declared total healing for Leah. "We know that by the stripes of Jesus, she is healed."

Dr. Zack said that two of them could see Leah for only a moment. Grace told Katherine what Grant said, and Katherine assured her she would try to make Leah understand.

As soon as Leah saw her parents, tears rolled down her face. Dr. Zack was close by. Her voice was a whisper and her breathing labored.

"Mama, Daddy."

Her mother kissed her forehead.

"I'm sorry for not telling you—"

"That's not important now. All I care about is you getting well." Bishop Robinson was standing at his daughter's side, silently praying. She looked so weak. He touched her face and tried to smile. "Dr. Zack said your surgery went well, so you need to concentrate on getting better."

"I can't move my legs," she said, barely audible. "I can't feel my body."

Lee looked at Dr. Zack for some help. He found himself at a loss for words. It was a place foreign to him. Katherine noticed it too. She had never seen her husband not in control of his emotions. But she knew how much he loved his daughters.

"Leah, the paralysis is temporary. Dr. Raja will get you started on some therapy in a few days if that doesn't change on its own." Dr. Zack said this as much for Lee and Katherine as he did for Leah.

"Leah, we've been talking to Grant, and he wants to come home, but we told him to wait."

Leah started to cry again.

"Grace told him we would call if you want to."

"Yes, please."

Katherine dialed the number for Leah.

But it went straight to voice mail. Katherine left a quick message.

When Grant got the message, he felt so helpless.

NINE

Eight o'clock exactly. Enoch and Clay were at Ben's door, pizza in hand. He was ready. Snacks, drinks, television, games—check. As soon as the games started, the trash talk began.

"Enoch, what happened, bro?" Clay asked with a self-congratulatory gulp of cherry soda, a laugh, and a high-five with Ben.

"Just wanted to make it more of a challenge for the next time," Enoch replied with a laugh.

Ben popped a slice of pizza in the microwave, and they settled in for part two of their evening: talking about whatever they wanted or needed to—the Bible, the Dallas Cowboys, the Los Angeles Lakers, politics, which HBCU band was the best. That night, Clay mentioned Jeremy's game, and the conversation proceeded to Delia.

"Man, you know better. Why did you get involved with the kid's mom?" Enoch asked. "That's the number one sin in that business. Plus, what happened to, what's her name, Carrie?"

"Her name is Cara," he replied, "and nothing happened to her. It just didn't work out."

Enoch looked at Ben. "She just didn't put out."

"I forgot about her," Ben said. "What happened to Alexandra?"

Clay laughed. "Man, that girl is whack!"

Ben sat back in his chair in what they called "minister mode."

"Let's hear it, BC," Clay said.

"You know what I'm gonna say. I've said it before, Clay."

"Man, you're out of order for all the obvious reasons and because sex is for married people."

"Sex is for grown people," Clay and Enoch said together, Enoch mocking Clay.

"You knew he was gonna say that. How many times have we had that discussion?" Ben leaned forward, looked Clay in the eye, and said, "You need to get your flesh under control. The facts are that you are violating God, the policy of the agency, and your relationship with Jeremy. What if she gets pregnant? Worse, what if she's positive and doesn't know it?"

"That's right, Clay, man. She has two kids by two different dudes, so you know what she's been up to," Enoch added.

"I'm not stupid. We're safe."

"No, you're not stupid, so why are you making dumb decisions?"

Before Clay could answer Enoch's question, Enoch's phone rang. It was Kirby letting him know she was back at home from helping Belinda do the twins' hair. Their ballet recital was the next evening.

"Make sure you plug in the batteries for both cameras." Enoch reminded Kirby.

"You were supposed to do that," Kirby said.

"I know, but I forgot." Enoch laughed. "Alarm set?" he asked.

"Yes," she said.

"Okay. I'll see you later."

The conversation shifted to Kirby and Belinda. Ben wanted to know more about Belinda, but he really didn't know what to ask.

"I saw Belinda and the twins earlier this evening at the sub shop. They are really cute."

"Yeah and really smart, but their mother needs to let them have a burger once in a while."

"I don't know why you even went there. You know Kirby's not gonna let your kids have burgers either." Clay laughed.

"You know you're right, if we ever have any." Enoch was thinking out loud.

Ben and Clay looked at him. It was out there. He didn't mean to say it, but he couldn't take it back.

"I'm not sure Kirby can even have children. We've been trying for months, and she's not pregnant."

"Have you ever considered it might be you?" Clay asked.

"No. I'm healthy."

"Being healthy has little to do with it. You need to get checked out. You can't assume its Kirby."

"That's true, Enoch," Ben said. "And then if it's not you, you can support Kirby in figuring out what she needs to do."

Ben wanted to get back to Belinda, but he couldn't figure out how to do it without being obvious.

"That's what's up, and then you and Kirby can have twins too." Clay laughed.

"Man, those two little girls are too much. I don't know how Belinda can handle them by herself. That's why we insisted they move back out here when Canady died."

This was his chance. "Do the girls remember their father?"

"Not really. They weren't quite four when he passed, and he had been in Iraq for over a year. They have a couple of pictures of him in their room and a photo album. They ask questions from time to time, especially Brianna. She's open about how she feels, her anger, her hurt. Britt is more like Belinda, quieter, keeps things to herself."

In minister mode, Ben asked if Belinda had had any counseling.

"Yeah. Uncle Sam made sure she did, and she can go back if she needs to. They still have benefits for now."

"But did she and the girls have any spiritual counseling? Psychology is fine, but—"

"Hold up, Minister Coffey," Clay interrupted. "Are you volunteering?"

Busted. "I just want to make sure our congregation is whole."

"No problem, boss," Clay said, holding his hands up in surrender. "I'm not mad at ya. She is *fine!*"

"Is that *all* you think about?" Ben asked.

"No, but you act like you never think about it. God don't care if you see a woman and think she fine. That's how He made her. You and Enoch so holy, but y'all perpetrating. I'm the one tellin' the truth."

Ben knew Clay was right. He struggled with doing the right thing, always concerned about his position in the ministry and the ministry itself. Anybody he spent time with had to understand his commitment to God, to the church, and to Bishop Robinson. The only serious relationship he had had ended while he was in grad school, and he hadn't been in a relationship in the two years he'd been back home. Grammy and Aunt Avis reminded him often that he was not getting any younger.

Kathy walked into Leah's townhouse and looked around. As always, Leah's home was immaculate, and she would expect it to be that way when she came home.

When she came home…when will that be? Kathy willed herself not to cry.

There had been a package-waiting notice from the post office in the mail.

I'll have to go get this for Leah on Monday. Probably wedding stuff, Kathy thought.

Kathy's cell phone rang. She looked at the screen, and it was the school. She hadn't called all day, and she knew her coworkers were concerned, but she also needed to let them know when she would return to work.

Kathy taught English at Hattiesville High School and was the cheerleading coach. She got the position straight out of college. She told her parents she wanted to teach a few years and then go to grad school. She loved teaching, but she knew her parents were expecting her to get a master's degree. Kathy knew teaching was her calling. She knew she had influence on the lives of youth, especially young ladies. She was always transparent with them. The cheerleaders couldn't believe it when she told them she was a virgin, and they were really floored when she told them she had never even kissed a man.

"Miss Robinson, are you telling us this just to keep us from doing it or are you telling the truth?" one student asked.

"I'm telling you the absolute truth. Do you realize if you have intercourse, the man deposits his spirit into you and the spirit of anybody else he's been with, whatever that spirit is?" She knew some of them didn't understand, but at least she had planted the seed.

"Hi. This is Kathy."

"Hello, Kathy. This is Robin Brackett. How are you?"

"I'm doing okay, Robin. Thank you for asking."

"Please update me on Leah."

Kathy and Robin talked for several minutes. Robin was calling as a friend, but she was also acting vice principal. Her regular position was the French teacher at the middle and high schools.

Kathy told Robin she would be back at work on Monday. Like it or not, she had to return to reality. No matter how much her heart was hurting, no matter how worried she was about Leah, she had to get back to her students.

$\mathscr{T}$EN

Early Saturday morning, Jill and Trey walked into the hospital
cafeteria to find Raja with a steaming cup of peppermint tea,
talking on his cell phone. He motioned for them to join him. Jill
went through the line to get Danishes and soy milk for both of
them. Trey didn't want soy milk; he asked for hot chocolate.

When Jill came back to the table, Raja stood to pull out her
chair, and she caught a whiff of his cologne. She thanked him,
and their eyes met for a second. Raja laughed at Trey for having
soy milk. Trey assured him it was only because Jill bought it. He
made sure they both knew he did not eat for medicinal purposes.

For a few minutes, the conversation centered on Raja's vegetarian diet and daily workouts versus Trey's carnivorous eating habits.

"Yeah, I'm a meat eater, but I go to the gym every day too."

Jill needed to get in the conversation. She wanted to talk to
Raja. She wanted to know more about him. "I work out every day
too, Trey, but I also eat well."

Her cell phone rang. Talk about rotten timing. It was her
assistant wanting to know if she should cancel her afternoon
appointment. While they were talking, Raja and Trey's pagers
went off at the same time. It was Kim Horng, paging them to
Leah's room.

Oh my God, Jill thought. *Please, Lord, no.*

"Don't say anything 'til I call you," Trey said to Jill as they left
the table.

Jill willed herself to sit there. She bowed her head and prayed. She ate her Danish and Trey's and drank the milk. Time wasn't moving. She decided to go back upstairs to the waiting room. She didn't know who would be there. Everyone had gone before she and Trey went downstairs.

The phone rang again. Maybe it was Trey.

"Hello," she said.

"Hi, sugar."

"Hey, Mom."

"Where are you?"

"At the hospital, sitting in the café. Trey and I were having a snack with Raja, and they got paged to Leah's room. Mom, I thought she was getting better."

"What did Trey say?"

"Nothing except that I couldn't say anything until he calls me back."

"Do you want me to come over there?"

"No, but you could do me a gigantic favor and make the presentation to the Trenton Group for me this afternoon."

"I can do that. Where's the file?"

"It's on my desk. Valerie can find it. She called a few minutes ago, so she's at the office. I'll call—"

"I'll take care of it, Jillie. Don't worry. Love you."

"Thanks, Mom. Love you too."

As Jill cleaned off the table, she noticed that Raja left his pen. She picked it up. It was a really nice Mont Blanc, black with "M K R" engraved in silver. She carefully placed it in her pocketbook. She couldn't help laughing to herself. God, with His sense of humor, had given her a way to approach Dr. Rajagopal.

The house phone rang, and Kathy got up to answer it. It was her mother.

"Hey, Ma."

"Kathy, Jill just called from the hospital," Katherine said.

Raja and Trey walked into Leah's room, and Kim updated them quickly. Leah's blood pressure had gone back up suddenly, and she was not responding to the medication they ordered. Raja ordered a stat CT scan and MRI.

"Dr. Strauss, her nose is bleeding," Kim said.

"We might be dealing with brain bleed." Raja gave a few more orders and told Trey to alert the Robinsons.

Jill walked into the waiting room, where the Bishop and Minister Ben were waiting. She hugged them both and sat beside Ben. She told them she hadn't seen Leah and that she had gone to the cafeteria for a while. She asked where First Lady Robinson was and how Mrs. Coffey and Mrs. Johnson were, making small talk. She and Ben chatted about her work with the foundation.

Trey walked into the waiting room with a worried look on his face. Bishop Robinson saw it too and leapt to his feet, Ben and Jill right behind him.

"Sir, Leah has had a setback. Her blood pressure shot up, and she is not responding to the medication. Raja has sent her for some tests. We should know what we're dealing with in about an hour."

"Trey, do I need to call my family?" her father asked.

"Let's wait until we get the test results."

"What's the worst-case scenario?" Jill asked.

His pager went off. He looked at it; it was the emergency room. "I can't really answer that, Jill, but I will say she might have to have more surgery."

"Is that Raja?" Jill was asking.

"No. It's the ER, and I'm not on call, so it must be a patient of mine. I'll be right back."

Ben looked at the bishop, and he looked defeated. He sat back down with his phone in his hand.

"Sir, why don't you wait before calling First Lady," Ben suggested.

"You're probably right because I can't lie to her, but I don't want to upset her again either."

"What if I call and just tell her Trey has ordered more tests and we'll let her know in about an hour?" Jill asked.

"That's a good idea, Jill. Do that please."

Before Jill could dial Katherine, her phone rang. It was Trey.

"Hi, Trey," Jill answered.

"Jill, tell Bishop that Kirby Casebier is down here. One of the Stewart twins is hurt."

Jill relayed Trey's message, and Ben reacted so quickly it surprised the bishop, and he surprised himself.

"What happened?" Ben asked.

"I don't know. That's all he said."

"I'll go down and see what's going on. You and Jill wait to hear back from Raja," Ben said.

Ben walked quickly to the elevator, his heart beating rapidly. He had to calm himself. He started to pray. Belinda had had enough tragedy. She didn't need this. Ben walked into the waiting room to see Kirby and Brianna, who saw him at the same moment and ran screaming into his arms. She was shaking terribly and smelled like smoke. He could feel his phone vibrating, but he couldn't reach it. He hugged Kirby and asked what happened. She explained that there was a fire at the auditorium where the girls were to have their recital. It started in the area where the children were. They panicked and started running. Brittani fell, and they thought her leg was broken.

At that moment, Ben noticed that there were several children in the waiting area. Brianna calmed down enough for him to sit her down. He reached in his pocket to see who had called. It was Enoch. He called back, not knowing Enoch was calling from the hospital. He was in the exam room with Belinda and Brittani. He was glad to know that Ben was with Kirby and Brianna. Brianna was explaining to Ben what she saw and that she couldn't find Brittani and how scared she was. He consoled her as much as he could, but she started to cry again. He picked her up, grabbed Kirby by the hand, and walked into one of the clergy conference rooms down the hall. Something really strange was happening there, and Ben couldn't explain it. He sat down with Brianna on his lap and Kirby across from him. He started to pray and immediately could feel Brianna's heartbeat slow down. Just as he finished, Kirby started to pray for him, to thank God for Ben being there.

Faces cleaned up and tears dried, they walked back into the main waiting area. Brianna was holding his hand. They sat a few minutes, and it occurred to Kirby that Ben had appeared so suddenly. He explained that he had been upstairs with Bishop Robinson and updated her on Leah's condition. As they talked, the nurse came out and called for the family of Brittani Stewart. Brianna jumped up and ran ahead of Kirby and Ben. They all walked back to where Brittani was lying on the bed, dozing. Belinda looked very surprised to see Ben come in, but she appreciated his presence. They hugged. He probably held her too long.

Trey walked in with X-rays. "Her leg is fractured, but it is a clean break, so she won't need surgery."

A sigh of relief went through the room.

"I want to keep her overnight for observation. We will put her in a cast in a little while."

Enoch asked Brittani what color she wanted, but she didn't answer. Brianna said she was asleep, but she knew her sister would want pink and green.

Kirby told Belinda about Leah and asked Enoch and Ben if they would stay with the girls for a few minutes so they could go upstairs to see the bishop. He was relieved to see them and to learn that Brittani was going to be okay. It distracted him for a few minutes to talk about the fire. He wanted to know if any other of their members' children were involved. There were a few, but there were no other serious injuries.

Brianna went home with Kirby and Enoch so Belinda could spend the night at the hospital with Brittani. Ben made sure they were settled, checked back with the bishop, and went home to prepare himself for Sunday morning. He had given Belinda his card and had written his home number and cell number on the back and told her to call him if she needed anything. She thanked him. Enoch noticed the exchange but didn't comment.

Raja came to the waiting room, expecting to see Trey there with the Robinsons, but Jill explained that he had been paged to the ER. Jill had called her dad, and Dr. Zack was there. Raja explained that Leah's test results did not show any other aneurysm or brain bleed. But she was not responding to the medicine, so they were going to sedate her heavily so that she would sleep for the next day or so. That was the only way to control her blood pressure. There were other medicines, but it was too soon to add anything else. It was their best approach. He also told them that he was going back to Chapel Hill on Sunday but he would be checking on Leah regularly and he would be back in a few days.

As Raja turned to leave, Jill remembered the pen. "Oh, Raja, wait."

He turned around.

"You left this in the cafeteria." She handed him the pen.

"Thank you." He smiled. "Hey, would you like to have brunch with me before I have to leave?"

"Sure. Would you like to join me for the early gathering at my church before?"

"I appreciate the invite, but I want to get here and check on Leah early."

"I understand. Does eleven a.m. sound okay for brunch?"

"Sounds perfect. Looking forward to it."

They exchanged numbers and agreed to meet at Lola's.

Jill went back to the waiting room and asked if Kathy or Bishop Robinson were going to call Katherine and to say she should call Grant.

Kirby bathed Brianna and got her settled in bed before Enoch came in for the three of them to pray. Kirby was very emotional and left the room quickly following the prayers. She showered, got in bed, and pretended to be asleep. Enoch knew they needed to talk, and putting it off was not the answer. He got into bed and pulled her into his arms.

"Mrs. Casebier, I know you're awake. We need to talk."

There was no need to pretend. She knew he was right. "Enoch, I keep thinking that we could have lost Brittani tonight—actually both of them. Can you imagine what Belinda must have been thinking?"

"Yeah, I can, 'cause I know how scared I was. I am so thankful it is what it is."

As they talked, recanting the events of the evening, Kirby suddenly started to cry uncontrollably. Enoch got up to close their bedroom door so Brianna wouldn't hear her. He held her and let her cry. She cried hard, and Enoch knew that what she was crying about had little to do with Brittani or the fire. When she quieted, he told her what was on his heart.

"Kirby, I kicked over the trash can, and I saw the pregnancy test."

She buried her head in his chest and wouldn't look at him. He kept talking.

"I understand why you didn't tell me, but you know we don't keep secrets. Our relationship is based on trust. You know that. I know how bad you want a baby. Relax, sugar, and talk to me."

"I am so tired of telling you I'm not pregnant."

"But, baby—"

"Please, let me finish. I'm so tired of disappointing you."

He started to protest again, but she put her hand over his mouth.

"I watched you tonight with the girls. You took over and handled that situation like they were your children."

"For all intents and purposes, they are my children."

"I know, but more than anything, I want us to have our own child, Enoch. I don't know what's wrong with me. Why can't I get pregnant? And don't tell me to pray. I've been praying and fasting and still nothing. Do you realize it's been over a year?"

"Yes, I do realize how long it's been, but why are you so sure it's you? There could be something going on with me."

It was tough for Enoch to admit that to himself, let alone admit it to her. Kirby sat up and looked at her husband. She had never seriously considered that their infertility could be Enoch. Even after Belinda mentioned it, she dismissed the thought.

"You can't seriously think anything is wrong with you."

"There's nothing wrong with either of us, but we do need to seek a doctor's direction on how to proceed so we can overcome this situation."

They talked for a few more minutes and agreed that as soon as Brittani was better, they would both make appointments with their doctors.

Ben left the hospital more emotional than he should have been. His thoughts raced from one thing to another. He asked himself if this is how combining family and ministry would be.

Wow. I need to get my imagination under control. That is not my family. My message for tomorrow is in pretty good shape. But I want them to be my family. I need to tighten it up and spend some time before the Lord. Man, you are out of control, he said to himself.

Ben went in the house, put praise music in the CD player, showered, made a milkshake, and sat at his desk with the notes for his message, his Bible, and a couple of reference books. He leaned back in his chair and closed his eyes.

"Lord, why did You put me in that situation today? I don't question Your will, Lord. I just want to know and understand the lesson."

Ben allowed himself to replay the events of the day. Leah Robinson, his good friend, was fighting for her life, and Brittani Stewart, the seven-year-old daughter of the most beautiful woman in the world, had a broken leg, which was good considering that she could have had smoke inhalation or worse because of the fire. He wondered what the cause of the fire was. Did someone start the fire? God forbid, with all those little girls in that part of the building.

Ben leaned forward, bowed his head, and began to praise God. He sang. He walked around and ended up sitting on the ottoman. He prayed and cried. His heart ached for the Robinsons, for Grant, for Brianna and Belinda, and especially for Brittani. He prayed to be of help to Belinda in that season. As Ben continued to pray, he was startled by the ringing phone. He looked at the clock. It was 11:10 p.m. He didn't recognize the number on the ID. He cleared his throat.

"This is Minister Coffey."

"Hi…uh…Ben, this is Belinda Stewart."

LEVEN

When the phone rang, Grant hoped it was somebody calling about Leah. He didn't look at the ID; he just answered.

"Hey, Grant, how are you?"

"I'm doing well, thank you. Who am I speaking with?"

"How soon we forget."

Silence.

"Grant, its Janis Mitchell."

"Oh." He laughed. "How are you, Janis?"

"I'm fine. Thank you."

"I'm surprised to hear from you. What's up?"

"You've been on my mind, and I heard something about another troop surge and wanted to make sure you weren't headed to Iraq."

"I appreciate your concern, but my job is here in Germany. I'm here to help the soldiers who are wounded get rehabbed. I don't expect to be sent anywhere else. I am still puzzled about your call."

"Chill, Grant. Like I said, you were on my mind, so I took a chance that you had the same cell number and called to chat."

"I have a lot going on right now, and I'm not in a mood to chat."

"Work or personal?"

"I'm sure you heard about Leah."

"No. What about Leah?"

"She's sick—very sick."

"No, I didn't know."

He didn't believe her. Janis Mitchell was what his mother called a busybody. She didn't miss much. She was not a member of Hattiesville Community Church, but she had friends there. She knew about Leah. That's why she really called: to see what he was going to say.

According to Janis, Leah was the reason she and Grant weren't together. She even went so far as to tell Leah that Grant was her daughter's father. He wasn't, but that was a horrible time for him and Leah. His fling with Janis was just that: a fling, an affair. That was the past. There was no way he was going to revisit that.

"So does that mean you're coming home?"

There it was—the real reason for the call.

"I'm expecting a call, so I need to go. Take care of yourself."

"Hold it, Grant. You didn't answer me."

He hung up.

"I can't believe she called me. That girl is whack," Grant said to himself.

After hanging up, he noticed there was a text message from Jill on his phone: "Can't get thru. Call when you get the message. Update, not urgent."

He called immediately. Jill told him everything she knew.

"Jill, I'm coming home."

"G, there's nothing you can do. Please wait."

"Why do you, my mom, and everybody keep telling me not to come home? What are you hiding from me?"

"We aren't hiding anything. You won't be able to do anything but be here."

"I'm coming home, but don't tell my parents or Leah's. I'll call you with the details."

Grant knew he wouldn't be able to get the process going until Monday, but he got online and checked airfares, schedules, and his bank account. He would have to get Gretchen to move some money from his savings.

TWELVE

"Is everything okay, Belinda? Is Brittani okay?" Ben's voice sounded tense as he sat down at his desk and rubbed the back of his neck.

"Brittani is okay. She's sleeping. Dr. Strauss said she would sleep through the night. I apologize for calling so late."

"No need to apologize. I meant what I said."

Before Belinda called Ben, she couldn't sleep. She smelled smoke, but she had sent the dirty clothes with Kirby. Maybe it was her hair or Brittani's hair. She dozed again and saw the military officials telling her the girls had died in a fire. That made her cry. She got up and walked down the hall but didn't stay out of the room but for a few minutes. She didn't want Brittani to wake up when she wasn't there. She prayed and prayed.

"I can't go there again," she said to herself. "I will not fall in that black hole again."

She needed to talk to somebody. She looked at her watch. It was almost 11:00 p.m. If she called Kirby and Enoch, they would think something was wrong. She decided to turn the television on. The end of *Law & Order* was on. The 11:00 p.m. news preview said, "A fire at a public auditorium in Hattiesville appears to be arson."

"Somebody tried to kill my babies!" Belinda didn't realize she was screaming until Brittani whimpered and squirmed in her sleep.

Belinda reached for the phone and looked in her pocketbook to get Ben Coffey's card. She wouldn't allow herself to get depressed. She would not fall in the black hole again.

"No, Belinda continued, "everything is not okay. I can't sleep, and I keep thinking, dreaming that...that..."

Silence.

"Talk to me, Belinda."

She went on to tell Ben about the dreams and about the news preview. "Why would somebody want to kill my children, any children for that matter?"

"First of all, nobody is targeting your children. Secondly, that's a question we can't answer and one that should be left to the police."

"What am I going to tell my girls anyway?"

"You'll tell them the truth."

"They have been through enough. How do you explain to seven-year-olds who have already lost their father that people are so hateful and have no regard for life? How do I keep them from becoming hate-filled people?"

"Belinda, listen to me. Breathe." Ben wanted to make sure he said the right thing the right way. "Is this about the twins or about you? Is it their understanding or yours that you're questioning? Are you fearful of becoming hate-filled yourself?"

Belinda was very quiet. "Are those rhetorical questions, or do you expect me to answer?" she asked finally.

"I expect you to answer."

Ouch, she thought. *Maybe he's right.* "I really don't know how to respond. Ben, my husband was killed, and for months I felt like I was living in a black hole. Tonight I felt like I was headed back there."

"God brought you too far to let you go back, and I won't let you go there either." *Oh no*, he thought. *Have I said too much?*

"Can you imagine how it feels to lose somebody?"

"As a matter of fact, I can. My mom died in a car accident when I was three, and I don't really remember her. Then my grandfather who raised me died when I was twelve years old. I didn't live in the black hole. I acted out."

"I didn't know. Please forgive me. I guess I get so caught up in my own pain that I disregard other people's pain. I don't mean to be selfish."

"There's nothing to forgive you for. You're entitled to some selfishness."

They talked a while longer, and Ben suggested Belinda have some additional counseling. He also said he would find someone to talk to the girls. And he promised to talk to the police chief and the fire chief about the fire.

When they hung up, they had been talking for almost two hours. Ben needed some sleep, but he was pleased. He learned some things about Belinda, and he was glad about that. And she said it was okay for him to call to check on Brittani after church.

Ben delivered a powerful message, but there was heaviness over the congregation. They were all concerned about Leah and the Robinsons. Ben assured them that God was in control. He said that they had to continue to cover the Robinsons and to realize this season was an exercise of their faith.

Ben saw Enoch, Kirby, and Brianna in the congregation, but they must have left immediately after dismissal. He called Enoch's cell, and Brianna answered.

"Uncle Enoch is helping my sister get in the car."

"Is your Mom close by?"

"Yes, but she is helping too. You can talk to Auntie K." She walked over and gave Kirby the phone.

"Hey, Kirby. This is Ben. I wanted to check on Brittani."

"She's pretty good. We're on our way to their house."

"Can I bring anything? Have you guys had dinner?"

"Hang on, Ben. Let me see what the girls want. I'll tell you what. Will you go by Lola's and pick up the order? I'll call it in. What do you want, Ben?"

"Whatever you order is fine. I'll work with it!" Kirby gave Ben Belinda's address and the directions.

Ben finished up a couple of things, picked up the food, and arrived at Belinda's townhouse at about the same time they were getting there from the hospital. Enoch carried Brittani in and sat her on the sofa, and Brianna got her a TV tray. Kirby and Belinda unpacked the feast while Enoch and Ben argued over Enoch trying to repay Ben for the food. Brittani didn't eat very much. She said she wasn't hungry, but she could hardly move with Brianna hovering.

Ben took a minute and looked around. The home was very well kept. It was modest but good quality and tasteful. He wondered if she owned the property or if she was renting. But he knew Enoch's influence on her, so he was 99 percent sure she was purchasing the property.

He came out of his daydream to hear the conversation about what the plan was for Brittani on Monday. Enoch, Kirby, and Belinda were working out a schedule in increments of who would be there throughout the day. It all sounded very hectic.

"May I make a suggestion?" Ben asked.

"Sure," Belinda answered, looking right into his eyes.

"I think my grandmother and aunt would come over and sit with Brittani tomorrow, and everybody else can stay on their regular schedule."

"Man, that sounds like a plan," Enoch responded.

"I can't impose on them," Belinda said.

Kirby and Ben laughed out loud.

"They don't really know us."

Kirby was still laughing.

"Belinda, let me assure you they won't mind, and whether they know you or not is not the point. And I'll know what they're up to all day." Ben laughed.

These were the kind of moments when Belinda remembered she was new to the community. She listened to the other three go on to sing the praises of Grammy and Auntie Avis. Enoch told how Grammy spanked him, Clay, and Ben when they were little boys.

"Excuse me, Uncle Enoch," Brianna said. "I think Brittani needs to be excused."

Enoch got up to carry her upstairs. Brianna and Kirby followed, leaving Ben and Belinda sitting at the table.

"Ben, thanks for offering to ask your grandmother, but—"

"But nothing. If she knew you were going to miss class, she wouldn't like it and she wouldn't want Kirby and Enoch to miss work. My darlings, as I call them, are from the old school, and they will consider it their duty to help. I'm calling right now."

"How will they get over here?"

"They both drive."

"Oh, I didn't know that."

"That's 'cause they prefer to ride, but don't underestimate either of them. They handle business."

Ben dialed their number as he talked. Aunt Avis answered.

"Hey, Auntie. I'm at Belinda Stewart's home with her daughters, Kirby, and Enoch. We need your and Grammy's help."

"How is the little girl, Benji?"

"She's pretty good."

He went on to explain the situation. Without hesitation she said they would be honored and could be available for as many days as Belinda needed them. Ben gave Belinda the phone.

"What time do you need to leave in the morning?" Aunt Avis asked.

"I leave at seven thirty to take the girls to school, but if that's too early—"

"No. That's fine. We'll see you in the morning."

"Thank you, Mrs. Johnson. Thank you so much." Belinda handed the phone back to Ben. "And thank you, Benji," she said with a laugh.

He laughed too and felt a real sense of satisfaction.

Grammy and Aunt Avis arrived Monday morning at 7:10. They both had grocery bags in their hands and the most incredible smiles on their faces. Any apprehension Belinda had had been removed. The three ladies talked, and Grammy assured Belinda that they would be fine.

Belinda told them she would be back close to 6:00 p.m., after she picked up Brianna from after school.

Brianna frowned. "Why do I have to go to after school if the ladies—?"

"Mrs. Coffey and Mrs. Johnson," Belinda interrupted.

"If Mrs. Coffey and Mrs. Johnson are going to be here with Brittani?"

"Brianna, Mrs. Coffey and Mrs. Johnson are doing us a favor by staying here with Brittani. Please go get your jacket so we can go."

"Belinda, honey, its fine for her to come home after school. Brittani will probably appreciate the company," Grammy said.

"But somebody will have to pick her up. Maybe I can get Enoch or Kirby—"

"One of us will pick her up. It's no problem really," Auntie added.

Brianna's face lit up, and her mother agreed.

"I go to Sunset Elementary School, and we get out at two thirty."

"I read to some of the children there when I volunteer in the library, so I'm familiar with the school and they're familiar with me," Auntie Avis said. "You just make sure you let them know I'm coming."

"Mrs. Johnson, would you like me to meet you at the library?" Brianna asked.

"Yes. That's fine."

"Let's go, and I will have time to go in and tell the office you will be a car rider today."

$\mathcal{T}$HIRTEEN

Grant knocked on his commanding officer's door, determined not to take no for an answer. He had to get home. He had to get to Leah.

"Come in."

Grant whispered a silent prayer as he entered the office. The conversation lasted about ten minutes, and the executive officer told Grant that he couldn't authorize the leave. Grant had pled his case. The answer was no. But he refused to accept that.

"With all due respect, sir, I am going to appeal your decision to the brigade commander. This is critical to me." Grant could hear himself talking, but he couldn't believe he was saying it. He was the one who didn't make waves. He very seldom asked for a favor. He worked additional shifts so other soldiers could be off. It was his turn now.

"Sturdivant, the fact that you appealed the executive officer's decision indicates to me you are determined to go home."

"Yes, sir."

"I will approve ten days, including travel days, effective on or about one December. Get the paperwork to him by end of the business today."

"Yes, sir. Thank you, sir."

As Grant turned to leave, the brigade commander said, "I hope you find things well at home. I will pray for you both."

"Thank you, sir."

"Gretchen, where are you? Can you talk?"

"Yeah, I'm at home. What is it, Grant?"

"I'm coming home, but don't tell anybody."

"What are you talking about, G?"

"I got ten days emergency leave granted, and I will be leaving here the first of the month. I'm going to have to work some extra shifts to make it happen."

"Okay. Cool. But why don't you want Mama and Daddy to know?"

"They told me not to come, like I'm supposed to just sit over here and imagine how Leah's doing."

"You know what's best for you and Leah, and I think you're right."

They talked a few more minutes, and he asked her to go to the credit union and withdraw some money from his savings and deposit it in his checking account in case he needed it. She promised to do it today, and he promised to call back with the details.

"I hope you got my back, GG, 'cause you know Ma and Bishop are going to flip when I get there."

"Always got your back, GP, and Mama will be glad to see you when she gets over the shock. I love you, Grant."

"Love you too, Gretchen. I'll call you later."

The credit union was in Davis Town, out of her way, but it was going to be her first stop. Grant didn't ask for much, and she supported his decision to come home. God forbid that Leah would die, but he would never forgive himself if she did and he hadn't seen her.

Just like most Monday mornings, the credit union was busy, so Gretchen had to wait in line. She looked around at the renovations that had been made. In one of the offices across the lobby was Janis Mitchell.

Gretchen hadn't seen Janis recently. They had been pretty good friends years ago, but after the fiasco with Grant, Gretchen didn't have much use for Janis. She turned around to face the teller line, hoping Janis didn't see her.

Transaction done. No Janis. Thank you, Lord.

"Thank you, Ms. Sturdivant. Have a good day."

"Thank you," Gretchen said as she stepped aside and counted the money. She recounted it. *One thousand fifty, not one thousand five hundred.* "Excuse me. This should be fifteen hundred dollars," Gretchen said, handing the envelope back to the teller.

"I apologize. Let me call my supervisor so I can get this corrected."

The teller picked up the phone, and ten seconds later, Janis Mitchell was standing behind the teller's counter.

"Hello, Gretchen. How are you?"

"Doing well. Thank you. How are you?"

"I apologize for this error. I'll have it taken care of in just a moment."

Janis looked at the computer screen: $1,500.00 withdrawal from savings, names on account Grant Sturdivant and Gretchen Sturdivant. She counted $1,500.00 onto the counter.

Gretchen nodded, and Janis put the money into an envelope. The teller apologized again. Gretchen turned to leave.

"Gretchen, I heard about Leah. How is she?"

"Her prognosis is good. Thank you for asking."

Janis knew why Gretchen was so cool with her, and she knew that if the situation was reversed, she would be the same way.

She went back to her office, got on the Internet, and checked flights coming from all points in Germany from Wednesday to Friday. There were four. She didn't expect him to come in on Thanksgiving Day, so there would be three. She put her money on the one on Wednesday.

At the end of the day, Janis still wanted Grant. They could have had a baby together.

Janis remembered that period in her life. Janis and Grant's relationship had been casual for months. They saw each other if he came home on a weekend. She went to Georgia to see him one time. When they became intimate, Janis started making wedding plans, but Grant was still in casual mode. A year later, the status had not changed. Janis gave Grant an ultimatum, and he chose to move on.

They both moved on, sort of. Janis started dating someone else, and Grant started courting Leah Robinson. But Janis and Grant were together one last time, one weekend when he came home on leave.

Her boyfriend admitted he had been seeing someone else. On Saturday night she told him, "Get the hell out of my house and the hell out of my life." He left. Two weeks later, on Monday afternoon, he called her.

"Janis, I wanted to tell you myself. We got married today."

"I can't believe you!" Janis screamed.

"I didn't call you to argue, just to let you know."

"Well, I don't care because Grant and I are back together anyway."

Janis had been sick for weeks, and she finally went to the doctor. It was the day after the big blow.

"I think you're pregnant," the doctor said after his examination.

"You think I'm what?"

"We need to do a blood test to be sure. We'll have the results tomorrow."

On Wednesday afternoon, the call came. "Ms. Mitchell, this is the doctor's office. Your pregnancy test is positive. You need to make an appointment to come in to see us."

On Thursday, at 4:55 p.m., Janis' supervisor called her into her office. "Janis, the cutbacks have hit our department, and we are going to have to lay you off."

Janis thought that was the worst week of her life. But little did she know the worst was yet to come.

Janis lay in bed on Friday morning, trying to decide what to do. She was pregnant, and he was married. And she had to find a job. She couldn't have an abortion. That wasn't an option. Why couldn't this be Grant's baby? He would marry her, do the right thing, make the situation right. She had to tell him. He had the right to know, and in a way, she wanted to hurt him. She called him at work. Voice mail.

"This is Janis. Call me at home as soon as you get this message. It's urgent."

He called back a few minutes later and immediately went off about her leaving an urgent message. Janis was furious. She took a deep breath.

"Since you were cordial enough to tell me you had gotten married, I thought I would return the favor and let you know I'm pregnant."

"Where are we going with this, Janis? I know it's not mine if you really are pregnant."

"I don't have any reason to lie about something this serious."

"Janis, you're a trip. I got married. You're mad, so you call me with this pregnancy nonsense. I gave you credit for having more integrity than that."

Janis fought back tears. She didn't expect him to accept the news with open arms, but she didn't expect this response either. She pretended to cough, to give herself a couple of seconds to regroup.

"I said I was calling to tell you. I didn't say the baby was yours."

Over the next couple of months, Janis became acclimated to the situation. She had gone back to work almost immediately. The greatest thing about the new job was the insurance went into effect immediately and there was not a preexisting condition clause. The pregnancy would be covered. Of course, she didn't tell anybody at work.

Everything was okay until one Saturday Janis saw Grant and Leah at a funeral together. They were walking to her car, holding hands. He opened the door for her and then got in on the passenger side. She wondered where he was stationed now. Since she was driving, he must have been stationed too far away to drive home.

Janis was hungry. It seemed she was always hungry these days. She decided to go to Lola's. While she was eating and reading the new *Essence* magazine, Grant and Leah walked right past her, and he barely spoke. All of a sudden, she got really angry—really angry. She would not be pregnant and alone and let Miss "Virgin Mary" Leah Robinson be with Grant. She was going to have to step it up a notch.

The following Monday, Janis called Grant's cell number, not knowing if he even had the same number. He answered.

"Hey, Grant. How are you?"

"What's up, Janis?"

"Are you somewhere you can talk privately?"

"Yeah, why?"

"Grant, I'm pregnant."

"And you're tellin' me why?"

She hesitated.

"What's your point, Janis?"

"It's your baby, Grant."

"Girl, you're crazy. I haven't seen you in months."

The tears were stinging her eyes. "The last time we were together…"

"Was probably six months ago."

"It wasn't that long—"

He interrupted her again. "I don't know what you up to, but this game you're playing ain't funny."

"I am not playing a game."

"Look, kid. Lose my number, just like you have lost your mind."

Grant didn't think much about it until Gretchen called him a couple of days later to say one of her customers told her Janis was pregnant and Janis said it was his baby. He told her about the call from Janis. He also told her he knew without a shadow of a doubt that the baby was not his.

"Gretchen, you know I wouldn't lie to you, and you know I wouldn't shirk my responsibility."

Gretchen advised him to tell their parents and Leah before somebody else did.

Things were going well between Grant and Leah, and he didn't want anything to ruin it. Trying to negotiate a long-distance relationship was tough enough without any added stress.

"Where is Mama?" Grant asked Gretchen.

"I don't know. Why?"

"I need you to distract her so I can talk to Daddy."

"Got it," Gretchen said.

Grant explained the situation to his dad and told him the whole truth.

"Son, I agree with your sister. You need to tell Leah. I know you don't want her to know you had sex with Janis after you two had established a relationship, but every time you lie, you have to lie again. Ask her to forgive you, son."

"But Dad, what if she won't forgive me?"

"That's a chance you have to take. Every decision has a consequence, Grant."

"You must ask God to forgive you, forgive yourself, and ask Leah to forgive you."

"I repented for that situation a long time ago."

"Then you know what you have to do now."

"This is the twilight zone live and in living color," Grant said to himself.

"Dad, will you—?"

"Okay, son. I'll tell your mother."

Grant called Leah and didn't get an answer. For a split second, he wondered where she could be. Then he remembered she was on the 7:00 p.m. to 7:00 a.m. shift. When she got off, he would be on duty. By the time he was off duty, she would be asleep. He hated to wake her, but he would have to.

Leah and Grant were on the phone for over an hour. He did most of the talking. Leah cried, and he begged for her forgiveness. He told her God had forgiven him and she should too. She said she didn't know what to think or what to do. He told her exactly when he was with Janis and that there was no way this baby could be his. He apologized for everything, including lying to her about where he was that day. She said more than once that she couldn't believe he had unprotected casual sex. The word *unprotected* rang in his head.

"Grant, I have to go."

"Baby, please don't hang up."

"Hear me clearly, Grant. I will call you when I have a chance to sort this out. I need to think about all of this."

"You have to believe I'm telling you the truth."

"I want to believe you. I do. And I don't feel in my spirit that she is telling the truth about you being the father. But you lied and you cheated. I don't know. I just don't know."

"Leah, sweetheart, you have to believe me."

"I will call you in a day or so."

She hung up and cried hard. She had to talk to somebody. She called Jill and told her half the story.

"I'll be there in a minute," Jill said.

They analyzed the situation backward and forward. Neither of them could believe any of this was happening. Leah was so upset that she called the hospital and told them she would be late. Jill insisted she get some sleep. Jill lay on the sofa, and she could hear Leah twisting and turning. Two hours passed, and Jill went into Leah's room to tell her she should call in sick. She did, and they decided Leah needed to talk to her mother. Katherine came right over and listened to Leah. Katherine asked all the right questions and said all the right things. Leah had to forgive Grant, even if she ended their relationship.

"Take a few days and gather your thoughts. Grant can wait."

"Mama, please don't tell Daddy."

"I have to or you do. We don't want him to hear this in the street. You know this kind of mess in the wrong hands will get back to him."

"Then he'll be mad at all three of us." Jill laughed.

Leah did get some sleep and was pretty rested the next morning, so she decided to run some errands. She stopped at the carwash, and much to her dismay, Janis Mitchell was there. Leah's car was in the bay, and Janis' was being dried. There was nowhere to go.

Janis approached Leah, and she got a good look at her. She looked thick but not pregnant.

"In case you don't know, I'm pregnant, and Grant is the father." Janis smiled smugly.

Leah looked her directly in the eye. "Grant and I have talked. He assured me that he is not the father. I believe him." Leah looked and sounded more confident than she felt.

"I wouldn't trust him if I were you."

Leah didn't respond. The young man waved his towel to indicate that Janis' car was ready.

"You can believe me or believe Grant, but time will tell." Janis walked away. She had told that lie so many times that she was starting to believe it herself.

Leah finished her errands, went home, went to sleep, got up, and went to work. She did her work and didn't say much. Her coworkers thought she didn't feel well. She took her breaks on time and left exactly at 7:00 a.m.

Grant had left six messages. All of them were basically the same: he was sorry, she had to believe him, please call him. She turned the ringer off. There was a message from her mother. She would call when she thought her dad had left. She hadn't talked to him, so she knew her mother had told him what was going on. Her dad thought a lot of Grant, and regardless of what Leah decided, he was going to have to deal with her father.

Grant came home that weekend. Nobody knew he was coming. His first stop was Leah's house. She let him in but didn't have much to say. She did tell him about seeing Janis at the carwash. He told her he fully intended to get to the bottom of it. Next stop: his parents. He knew Gretchen had his back. His parents were none too happy with him or the situation. Next stop: Bishop Robinson.

"Good evening, Grant," Katherine said, hugging him as usual. "I can't say I'm surprised to see you."

"Mrs. R, you have to believe me. Janis Mitchell is a liar. I don't know why she started all this, but I am not going to lose Leah over it. I know I need to talk with the Bishop."

"Yes, Grant, you do, and so does Leah. She has avoided him all week."

"I take full responsibility for this mess, and I will tell him that. I didn't know Leah hadn't talked to him. I promise that before I leave on Sunday, they will be friends again."

"I think he's still at the office, but we should call first."

There was no answer at the office. Katherine called his cell.

He answered abruptly. "I'm in the driveway." *Click!*

Lee walked into the house and immediately addressed Grant. "Son, what is your plan?"

"Sir, I am not…am not that child's father. I admit I had sex with her, but that was months ago. I have no explanation for why she is doing this to me."

Grant and Lee talked awhile.

"I can forgive you, son, but it's my daughter you need to be concerned about. My daughter is hurt, and she has never experienced anything like this. She is unaccustomed to gossip and humiliation. You get this straight, and you get it straight before you leave here. And if Leah tells you to go to hell, you go."

Grant had not seriously considered that Leah really might tell him it was over. He knew he had to get her to believe him, and he had to get Janis to tell him why she was lying on him. He knew Janis was reckless, but he underestimated how crazy she really was. He left the Robinson's for his final stop: Janis' house.

Janis looked out the window and was genuinely surprised to see Grant. She also was slightly apprehensive. She really did not know what to expect. The doorbell rang again. Janis opened the door and stepped aside.

"Why are you doing this, Janis? You know that's not my baby," he said, looking at her stomach. She didn't look pregnant to him.

"Why not, Grant? You could be the father of my child."

"What are you trying to prove?" he yelled.

"That the little debutante sorority girl honor graduate nurse manager who thinks she can have any and every thing she wants won't have you."

"Janis, think about what you saying. How much sense does that make? You can't make that decision for me. Even if Leah and I don't end up together, I don't want you."

"So I'm good enough to take to bed but not good enough to take home to Mama."

"Exactly."

She was furious. They went back and forth for a few minutes. He told her that she needed to tell the truth, tell Leah she lied. She refused. He told her he would have a blood test when the baby was born and the truth would come out.

"How are you going to feel when everybody knows you lied since you care so much about what people think?"

"I won't care because Leah will hate you, and that's what I care about."

Grant couldn't believe his ears. *She really is crazy.* "Janis, think about your child. How do you think he or she will feel when they find out what you did?"

He had her attention. That comment stung. She really had not considered the baby ever finding out.

"Your child needs to have a relationship with the real father."

That comment hit her hard. "My child won't ever know about any of this. My child will believe *me*!" she screamed.

Grant had calmed some. "As small as this town is, somebody will tell it. You don't want your son or daughter to ever think they can't believe you."

They both just stood there for a minute. He thought he had gotten through to her.

"Let this go before it goes any further."

"Grant Sturdivant, I am not letting anything go!" She was screaming again. "As far as I'm concerned, you are this baby's father and I don't care who knows it. I don't care what Miss Leah and her holy family think or those people at, your 'bougie' church. You need to leave."

"Okay, Janis, but Leah and I are not breaking up over this, and when we have the blood tests, the joke will be on you."

She was fuming. She opened the door and waited for him to leave. She locked the door just as the tears started to roll down her face.

Janis kept up the charade for the next six months. She made a point of being where she knew Leah would be. She even told her friends the baby was a boy and his name was Grant.

Things were tough for Grant and Leah, but he promised her that they would get through it. Grant was stationed in Georgia, so he didn't have to deal with it every day, but Leah did. Gretchen dealt with a lot of it too.

The day her daughter, Carmen, was born, Janis called to let Grant know. He didn't answer, so she left a message. When he got the message, he called Gretchen to put their plan in place.

Because it was before 5:00 p.m., she called the attorney who pre-pared the paperwork requesting the blood test. But because it was Friday, nothing would happen before Monday. So the chance of them getting the blood test done while the baby was still in the hospital was not good. Janis fought the request for the test and put it off as long as she could. When the court order was delivered to her, she had to comply. Three weeks later, the results of the paternity test revealed that Grant was not the father of the child. Between the lawyer and the test itself, it cost him hundreds of dollars, but it was worth it. Now he and Leah could get on with their lives, without the drama.

Janis surmised that if Gretchen was moving that kind of money out of Grant's account he must be coming home. She was giving this considerable thought. *There has to be a way for me to figure out when he's coming. Wouldn't he be surprised for me to meet him at the airport? Next week is Thanksgiving. He will be here for the holiday.*

$\mathscr{F}$OURTEEN

Clay had definitely gotten his role with Jeremy confused. Delia's money issues had come up several times recently. He had paid her car insurance and cell phone bill in the last couple of months, and today he had paid for Jeremy's team pictures.

After the pictures, the game, and the victory pizza, Clay, Delia, and the kids met back at Delia's house.

"Delia, what's going on with you financially?" Clay asked.

"Why do you ask?"

"Don't answer a question with a question. You know why I ask. All of a sudden, you can't pay your car insurance or cell phone bill, can't get Jeremy's pictures. What's up with that?"

"Clay, I got in a jam and asked you for help. If you didn't want to do it, you should have said no."

"Delia, you still didn't answer my question."

"What do you want to know? Do you want a rundown of my finances? Besides, if we are in a relationship, you should help me financially."

"I should help you?"

"Yes. If you are the man in my life, don't you think you should help me?"

"Is that what this is all about, money?"

Delia let out a big sigh. "Clay, I take care of your needs. Why shouldn't you take care of mine? Every man who has ever been in my life has given me money."

"Delia, listen to what you're saying. You sound like a prostitute."

"I can't believe you said that!"

"Why? What's the difference in what you're saying and selling your body?"

"We are in a relationship. You are not some random man."

"But you are comparing me to every man who has been in your life. Obviously there's nothing special about our relationship. Dee, you need to check yourself. Whether it's me or somebody else, you can't go into a relationship expecting money in exchange for intimacy."

"Call it what it is Clay: s-e-x! I am a single mother with two children. I need all the help I can get, and you obviously can afford to help."

"You're going about this all wrong, Delia. And you need to understand, s-e-x or not, I'm not going to bankroll you."

$\mathscr{F}$IFTEEN

Jill couldn't sleep. She had to laugh at herself. *You would think I was sixteen and going on my first date*, she thought.

Then she couldn't find anything to wear. *Hair up, down, or ponytail? Okay, Jill. Get yourself together.* This was not Jill's Sunday to serve as an usher/greeter, so she dressed up a little more than usual. She was glad Raja was tall so she could wear heels.

This was the first time ever she had been on a first date without Leah's input. A sinking feeling hit Jill in her stomach. She prayed silently for Leah to be well.

Jill pulled into the parking lot at Lola's and realized that she didn't know what kind of car Raja was driving. She decided to go in and get a table. Just as she walked in, he called. He had missed his turn. She talked him around the block and to the restaurant. He was driving Trey's truck. She should have known.

He looked incredible, more casual than usual. He was on the phone when he walked in and for a few minutes after they sat down.

"Forgive me, Jill. That was my cousin calling from London. He told me he is getting married!"

"No problem. How is Leah?" Jill asked.

"She is better, but not great. Her blood pressure is down due to the sedation. I left strict orders, and I'll be back on Thursday. By the way, Trey invited me back here for Thanksgiving dinner."

They ordered their food and had a lengthy conversation about his cousin's arranged marriage. Jill was very curious, and Raja obliged her by answering all of her questions.

"My parents' marriage was arranged. They had only known each other a few months, and the day they were married was the second time they had ever seen each other."

"I don't mean any disrespect, but did your grandparents pay a dowry too?"

"Yes"—he laughed—"and that is what my cousin and I were just discussing: his fiancée's parents have two daughters, and they are having a little difficulty with two dowries."

"This is the twenty-first century. You have to be joking."

"I wish I was, but my family is very traditional."

"Your family? What about you?"

"I am the radical one." He laughed. "Me and one other cousin. She is dating an African American guy she met in college. Her parents have disowned her."

"What do you mean disowned her?"

Raja went on to explain that his aunt and uncle had not spoken to their daughter in two years. They didn't want her to come to America to attend college. They wanted her to stay in London, and then they completely shut her out when she told them about her friend.

"The totally interesting thing about the situation is my uncle taught at two historically black colleges during the years he lived here. I am her only connection to the clan."

As the conversation continued over a great meal, Raja told Jill more about life in India and London and how marriages are arranged. He also told her he thought it was a barbaric tradition and he had no intention of participating. Jill was curious how his parents would react.

"Just like they did when I told them I had confessed Christ. They were incensed. They said I was their only child and I had disappointed them."

"But they didn't disown you."

"No, but they still ignore the fact that I am a Christian. My mother thinks it's a phase I'm going through—a phase that has lasted almost ten years. But Jill, marriages are arranged in this country too."

"You mean people from other cultures who maintain their traditions in this country?"

"No. I mean how Americans want their sons and daughters to marry within their own race or religion or socioeconomic background."

"Raja, you can't really believe that."

"Sure I do. If I were not a doctor, I would not be introduced to some of the young ladies I get introduced to or invited to some of the functions I get invited to."

As Jill listened to him talk, she noticed how dark his eyes were and how neatly trimmed his very short beard was and how perfectly manicured his nails were. She suddenly became very self-conscious and looked down at her own hands. She had missed her appointment this week, but for a three-week-old manicure, her hands looked pretty good.

"If I were not a successful friend of your brother, your father would not approve of me having brunch with you."

Jill laughed. "You don't know my father very well. He doesn't choose my friends."

"Maybe not your friends, but I know he would have input into who you marry."

"My father—my family, for that matter—just hopes somebody will want to marry me who can afford me. We have never really had the conversation, but I know my father well enough to know that his stipulation would only be that I marry a Christian. You have to understand, Raja, that our community is very diverse. I wish you had come to church with me this morning so you could see for yourself. Our congregation is like the United Nations. There are flags in our family life center that represent every country in our church family, and I know there are at least twenty, maybe thirty. My church family is my extended family and my friends. Leah and I have been best friends since middle school. I think the day it dawned on us that we were of different races was the day my Mom had a makeup party at our house and she let me and Leah come. She allowed us to get our faces made up and we discovered we had to use different shades of foundation."

The waitress had cleared their plates, and they continued to talk. When the crowd picked up, Jill looked at her watch and realized that it was about time for the after-church groups to start coming in. She hated to end their time together, but she knew they had held the table long enough. Raja knew it too, and he left a good tip on the table. They stood outside and chatted for a few minutes more. She told him she looked forward to him having Thanksgiving dinner with their family. He told her he would talk to her before Thursday. She was pleased.

"Are you driving the truck back?" Jill asked, rolling her eyes.

"Yeah. Strauss let me borrow it. Since I'm coming right back on Thursday, it worked out. He needed me to get here so quickly that I flew in on a medical ambulance headed for Atlanta and they dropped me off in Charlotte."

Raja walked Jill to her car, opened the door for her, and waited until she had driven off before he got in the truck to leave.

Jill drove straight to the hospital. She had to tell Leah about Raja, whether Leah could hear her or not.

$\mathscr{S}$IXTEEN

Grammy and Aunt Avis unpacked the bags they brought and filled the refrigerator with what they had prepared the night before for lunch and dinner. They went upstairs to see what Brittani needed and to get a good look at the rest of the house. The downstairs was in good shape, but you can really tell how people live when you see their bedrooms. The twins' room was a little fussy, but the bathroom was clean and Belinda's room was very neat and well decorated. The twins' room didn't have any problems that a little more space wouldn't solve. It was decorated nicely in pink, green, lavender, and white. There was a set of twin beds, a desk with bookshelves, two chests of drawers, and a toy box at the foot of each bed. There was a picture of a strikingly handsome man on top of each chest.

Brittani saw Grammy looking at the picture. "That's my daddy. He died in Iraq."

"I'm sure you're proud of him for being a soldier," Grammy responded.

"My mommy said it was a waste. She put the pictures in here because she gets too sad when she looks at them. We have a lot more pictures on the shelf in that blue book if you want to look at them."

"Maybe we'll look at them later," Grammy said, looking at Avis.

The morning went well. They read and played UNO. Brittani was impressed that Grammy and Auntie could play. Brianna would bring home Brittani's assignments and two new library books, so the next day they would have work to do. Brianna left the cordless phone where Brittani could reach it in case someone called. They had several calls during the day from Belinda, Aunt Kirby, and Uncle Enoch. And they had one visitor: Minister Ben.

Ben dropped by at about the time Aunt Avis was getting ready to bring Brittani downstairs. Grammy was heating up lunch. His timing was perfect. He carried her down the stairs. Grammy told Brittani he must have smelled her chicken pot pie across town.

"No. Actually, it was the oatmeal cookies I could smell," he said, winking at Brittani.

The four had lunch together, and shortly afterward Aunt Avis left to pick Brianna up from school. Brittani was tired. Ben and Grammy took her back upstairs, gave her a pain pill, and got her settled. They went back down so Grammy could see her soap opera.

"Thanks for doing this, Grammy. I appreciate you coming through for me."

"For you? I thought I was doing this to help Belinda."

"You are, but I wanted to be the one to offer her some help, some relief."

"What are you saying, honey?"

"I really, really like her, Grammy, and this has given me a way to get to at least talk to her. She's very standoffish."

"Her husband died, honey, suddenly, tragically. And I'm sure she still needs to work through that pain. And I'm sure she has built a wall around her heart. I did too when your grandpa died. Be her friend, but don't rush her and don't expect anything immediate."

That wasn't what Ben wanted to hear, but he knew that Grammy was right. He didn't want to blow it, so he needed to be careful and make good decisions. He decided that it was time to talk to Enoch.

$\mathscr{S}$EVENTEEN

On the drive back to Chapel Hill, Raja thought through his conversation with Jill. She was an intelligent, incredibly beautiful woman, and she was very wealthy. He noticed her car, her jewelry, and the comment she made about a husband who could afford her. He had always known that the family was well established, and Trey wasn't excessive, but even the townhouse they shared in med school was among the nicest in the area. Raja wanted to see Jill again, but he didn't know if their lifestyles were compatible. His car was almost ten years old, and hers was one year old. Her jewelry and clothes were better quality than anything his father had been able to give his mother.

Raja had only met their mother once, many years ago. He didn't remember how she was dressed or what kind of jewelry she wore. He just remembered her being incredibly warm and pleasant. *Did Dr. Strauss provide all this for Jill, or did she get these things for herself? What difference does it make?*

Raja kept thinking as he drove. *Why am I so concerned about material things?* He knew of her philanthropy, her work with the foundation. He had seen their annual report and knew how much money they contributed to very worthy causes and organizations. Many of the charities they contributed to were ones he was interested in himself, including both of the ones he contributed to regularly.

Jill was a woman in a position of authority and influence. She had to look prosperous.

Raja's thoughts were interrupted by his phone. It was Trey. He hoped the call didn't concern Leah Robinson.

"How are you, my friend?" Raja asked when he answered.

"Doing well, and you?"

"Good."

"Yeah. I bet so. You hanging out with my sister."

"Guilty." Raja laughed.

Trey told Raja about his exam of Leah, and they discussed the plan for the next three days. Then the conversation shifted back to Jill.

"Does Jill report all her brunch dates to you?"

"As a matter of fact, she does...not. No. I saw her at the hospital, and she told me you all had been to Lola's so she wasn't hungry. Now what are your intentions toward my sister?"

"I intend to see her on Thursday when I come back. You and Jill are a lot alike. Your interests and opinions are very similar."

"Yeah. Probably so. But my sister is her own woman, her own person. Don't underestimate her. Jill can hold her own."

Raja took a chance and shared with Trey the comment Jill made about a husband who could afford her.

Trey laughed. "Man, Jill can spend a bunch of money, but the truth is she can afford herself. Jill has built the Strauss Foundation into the empire that it is. She is well versed in how to invest, how to buy and sell stock. Her personal portfolio looks great. My granddad gave us stock for our sixteenth birthdays. I just let mine sit. It grew, but not like hers. She did research and talked with Granddad's broker. She got interested and kept it going. If the expectation had not been for her to take over the foundation, she would probably be on Wall Street. She makes a good salary, and she pays her staff well. That's why they work so hard. She gives a lot too of her personal resources. She is a steadfast believer of what Bishop calls the prosperity principle: the more you give the more you receive."

They talked a few more minutes, made a plan for Thursday, and hung up. Raja was actually glad he had talked with Trey about his concerns. He felt better about the comment, but he had to give some more thought to how independent she obviously was. The fact that she took over the foundation because that was her family's expectation went a long way with him. She was loyal to her family. That was good. He didn't know if he wanted a wife who didn't need him.

Wife! Why am I thinking of her in that way? I don't even know her. I might not like her once I do get to know her, and she might not like me. He decided he needed to get his mind on other things.

EIGHTEEN

Avis and Brianna came in and went upstairs to find Brittani and Grammy watching *Akeelah and the Bee*. The girls hugged, and Brianna proceeded to recap the day at school. Everybody asked about Brittani, and the principal even said on the morning announcements that everybody should send good thoughts to her. Brittani asked for her two new library books and her assignments for the week.

Grammy and Avis left the girls upstairs after Brianna changed her clothes. They also had a recap of the day.

"Victoria, I told you there was more to this than his ministerial duty."

"Yes, you did. And you were right. I'm glad, though. Benji is not getting any younger, and he needs to be thinking about settling down."

"But you know Belinda won't be an easy person to get close to. Her pain is real, and the heartache is most likely still there if she can't even look at the man's picture."

Victoria nodded in agreement. They settled in to watch Oprah at 4:00 p.m. and would get dinner ready at 5:00 p.m. The routine didn't change because they were not at home except there was homework to get done and checked. Avis went back up to check on the girls and see if they wanted to watch Oprah too since her guests were Venus and Serena Williams. They all came back downstairs. Brianna had devised a plan for Brittani to come down on her bottom, but Avis didn't think that was such a good idea this early in the healing process.

Belinda came home to dinner and a clean kitchen. The girls' homework was done, and Brianna was in the bathtub. Dinner was more than she expected, and the rest was gravy. Almost as soon as Belinda went upstairs, the bell rang, and it was Enoch. Kirby arrived a few minutes later and Ben a few minutes after that.

Belinda was amazed that there was enough food.

"I know my crew," Grammy explained.

Kirby and Belinda went upstairs to figure out how to bathe Brittani, and Enoch and Ben finished up the kitchen. Grammy and Avis left after Belinda thanked them over and over. They said they would be back in the morning.

While Ben and Enoch packed the leftovers for Belinda, Kirby, and Enoch's lunch the next day, Ben decided to ask Enoch what he thought Belinda would say if he asked her out.

"No." Enoch laughed.

Ben looked crushed.

"Man, Belinda is gun shy. She doesn't trust the process, and she's afraid of being hurt again."

"But what happened to her husband wasn't like he cut out on her. She can't be mad at anybody but God because He allowed it."

"Whew! Don't go there. She went through the whole not-feelin'-God phase too when she first got here. And sometimes now she can get pretty funky. My suggestion is that you make the best of this week while Grammy's here and you have a reason to be in and out. Just be her friend. Don't be trying to court her. Plus, you didn't ask me if you could take her out. I knew you were feelin' her. I could tell."

"Why in the world would I ask you?"

"'Cause her Pops ain't around and I'm the big brother."

"Where is her family?" Ben asked.

"Who knows? Neither Kirby nor Belinda know anything about their biological families. Belinda was born in Augusta, Georgia, and Kirby was born in Knoxville, Tennessee. That's all they know. They ended up in foster care in Greenville, North Carolina."

"So neither of them has ever searched for their families?"

"Not that I know of. They both were put in foster care as infants. Their foster parents took good care of them. They only ever lived with one family, so they considered them their family."

"Are the foster parents still living?"

"No. The dad died while they were in college, and the mom died about a year ago.

Ben continued to ask questions, and Enoch answered what he could. When the conversation shifted to Canady and Belinda's relationship, Enoch stopped answering.

"Man, that's the kind of information you need to get from her. They lived in California most of the time they were married, so I didn't see them interact on a day-to-day basis. But from everything I knew, he was great to her and the girls."

What Enoch didn't want to say was that they were madly in love. Canady adored Belinda, and she adored him. He was definitely the wind beneath her wings. Kirby had confided in him that Belinda was still grieving, still crying, and still having nightmares. Ben might have been just what the doctor ordered, but making Belinda see that would be a chore.

NINETEEN

It had become a tradition in the community since Lola's opened to have Thanksgiving dinner there. During the course of the day, hundreds of people would eat hundreds of pounds of turkey, dressing, collard greens, sweet potatoes, and about anything else that was served. And hundreds of pounds of the same food would be served to the men, women, and children from the homeless shelter transported to Lola's by the HCC buses and paid for through donations from everybody who ate the Thanksgiving dinner.

Bishop and First Lady Robinson made a point to be there while the shelter residents were there. A banner had been designed for the event and hung inside the restaurant that said, "We are taking our meals 'together with gladness and sincerity of heart' Acts 2:46."

Under the circumstances, it was good that Thanksgiving dinner would be prepared. Katherine Robinson didn't have the physical or mental energy to deal with it.

As expected, hundreds of people came to Lola's for the community Thanksgiving dinner, including the residents from the shelters. Volunteers from HCC and a few other churches helped serve and clean up.

Bishop and First Lady Robinson were there at noon and spent time with their special guests before having dinner with their family, the Sturdivants, and the Strauss family. Paul Sturdivant was able to come, and that was a treat for Grace and Gretchen.

Kathy had visited Leah before going to the restaurant. She had convinced her parents to take the day off and spend their day ministering to people who really needed them. Leah would understand and want them to. Kathy talked with the ICU nurse, who assured her that Leah was responding to the medication and that they were expecting Dr. Raja any minute to do his assessment. Dr. Zack had been in, and Dr. Trey would be there with Dr. Raja.

Janis Mitchell and her family came to the restaurant for dinner too. They sat away from the Robinsons and didn't acknowledge them. She noticed Grant's parents and Gretchen, and she noticed that he wasn't there.

Her theory had been wrong about his travel schedule. Janis had double-checked the flights from Germany and arrived at the airport thirty minutes before the flight was due. Every hair in place, dressed immaculately, and wearing Grant's favorite scent, she waited in the baggage claim area and watched the monitor. The flight arrived on time. Her heart was pounding. He would be surprised and maybe even angry at first, but he would warm up to the idea of her being there to meet him. She looked around and didn't see Gretchen or Clay, so they must have been in the cell phone lot, waiting for his call. She would meet him in person. They were going to pick him up at the curb. How impersonal.

The passengers started to gather in the baggage claim area. There were a lot of them, but so far no Grant. She waited and moved away from the crowd so she could see him come down the escalator. No Grant. Maybe she missed him. Maybe he went out of the departure area doors upstairs. No. The realization was Grant wasn't on the flight. She had guessed incorrectly.

Janis had been wrong about why Gretchen withdrew the money from Grant's account. *What is really going on? Why do I care? Nobody I talked to said anything about Leah being better, so he has to be coming home.* She vowed to figure it out.

Jill and Raja had talked every day since the brunch date on Sunday, and they were looking forward to having Thanksgiving dinner together on Thursday. Raja and Trey were meeting at the hospital to consult on Leah, and then they would meet the family at Lola's. Jill was more relaxed than she had been on Sunday. Her attire for the day was a pair of jeans and an HCC T-shirt. She was on the volunteer team, so he would have to see her dressed down today. Jill hoped she could get Raja to work some too so he wouldn't feel like a guest.

Raja and Trey looked over Leah's test results, consulted with the nurses, and did a thorough examination. Raja was pleased with her progress. He instructed the nurse to stop the sedation but to keep constant check on her blood pressure. They were to page him and Trey as soon as she was awake, which they expected in about twenty-four hours. He wanted to know if she was not awake in twenty-eight hours. He gave several other specific instructions, signed the chart, went to Trey's office and dictated his notes, and they left for dinner.

When Trey and Raja arrived at the restaurant, Ellen Strauss basically met them at the door and gave them bust pans. They went to work immediately. Jill was pretty amused. She wanted Raja to feel included but she wanted to ease him into the process. They did manage to say hello and to discuss his examination of Leah.

An hour or so later, when the HCC bus left with the last of the shelter residents, the crowd thinned considerably and the Strauss family, the Sturdivant family, and the Robinson family finally sat down to dinner themselves. Of course, Raja was the guest of honor because he was new to the group but also because he was Leah's doctor.

After the prayer and blessing of the meal, Raja told everybody about his exam of Leah. Gretchen made a note of what Raja said so she could tell Grant.

As everyone settled into their own conversations, Jill and Raja finally had an opportunity to talk. The chemistry was good, and they discovered that they had a lot in common. Raja was actually surprised. He saw Jill as the compassionate, brilliant woman she really was. Jill had a real servant's heart, and Raja saw it firsthand that day. It was a good day, and they both secretly hoped it was the beginning of a good courtship.

Kathy had taken a special interest in one of her students, Campbell Rice. She had invited him to volunteer with the HCC group and to have dinner with her family. He was a bright young man and a good student, and he was a Christian. But she could see him starting to be distracted, and she was determined not to let that happen. He was sixteen and really needed a job, but his mother wanted him around the house when she worked evenings and nights to supervise his brothers.

Campbell was helping the restaurant staff clear the tables. He worked hard and fast and took pride in his work. Kathy hoped the restaurant managers would notice. She decided that she would ask if they would consider hiring him.

Enoch, Kirby, Belinda, and the girls arrived at Lola's just ahead of Auntie Avis, Grammy, and Ben. Brittani and Brianna had invited themselves to eat dinner with Grammy and Aunt Avis. The four of them had become fast friends. Enoch, Kirby, Ben, and Belinda did their volunteer time with food and dishes, but Grammy, Auntie, and the twins used the time to meet everybody they could, talking to other children who were also in the fire. They all had a story, but Brittani was the celebrity because she was hurt the worst. They all signed her pink cast with a green pen. Auntie had even tied pink-and- green bows on her crutches.

Ben made sure he stayed close to Belinda. They made small talk and laughed a lot. He told her this was his second Thanksgiving back in Hattiesville. She confided in him that she had not really celebrated any holidays since Canady passed. But it had gotten harder every year not to because the girls wanted to. Ben wanted to be very careful how he responded.

"I'm glad you decided to hang out this year," he said.

"Well, if I hadn't, I would have been home alone. My daughters were determined to be here with their two new best friends." She nodded toward Grammy and Aunt Avis.

"Trust me. The feeling is mutual. I reminded them that Brittani is going back to school next week and they will need to find something else to do."

They both laughed. Talking about Grammy teaching the girls how to knit and Aunt Avis teaching them French was easy, but Ben wanted to talk about so much more. He wanted to know what she was thinking, how she felt about so many things. He wanted to know her favorite scriptures and her favorite color, what made her laugh. But he made himself content with hearing her talk about the girls' next project, learning to cross stitch, and how many new pot holders they made in two days. He remembered what Enoch said and thanked God silently for them just being there together.

After they ate and cleaned up, everybody left for the evening. It had been a great day. God was pleased with their service, and that was the whole point.

Enoch and Kirby didn't stay long when they dropped the girls and Belinda at home. Belinda got the girls settled in, and when she got into bed, she hoped to go to sleep quickly. She didn't want to be alone with her thoughts. She did go to sleep quickly, but she dreamed. She dreamed about the fire. She dreamed about Canady. And she dreamed about Ben.

Since there was no school on Friday, the twins, Grammy, and Aunt Avis didn't see each other, but they had a play date for Saturday. Brittani told Belinda she should see if Aunt Kirby wanted to go shopping or something because they were going to get cooking lessons from Grammy and Auntie Avis. They had changed from calling the sisters Mrs. Johnson and Mrs. Coffey to calling them by the pet names Ben had given them as a little boy.

Belinda did need to study, so she was grateful for the time alone, but she felt guilty for imposing on these two wonderful women. Every day they had been there with the girls, the house was spotless, dinner was cooked, homework was done and checked, and lunch was prepared for the next day. Belinda had gotten so much done and had been able to get to bed a little early each night. She told Kirby she could get used to it.

Brittani was recovering nicely, and they expected she would return to school on Wednesday after her appointment on Tuesday. Grammy and Aunt Avis told Belinda they would meet her at Trey's office so she wouldn't have to come back to Hattiesville and go back to Charlotte. Grammy told Ben she needed him to drive them to Charlotte to meet Belinda at the doctor's office. Avis just laughed. Ben knew they didn't need him, but he appreciated Grammy looking out for him.

Grammy and Belinda had had a brief conversation after a few days of them being there with the twins.

"Belinda, the girls told me that the pictures of that handsome man in their room is their dad."

"Yes, that's Canady." She didn't say anything for a minute.

"You still miss him, don't you?"

"Yes, ma'am, I do. I am still heartsick about him being gone. I still dream about him, and I miss him so much."

"I can relate," Grammy said. "You know I lost my husband and my only child. But Belinda, let me assure you, God is faithful, and in time those wounds healed, and yours will too. But let me also give you some advice: Talk to somebody. Don't try to work through this alone."

Delia, Jeremy, and Crystal had Thanksgiving dinner at Lola's with Delia's family. She didn't spend a lot of social time with them, but her parents had asked and she obliged them. Crystal and Jeremy were excited about seeing their cousins from Atlanta. Delia invited Clay to have dinner with them, but he explained that Thanksgiving dinner was a command performance for the Sturdivant family. His uncle Paul was coming, so he would be spending the evening with them. Delia told Clay that she wanted her parents to meet him. He asked what time they would be there and said that he would try to see them there. The truth was he wasn't feeling meeting the family. Delia was really pushing the couple thing.

Clay thought he had missed Delia and her family, but just as the wheelchair transportation was pulling away with his uncle Paul, he heard Jeremy call his name.

"What's up, man?" Clay asked Jeremy as they shook hands and then hugged in their usual way of greeting.

Clay followed Jeremy back into the restaurant and to the table where his mother and the family were being seated. Jeremy was beaming as he introduced his cousins, uncle, and grandparents to "Mr. Clay Sturdivant, my Big Brother." After the introductions, Clay moved to the other end of the table, where Delia was sitting with her sister-in-law.

"This is my friend, Clay," Delia said, smiling.

"I'm Jeremy's Big Brother, and it's my pleasure to meet you."

The disappointment on her face was evident. She couldn't believe he wouldn't own their relationship. She was furious, and she fully intended to tell him so.

$\mathscr{T}$WENTY

The trip to the doctor became an adventure. Brittani, Aunt Avis, and Grammy entertained Ben on the thirty-minute drive to Charlotte. They played word games and laughed a lot. Belinda was waiting when they arrived at Dr. Trey's office. Ben, Auntie, and Grammy sat in the waiting room while Brittani was being examined.

Dr. Trey looked at Brittani's X-rays and was pleased with what they showed. He had a soft cast put on her leg but told her that she could go back to school but not back to ballet yet. Ballet. They hadn't talked about going back. The thought sent a chill down Belinda's spine. Brianna had assured Brittani that they could go back to ballet because the fire was an accident. So Brittani knew Brianna would be disappointed. But Brianna could go, and she would teach Brittani the new dances as soon as her leg was stronger. As she explained the plan to Dr. Trey, Belinda hoped she would be able to talk them out of it.

Brittani told Grammy and Avis what the doctor said. She could go back to school the next day, but he thought that she shouldn't ride the bus yet or go back to ballet. She was going to miss them. Maybe they could still come to her house after school. She would talk to Brianna about it.

Leah's blood pressure had been steady for eighteen hours. It elevated slightly at hours nineteen and twenty. She started to stir a little at twenty-one.

Kim Horng's shift started at 11:00 a.m., and she was determined to awaken Leah. She wiped her face with a warm cloth and rubbed her hands. She talked to her about patients, the weather, her wedding. A little over twenty-five hours after stopping the sedation, Leah woke up.

Brittani called Enoch and Kirby to tell them that she was going back to school the next day and that Grammy and Auntie were going to pick her and her sister up from school and be the after-school teachers until she could ride the bus again. Having delivered all the information she thought was pertinent, she gave her mother the telephone and went to her room to prepare for the next morning.

Belinda and Kirby talked for only a few minutes. Kirby reminded Belinda that she had an appointment with the gynecologist the next day. She hung up and headed upstairs so she and Enoch could talk and because they needed to pray.

Leah's mouth was dry, and she couldn't feel her legs. Her head hurt, but not bad. She wanted to sit up, and she was hot. She didn't know who Kim was or where she was.

"Leah, its Kim Horng. Do you know where you are?"

There was no response, but Leah did make eye contact.

"Can you blink?"

Leah blinked her eyes.

"I'm going to remove the tube from your mouth."

She did, and Leah coughed slightly. Kim raised the head of the bed, paged Trey, and checked her vitals. Leah licked her lips, so Kim gave her a few ice chips. Kim performed the basic neurological exam and discovered that the paralysis was still there in her lower extremities. She also knew that Leah didn't remember what had happened.

"Leah, you're in the hospital. You had an aneurysm. It was repaired surgically. Do you remember Dr. Trey telling you that?"

Leah nodded yes. Her throat was scratchy, and she couldn't talk.

"Good. You had some complications, so we induced a coma and you've been sleeping for a few days."

Leah was very quiet, but Kim could tell that she was trying to comprehend what she was saying.

Leah cleared her throat. "I can't feel my legs."

"That is temporary paralysis. We'll get you working with a therapist in a day or so, and that should pass."

"I want my daddy," Leah said as tears began to swell in her eyes.

"I'll call him right now." Kim hoped Leah could answer the next question. "Can you tell me his number?"

Leah thought, but she couldn't remember. The tears fell down her face.

Not good, Kim thought. *If she doesn't remember her dad's number, chances are that there will be other things she won't remember.*

"That's okay. I'll get it." Kim called the nurses' station and asked them to call the Robinsons.

Kim continued to talk to Leah, and Leah gave her one- or two-word answers if she could.

"Kim, Dr. Strauss is in surgery. They just called from the OR. I have paged Dr. Rajagopal to call you."

"Thank you," Kim said into the microphone.

Dr. Zack arrived in Leah's room first. The OR had paged him. Leah recognized him but didn't know his name. He talked to her about her illness and the surgery. He recounted the whole course of events. Leah didn't remember any of it. When Trey finally arrived, Leah's reaction was the same. He was also concerned with her lower body paralysis.

Talking to Raja by phone as he drove in, Trey did a more extensive exam. The conclusion: Leah could not write, walk, or remember numbers or names. She could not recite the alphabet or count to ten. Interestingly, she did remember the end of a song and two verses of scripture her mother knew she loved. Raja told Trey to order some tests. The results would dictate their course of action.

Kim asked Trey if she could take Leah for a shower while they were waiting for the tests to be administered. He hadn't thought of that but knew that that would relax her some and thought maybe the warm water would work as a stimulant. Kim made arrangements for a shower bed, and she said she would do it herself if none of the nurses' aides were available. Registered nurses did not shower patients, but everybody on the floor knew that Kim and Leah were friends, so they were making allowances and picking up her other responsibilities. Leah could feel the warm water from her waist up but nothing from the waist down. Kim could hear her stomach growl and promised her a snack after the tests.

Raja arrived at about the time the first test results were back. Her heart and lungs were fine, as was her liver. The test on her kidneys and the brain scan would be available shortly. Her pupils were reactive, and her blood pressure was slightly high. She told Raja that her headache was slight, a five on a one-to-ten scale. He asked her if she could tolerate the pain a little. He didn't want to give her any pain medicine if he didn't have to. She said she could. Then she started to cry. Her mother knew it was out of sheer frustration. There was nothing they could do to console her, so they let her cry. Dr. Raja gave his orders to Nurse Kim, including physical therapy to start the next day, solid food for breakfast, and a psychological consult.

Grant boarded the plane for the eight-hour flight. He would change planes in Atlanta, and Gretchen would pick him up in Charlotte. As anxious as he was to get home to see Leah, he didn't know what to expect. He hoped he wouldn't shock her by just showing up. He hoped she would be glad to see him and that she would get better because he was there.

Gretchen had told him last night that she still hadn't awakened. Grant loved Leah—really loved her. He messed around with Janis and regretted it. He would never do anything to hurt her again. He had to see her for himself, and he finally was on his way.

Clay's company's annual conference in Las Vegas came at the right time. He needed some distance from Delia. She had really been sweating him since the Thanksgiving dinner episode. She was really angry about his introduction as Jeremy's Big Brother. He knew he was in over his head with her. He just wasn't that into her. He liked her. He adored the kids, and the sex was good. He asked himself over and over what it was about her that wasn't clicking for him. The only thing he could come up with was that she was too needy. She had some unresolved issues with her parents and the fathers of her children, but none of that had anything to do with him. He knew it was a Friday night discussion point for him, Enoch, and Ben. He had left Gretchen a message to remind her that she had promised to fix them some food. Not only was she the best hair dresser in town, but his cousin was an excellent cook.

Speaking of Gretchen, Clay needed to forward her his itinerary for Vegas. He always made sure she knew where he was and how to reach him.

Clay checked his personal e-mail, and he had two new e-mail messages—one from Gretchen titled "Grant" with a high priority: "GP is en route to Charlotte. He is arriving tonight at 9:20. I am picking him up but wanted you to know. Nobody else knows he's coming. I'll call you later. Smooches, GG. P.S. Got the food covered. Hope you can make room for Grant. Sure he can use the fellowship."

Clay hit reply and sent the message to her phone.

"Got the msg. Tell GP to holla when he lands. Will meet you at the house if you want me to. Love ya back."

Clay hadn't been to see Leah, but his aunt Grace had kept him informed of her situation. If Grant was coming home, things must not be too good. But on second thought, if he was coming and nobody knew, he decided to do it on his own.

Clay sent an e-mail to his assistant and asked her to change his flight to come back the day the conference ended. He had planned to stay a few extra days, but if Grant was going to be home, he wanted to come back. He had told Jeremy that he would be out of town the next weekend and wouldn't make his game, but now he would be here. He hated to lie, but he decided he just wouldn't tell them any different. Delia had asked if she could go with him, and he told her no and didn't tell her the conference was ending three days before he was coming back. He didn't tell her partly because he needed some air, but also because a friend from the Chicago office would be there and he hadn't seen her in a year.

The text message from Grant said he was in Atlanta, but the flight was delayed due to the weather. He would call her when he was on his way. Gretchen forwarded the message to Clay and stepped out of her shoes. She could get a jump on the refreshments for the Friday night Xbox /PlayStation tournament, or whatever they called it. Clay wanted chicken salad "with the grapes and nuts and stuff." She decided to double the recipe and take some to her dad.

Before she got started in the kitchen, she remembered she needed to put towels in the guest bathroom for Grant. She hadn't asked; she just assumed he would stay there. Kathy was staying at Leah's, and she didn't think he would be able to really relax at their parents' home.

"Ma is going to flip when she sees him." Gretchen laughed out loud.

Janis had made another unsuccessful trip to the airport a few days ago. There was nobody to ask, but Grant had to be headed home. She would try tonight and then let it go if he wasn't on this flight. Three strikes and you're out.

Dressed, hair done, and smelling good, Janis walked into the airport a few minutes before the flight from Frankfurt was to arrive. She looked at the monitor: "On Time." *Good*, she thought as she smiled to herself.

She stood at the bottom of the escalator and waited for Grant to come down. She had checked her hair and lip gloss. They were perfect. She waited, and she waited. No Grant. Janis went upstairs to the ticket counter to inquire about the flight schedule. The man at the counter told her that it was the only flight that day directly from Frankfurt. There wouldn't be another one until next week.

Janis was angry. She just didn't understand why she couldn't figure out what was going on. Her friend told her that just because he took money out of his savings didn't mean he was buying a plane ticket.

"He is getting married. Maybe he needed the money for the honeymoon."

Janis was furious and hung up on her friend. But maybe she had been right because three airport trips later, there was still no sign of Grant. But Leah was sick, in a coma. She heard Leah had had a stroke and couldn't walk. So surely the wedding was called off. He couldn't still want to marry her.

She decided to call him. She would ask if he was coming home for Christmas. He wouldn't tell her. She would think of something. Grant Sturdivant wouldn't be able to hide forever.

TWENTY-ONE

The appointment at the gynecologist was more intense than Kirby expected. The doctor basically said she had some problems that might or might not be corrected by surgery. He wanted to run some additional tests, but he was pretty sure her fallopian tubes were blocked, preventing her from becoming pregnant. Kirby willed herself not to cry. She knew that God could and would heal her. She asked the doctor what her options were. He said that they would discuss it after he saw the results of the test.

Kirby had purposely scheduled the appointment when neither Enoch nor Belinda could go. Enoch asked her to reschedule, and he offered to reschedule his appointment, but Kirby insisted she could go alone. He knew she would tell him what the doctor said and be totally honest, but his concern was the doctor might tell Kirby something that would devastate her and she would be alone.

She explained it all to Enoch, who was relieved. The research he had done and things he heard at the barbershop had him concerned that they would not be able to conceive. He held her tight and assured her that they would do what they needed to do.

"But like Bishop said, we gotta keep practicing."

She just rolled her eyes at him. They prayed and talked a little more.

"Are you okay with having surgery if that is the doctor's recommendation?"

"Yes, if you are," she said. "I want a baby bad, Enoch, and the thought of not having one makes me sick."

"Whoa, whoa. Don't let it make you sick, K. We can adopt, and I'm okay with that."

She knew that was coming, but she didn't want to hear it. Every time he said that, she wanted to scream. He didn't understand. Her mother gave her away, and she wanted to do better. It was easy for Enoch to say, "We can adopt." He was raised by both his parents and grandparents who loved him. He was a bratty only child who knew nothing about adversity. His family didn't have much. His parents never owned their own home. They always lived with his grandparents in the family home, but he was raised well. Kirby was grateful for the foster family who raised her and Belinda, but as they had often discussed, there was still something missing. Belinda had her own children, so Kirby knew that she didn't fully understand either. For Enoch, it was not about biology; he simply wanted a house full of children running around, making noise. But for Kirby, it was very much about biology. She knew that not wanting to adopt was selfish. She was being selfish toward the children they could bless and toward Enoch. Kirby could never tell Enoch, but she was so unhappy and so angry. She was angry with life, angry with God.

Why is this happening to me? she thought.

Enoch's answer to that question would be, Why not her? She was an abandoned baby who grew up in foster care, and then her life changed. She met and married an incredible man, and what they wanted most—children—was eluding them.

TWENTY-TWO

Grant finally arrived an hour after he was scheduled to. Gretchen knew she would be glad to see him, but she hadn't realized how glad. They had to come up with a way to tell their parents he was here. They wanted to surprise them but not shock them.

Clay's suggestion was that they call the house and tell Uncle Paul and let him tell Aunt Grace or tell them what to do. Grant thought Clay should make the call.

"Okay, I'll call," Clay said. He dialed the number laughing but hoping Uncle Paul would answer.

"Can you talk a minute?" Clay asked.

"Sure, son. What's on your mind?" Paul said.

"I just want to tell you Gretchen is on her way to your house… with Grant."

Paul chuckled. "I'm not surprised. How close are they?"

"Probably fifteen minutes out. I'm on my way too. We know Aunt Gracie is going to have a fit."

Paul laughed heartily this time. "She will for a few minutes, but it will be all right. Come on, and I'll tell her before they get here."

"Gracie, come here for a minute please. That was Clay on the phone, and he has a surprise for you."

"What kind of surprise?" She laid down the magazine she had been reading.

"Your daughter is on her way here with Clay and Grant."

"Grant is here?"

"Yes. Gretchen just picked him up from the airport."

"What in the world was he thinking coming across the world without telling anybody?"

"He told Gretchen." Paul laughed.

"He tells Gretchen everything. That is not the point. Ugh. That boy makes my blood pressure go up."

"Grace, he is not a boy. He is a grown man with a fiancée—a fiancée who is very sick. I'm not surprised at all. The only thing I'm surprised about is he's just getting here."

"Paul, Lee and I told Grant to wait, not to come now."

"Sweetie, did you hear what you just said? Neither you nor Lee, no matter how good your intentions, have the right to tell Grant what to do. I repeat, he is a grown man with the where-withal to make his own decisions. When they get here, don't jump on Grant. He has enough on his mind. Be glad to see him."

Just then, they heard the door alarm monitor beep.

"Mommy, Daddy, I come bearing gifts," Gretchen yelled.

"I heard you have a big gift," Grace said

All the other things Grace was going to say went out of her mind when she laid eyes on Grant. She hugged him tightly, thanked God silently, and let the tears that were stinging her eyes roll down her face. She finally turned him loose so he could hug his dad. The alarm monitor beeped again, and it was Clay. As soon as he walked in, Grace hit him on the arm.

"Ouch!"

"So you knew about his too?"

"Knew about what?"

"Don't play with me Clayton Paul Sturdivant."

"Aunt Gracie, you know I wouldn't keep anything from you!"

Clay and Grant hugged. They were really glad to see each other. They would talk later. Gretchen walked back into the room with everyone else. She had put the chicken salad in the refrigerator.

"Daddy, I brought you some chicken salad."

"Thank you, sugar," he said as she kissed his forehead.

"Is chicken salad supposed to make it all better?" Grace asked.

"Ma!" Gretchen was laughing.

"And I guess Clay is the reinforcement," Grace said, smiling.

Clay, Gretchen, and Grant looked at each other, and they all laughed.

"Let it go, Gracie," Paul said firmly.

She was still wiping tears. Grant put his arms around her again, and she cried.

They talked a few minutes about how Paul was doing. He updated Grant on his therapy and last doctor's visits. The conversation then turned to Leah. Grant took a deep breath and asked his mom what to expect.

"I don't think you should try to see her tonight. She's only been awake a few hours."

"She's awake?" Grant and Gretchen asked at the same time.

"Oh, I thought you knew."

"No. I haven't talked to anybody in over twenty-four hours," Grant said.

"Well, I haven't seen her, but I talked with Katherine this afternoon. She told me that Leah can talk, and she did recognize her and her dad, but she does have some memory loss. She doesn't remember anything about her surgery. Dr. Zack and Trey say that they think this is all temporary, including the paralysis in her legs."

"That's what I was afraid of the most. I see it all the time," Grant said.

"The trouble is Leah is not in shape. She probably can't do three sit-ups. So she is going to have to work really hard to make her legs work."

Grant started to pace back and forth. Nobody said anything. Grant looked at his dad.

"What if she doesn't recognize me or remember that we are getting married?"

"Son, you can what-if all night. Don't start that. It serves no purpose. I do suggest though that you not surprise her. Call and tell her you're here before you go."

"That's what's up, GP," Clay said.

"Okay. I will in the morning. Ma, if you speak to her parents, please don't say anything about me being home. Bishop told me not to come, so I want to speak with him myself."

They talked for a few more minutes, and Clay decided he could leave. He told Grant that they were playing video games at his house tomorrow night, and he wanted him to come hang out. Grant said he would. Clay and Gretchen worked out the food delivery.

"You acting like you don't have a key and the alarm code," Clay said.

"That's not the point. I need to give you some instructions so you won't mess up the presentation," Gretchen replied.

Grant and Clay looked at each other, and Grant shrugged his shoulders.

"Are you staying here or going home with your sister?" Grace asked.

Paul just looked at Grace. He knew the answer to the question, and so did she.

"I'm going home with GG. I'll see you tomorrow."

"How long you here for, son?" Paul asked Grant.

"I'm on emergency family leave, so I only have ten days, including travel."

Grant didn't realize how tired he was until he got out the shower. He hit the mute button on the remote and got on his knees to pray. He prayed on his knees every morning and every night. He got up and lay across the bed. The TV was on SportsCenter, but he was only half listening. He couldn't help but think that Leah might not remember him or that he loved her, that they were getting married in six months. He really didn't know what he would do. He knew Leah was worse than his mother told him. He knew Grace would try to spare him. He lay there, trying to analyze the situation, and drifted off to sleep.

TWENTY-THREE

"Good evening. This is Minister Coffey. Is this Miss Brianna or Miss Brittani Stewart?"

Giggles. "This is Brianna." More giggles.

"How are you, Brianna?"

"Fine. How are you?"

"I'm doing well."

"Is your mother available?"

"Yes. Just a minute please." Giggles.

"Hello, Ben. How are you?"

"Hey, Belinda. I'm good. How are you?"

"Pretty good actually."

"Why actually?"

"I had a test a few days ago that I was really concerned about, and I found out today that I made a hundred on it."

"Good job!"

"Thank you!"

During the conversation, the girls interrupted once to tell their mom good night. She offered to get off the phone to pray with them, but they told her they had already prayed.

Ben complimented her on how well she was raising her daughters. She let out a big sigh and told him that if it was not for them some days, she wouldn't put one foot in front of the other one.

"The honest truth is there are still days that I don't want to get out of bed, but I have to. Losing Canady was the proverbial icing on the cake because I have experienced so much loss. I lost my parents as an infant, but I don't know whether to death or decision. My foster father died while I was in college, and my foster mom has passed since Canady passed. If I didn't have the girls and, of course, Kirby, I would jump in a hole and pull it in behind me."

Ben chuckled. "I just had a visual of you as a cartoon character jumping in a hole."

Belinda laughed too.

Ben and Belinda continued to talk. He told her again about his mom being killed in the automobile accident and his grandfather dying. He told her about how he acted out, got in trouble, and actually got arrested.

"Arrested. You? Talk about a visual!"

"Yep. I got arrested the first time for throwing rocks and breaking windows and the second time for stealing candy from the drugstore."

"Did you get punished?"

"Did I ever! Grammy beat me like I was a runaway slave! The only time I saw outside was to cut the grass, wash windows, and clean out the storage house for weeks."

"You didn't go to juvenile jail or anything?"

"No. The police chief knew that there was no sentence in life that would be worse than me being at home with Victoria Coffey. She let me slide the first time. All I had to do was to meet with the pastor. He told Grammy I was grieving and angry because of my grandfather's death. So she thought she could love me through it. Well, that love lasted until she got the call to come get me from the police station. Then, to top it all off, I was supposed to go to Auntie's for the summer and go to the beach. The only water I saw was for window washing and bathing."

Throughout Ben's recollection of his early teen years, Belinda laughed. Neither of them realized how long they had talked.

When Ben finally noticed the clock, he apologized for keeping her so long. They talked only a few more minutes, and as they were about to hang up, Ben decided to go for broke.

"I understand that the girls have a play date on Saturday with Brianna and Brittani."

Belinda laughed at the way he put it. "Yes. I heard that. Do you know what the plan is?"

"No. I have learned not to ask. My point in bringing that up is you will have a little free time on Saturday, so would you like to have lunch or dinner, depending on their schedule?"

Belinda's immediate thought was no. She had not been anywhere with a man one-on-one since Canady died. Her mind said no, but her mouth said, "Sure. Thanks for the invitation. I'll find out the plan and let you know tomorrow if that's okay."

"Sounds like a plan."

They said their good-byes. Belinda went to bed, went to sleep, and slept all night and didn't dream.

TWENTY-FOUR

Grant didn't realize how long he had slept. It was almost 9:00 a.m. when he awakened. He went downstairs and wasn't surprised to see a loaf of banana bread and a note. Gretchen knew he liked it, so she made it for him. The note said, "Eggs, juice, and milk in the fridge. Grits in the pantry if you're really hungry." It also said, "Call me and I'll get you to the hospital."

Grant washed his hands and cut a big slice of the banana bread. It was good. As much as he loved Leah, she wasn't as good a cook as Gretchen. He opened the pantry, looking for coffee, knowing there was only a one-percent chance he would find any. He opened the fridge, poured a glass of milk, and took out eggs and cheese. As he scrambled the eggs, he replayed in his head what he would say to Leah. He knew Clay was leaving for Vegas that morning, so he would ask him for his car to go to the hospital to see his love, his sweetie, his wife-to-be, the woman he wanted to spend the rest of his life with, the woman he wanted to be the mother of his children.

He finished his breakfast, took a deep breath, and called Leah's cell phone. It went straight to voicemail. He picked up the house phone, called information, and called the hospital and asked for her room. Two rings and her mother answered.

"Hey, Mama K."

"Grant! Hey, darling."

Leah looked at her mother, puzzled. The name sounded familiar. Her mother obviously knew who this was. She was smiling.

Grant. Grant. The name echoed in Leah's mind.

"Yes. She's right here. She's talking a little slowly, but hold on. It's okay," Katherine said as she handed Leah the telephone.

"Hi, Grant."

"Hey, baby. How you feelin'?"

Leah recognized his voice. It didn't all come back, but she felt relieved. After a big sigh, she answered, "I'm okay."

"I have a surprise for you."

"What is it?"

"I'm at home."

"At home?" She was thinking, *At home from where?*

"At home!" Katherine said, smiling at Leah.

Again, she knew it was okay because her mother was smiling.

"I'm at GG's, but I'm coming to see you in a little while."

Leah wasn't saying much at all, and Grant wasn't sure what that meant.

"Okay," was all she said.

"Can a brotha get a kiss when he gets there?"

She remembered him saying that. She smiled and said, "For sure."

He grinned from ear to ear. That was her usual response. He told her he would see her in about an hour and asked to speak to her mom.

Leah used both hands to give her mother the phone back.

"Grant, you're home?"

"Yes, ma'am. I needed to come see Leah. I was miserable wondering."

"I understand, and I think it will do her a world of good to see you."

"I hope Bishop feels that way. Is he there?"

"No, but I'm expecting him at any minute. I'll tell him you're here if he gets here first. It's fine, Grant. He'll be glad to see you."

Raja was on his way to Charlotte, Leah was awake, and life was wonderful. Jill was driving to her office, and Raja called to let her know he was en route. They settled into a routine of talking regularly, though they hadn't seen each other much. When he called to say he was going to stay until the next day, they made a date for dinner. He wanted sweet potatoes from Lola's. Jill wanted some privacy. The compromise was she would pick up the food and they would eat at her house. He had not visited her home before, and she would have preferred to cook for him. She would suggest that for the next visit.

The day had gone quickly. Jill had back-to-back appointments. She went to see Leah and went to the elementary school to have lunch with her lunch buddy. She was pleased with what she saw during her visit with Leah, but she would ask Raja for the whole story. He called for directions from the exit to her townhouse just as she was pulling out of Lola's parking lot. They should arrive at about the same time.

The week after Thanksgiving, the managers of Lola's agreed to meet with Campbell to discuss his working at the restaurant. He was definitely interested but was up front with them about his responsibility to his brothers when his mother worked evenings. They assured him that they could and would work around that schedule. Campbell was beaming with pride when he was offered the job.

Jill and Raja's dinner date went exceptionally well. He showed up with flowers, which Jill thought was romantic. There was only one interruption: a call from his office. He handled it quickly. The conversation was easy, and they laughed a lot. They talked about Leah, but the subject didn't consume the conversation.

Jill was fascinated with Indian culture and living in London and being of another nationality living in the US. She asked a lot of questions, and that gave Raja an idea.

"How would you like to accompany me to London to my cousin's wedding?"

"Wow! I would love to. Thank you for asking."

They discussed the details, and Jill got more excited. She had visited London in high school, but this would be different. After they had talked and Raja was getting ready to leave, he told her there was only one more detail to work out.

"I will have to ask Trey if it's okay for you to go." He looked very serious.

"Ask Trey! Trey Strauss is nobody's daddy and for sure not mine."

Raja started to laugh. "Well, Strauss asked me what my intentions are toward you."

Jill was standing there with her mouth open, not realizing that Raja was teasing her.

"If he asks you that again, you tell him to ask me. And for the record, you don't have to ask my dad either."

By then Raja was really laughing. When Jill realized that he was bantering her, she laughed too. But she would still have a talk with her big brother.

Grant arrived at the hospital, and the first person he saw was the bishop. He was anxious to see Leah, but he wanted to settle things with him now. He didn't want Leah to feel the tension.

"Bishop, what's up?"

They embraced and then shook hands.

"Katherine told me you were here," the bishop said.

"Sir, I know you told me not to come, but I—"

"Grant, you don't owe me an explanation. You made the decision you were led to make. I know you want to see Leah, and I pray you being here hastens her recovery."

They boarded the elevator together and talked about the war.

The bishop walked into Leah's room first. She smiled but seemed to be looking past him at the door, like she knew somebody else was there. Grant walked in, and the tears came. She recognized him immediately. He hugged her Mom and then sat down on the bed, took both Leah's hands in his, and kissed her forehead. Katherine motioned for Lee to come into the hall.

Clay's trip to Vegas didn't go as he had hoped. The friend from the Chicago office was at the conference. She and Clay had dinner the night they arrived, but she wasn't interested in anything else. She told him in no uncertain terms that she knew there was no future with him and as far as she was concerned, they were just friends and colleagues. He wasn't accustomed to being rejected, and he had no plan B.

The second evening, he called Delia and told her that his plans had changed and he would be coming back earlier than he originally thought. He asked her to pick him up at the airport, and she said she would. She did, and he spent the night.

The next morning, before he left, he told her that Grant was in town and they would be hanging out over the weekend. She wanted to know why she wasn't invited and why she couldn't meet Grant. His explanation was that the Friday night Xbox game was for "the brothers only" and he didn't know what the family had planned for Saturday and Sunday. Again, Delia was angry. Why couldn't she meet the family?

"Not yet," was all he said.

$\mathscr{T}$WENTY-FIVE

The girls, as Ben referred to Grammy and Auntie, were taking Brianna and Brittani to an exhibit called Gees Bend Quilts. It was at a museum in Charlotte. No, they didn't need Ben and Belinda to come. They were having lunch first and tea following. No, they didn't need any money or anyone to drive them. If Ben and Belinda would like to see the quilts, they should do it on their own.

Belinda laughed as Ben relayed to her his conversation with Grammy. He told Belinda that she seemed a little undone that he needed to know all that. Belinda shared the part that she knew that he didn't. They had to get dressed up and be ready at 11:30 a.m., and they would be back before 8:00 p.m. They also had to do research on the Gees Bend Quilts so they would be knowledgeable about the exhibit before they got there.

"Is that why they are so quiet?"

"Yes. We came in from school. They didn't want to stop and eat. They wanted to come straight home. Apparently Aunt Avis had volunteered in their school library today and had helped them get a book each and do some research on the Internet."

"Do you have parental controls on your computer?"

"Yes, we do. Kirby loaded all that stuff when she bought them the computer. They told me they had some reading to do and if I wanted to make a salad or sandwiches for dinner, that would be fine."

"Belinda, your girls are amazing."

"Thank you, Ben."

She was sincerely very humbled by what he said. Her world revolved around them, and she had worked very hard to be a good mother and to make sure they were good girls. She did her best to expose them to a lot of things—spiritual things, education, culture, sports—and to surround them with positive people. Not having known her biological parents made her quest to be a great mother even more important. And when Canady passed, she knew she couldn't let him down. She thanked God for Grammy and Auntie. They had definitely added value to their lives and had been a tremendous help to her. They were the grandmothers the twins didn't have.

"Well, based on what we know, what would you like to do tomorrow?" Ben asked.

Belinda held her breath and closed her eyes for a couple of seconds. "Why don't we have a late lunch/early dinner, and then I can get some reading time in before they get back."

"Sounds like a plan. I'll pick you up around two, and we'll go from there."

As they were about to hang up, Belinda asked Ben if he told his girls that they were going out.

"No, but I will unless you have some objection."

Belinda hesitated and finally said that she thought they should know in case anything happened, but she really didn't want to tell Brittani and Brianna they were going out.

"Why?"

She didn't know how to answer that question.

Ben wanted to hear her answer. "This better be good, Belinda." He regretted saying that as soon as it came out of his mouth.

She sighed loudly and said that it was the first time she had been out of the house without them except with Kirby since they moved to Hattiesville and she didn't know how they were going to take it.

Ben decided to go for broke. "I doubt if they will be opposed to it, but the truth is it's not them—it's you. If this makes you feel any better, we won't call it a date. We're just two friends grabbing a bite to eat."

She was ashamed of being so closed-minded, and she knew he was right. Brittani and Brianna probably would encourage her to go, especially with him. They adored him.

"Hello? Are you still there?"

"Yes, I'm here. Ben, please understand that this is all new to me."

"I do understand, but you have to embrace new."

"You're right, and I'm trying."

"Mrs. Casebier, you have fallopian tubes that don't work. It's a condition known as hydrosalpinix. The dye we injected could not travel through the tubes, which means sperm can't either, so your eggs can't be fertilized."

The doctor continued to explain to Kirby what her options were, including surgery and in-vitro fertilization. The in-vitro intrigued her. She and Enoch could still have a baby of their own. She asked the doctor questions, and he answered her honestly. He told her that she could have multiple births and though the incidence of the procedure not working was not great, there was always that possibility. The next statement gave her pause.

It was a very expensive procedure, and most insurance policies did not cover it. Kirby didn't care how much it cost. She didn't care if they had to exhaust their savings and max out their credit cards. It was the answer, and she couldn't wait to get home to tell Enoch.

Enoch's work truck was in the driveway when she pulled in, and that was unusual. He was on the phone but managed to tell her to give him a minute. She was thrilled, and he could tell.

Enoch hung up and hugged his wife and sat down on a barstool in the kitchen. "Obviously, you have good news."

"I have great news!" Kirby told Enoch everything the doctor had said, saving the best news for last: "We can have in-vitro fertilization."

She explained the procedure, including the risks, and told him that they should get it scheduled right away. Kirby knew that Enoch was going to do his own research, and there was no urgency in his thought process. Enoch Casebier prayed about *everything*, and she knew this would be no different. She just thought that maybe she could light a fire under him.

TWENTY-SIX

Grant and Leah hugged until her arms got tired. She leaned back against the bed but didn't take her eyes off him. He reached for her hands with one of his and reached for the tissue box with her other one. He wiped his eyes and hers. She looked so frail to him, so weak. The bandage around her head reminded him of how close he had come to losing her.

"I am so glad to see you, baby. I have been miserable not knowing for myself how you are."

"I had a headache, and I had surgery…"

Grant could tell Leah was struggling to tell him what happened. "Don't worry about all that right now. We'll talk about that later. Do you know who I am?"

"Grant."

"Do you know why I'm here?"

"To get a kiss!"

Grant laughed, but he didn't know if she was teasing him or if that's what she really thought.

Her words were slow and deliberate. "You are my…" She couldn't think of the word. "You are getting married to me."

"Yes!" Grant said out loud.

Still holding her hands, he told her he loved her and very carefully explained to her that she was right, they were getting married in June, that he was in the Army and he worked in Germany. According to her facial expression, she understood some of what he was saying, and some she didn't.

As they talked the door opened and her parents, Jill, Raja, and Trey walked in. Jill didn't know Grant was there and practically jumped into his arms. Grant and Trey shook hands, and Trey introduced Raja. Grant thanked him for saving her life as he shook his hand. As they talked about her prognosis, Jill sat down beside Leah and teased her about Grant surprising her. Leah only smiled.

"I'm glad everybody is here. I have Leah's test results," Raja said. "I'm pleased with her progress, but what is essential now is that we get her lower body moving again. She will continue to see the psychologist and start working with an occupational therapist and a physical therapist. But let me warn you, although she is doing well, all things considered, she has a long way to go."

"At some point will she be moved to the rehab unit?" Trey asked.

"At some point, yes, but I want her blood pressure stable before we move her anywhere."

Just as Grant got ready to say something, Trey spoke up again. "G, I know PT is what you do, but Leah is not a soldier and you are too emotionally involved to work with her."

Grant looked at Trey, wondering how he knew that that was what he was thinking, that he could help her with her therapy. "Can I at least be around? I'm only going to be here a few days."

"I think that should be fine unless she gets embarrassed or frustrated because you're there," Raja answered. "One of two things tends to happen. She'll either do really well or she'll be afraid to fail in front of you and not try."

"Sir, I have seen it at all phases. I know when to back off."

"See that you do," the bishop said.

Everybody turned in his direction. He didn't say anything else.

Leah is my baby, Grant thought to himself. *I know how to help her.*

Gretchen meant to be gone from Clay's house before Ben and Enoch arrived, but she was running a few minutes late.

"What's up, GG?" Enoch said as they hugged, and then she hugged Ben.

"I'm getting out of here and letting you gentlemen have it."

"I'm glad to see you," Enoch said.

"She would have been gone, but one of her nappy-headed customers was nappier than usual," Clay chimed in.

They all laughed. Gretchen hugged Grant. Ben and Grant shook hands, and everybody gathered around the food.

"Tell me about GG and GP," Ben said.

Clay and Grant laughed.

"When we were growing up, we would go to South Carolina in the summers for a couple of weeks to our grandparents' house. Grandma would give us a paper cup for the day so that when we would go outside to play and come back in for water, we wouldn't keep getting cups. She had us put our initial on the bottom of the cup. So one day, Gretchen was drinking some water from the cup with the 'G' on the bottom, but it was actually Grant's cup. I told her that she had Grant's germs and when she woke up the next morning she would be a boy," Clay said, laughing.

Grant continued with the story. "So drama queen Gretchen cried all day and didn't sleep that night because she was scared she was gone turn into a boy. The next day, when Grandma found out, she made me and Gretchen start writing GG for Gretchen Grace and GP for Grant Paul on the bottom of our cups."

"And I started calling them that, and it stuck," Clay finished.

"That's the kind of stuff I missed being an only child," Ben said.

"Me too, man," Enoch added. "But at least you had cousins." Enoch nodded toward Clay and Grant. "All I had were these cats next door."

"That's why I want us to have a bunch of kids," Enoch said.

"How's that going anyway?" Ben asked.

"We're still practicing." Enoch laughed.

"That's what's up," Clay responded, giving Enoch a high-five.

As they ate, Enoch went on to explain what Kirby told him about the in-vitro process. In minister mode, Ben asked how he felt about that.

"I'm not sure how I feel about it, honestly. I know it accomplishes the ultimate goal of us being pregnant, and the twin thing doesn't scare me. But are we messing with God's plan? Are we getting in front of Him?"

Grant had been pretty quiet through most of the conversation. It had been so long since he had been home and with his "boys." Talking about babies seemed so farfetched to him. He just wanted Leah to walk again, even if they never had a baby.

"But don't you believe God makes things available to us, uses people to accomplish His plan?" Grant asked.

"Yeah, Grant, I do. But my spirit is not settled about this yet," Enoch answered.

"Keep praying and asking for clarity. I will pray with you."

Ben continued. "While Belinda and I are out on our date tomorrow, I'll get her perspective on the process."

"Let's get the game going." Clay got up to get the game started while Enoch asked Ben about "this date."

"Grammy and Auntie are taking the twins to Charlotte tomorrow for some kind of exhibit, so Belinda and I are having lunch."

"Kirby didn't bother to share that."

"Do I know Belinda?" Grant asked.

"Probably not. She's Kirby's foster sister who moved here from California after her husband died in Iraq."

"I do remember all that. How's she doing?"

"She's cool, but I'm beginning to be concerned about the company she's keeping," Enoch said, laughing and looking at Ben.

"I ain't mad at ya, bro. She is fine!" Clay gave Ben a high-five.

"Shut up, man, and play," Enoch said, laughing at Clay.

Grant had successfully outplayed Clay on Xbox and Enoch on PlayStation.

"I know you aren't doing anything on that government job of yours 'cause you're playin' too well," Clay told Grant as the four of them were eating again.

"Man, you still hate to lose," Grant said to Clay, laughing.

As they settled back in their chairs, Enoch asked Grant about Leah. He answered by telling them that her first day in therapy was rough. She had cried, and he had felt so helpless.

"They wouldn't let me do anything but stand there. The physical therapist was pretty good, but I would have tried a couple of different techniques."

"Leave it alone, G," Enoch cautioned him. "You will put too much pressure on her, and if she can't do it, she will feel like she is failing you."

"You sound like Trey," Grant said.

"He's right, GP. Plus, the liability is too great. Your licenses are for military installations, not private hospitals." Clay was very serious.

"Do you know? Can you even imagine how I feel seeing her like that?" Grant hit his left palm with his right fist.

Ben leaned in as if he was going to tell Grant something he didn't want the other two to hear. "This situation, Leah's illness generally, but the therapy thing specifically is a test of your faith. Not hers. Yours."

Nobody said anything for a few seconds, and then Grant let out a big sigh.

"Hang in there, Grant," Ben said, sitting back again.

"Are you changing the wedding date?" Clay asked.

"No, and I'm glad you brought that up. Since the three of you are here, let me give you your assignments."

"I know my assignment: to look fly, dance with all the ladies at the reception, and not catch the garter."

They all just looked at Clay, but they couldn't help but laugh as he danced around the room.

"Ben, Leah and I would be honored if you would perform the ceremony."

"It would be my honor to do it, but have you talked to Bishop about this?"

"Yeah, yeah. He's cool. He's walking her down the aisle and giving her away."

"Consider it done," Ben said as he took out his phone to store the date. He and Grant shook hands.

"Enoch, will you serve as my best man, and Clayton, will you be the head usher?"

"Does the head usher get to plan the bachelor party?"

"Yeah. Under the strict supervision of the best man!" Enoch answered.

They all laughed.

Clay and Grant hugged, and then Enoch and Grant did the same.

Leah was wide awake. She had not had any medication in over forty-eight hours, and she was feeling pretty good. It had also been her best session in therapy so far. Grant hadn't been there. He was so hard on her, and that made her nervous. He said he didn't mean to be—he "just wanted her well." From what she could remember about Grant, he made her feel comfortable. All of it had not come back, but the doctor had told her to go with her feelings. Her feelings about Grant were good. There were things she still didn't remember about everybody. Grant and Kathy kept talking to Leah about the wedding, but she didn't remember. Her mother explained it to her too, but it was all foggy. Her mother had brought her engagement ring back to the hospital, and Grant put it back on her finger.

She kept looking at it. She did remember the ring. *It is beautiful,* she thought. She also remembered the smell of her father's cologne.

The doctor said that little things were important. These were little things.

The worst part of the therapy was working with the occupational therapist. The physical therapy was physically hard, but the occupational therapy was mentally hard. She was learning how to read and write again, but the hard part was that she remembered things like sophisticated medical terms but not the days of the week. She read the thermometer when Kim Horng handed it to her, but she couldn't write her numbers. She was frustrated. Trey and Raja kept saying that she was on track, but she wasn't convinced.

"Girl, Grant is in town." Janis' friend was calling.

"Shut your lying mouth. How do you know?"

"I saw him at the hospital this morning."

Janis wanted to scream, but she was in her office at the credit union. *How did I miss Grant? When did he get here? Why haven't I seen him?* "Are you sure it was him?"

"Yes, I'm sure. I guess you were right. He did take the money out of his account for the plane ticket."

"I am going to call him or, better yet, just show up somewhere."

"You can't go busting up in his parents' house or his sister's house, so where else do you think you're going to find him?"

"I don't know, but I will."

Janis was fuming when she hung up the phone. Grant owed her absolutely no explanation, and it was not her business what he was doing, but she wanted to know. Tomorrow was Saturday. She would find him. Hattiesville just wasn't that big. He had to be somewhere.

"I will find Grant Sturdivant tomorrow."

Janis slept off and on during the night. Each time she awakened, she had a different series of thoughts about Grant. He was from a well-respected family, and her being with him would raise her status in the community as well. Besides, she and Grant were good together, not just physically, but they talked, they laughed, they partied together—they had fun. If she could just talk to him, she knew she could convince him that being with her would be better than being with a cripple like Leah.

"Miss Leah Robinson, Miss Perfect, look at her now."

At 8:00 a.m., Janis put her plan into action. She drove to the farthest point: Gretchen's house. Her car wasn't there, so that didn't really tell her anything. Gretchen might have been at the shop. The next stop was the Sturdivants' house. The garage was closed. There were no cars in the driveway. Driving by Leah's condo wasn't in the original plan, but Janis decided it wouldn't hurt. Kathy's car was in the parking lot, so she knew Grant wasn't staying there. Janis didn't know where Clay lived, but she knew his car and some of his hangouts: the gym, the ball field, the barbershop.

"The barbershop. That's the place to start."

Gretchen owned the barbershop too, but it was a couple of blocks away from the salon. Clay got his hair cut there, so there was a good chance Grant would be there too. Janis had nothing to base her theory on but pure speculation. If she couldn't find Grant in Hattiesville, she would go to Charlotte to the hospital. She wanted to see him, but she didn't want to make him angry. If she showed up in Leah's room, that's exactly what would happen.

Janis' phone rang.

"Hello?"

"Where are you?" her friend asked.

"Headed to the barbershop to see if Grant and/or Clay are there," Janis said.

"No need. He's in Lola's. Come over here like you're meeting me."

"I'm on my way."

The restaurant had the usual Saturday morning crowd. Janis walked toward the table where her friend was. She actually didn't see Grant. When she sat down, she realized where Grant and Clay were sitting. Grant had not looked up, but Clay spotted Janis and warned him.

"Good lookin' out," Grant said to Clay.

Janis walked over to their table.

Ben had a great time with Enoch and Clay the evening before, and it was great to see Grant. He was so humbled to be asked to perform their wedding ceremony. His prayer was that Leah would get well and that there would be a wedding. He hoped that Grant wasn't in denial about the seriousness of Leah's situation.

But the big thing on Ben's mind that morning was his lunch date with Belinda. He was so nervous, like it was his first date. It was actually his first date in a long time—a very long time. His thoughts were interrupted by the house phone ringing. It had to be Grammy or Auntie. They were practically the only people who called that number.

"Good morning."

"Hey, Benji. How are you?"

"Fine, Gram. How are you?"

"Doing just fine. I need you to give me some directions to that museum and a close parking space."

"Okay. I'll print it off the computer for you and bring it over there. What time are you leaving?"

They talked a few minutes more, and Ben insisted that she valet park. He only got her to agree because he said Brittani didn't need to walk too far. The truth was Brittani was doing well. He didn't want them fumbling around downtown Charlotte.

He decided that he had better reinforce it. After he got off the phone with Grammy, he dialed Belinda's number. Did he just want an excuse to call her? Probably so.

"Hey, Belinda. It's Ben. I hope I didn't call too early."

"Hey, Ben. No, not at all."

"I actually need to talk to one or both of the girls."

She seemed a little disappointed, or was it his imagination? He went on to explain the situation, and laughing, Belinda called Brittani to the telephone. Ben talked to Brittani, who assured him that she and Brianna knew what to do.

"Brianna is downstairs, printing the directions off the Internet right now, so we'll find a close parking lot with valet parking."

Ben couldn't believe his ears. Those two were amazing.

"Hold on please." Brittani handed the phone back to Belinda.

"Where did you get them from? They don't miss anything."

"No, they don't miss much. You're right. Have you decided where we're eating?" Belinda asked.

"Yeah, but it's a surprise."

"But what if I don't like it?"

"Then I guess you'll be hungry."

She was laughing when Brianna walked in and asked if it was still Minister Coffey because she needed to ask a question. Belinda gave her the phone, and Brianna proceeded to explain that she couldn't find valet parking on the map. Ben went to his computer and pulled up the site where Brianna had gotten the directions, and they looked together. She was right. There was no info on valet parking.

"Bree, can I call the museum and call you back?"

"Don't you have three-way calling?"

"No, but I can call from my cell while you're on the line."

"Okay. I'll hold."

When he got the information and relayed it to Brianna, they ended the call. She had even asked him how much it cost and how much they should tip the man. She knew Grammy would want to know. Not only was she computer savvy, but she had gotten to know his grandmother well. Brittani and Brianna were adorable. He prayed that their mother turned out to be just as adorable.

TWENTY-SEVEN

Grant looked up at Janis and wiped his mouth with his napkin but didn't say anything. Clay leaned forward and looked up at her too.

"Hi, Grant. How are you?"

"I'm good. What's up?"

"When did you get back?"

"I've been here a few days."

"You could call and say hello."

"Why?"

"Grant, can we talk privately for a minute?"

"Anything you need to say to Grant you can say in front of me," Clay answered.

Janis cut her eyes at Jeremy.

Clay had invited Jeremy to have breakfast with him and Grant. Since Clay had been Jeremy's mentor in the Big Brothers program, he had made a point of exposing Jeremy to people who had different careers. He wanted Grant to tell Jeremy about making the military a career option.

"What you gotta say ain't X-rated, so why can't you talk in front of the kid?" Clay continued.

Grant just sat there, enjoying the exchange. Nobody said anything for a few seconds. Jeremy felt the tension and told Clay that he was going to the restroom. Janis knew that Clay wasn't going to move, so she looked directly at Grant.

"I hope we can put the past behind us and start over, Grant."

Clay laughed.

"Janis, you are absolutely disrespectful. Why are you acting like I'm single and like I don't know you?"

"You are single."

"No. I am unmarried, and in six months that will no longer be true."

Janis walked around the table and sat down in Jeremy's chair beside Clay. She rolled her eyes at Clay and continued.

"Leah is in a coma and paralyzed. Why do you still want to marry her? Do you think she is even going to live?"

Clay and Grant looked at each other. Grant didn't know whether to laugh or to take offense to Janis' comment. Obviously, she and her gossiping friends had gotten their information all wrong.

Just as Clay started to correct Janis, Grant looked at him and, with his eyes and a nod of his head, said to Clay, "I got this. Janis, you got some big ones to sit there and act like you are not a liar and didn't try to ruin my relationship with Leah."

"Grant, we worked through that."

"We worked through nothing. I told you then and I'm telling you now that I don't want to have anything to do with you."

Janis looked embarrassed. She didn't expect Grant to greet her with open arms, but she also didn't expect him to speak to her with such contempt.

"Janis, you're dismissed," Clay said as Jeremy approached the table.

"Before you go, Miss Mitchell, let me clear up the misinformation your crew gave you. Leah is not in a coma, not paralyzed. She is going to live, and we are getting married in June."

Janis refused to just walk away. "Grant, we need to have a private conversation."

"Janis, did you not hear anything I said to you?"

Jeremy looked at Janis like she was crazy. After standing there for a full minute, she walked back to the table where her friends were still sitting.

A very few minutes later, Janis and her friends walked out of Lola's. Grant, Jeremy, and Clay sat for a while longer. They walked to Clay's car, and Janis approached them again. Grant couldn't believe his eyes.

"Grant, I am not leaving until you hear me out!" Janis was screaming.

Grant couldn't believe she was going to make a scene in the restaurant parking lot. Grant got in Janis' face. He was close enough to kiss her.

"Janis, hear me clearly. You and I are through now and forever. Don't call me. Don't ever approach me again. You have totally disrespected me, Leah, and my family, and you are making a fool out of yourself in front of this young man." Grant pointed to Jeremy. "Go away, Janis."

"Grant, you and I were good together, and you should still be in my life." She was still screaming as she pushed Grant in his chest with both hands.

Clay jumped between them and told Grant to get in the car. "Don't hit her, G. Don't do it."

"Janis, you said one thing that's true. 'We were.' But we're not now and never will be again. You are pitiful. You need to get a life."

Grant got in the car, Clay got in on the driver's side, and Jeremy got in last in the backseat. He couldn't believe what he had just seen.

"That's why I don't like girls," Jeremy mumbled.

Clay and Grant looked at each other and wanted to laugh, but they didn't.

"Jeremy, all girls ain't whack like that. When you get older, you'll change your mind."

Janis walked toward her car, and Clay pulled out. He looked in the mirror to make sure she wasn't following them.

Clay drove to Delia's house and told Jeremy to jump out and he would holler at him later. Jeremy shook hands with Clay and Grant and said okay. Two minutes after Clay pulled away from Delia's house, his phone rang. Delia wanted to know why he dropped Jeremy off and didn't come in.

"Grant and I have some business we need to handle."

"You could have brought him in and introduced us."

"Delia, you sweatin' me. Let it go. I'll talk to you later." Clay cursed when he hung up.

Grant laughed. "What's up with her?"

"Man, we hung out yesterday morning before work. Now she trippin'."

"Clay, you realize that you are to blame in all of this."

"I know, and I take full responsibility for it, and I know I need to get out of it, but I'm real concerned about the kid. I know his mama will flip, but I might have to take that chance."

"You need to do something!"

TWENTY-EIGHT

Enoch made a consultation appointment with the OB/GYN. He wanted to discuss the in-vitro process firsthand. It wasn't that he didn't trust Kirby, but he knew how emotional she was about it. He wanted to think it through with a level head. The doctor answered all Enoch's questions and answered them candidly. In-vitro was not a 100 percent guarantee of conception. Enoch didn't know if he could put Kirby through that. If it didn't work, she would be devastated.

As he drove home, Enoch replayed in his mind all the conversations he and Kirby had about being parents, about getting pregnant or adopting, and about Kirby's objection to adopting. Enoch knew that this was a delicate situation and the decision he made would affect their marriage and his wife's stability. The doctor suggested that they seek counseling before making the final decision. They both agreed that Kirby was fragile. It was hard for Enoch to view Kirby as fragile. She had always been strong, opinionated, and in control. But not being able to get pregnant had taken her to a whole other place. She had remarked to Enoch that it was the only fight she had ever lost.

Enoch prayed as he drove. By the time he got home, he had made two decisions. First, he would fast and seek God's direction before he agreed to the in-vitro process, and he would tell Kirby they couldn't move forward until they had some counseling. He knew he would have to find a counselor and have it all set up before he approached Kirby.

Should I call the church, or should I call a psychologist? He decided to call Ben to see what he suggested.

Ben had rearranged his plans several times during the week. He wanted Belinda to have a good time but not feel like they were on a date. He wanted their lunch to be nice but not necessarily romantic. He canceled his reservations for the lake cruise. It was too much for their first outing. He decided against the fish camp. It was too noisy and too common. He wanted them to have more privacy than that. He finally decided to go back to his original plan: Sheldon's, a restaurant on the Davis Town side of the lake. He had requested the table in the bay window so they could see the water. Belinda had mentioned to him once that she liked the beach. It was too cold to go to the beach, so looking at the water would have to do.

When Ben arrived at Belinda's townhouse, he expected the girls to be gone. But of all days, Grammy, who was never late, was off her schedule. Brittani opened the door. There he stood with a bouquet of flowers, looking Brittani in the face.

"Minister Coffey, what are you doing here?"

Busted! All he could do was tell the truth. "Hey, Brittani. I came to take your mother to lunch."

"Come in," she said, stepping out of the way. He was actually glad it was Brittani. Brianna would have asked half a dozen questions by now.

"How's your leg today?"

"It's good. I rested last night so I could walk a lot today. Are those flowers for my mama?"

"Yeah. Do you think she will like them?"

"Yes, I do."

By that time, Belinda and Brianna came downstairs, expecting Grammy and Aunt Avis but found Ben standing there. Belinda looked totally embarrassed.

"Have you heard from Grammy and Auntie? It's unlike them to be late," he said to no one in particular.

Brianna answered, "They are on their way."

"Minister Coffey brought you flowers, Mama," Brittani said, looking at Brianna, not at her mother.

Ben handed the flowers to Belinda with a half grin on his face. She thanked him and asked Brianna to get a vase and invited Ben to have a seat. Brittani followed Brianna into the kitchen, and Belinda and Ben could hear them giggling.

He looked at Belinda and mouthed, "I'm sorry," pointing to his watch and shrugging his shoulders.

Just then, they heard a car door and, two seconds later, the doorbell. Belinda went to the door as Brianna walked back into the living room and set the vase on the coffee table.

Avis and Grammy looked surprised to see Ben, but neither of them drew any attention to it. They apologized for being late, hugged everybody, and told Belinda that they would be coming back later since they were almost thirty minutes late getting on their way.

"Are you two okay? It's not like you to be late," Ben said.

"Yes. Fine. I went to the hairdresser this morning, something I don't usually do, go on Saturday, and it took longer than it should have," Grammy answered.

"Can we go now?" Brianna asked.

"Sure," Avis answered.

Hugs all around and the foursome were out the door. Belinda and Ben looked at each other and laughed. That's all they could do. Belinda put the flowers in water and sat them on the counter between the kitchen and living room, and they were out the door. Ben called the restaurant and told them he was running late, but they assured him that they would hold his table.

"Of all days for Grammy to do something different, why would she pick today?"

"Well, it's not like us going to lunch was a secret."

"But I know you didn't want to spring it on your girls."

"They're cool. They like you."

"You know they're going to ask you about our outing when they get back, just like I know my grandmother is going to ask me."

"I will simply tell them we went to lunch. They are seven years old. They are going to an exciting exhibit. What I did today will not even matter tomorrow. They will be on a whole new adventure. Trust me."

TWENTY-NINE

Clay and Grant went on to Charlotte to the hospital to see Leah. She had had several good therapy sessions, and she was regaining her strength. She looked good when they walked in. She was sitting in the chair rather than in bed. The therapist and Trey had been right: her therapy went better when Grant was not there. The speech pathologist was in the room, so Clay and Grant stood quietly for a minute, but Grant decided that maybe they should wait outside.

"Does Leah know you're leaving tomorrow?"

"She knows because I told her, but I don't know if she really understands. I plan to come down here early tomorrow and go to the airport from here. Man, I hate leaving her, especially because she's not walking. I think I thought me comin' would make her miraculously better," Grant continued.

"G, she is better. You just had some unrealistic expectations. Face it, man. Leah had an aneurysm. That's some serious stuff."

They talked a few more minutes, and the room door opened. The speech pathologist came out and told Grant and Clay that they could go back in. Clay went in, and Grant asked a few questions before he went it. She assured him that Leah was making progress.

When Grant walked in, Leah was standing, leaning on a walker. She was smiling at him, and he smiled back.

"Oh, you grown now? You gettin' up on your own?"

A big grin came across her face.

147

"Do you need to go somewhere?"

"No. Just practicing." Her voice was strong and clear.

Clay sat down in the chair, and Grant sat on the foot of the bed. As he always did, Grant read her chart. The doctors' and nurses' notes all pointed to improvement. He asked her a few questions, and she answered. She told him that her blood pressure was still good and that she might be going to rehab in a few days.

"Are you the doctor?" Clay asked Grant.

Leah looked at Clay and laughed with an expression on her face that was so familiar, like their times together before everything happened.

As Leah got better, Raja's visits became fewer, but he and Jill talked every day. Jill didn't want to be too forward, but she didn't want to be too passive either. Lola would always tell them, "You have not because you ask not." Jill had called Trey and asked if Raja could spend the weekend at his house. After the customary bantering back and forth, he agreed. Having that taken care of, Jill took a deep breath and called Raja.

"Jillie, how are you today?"

"I'm fine, but you sound like Trey."

They chatted for a bit, and then she asked if he had weekend plans.

"I'm on call Friday, but I'm free Saturday and Sunday. What's up?"

"I thought maybe you could come down and we could have dinner or something and you could stay for church on Sunday."

"That sounds like a plan. I want to give you the details about the trip to London."

"Cool! I talked to Trey, and he said you can stay at his house."

"Okay. That works, but how do you know he doesn't have plans?"

"We're talking about Trey. All he does is work. But even if he did have some plans, that doesn't have anything to do with you."

Raja laughed.

Jill liked to hear him laugh. Like his accent, his laugh was very distinguished. They made plans for Saturday and then went on to talk about other things. Jill called Trey back to confirm, and he started talking about all the things he and Raja could do. They had a lot to catch up on.

"He is coming to see me, not you, Trey."

Trey laughed. He had not heard Jill whine in years. "Okay, Jillie," he said, mocking her.

THIRTY

Belinda was nervous. She had not been out on a date in almost four years. She started to remember the last time she and Canady had been out.

No, not now, she thought. *Not today. Not in the black hole.*

She willed herself to concentrate on this moment and tuned back in to what Ben was saying. As they drove across Lake Norman, he made a remark about the cost of lots on the lake. The conversation was easy, and Ben had a great sense of humor. Belinda glanced at him. She noticed how striking his profile was. His short beard was very neatly trimmed and added to how handsome he was. He wore his hair cut close. Canady was bald.

Stop it, Belinda, she said to herself.

He was dressed immaculately, and he smelled great. His leather jacket, belt, and shoes were the exact same shade of brown. Belinda was definitely impressed.

Ben was doing most of the talking, but from time to time, he would look at her. She was dressed in a fuchsia pant suit with pearl accessories. He noticed that she wore a pearl ring on her right hand but no jewelry on her left hand. He wondered when she stopped wearing her wedding rings. He didn't know what perfume she was wearing, but whatever it was, it was working with her body chemistry. They pulled into the parking lot of the restaurant.

"This is beautiful, Ben."

"I'm glad you like it. The food is good too."

They pulled into the valet parking area, and they both laughed.

"I hope they found the valet parking," Belinda said as she reached for her pocketbook.

"I'm sure Brianna took care of it," Ben said, laughing.

The valet opened Belinda's door, but Ben was there to help her out of the SUV. The host greeted Ben and escorted them to their table in the bay window overlooking the water. It was a nice fall day, and a few sailboats were on the lake. It was a beautiful scene. The waiter appeared almost immediately and introduced himself as Fredric and took their beverage order. He had a heavy French accent, and they agreed that he might have been from Africa.

"Your lemonade, *madame*. Iced tea, *monsieur*."

Ben liked the idea that Fredric thought Belinda was his wife. They chatted about the menu. There was so much to choose from. Ben recommended the shrimp cocktail for an appetizer and the salmon for her entrée.

He knew she would react, so he said to Fredric, "I would order a steak, but Ms. Stewart would not approve. So I'll have the salmon too."

"Very well, sir," Fredric said with a smile. "We wouldn't want her to disapprove."

Belinda rolled her eyes at Ben and asked Fredric where he was from.

"Kenya, ma'am. I am a student at Davis Town College."

"What is your major?"

"My major is Education, ma'am. I want to teach. We need good teachers in my country."

"We need good teachers everywhere. That's a noble profession."

Ben noticed how easy Belinda talked to Fredric. He excused himself with a slight bow to her.

The meal was delicious and the service superb. Ben talked Belinda into them sharing a slice of key lime pie.

"How did you find this wonderful restaurant?" Belinda asked as she looked around.

The restaurant was full but not packed. For a late lunch Saturday crowd, business was good.

"A childhood friend of mine is the owner." He would wait to tell her the rest of the story. "Would you like to meet him?"

"Sure. Do you think he's here?"

"He's usually here, but we'll see."

When Fredric brought dessert, Ben took the opportunity to invite him to church. He told Fredric about the college ministry.

"Thank you, sir. I will plan to come on Sunday but might not attend during the week. With work and study, I haven't much time for anything else."

Ben gave Fredric his business card. "Feel free to call me anytime."

He thanked Ben with a slight bow and tucked the card into his pocket.

"Mr. Eisner is a friend of mine. Is he here today?"

"Yes, sir. I will get him for you."

Sheldon Eisner had a broad grin, and it was obvious that he was glad to see Ben. They hugged and shook hands. Fredric brought a chair. Ben made the introductions, and Belinda complimented Sheldon on the ambience and good service.

"I knew Ben had a special guest when Fredric told me he was in the window. He wouldn't have a business meeting in this spot. This is the best-looking person you ever brought here." Sheldon laughed.

Belinda blushed, but she was actually glad to know that the cozy bay window seat was not a regular spot for Ben. The three of them talked for a few minutes, and then Sheldon excused himself. Fredric came back to the table to see if Ben and Belinda needed anything else.

"No, Fredric, but you may bring the check."

"*Monsieur*, Mr. Eisner has taken care of your check."

"*Merci beaucoup.*"

"*Avantage servir, monsieur et madame.*"

"*Avantage.*"

Belinda was impressed with Ben's French. Belinda was impressed period. This had been an incredible experience. She couldn't wait to tell Kirby. Ben gave Fredric a $100 tip.

"Merci, monsieur. Merci beaucoup." He gave a slight bow to Belinda and shook hands with Ben.

"We'll be looking to see you at church."

"Yes, sir. You will see me."

As Ben and Belinda left the restaurant, Belinda took another look around. It was very nicely decorated. The valet brought Ben's car and opened the door for Belinda. As soon as she got in, Belinda noticed the clock on the dashboard. They had spent two and a half hours in the restaurant.

"I know I should have paid the check before I asked to see Eisner. I brought Bishop and First Lady up here for her birthday and he did the same thing."

"Are you fluent in French?"

"Not really. Auntie taught me some when I was growing up, and I took a couple of semesters in high school and college, but I don't have much occasion to use it."

"Well, Auntie is teaching the girls, so maybe you can talk to them."

"From what I know about your girls, they will teach me."

"That was a very generous tip you gave Fredric."

"He deserved it. He worked hard, but more than that, he needed it. If he is here even on scholarship, he still has expenses. Davis Town is an expensive school. Most of the international students there come from very humble backgrounds."

They continued to talk. The conversation was easy.

"May I make a confession?" she asked.

"Sure. What's up?" Ben looked at her very seriously.

"First, let me say thank you for lunch. I really enjoyed myself. That was an incredible choice."

"You're welcome. We can go back anytime."

Belinda sighed heavily. "I was apprehensive about coming, about accepting your invitation. I haven't been anywhere without my sister or my girls since Canady passed." Her voice cracked slightly. She cleared her throat and kept talking. "I tried to think of an excuse to back out, but I couldn't lie, so there was no real reason for me not to come."

"Why were you apprehensive?"

"I guess I thought I was doing Canady wrong. I don't know." She shrugged her shoulders.

"Do you know beyond a shadow of a doubt that Canady loved you?"

Belinda looked at Ben like he was crazy. The look in her eye was fury. "Why would you ask me something like that?" she snapped.

"Hear me out please." Ben's voice was firm but not demanding. He knew he was in unchartered water, and he didn't want to ruin what had been a great day. "Answer my question. Do you know for an absolute fact that Canady loved you?

"Yes, I know that," she answered rather sarcastically.

"Then don't you think he would want you to be happy? Don't you think he would want you to go on with your life? It wasn't his choice to leave you. That was God's plan, and as much as it hurts, you have to believe that God's plan is perfect."

"Ben, I believe that in theory, but in reality, why would God's plan bring me so much heartache and take Brittani and Brianna's dad from them?"

"I don't know, Belinda, and I feel the same way. My mom passed when I was three. I don't really remember her, but in my heart of hearts I know that she loved me and the things she wanted for me have manifested."

Belinda's body relaxed a little. She looked at Ben, but neither of them said anything for a few seconds.

"I'm sorry," she said finally.

"For what?"

"I don't mean to minimize your loss. Sometimes I get so caught up in my own pain, my own situation, that I forget that other people hurt too."

"You don't need to be sorry. I'm glad we can talk about it. I miss my mom. I guess I miss having a mom. My grandmother is the best, but I always wanted to know my mom."

"I'm sure Britt and Bree feel that way too."

"Maybe, but they have you."

"You don't have a relationship with your dad?"

Ben laughed. "I don't know my dad. Never met him, never seen him, and never even smelled him. My granddaddy used to say he was the only daddy I had. They were good not to say anything bad about him in front of me, but I heard Grammy say to Grandpa that he wasn't worth the salt in his peanut butter."

"Aren't you curious about him?"

"I was when I was young, but I'm over it now, especially since I've met the bishop. He's the greatest dad I could ask for."

"Having grown up in foster care, I've always been curious about both my parents."

"That's understandable, but don't let that define you. Don't let that make or break your life. You are an incredibly beautiful woman. You're intelligent, and you are raising great kids. Don't discount any of that."

Belinda was blushing.

They had driven all the way back to Belinda's house and were sitting in the parking lot. Neither of them said anything about going in. Belinda was so glad to be talking, and Ben was glad to listen. They were facing each other, and it was a little harder talking to his face rather than his profile. Belinda was doing something she didn't usually do: talk about Canady. Her mind kept telling her to stop, but her mouth kept talking. Ben had that effect on her. She told him the whole story about the day she found out Canady had been killed. She told him about the dreams and about her anger, even about being mad at God. Ben let her talk and gave her his handkerchief when she started to cry, but he didn't say anything until she told him that Enoch and Kirby had insisted that they move to Hattiesville. He decided to go for broke again.

"Belinda"—he reached for her hand—"I know that I know God brought you to Hattiesville for me. I know you can't get your head around that because of the circumstances that brought you here, but I need you to trust me on this."

Belinda didn't know what to say. She looked at Ben for more explanation. The silence was huge. Ben had opened that door, so now what?

"Whew! Where did that come from?" He looked around like somebody else had said that.

Belinda was looking at Ben but still didn't say anything. The strange thing was what he said didn't bother her. She wanted to be angry with him, but she wasn't.

"Belinda, I didn't mean to just spring that on you, and I pray you will forgive me if I'm out of order."

Belinda needed a minute to think. She had to respond. "Ben, let's go in."

He started to protest, but he needed a minute too. It was as if she read his mind.

"We'll finish talking inside."

She found her keys in her purse while he came around to open her door. Ben glanced at the clock. Grammy, Auntie, and the girls would be back in about an hour. Belinda sat down on the sofa. Ben sat on the loveseat.

"Ben, you are not out of order. I appreciate your honesty and your discernment. I am quite surprised, though."

"Surprised? Why?"

"Let me finish. I'm surprised because I never expected you to say that. I had no idea you felt that way, but I'm also surprised because it's okay. I'm actually okay with what you said. I never considered that God brought me here for you, for any man for that matter. But since we got here, everything, *everything* has gone well. I was able to buy this townhouse, get a scholarship for school so I could go full time and not have to work. Brianna and Brittani have adjusted, and other than the fire situation, they are doing fine. God has tremendously blessed me, abundantly blessed me. So I trust that He told you I'm in Hattiesville for you. I believe you. I just need to understand what that means. Am I here to be your friend, your nurse?" She laughed slightly.

"Belinda, let's not be coy." Ben sat on the edge of the seat and looked into her eyes. "I know you know it's more than that. Yes, I want us to be friends, best friends. And if I ever need a nurse, I'll let you know. But being my...well us always being together is what I mean."

He couldn't say *wife*, and she didn't want him to.

"You don't even know me."

"You don't know me either, but I hope we can get to know each other."

Belinda looked at Ben and smiled.

THIRTY-ONE

Grant was leaving the next day. He had a sinking feeling in his heart. He and Leah had eight great days together. She had gotten better. Nobody could argue with that. His coming home was a good thing. Seeing Grant had motivated her. Leah's memory was still a little foggy, and she still couldn't write or tie her shoes, but she was out of the woods. She knew too.

They were alone in her room. She was sitting in the recliner, and he was sitting in a chair, holding both her hands. He wanted to make sure that she knew he loved her and that it was so important for her to get well. She nodded, but he wasn't sure she comprehended it all. She wasn't talking much, but her speech was very clear and deliberate. She looked down at her hand and smiled at the ring sparkling on her finger and smiled at Grant.

"I have to work hard to get well so I can walk down the aisle to marry you," she said.

"Yes! Exactly. After you marry me, I am going to take you away for two weeks on vacation."

"On our honeymoon," Leah said with a big grin on her face.

"Sho you right," Grant said in his best Barry White voice.

Leah looked like she didn't get it. He kissed her forehead, took a deep breath, and asked Leah if she realized he was leaving the next day.

"Yes, to go back to Germany. When will you be back?"

"Maybe for your birthday, but maybe not until time for the wedding. I have to see how it goes, how the war goes."

Leah was moving her lips, repeating what Grant had just said. She looked puzzled, so he kept talking.

"But I will call you every day."

She said okay and smiled.

Just then, there was a knock and the door opened at the same time. It was Kim Horng. She apologized for interrupting but wanted to check Leah's vital signs before her shift ended. Leah told Kim she wanted to go to the bathroom.

"Why didn't you tell me you needed to go to the bathroom?" Grant asked.

Leah rolled her eyes at Grant. He loved it. That was a facial expression from the old Leah. There was another knock at the door as Leah was pulling herself up on the walker.

"Come in," Grant said.

In walked Jill and Raja.

"Leah, what are you doing?" Jill asked, all exasperated.

"Going to the bathroom."

Leah and Jill kissed on both cheeks as she said hello to Dr. Raja. She looked back at Grant and smiled, nodding toward Jill and Raja, another "old Leah" expression Grant had seen before. He smiled and nodded too.

Kim helped Leah into the bathroom, and Raja took a look at her chart.

"This looks pretty good," was all he said.

Jill sat beside Grant, and they talked while Raja continued to look at Leah's chart. When she came out of the bathroom, she asked Raja what he was looking for on her chart.

"This is a social call, Leah. I'm not here to examine you."

Leah smiled as she slowly dragged herself back to the recliner. Kim left the room, and Raja joined Grant and Jill's conversation. Leah looked from one to the other as they talked, and she tried to concentrate on what they were saying. It felt good, so she relaxed and let it flow.

Raja and Jill visited for about an hour. As they were getting ready to leave, Leah told Jill that she needed to tell her something privately. Raja and Grant walked out.

"Grant is leaving the next day," Leah said.

"Yeah, he is leaving tomorrow," Jill repeated.

"I want to…want to…" she couldn't think of the word, but she put her hand on her bandage around her head.

"You want to take the bandage off?"

"Yes, and no pajamas."

"You want to do your hair and get dressed tomorrow before he leaves?"

Leah nodded.

"That's a great idea. Do you know what time he's coming?"

Leah looked puzzled.

"I'll find out."

Jill walked to the door and asked Grant what time he would be there the next day. He told her after the first gathering at church and he would stay until time for him to go to the airport. Jill came back in and called Kathy. They devised a plan to get Leah some clothes, and Kathy said she would come to fix her hair, but they said the bandage had to stay. Kathy told Leah she would bring her camera, some perfume and makeup, and some earrings. Leah asked for her cross. Grant had given it to her when they got back together after the whole Janis fiasco. Kathy told her she would be there in the morning before Grant got there.

Jill explained to Leah that Raja was going to church with her but she would be there the next day after he left to go back to Chapel Hill.

"Are you getting married to him?"

Jill laughed and put her hand on her forehead like she was going to faint. "Right now we're just friends."

Leah looked at Jill as if to say, "Yeah right."

160

Delia hadn't heard from Clay all day, and she was not happy. He had dropped Jeremy off that morning, didn't come in, and told her that he and Grant had some things to do. Grant had been in town for over a week, and she had not met him. She and Clay were definitely not on the same page. Jeremy and Crystal wanted pizza, so she was going to take them out for a while, but she would deal with Mr. Clay Sturdivant when she got back.

The pizza parlor was busy, as usual, on Saturday afternoon. Crystal and Delia found a booth, and Jeremy went straight to the buffet. When Jeremy came to the table, Delia went to fix her plate.

She was getting a salad when she heard the man at the counter say, "Gotcha ready, Clay."

She looked up, and there was Clay, getting two pizzas to go. "Clay."

He looked up to see Delia at the salad bar. "Hey, Delia. The kids with you?"

"Yeah, but we need to talk."

"Let me holler at them first."

Delia took her salad and followed Clay back to the table. Clay was telling them he had to go, that he couldn't eat with them. He fist-bumped Jeremy and started back toward the door.

"Clay!"

"I'll call you."

Delia stood there for a few seconds and then decided to walk outside and confront him. She got to the door just in time to see Clay open the passenger door and hand the pizza to his female passenger.

Jill and Raja had a good visit with Grant and Leah. It turned out to be sort of a double date. Raja told Jill that he was pleased with Leah's progress and would probably move her to the rehab center soon. He also said that Grant coming home had been good for her.

Jill had cooked dinner for Raja, and he complimented her culinary skills. She cleared the table, and Raja brought out the folder with the information about the trip to London. They would leave on Saturday and come back a week later, on Sunday. He had booked their rooms at the hotel where the festivities would take place. Jill offered to pay her part, but he said no. She was his guest. She offered to pay for her airfare, but he declined that too.

"You will need to have two traditional wedding garments, so you can choose those and pay for them."

"Where do I get them?"

"My cousin is sending some pictures by e-mail, and I will forward them to you. The ordering information will be included, and you should have them delivered to you here."

"I'll probably have them delivered to my office so somebody will be there to sign for the package."

"Good idea."

Jill was ecstatic. She was curious about the culture, the traditions, and a little apprehensive about meeting his family. March was three months away, so she had time to prepare herself. Raja went on to tell Jill about the festivities prior to the wedding.

"That has to cost a fortune!"

"Yes, it does."

Raja explained that the celebration lasted for several days.

"Will we have time to do any sightseeing in London?"

"Sure. We'll make time," Raja replied with a sly smile. Raja continued to explain the process, how the families have to approve of the couple's desire to get married because getting married is the joining of two families. "Unlike American tradition, Indian tradition is that the wedding be held in the groom's hometown."

"Really? That's interesting." Jill laughed.

"If you like flowers, you will be in a fragrant heaven. There will be thousands," Raja continued.

"I am really looking forward to going. I have been to some fancy weddings, but I think this will top them all."

They continued to talk more about the sights of London and what they wanted to do and see on their visit.

THIRTY-TWO

Campbell hadn't had a Saturday evening off since he started working, so he wanted to spend some time with Chloe. He invited Chloe to come to his home.

Chloe arrived on time. She knew she had to keep her promise to her parents to be home by 10:00 p.m. Her dad wasn't excited about the idea of her visiting Campbell anyway. She looked around at the duplexes in the neighborhood. Her parents owned a couple on the next street, but she hadn't been there in years. The lawn was very neatly manicured, and a welcome mat, two pots of white mums, and a Christmas wreath greeted her. Campbell was excited to see her.

The living room was small, and there seemed to be too much furniture for the space, but everything was nice and neat. The kitchen floor was so shiny it looked like glass. They eased into conversation. Campbell had brought Chloe some strawberry shortcake from the restaurant. That was another advantage to his working there. Most days Campbell was able to bring something home that was left when the restaurant closed.

"What are you and your family doing for Christmas?" Campbell asked Chloe.

"I'm not certain, but I think we're going to DC to my aunt's for Christmas. We go to a different place every year."

"When do you leave?"

"We usually fly in the day before Christmas Eve and come back the day after Christmas. It kind of depends what day of the week it is. We don't like to miss church. Plus, staying in a hotel during the holidays is expensive."

Campbell was half listening to Chloe. He was thinking that he had never flown and he had only stayed in a hotel once on a school trip. "Well, maybe we can spend some time together when you get back."

"Sure we can," Chloe said, sort of blushing. "What are you doing for Christmas?"

Chloe left in time to be home well before her curfew. Campbell made sure of that. She called him when she got home. It was only fifteen minutes.

Campbell knew he had to buy the right Christmas gift for Chloe. He would ask Miss Robinson for a suggestion.

THIRTY-THREE

Grant packed his things, dreading to go back to Germany. He didn't want to leave Leah, and not seeing her until June made him sad. The time had gone by so fast. He had to figure out a way to get back.

When Grant arrived at the hospital, he was taken aback by Leah's appearance. He brought her flowers, but she had a big surprise for him too. She was dressed in a black pant suit, was wearing black-and-white accessories, and had a black-and-white scarf tied on her head so that the bandage was covered. She was wearing makeup and perfume, the one from Victoria's Secret that he really liked. She was also wearing the cross he had given her.

Grant didn't know what to say. He just stood and looked at her. Leah giggled, and Grant set down the vase of flowers.

"Babe, you look fantastic."

"Thank you." She was standing with her walker and leaning against the bed. "I wanted to surprise you."

"You did," he said as he walked over to give her a hug. She was still unsteady on her feet, and Grant helped her to the chair.

"Thank you for the flowers."

"No problem, but tell me how you pulled this off." He waved his hand from her feet to her head.

"Kathy and Jill helped me."

They talked for a long time about many things. It was obvious that Leah was still struggling with her memory. There were still words and terms she couldn't remember or couldn't say. There were still events she didn't recall, and it was obvious that it frustrated her.

Clay knocked and walked in at the same time. He noticed how good Leah looked and acted like he was flirting with her. She didn't quite understand, but she laughed because Grant laughed.

Clay's arrival signaled that it was time for Grant to leave. Clay knew he would have to control the situation so that they wouldn't be late.

Leah asked Clay to take a picture of them. He took eight or ten. He asked Leah if he could take the camera with him to send the pictures to Grant and print them for her. She agreed with a big smile on her face.

"Aw-ight, GP," Clay said finally. "We need to make a move."

"Let me say bye to my baby."

"I'm going out here to talk to Nurse Cicely. Don't be long."

Grant knew he couldn't prolong it. He had to go. He took both of Leah's hands into his hands and he prayed. They both cried. She put both her arms around him and hugged him tight.

"I love you," she said.

"I love you too, Leah. I will miss you so much."

"Call me every day."

"I will, and you have to work hard to get well."

"I will. I'm going to work hard."

Another hug and kiss and Grant walked out of the room.

Ben walked the bishop and first lady to their car as they talked about how well Leah was doing. As he opened the door for the first lady, the bishop told him to make sure they talked in the office on Tuesday. Ben said he would.

As he drove to Grammy's, he wondered what Bishop Robinson wanted to talk to him about. They talked regularly, so for him to ask Ben to come to the office and not say what it was about, it had to be important.

Ben knew there was some work involved in the dinner invitation. Aunt Avis loved to decorate for Christmas, and it was about that time. Everything had to be prepared for the arrival of the Christmas tree the second week in December. Ben laughed to himself and wondered what the theme would be this year.

He was quite surprised when he turned into the driveway to see Belinda's car. He had seen her in church, but they didn't talk. When Ben left Belinda's house the night before, they had agreed not to try to define their relationship, not to call it anything but to pray about it, spend time together, and let the process work. Ben felt like they had made good progress, especially because she had talked about Canady. He left before the girls came back from their outing. He felt a little uncomfortable about them knowing he had been with Belinda all afternoon.

Belinda had gone upstairs to study, but she couldn't concentrate. She replayed the day's events over and over in her mind. The beautiful flowers, the beautiful restaurant, the meal, and Ben saying God brought her to Hattiesville for him, the strangest part being the fact that she wasn't disturbed by it. She had called Kirby, but they didn't really get to talk. It was obvious that she was distracted, so Belinda told her they would talk later.

She prayed for clarity and discernment. It was also interesting to her that when Brianna and Brittani came in, they wanted to know where Ben was. They told her all about the exhibit and the history of the Gees Bend quilts. They also said that Aunt Avis and Grammy were going to teach them how to make a quilt. They had pictures and souvenirs. Everything had gone fine with the valet parking. "The man at the restaurant gave us free dessert," Brianna had told her. "He said we were his most special guests for the day."

"Well, Mommy, how was your lunch?" Brianna asked as she plopped down on the foot of Belinda's bed.

"It was really nice. Thank you for asking."

"Where did you go? What did you eat?" Brianna was full of questions, and she shot Brittani a look.

"Oh, I almost forgot," Brittani said as she reached for the phone and dialed.

"Hello, Minister Coffey. This is Brittani. I just wanted to tell you that everything went fine with the valet parking. Thank you for the information. Please let me know you got this message."

Brianna was still talking, but Belinda was tuned to Brittani. Belinda thought Ben would call back, but he didn't.

Ben was a little apprehensive when he got out of the car. Neither Grammy nor Auntie had said anything about Belinda and the twins being there for dinner.

He looked in the window before he opened the door. Nobody was in the kitchen but Auntie. When he walked in, he could smell peach cobbler. He knew he was being set up.

"Hey, Auntie."

"Hey, sugar."

"I see we have guests."

She laughed. "Victoria invited the girls for dinner today so we could look at our pictures and things we brought from the exhibit, so of course Belinda had to come too. We knew you wouldn't mind," she said with a sly smile.

Ben walked into the dining room, and Belinda was setting the table. There was no sign of Grammy and the twins.

"Hey, you," he said.

"Hey, yourself."

It was an awkward moment. He hugged her slightly and just for a couple of seconds.

"How did you get this job?"

"I volunteered. The girls and your grandmother are 'in the attic,'" they said at the same time.

"I knew this was a setup when I smelled the peach cobbler."

Belinda looked puzzled. Ben went on to explain how the house would be transformed into a Christmas village and how he would have to hang lights and a wreath on the chimney. Belinda listened with amusement.

"What I want to know is how Enoch got off the hook."

Belinda let out a big sigh. "I haven't actually talked with Enoch, but Kirby has been really distant the last couple of days." Belinda moved closer to Ben so nobody else would hear her. "You know about them trying to get pregnant?"

"Yeah. Enoch told me that Kirby wants to do in-vitro, but he hasn't agreed yet."

"Right, and she is real undone that he hasn't. I didn't see them at church this morning, so Grammy probably didn't have a chance to ask him."

"I need to call him."

"Please do and let me know. I haven't been able to get Kirby to talk."

Grant laid the seat back and closed his eyes.

"I'm getting out, man."

"You can't get out 'til your time is up."

"I'm going to see when I get back if I can get an emergency discharge. I gotta be home, man. I need to be with Leah. It's killin' me to leave her. I can't do this!"

Grant stomped his foot. Clay looked over, and tears were rolling down Grant's face.

"If they won't let me out, I'll just leave."

"Whoa, man. Hold up. You're talkin' crazy. You can't throw away over ten years. What are you gonna do with a general discharge or, worse, a dishonorable discharge if you go AWOL? Man, that's your heart talkin', not your head. You can't make a future for Leah with no job and a bad rap from Uncle Sam. And you know her dad ain't about to let her marry you if you're out of order."

Grant leaned up, held his head down, and cried hard. Clay just let him cry.

The original plan was that Clay would drop him off and keep going, but Clay decided he would park and make sure Grant got on that plane.

Grant had gotten himself together by the time they parked. They walked across the parking lot, and Clay thought he saw someone familiar, but he didn't say anything. As they started up the stairs to check in, someone called Grant's name. They both looked back.

It was Janis.

"Hi, Benji."

Grammy walked in with a box in her hands. An echo came from behind her: "Benji," followed by giggling. The twins walked into the dining room, following Grammy. Brianna was also carrying a box. Brittani took a seat.

"Hi, Minister Coffey," they said in unison.

He kissed his grandmother on the forehead and said hello to the girls. Brianna and Grammy went through to the kitchen.

"Brittani, are you okay?" Belinda asked.

"My leg is tired."

"You probably walked on it too much yesterday," Ben remarked. "By the way, I did get your message. It was too late to call you back. Thank you for letting me know."

"Do you need some medicine, Brittani?"

"No, Mommy. I just need to rest."

Belinda was a little unsettled about this. Since the cast had come off, she had not complained about her leg at all. Maybe Ben was right. She had been on it too much yesterday. But if her leg was still "tired" tomorrow, they were going to see Dr. Trey.

"Wash your hands, everybody. Dinner is ready," Avis said from the kitchen.

Ben realized that he was still standing there, holding his coat. After Ben blessed the food and plates were served, the conversation around the table was the exhibit. Shortly, though, Ben shifted the conversation to Christmas decorations.

"What was in the boxes, Grammy?"

"Some material scraps we're going to wash so Avis and I can show the girls how to make a quilt."

"Oh. I thought that was the beginning of Christmas to the tenth power."

"Mrs. Coffey, Ben thinks you and Mrs. Johnson set him up with the dinner invitation and the cobbler to get him to help with the decorations," Belinda said.

Ben looked across the table at her. "I thought you were on my side."

"Belinda, now if you are going to be around here, you have to let go of the Mrs. Coffey and Mrs. Johnson. Grammy and Auntie will be just fine," Grammy said matter-of-factly.

Belinda was stuck at, "If you're going to be around here." Ben was stuck there too.

"Hear me clearly—"

"Uh-oh. Here we go," Ben interrupted his grandmother.

"I don't have to bribe Benji. He knows every year what has to be done, and cobbler or not, it's his responsibility."

"How did Enoch get off the hook?" Ben asked.

"I didn't see him in church this morning, and when I called yesterday, they didn't call me back. Don't worry. I'll catch up to him," Grammy answered.

THIRTY-FOUR

Things at the Casebier household were quiet. Enoch and Kirby were having what Bishop Robinson called a valley experience. He had gone to church at the early gathering and left immediately. Kirby stayed at home. She was angry with him for not immediately agreeing to the in-vitro process. They had been talking about it for days. Kirby knew Enoch was right. They needed to be prayerful and proceed through direction, not emotion, but she couldn't help but think that he was being selfish. She felt that nobody was seeing her side of the story. Nobody understood how she felt. Enoch said she was being selfish. Not even Belinda understood.

Kirby knew she had to fix things with Enoch. *We've had disagreements or misunderstandings before, but nothing like this. Why are we fighting over something we both want?* Kirby knew that if Enoch said no, that was the end of the discussion. *I love Enoch so much. I don't want our marriage to suffer, but why should I apologize? He is the one being unreasonable. Why should we adopt when we could have our own child? Why is my body being so unkind to us? Have I inherited this from the mother I never knew? Obviously not. She had me.*

As bad as she wanted to have a baby, Kirby couldn't fathom having one and giving it away. She couldn't just lie in bed. She had to get up and do something. When she sat up to pray, it dawned on her that it was the first morning since they had been married that they had not prayed together. Even if one of them was away, they would pray over the telephone. This was all wrong.

Enoch took a deep breath before he went in. He was tired of fighting with Kirby, but his heart and his spirit weren't settled about the whole process. But he knew better than to get in front of God, and she had to trust him. Ultimately, God was holding him responsible, and he wouldn't mess this up. The one question he had to ask Kirby was: What if they did the procedure and it didn't work? Then what? She refused to even entertain that thought. But she would have to before he would agree to put her through it. Do they try once, twice, three times? The emotional stress of all that was just too much, not to mention the thousands of dollars it would cost.

Enoch was surprised when he walked in. Kirby was in the kitchen, cooking, and the table was set. She greeted him with a smile.

"I hope you're hungry," she said as she put her arms around his waist.

They hugged and lingered there for a moment.

"I am. Thanks for the brunch, babe. I expected to come in and make a sandwich."

They both knew that they were making small talk, but there was an elephant in the room.

"Did you remember to call Grammy back?"

Enoch laughed. "No. I will when I finish eating. You know it's Christmas decoration time."

Kirby sat down beside Enoch. She wanted to be on offense, not defense. "I would like to call the doctor tomorrow to make an appointment to get the first round of treatments started."

"Kirby, what if we do this and it doesn't work? How many times are you willing to go through the procedure emotionally, physically, and financially?"

"Enoch, the financial part I don't care about. I don't care how much it costs."

"K, you have to care. If we exhaust our savings and an emergency arises, then what?"

"When did you become a pessimist? Where is your faith?"

"I am not a pessimist. I'm trying to be realistic, but you are sidestepping the question. What if it doesn't work? What if it doesn't work?"

$\mathscr{T}$HIRTY-FIVE

Clay and Grant kept walking, leaving Janis standing at the bottom of the stairs.

"Grant Sturdivant, don't turn your back to me!" Janis yelled.

Clay stopped. Grant kept walking.

"Janis, you're a piece a work. Why can't you leave Grant alone?"

"Clay, this is none of your business." She was still screaming. The look from a lady walking by made her realize how crazy she was acting. "Clay, I just want to talk to Grant. That's all. He owes me that."

"He does not owe you anything. Why do you even believe that?"

Janis walked up a few more steps to see if she could see where Grant was, ignoring Clay's question. Grant had reached the check-in point and motioned for Clay to bring his bag. Janis walked up the stairs behind Clay. When Grant finished at the ticket counter, he walked over to where Janis was standing.

"Let's hear it, Janis. State your argument. This is your one and only chance."

"Can we talk in private?"

"No," Clay answered her.

"We can't talk at all. I don't have anything to say," Grant said.

"Grant, I know you don't understand why I made up the story about you being Carmen's father, but I wanted you in my life and you wouldn't give me a chance. I had to do something. I still want you in my life. I still love you. Grant, we can have a good life together. I can and will make you happy."

Grant looked at his watch. He walked very close to her. He got right in her face. "Janis if you want to make me happy and give me a good life, disappear. Don't ever call me, approach me, or admit you even know me. As far as I'm concerned, you can go to hell in gasoline drawers."

Clay left the airport and decided to stop at Delia's before he went home. He knew he was going to have to hear it from Delia, but so what? She just needed to realize that she was not his priority. Bishop had talked about provisional relationships and optional relationships. Delia wasn't exactly optional, but she was not exactly provisional either.

Crystal and Jeremy came to the door, and Clay hugged them both. Crystal had her hair loose, and Clay complimented her on it.

"Thank you."

"Don't worry. She'll be back to ponytails tomorrow." Jeremy laughed.

"Shut up, Jeremy."

"Crystal!" Delia said.

"I'm sorry, Mommy. Be quiet, Jeremy."

"What's up, Delia?" Clay said.

"Clay." The attitude was immediately evident. Delia kept walking into the kitchen.

"Why aren't you watching the game?" Clay asked Jeremy.

"Cable's out."

"Mama didn't have the money to pay the bill," Crystal chimed in.

"Crystal, get out of my business," Delia yelled at her.

Clay looked back toward the kitchen, but he couldn't see Delia. *What was that all about?* "The Panthers and the Falcons are on regular TV."

"We can't get it to work," Jeremy said.

Clay walked over to the television, disconnected the cable from the back of the set, and reprogrammed the remote and the television worked.

"Ma, Clay got the TV to work!" Jeremy said excitedly.

"Good. I'm going to the store." Delia picked up her pocketbook and keys and walked out.

Clay wasn't in the mood for Delia's attitude. He had dealt with Janis and dealt with Grant. He decided he would leave when Delia came back. If she was angry about him not introducing her to Grant, she would be angry some more days.

Delia couldn't believe how cool Clay was.

He shows up like nothing had happened, like I didn't see him with another woman. He doesn't know I saw him with her, she thought. *He didn't come see me anyway. He came to see Jeremy.* Clay didn't spend much time with him while Grant was there either. She was glad Grant was gone.

Delia stayed gone for about an hour. She hoped Clay would be angry at her for leaving him with the kids. She hoped he thought she was with another man.

Would he care?

When she walked in, the three of them looked up, but nobody said anything. Clay wondered if she had adjusted her attitude.

"Crystal, get your book so I can listen to you read. Jeremy, have you finished your homework?" Delia said.

"Yes ma'am," Jeremy answered.

"Go get it, man. I'll check it for you," Clay told Jeremy.

With both children out of the room for a minute, Clay decided to ask Delia about her mood. "What's up with you?"

She didn't answer.

"Don't bite the kids' heads off 'cause you're hot with me."

Before Delia could respond, Jeremy and Crystal walked back in. Jeremy and Clay finished checking homework first, and Clay stood to leave. Delia didn't want him to go, but she was determined not to ask him to stay.

Delia waited as long as she could after talking herself out of calling Clay more than once. She gave in and called him. He sounded half asleep when he answered.

"Hi, Clay. I didn't mean to wake you."

"Oh. Hey, Dee. That's okay." He sat up, yawned, and glanced at the clock. "You feelin' better?"

"I feel fine. What are you talking about?"

"I thought you had PMS or something, you hollering at Crystal for nothin'. By the way, why didn't you say something about your cable bill?"

"Because you told me you wouldn't pay my bills."

"Yeah, I said that, but Jeremy needs to use the Internet, so I would have paid that."

She changed the subject. "Clay, don't tell me how to talk to my children."

"I will tell you when you're takin' your frustrations with me out on them. If you're mad at me, holler at me. I told you when Grant came home that I would be hanging out with him."

"That's not the point, Clay, but since you brought it up, Grant was here for two weeks and you didn't find one minute to introduce us."

"Why did you need to meet Grant? Why was that necessary?"

"Why not?"

"Grant doesn't know everybody in my life."

"Does he know the young lady you bought pizza for yesterday?"

"No, as a matter of fact, he doesn't." He sounded cool, but he had no idea that she had seen who he was with. "Oh, so that's what you got the attitude about."

He was not going to defend himself. She could do and say what she wanted to. But he had to smooth it over enough that she didn't ask for another Big Brother for Jeremy, because of Jeremy and because he didn't want to be in hot water with the agency.

"Look, Dee. Let's not fall out about this."

"We don't have to fall out about it. I just want to know if you are sleeping with her."

"Delia, I'm not going to answer that."

The conversation didn't last much longer after that. Delia was furious, and Clay was puzzled. He was not accustomed to being challenged, and he didn't know what had gotten into her. He would let her cool off for a couple of days, and then he would call her.

Janis was totally embarrassed, humiliated, and hurt. Grant had dismissed her in front of dozens of people. But it was her fault for even going to the airport. Grant was totally unreasonable, and the fact that Clay was always around didn't help.

She knew Grant would be in the air by now, so she decided to leave him a message. She apologized for coming to the airport but told him that she was not giving up on him and them being a couple.

On her way home, she decided to make a stop at the hospital. She knew that if she talked to Leah, it would get Grant's attention. Plus, everything she heard was that Leah was never going to get better, but Grant said she was better and they were still getting married.

"I'll see for myself."

THIRTY-SIX

Dinner had been fun. The twins were quite entertaining, and the whole group got a kick out of Ben being the only man there. Even getting started with the decorations was fun because Belinda helped him. She wasn't as prissy as he thought. She could handle a staple gun. But Ben still wanted to talk to Enoch. He decided he would call before he settled down for the evening.

"Hey, Ben," Kirby said. "How are you?"

"I'm cool. I missed you guys at the kick off of Christmas USA!"

Kirby laughed.

"Belinda and the girls were out there too."

"That's interesting. I'll have to talk to her about that." Kirby sounded fine, so Ben didn't really know what to think.

"Yeah, you do that. Casebier around?"

"He's in the shower. I'll have him call you."

Kirby called Belinda as soon as they hung up. Belinda was glad to hear from her and glad she sounded better. She told her about the Saturday lunch date, the window seat at the restaurant, and dinner with Grammy and Auntie. She even told Kirby about Grammy's comment. But she didn't share what Ben had said. Belinda needed to hold on to that for a while.

"How did you leave it?"

"We are going to spend some more time together."

Kirby told Belinda about the conversation she and Enoch had. She shared how hurt she was that Enoch didn't immediately agree to the in-vitro and that he would even entertain the idea that it might not work.

"We talked all afternoon, and he finally agreed to the procedure."

"So when are you going?"

"I will call the doctor tomorrow to make the appointment. I read the literature he gave me, and I know there is some prep work to be done."

"Yeah. You will have to take some hormone therapy. Are you taking vitamins?"

"Yeah. I never stopped. I've been taking these prenatal vitamins for almost a year."

"Kirby, did you answer Enoch's question? What are you going to do if it doesn't work?"

Kirby let out a big, long, deep sigh. "Belinda, I didn't expect you to ask that question."

"I'm being realistic, Kirby. Sometimes these procedures don't work."

Kirby was silent for a minute. "Belinda, I believe in my heart that the procedure will work the first time. I have total faith in that. But Enoch and I agreed to a second procedure if it doesn't work the first time."

Belinda was shocked at how at ease Kirby sounded. She was almost too calm. "Kirby, I'm really, really glad you and Enoch came to an agreement about this."

"Me too. I just don't know what I would have done if we hadn't."

Belinda called Ben to tell him she and Kirby had talked.

"Hey, babe." Ben surprised Belinda by answering that way.

"Hey yourself. I talked to Kirby."

"Yeah. I have Enoch on the other line. Can I call you back?"

"Sure." She smiled as she hung up.

"That was the future Mrs. Coffey."

"Is that right?"

"Man, I'm going to marry Belinda one of these days!"

Enoch and Ben talked about finishing the decorations at Grammy's and about his agreement with Kirby to begin the in-vitro process.

"You good with it, or did you give in?"

"Naw. I'm cool, but Kirby knows what the parameters are. We agreed to two procedures. And she knows how much money I'm willing to spend. Nobody gave in. We compromised. I know what I'm being led to do, and that's what I intend to do. Kirby knows who she's married to."

Enoch changed the subject. "But hold up. Let's go back to Mrs. Coffey.

Ben laughed. "You know I'm talking. I wouldn't say that to her. I just got her to agree to see me again."

"So evidently lunch went well."

"Very well. We went up to Sheldon's, and we sat in the bay window."

"No, man, you didn't take her to your spot on the first date. What you gonna do for a follow-up?"

"I don't know, but I had to make an impression if I expected to have a follow-up."

They talked a while longer, but Ben did not tell Enoch the most serious part of his and Belinda's day. Right then he thought that that needed to stay between them.

"Enoch, man, you need to call Grammy."

"I know. Kirby reminded me too. I'll go by there tomorrow and take my beatin'! I just wasn't up to the whole family thing today. Kirby and I had been at it all weekend, and when she didn't want to go to church this morning, I was really put out."

"Do you think Kirby needs somebody to talk to?"

"Yes, but she doesn't. But I told her that that is a condition of us doing the in-vitro. So I know she'll make it happen."

Ben and Belinda talked a few minutes. She was studying, and he apologized for interrupting her. As they were getting ready to hang up, Belinda asked Ben to pray for her this week. She had exams to take.

"Let's pray now."

She was not expecting that response, but she said okay. Ben prayed for her and for her success with the exams. He prayed for the girls, and then he prayed for them, him and her as a couple, and he asked God to show them His will for their lives.

"Father, show us what you ordained for us before the foundation of the world. We pray that Your kingdom will come and Your will be done. In Jesus's name."

For a couple of seconds, there was silence, and then Belinda whispered, "Thank you."

$\mathcal{T}$HIRTY-SEVEN

Kathy, Gretchen, and Jill were listening patiently as Leah told them about her afternoon with Grant. It was almost like old times.

"Where's the camera?" Gretchen asked.

"He took it to send me the pictures on the computer," Leah answered.

"Why would that nut take the camera all the way back to Germany?" Gretchen asked, puzzled.

Leah laughed. "No, not Grant." Leah couldn't think of Clay's name. "The other man."

Gretchen, Jill, and Kathy looked at each other, and then Gretchen realized she was talking about Clay.

"Oh, the other nut took the camera. Clay," Gretchen said.

Leah repeated his name.

They were all talking. After a couple of minutes, the room door opened. They thought it was a nurse coming to kick them out for making so much noise. Janis walked in, not expecting all of them to be there any more than they were expecting to see her. The expression on Leah's face was pure horror.

Janis only caught a glimpse of Leah. Before she could get all the way into the room, Gretchen was in her face.

"How dare you walk up in here! Get out!"

"I have a couple of things I need to say to Leah."

"No, you don't."

Gretchen pushed her back out the door, and Jill was right on Gretchen's heels.

The door was open, so Janis spoke loud enough for Leah to hear her. "Grant and I are back together. We spent the whole day together, and I went to the airport with him. He's calling off the wedding."

Jill tried to close the door quickly, so they didn't know how much Leah actually heard.

"Oh my God! You are such a liar!" Jill retorted. "Grant spent the day right here with Leah, and Clay took him to the airport."

"An ice cube has a better chance of surviving hell than you do of you and Grant being together," Gretchen continued. "You need professional help."

A man in uniform was approaching them. Jill realized that he was hospital security. Kathy must have called from the room phone.

"Is there a problem, ma'am?"

Gretchen asked him to escort Janis out of the hospital.

"I'm not going anywhere."

"Yes, ma'am, you are. Now you can come on your own or I can have you arrested."

The word *arrested* snapped Janis back to reality. She started to walk away, the security guard beside her. She looked back at Jill and Gretchen.

"I'll be back."

The guard took her by the elbow and started to walk a little faster.

"Do we need to get security for Leah's room?" Jill asked.

"I don't know. I need to talk to Clay," Gretchen answered.

"I know how to get to my car," Janis yelled at the security guard.

Tears were stinging her eyes. She ran to her car, using the stairs rather than waiting for the elevator. By the time she got in the car, she was crying.

Gretchen was right. I'm a liar. Why does Grant Sturdivant make me act so crazy? This has been a horrible day.

First the fiasco at the airport, then Leah's whole entourage knowing she had come to the hospital. But what made it worse was them catching her in the lie about spending the day with Grant. She knew Gretchen would tell him. He would never forgive her for going to the hospital. She had really blown it.

Janis leaned back against the headrest. She closed her eyes, trying to picture Leah in her mind. All she really saw was that Leah was sitting up in a chair. She was not in bed. Maybe she really was better. Janis knew that Gretchen would call Grant, but she needed to tell her side of the story. She knew he would still be in flight. She had to get her thoughts together.

Kathy was glad Gretchen and Jill had reacted so fast to Janis' appearance. It was obvious from the look on Leah's face that she recognized Janis. When Jill and Gretchen walked back into Leah's room, Kathy was on the phone.

"There's no need for you to come over. Just please ask Gentry to call me."

Kathy had called her friends, Gentry and Robin Brackett. She knew Chief Brackett would know what to do and how they should handle Janis' appearance. Leah was improving, and the Janis event could upset her, and nobody was willing to take that chance.

"Are you okay, Leah?" Jill asked.

"Yes, I am, but tell me her name."

The two looked from one to the other, and Kathy spoke up. "Her name is Janis Mitchell. She's the one—"

"I know who she is. What did she want?" Leah's hands were shaking.

"I don't know what she wanted, but I know it wasn't good. I didn't give her an opportunity to say what she wanted," Gretchen stated firmly, dialing Clay's cell number at the same time.

When the phone rang, Clay looked at the caller ID. He expected it to be Delia. He was relieved to see "GG" on the screen.

"What's up, G?"

"Clay, that crazy Janis Mitchell just walked into Leah's room."

"She did what?" Clay sat up and hit the mute button on the television remote.

Gretchen explained what happened, and in the process, Gentry Brackett was calling Kathy on her cell. There were two conversations going on around Leah, the television was on, and Jill was talking to her. All of a sudden, everything went black. Leah slumped in her chair. Kathy started crying, Jill was scream-ing for the nurse, and Gretchen told Clay to come to the hospital.

The nurse made everybody leave the room. They got Leah into bed, checked her vitals, and called Dr. Trey. She was only out for a few minutes, but she didn't remember fainting. She said she remembered a lot of noise and then waking up in bed. Her blood pressure had gone up.

Trey was in the hospital and showed up rather quickly. By the time he was getting the explanation from Kathy, Chief Brackett showed up too. He had come to Charlotte from Hattiesville, blue lights flashing. Trey went in to examine Leah but wouldn't let anybody else come in. She made no mention of Janis, and Trey wondered if she remembered.

Chief Brackett suggested that they go to a conference room to talk, and he told Kathy that she should call her parents. Clay and Gretchen hung up so abruptly that he didn't have a chance to tell her that Janis had been at the airport when he and Grant got there.

"Do you think Janis would hurt Leah?" Brackett asked to no one in particular.

"Yes!" Gretchen answered. "That girl is crazy! She stood in the hall and just lied. Why did she come here? What do you think would have happened if we hadn't been here?" She waved her hand at herself, Jill, and Kathy.

"She made Leah and Grant crazy with her foolishness," Jill said.

Just then Clay walked into the conference room. His new nurse friend told him where they were. Gretchen told Clay what Janis had said, and he told all of them about the incident at the airport.

"It's clear that your dad needs to get a restraining order against her." A knock at the door interrupted Chief Brackett.

"Excuse me. Dr. Trey wants to see you, Kathy," the nurse said, looking at Clay.

Kathy walked into the hall.

"I have given Leah a sedative, so she should sleep through the night. I am going to limit her visitors to family only for the next day or two. She can't take too many spikes in her blood pressure." Trey's voice was very forceful, almost angry.

Leah had been doing well, and he wanted to move her to rehab, but this setback was dangerous. Trey gave the nurse the orders and explained to Kathy what he was doing. He also told her he wanted to talk with the police chief.

"He's down the hall. I'll get him," the nurse offered.

Brackett was coming down the hall, and the bishop and first lady were approaching, so he showed them to the conference room and asked Trey to join them there. Trey updated them on Leah's condition and told them that she was in muddy water.

"Leah was doing remarkably well, all things considered, but she is not completely out of the woods. If the visit from that woman will make her react like this, we have to make absolutely sure she does not come back."

"Bishop, my recommendation is that you get a restraining order against Ms. Mitchell," Chief Brackett said.

Before Bishop Robinson could respond, Clay told him what had happened at the airport and that Grant was adamant about not having anything to do with Janis. Gretchen was glad because she didn't want Leah's parents to be angry with Grant.

"I am going to see Leah," her mother said, looking at Lee and walking out of the conference room.

Jill walked out behind her. Gretchen and Kathy were standing there, waiting for the conversation to continue. Clay caught Gretchen's eye and looked at the door. She grabbed Kathy by the hand and left the room.

Bishop Robinson looked at Trey and then at Chief Brackett. "I want you to do everything in your power to keep that woman away from my daughter. If you need to post an officer outside her door to enforce the restraining order, then do that too. I don't—hear me clearly—don't intend for my daughter to go through this again. If what you do doesn't prevent her from coming here and I have to take matters into my own hands...well, consider the department warned."

Chief Brackett wasn't sure how to take that comment, so he didn't respond.

The bishop continued. "I will call Attorney Sandra Matthews first thing in the morning to see what else I need to do, but I want the restraining order executed tonight."

"Yes, sir," Chief Brackett said.

"Clay, I want you to call Grant and let him know all of this, every detail. I don't know if he can talk some sense into her, but he needs to know. And you make sure he knows I told you to call and that I hold him responsible for this mess."

"Sir, with all due respect, how can you hold Grant responsible? He was clear with Janis that she was out of order and he didn't want to have anything to do with her. He doesn't control her moves, and you shouldn't expect him to." Clay wanted to be respectful of the bishop, but he was actually pretty angry at his comment.

The silence in the room was very uncomfortable.

Finally, the bishop looked at Clay. "You're right, but I still want you to make him aware of the situation."

Grant lay back and closed his eyes. The flight wasn't full. There was no one in the seat behind him, so he took advantage of being able to lay the seat all the way back. He smiled to himself. His visit home had turned out better than expected. He almost laughed out loud thinking about Leah getting dressed up for him today. He loved Leah so much, so very much.

As Grant dozed off, the plane hit a little turbulence, which awakened him. Janis crossed his mind. He replayed in his head the scene at Lola's and the scene at the airport. He hoped that Janis would leave him alone.

Janis fixed Carmen a snack and went to her room to call and leave Grant a message. She decided to tell him she had gone to the hospital to make peace with Leah and that Gretchen had overreacted and didn't give her a chance to say what she wanted to say. She knew that would make Grant happy. She would wait for him to call her back to tell her he accepted her apology. As Janis continued to think through exactly what she would say, the doorbell rang.

$\mathscr{T}$HIRTY-EIGHT

"Mommy, I think I need some medicine. My leg is still tired today."

Belinda gave Brittani an ibuprofen. "I am going to call Dr. Trey today to see if he wants to see you."

"I don't think I need to see Dr. Trey. I'll be okay."

As the school day went on, Brittani's leg was not getting better. When she went to the library, their class was to sit on the floor to hear a story, but Brittani couldn't get on the floor. She was in a lot pain. She started to cry and asked her teacher if she could see Brianna. In the midst of handling that situation, Aunt Avis walked out of the library work room.

A look of relief was on Brittani's face. "Auntie, my leg feels terrible."

"Don't cry. Let's get you to the back and see what we need to do."

Brittani told her that Belinda was going to call Dr. Trey.

"Okay. Let's see if we can get your mom on the phone."

The call went straight to her voice mail. Brittani started crying. Brianna walked in, looked at her sister, and started crying too.

"Brianna, listen to me. We need to get in touch with your mom, and I'm getting her voice mail. Who else can we call?" Auntie asked.

Brianna was hugging Brittani, but she managed to answer. "Call my Aunt Kirby." She recited the number, but there was no answer. "Call my Uncle Enoch."

Auntie was able to get Enoch on the phone.

"Oh man, Auntie. I'm over an hour from the school. Go ahead and take her to Trey's office, and I'll call to let them know you're coming. As a matter of fact, I have his cell number."

Brianna got their things from the classrooms, Avis went to get the car, and the other library volunteer stayed with Brittani. Once they were in the car, Avis called Grammy.

"Keep calling to see if you can get Belinda on the phone."

After they hung up, Grammy decided that she would call Ben. "They can't get Belinda on the phone."

"She's taking an exam."

"Well, where are you? Avis is on her way with both of those babies crying."

"Call her back. I'll meet them at the office. I'm only ten to fifteen minutes away."

Ben's heart was pounding. He had met with the fire chief first thing that morning, and he told him they knew who set the fire and they would be meeting with all parties involved next week. If something additional is going on with Brittani's leg, how will that impact the charges? He would deal with that later. Right then he had to see about Brittani.

Ben arrived at Trey's office before Avis and the girls. When they pulled in, he picked Brittani up and carried her in while Avis parked the car.

"This is Brittani Stewart. Dr. Trey is expecting her."

"Are you her father?" the receptionist asked.

Brittani was crying, and her head was buried in his shoulder.

"I am responsible for her."

"Do you have her insurance card?"

"No. You should have it on file."

With each answer, the volume in his voice grew louder. The receptionist was going to ask another question, but the nurse walked into the reception area, saw Ben standing there holding Brittani, and told him to come on back.

"Dr. Trey is at the hospital. He'll be here in about ten minutes."

Ben tried to sit Brittani down, but she wouldn't let him go. The nurse took Brittani's blood pressure and temperature. Both were up. She had stopped crying, but she was holding on to Ben's arm. It crossed his mind that Grammy must not have gotten in touch with Belinda. He felt his phone vibrate. It was Grammy.

"Hey, Gram."

"I still can't get Belinda. What's going on there?"

Ben told her they were waiting on Trey. "Brittani is still in pain, but she's a trooper," he said, looking at her and winking.

Brittani smiled.

When Trey walked into the examination room, his poker face concerned Ben. Trey asked Brittani some questions and then asked Ben where Belinda was.

"She's taking exams today. Her phone is off."

"Okay. I need you to take Brittani over to the children's hospital. I'll make arrangements for you to check her in."

"Trey, what is it?"

"I don't know for sure, but she might have a blood clot at the point of the break. If the tests confirm that, I need to go in right away."

Brittani was looking back and forth between the two of them. She had reached for Ben's hand again.

The nurse brought in a wheelchair.

"Brittani, I don't want you to put any pressure on your leg," Dr. Trey said.

"Minster Coffey, will you please pick me up?" Brittani said.

He picked her up, and she rested her head on his shoulder. They walked into the waiting room, and Brianna jumped up and ran to them.

"I have to go to the hospital again," Brittani told Brianna.

"We need to call Mommy," Brianna said.

"She's taking an exam today, so we are going to have to take care of Brittani for now," Ben said to Brianna. "But I do think we need to call Uncle Enoch and Aunt Kirby." He handed Brianna his phone.

Enoch answered on the first ring. Kirby was on her way to Charlotte.

"Tell her to meet us at the children's hospital," Ben said.

$\mathscr{T}$HIRTY-NINE

Grant finally had a chance to check his messages. He couldn't believe that Janis had called, and he couldn't believe the message he had gotten from Gretchen saying that Janis had come to the hospital. He called Gretchen immediately, and she told him the whole story, including the fact that Bishop Robinson had gotten a restraining order against Janis and that the hospital agreed to step up security near Leah's room.

"Leah was doing great when I left, and one look at that witch, and now she has had a setback to deal with." Grant was incensed. "He said what?"

"That he holds you responsible, but Clay straightened it out and he apologized."

Grant let out a big sigh. "I told Clay I shouldn't have left."

"What are you talking about? You couldn't stay here."

Janis couldn't believe she had just been served with a restraining order. She couldn't go within five hundred yards of Leah, could not go to the floor where her room was in the hospital, and was banned from approaching her at home or in the hospital. She was furious. It was 10:00 at night, and they came to her house to give her the paperwork.

"I guess the Robinsons and their church own the police department too."

Janis couldn't sleep. She played the day's events over and over in her mind, and she kept thinking about the restraining order. *How dare they?* She sat up in bed, turned on the light, reached for the phone, and called Grant.

Jill walked into her office and saw the huge peppermint poinsettia on the conference table. The other offices and reception area were decorated with red poinsettias. She didn't notice the card right away. As usual, she and her mom talked by phone early in the workday. She told Ellen about the incident at the hospital as she flipped through some mail. She glanced over and noticed the card. She opened it casually, thinking it was from her dad. It read, "Jill, I hope this adds to the beauty of the season. Merry Christmas. Miss you. Raja."

"Jill, honey, how is Raja?" Ellen asked.

"He's good. He's great."

She read the card to her mother. They talked a couple more minutes and then hung up so Jill could call Raja.

She got his voice mail but left a message, thanking him for the flowers and ending it with, "I miss you too."

They were moving toward a serious courtship. Raja had relaxed a bit about her independence, and she had relaxed a bit about how slow he moved. Her mother reminded her more than once that it was Raja's place to pursue her, not her place to pursue him. What Jill really missed about getting to know Raja was being able to share it with Leah. She picked up the phone to call the hospital to see if Leah was awake.

Clay and Delia hadn't talked in a couple of days, but he figured that he would see her the next night at Jeremy's game. He would let her stew until then and see where her head was. Clay had options, so dealing with Delia's attitude wasn't what he intended to do. He knew women like her. She would come around.

They always do, he thought.

Jeremy was doing better in school with his grades and his behavior, so maybe it was time for Clay to move on anyway. He would need to give that some thought. Right then he needed to call Enoch to remind him that it was his week to host the Xbox and PlayStation games. The only reason he was glad Grant was gone was because he had beat them all so badly while he was there.

Grant and Clay had talked earlier, and Grant told him about all the messages Janis had left. She was upset that a restraining order had been taken out against her. She said over and over that nobody understood her side and that she needed Grant to fix it. He finally figured out how to block her number so maybe she would get the message. Clay had promised Grant that he would go to the hospital and check on Leah the next day. He made sure to get the pictures printed, and he put them in a little album so she could look at them as often as she wanted to. Gretchen said that she was better that but not out of the woods.

That Janis is a piece of work, Clay thought to himself. "Now I have dated some whacky women, but this chicken head beats all," Clay said out loud.

Janis finally gave up after trying to call Grant the third time. He had blocked her number from his phone. She would have to wait until she got to work the next day to call. If she didn't talk to him the next day, she would write him a letter and send it the fastest way possible, no matter how much it cost.

Everybody arrived at the children's hospital at about the same time. Check-in was easy. Trey had made the arrangements. Kirby had a copy of the insurance card, so she took care of all that while the nurses got Brittani settled.

"Kirby, I don't want to leave Belinda a message about Brittani," Ben said. "If you will handle things here, I'm going over to the school to see if I can find her."

"Sure, Ben. That's a good idea."

Ben went to get his phone from Brianna, and she wanted to know where he was going. Before he could answer, Brittani started crying and reaching for him.

"Don't leave me. Please."

He sat down beside her and took her in his arms. Brianna was standing close.

"I'm going to the nursing school to get your mom. I promise we'll be back in a few minutes." He put his arm around Brianna and held them both tight. He closed his eyes and prayed silently for a minute, and then he prayed out loud so that they could hear him. "Amen. Brianna, will you please take care of Brittani until I can get back with your mom?"

"Yes," she said, handing his phone to him.

He kissed both their foreheads. Kirby and Aunt Avis observed the whole scene from the door.

As Ben got in his car, he noticed the time. He decided he needed to let the bishop know where he was and what was going on. He called his office rather than his mobile phone.

"Ben, he's at the hospital with Leah, so I'll get a message to him," Bishop Robinson's assistant told him.

Ben went to the administrative office of the nursing school, identified himself, and asked how he could see Belinda Stewart. "It's an emergency."

He was directed to the class where she was preparing for an exam.

Raja had about thirty minutes before his next patient, so he decided to call Jill. He had gotten her message earlier. He noticed that he had a message. It was from his mother. He knew that he wouldn't get to talk to Jill if he called his mother first. He and Jill talked for a few minutes. He invited her to come to Chapel Hill for the weekend. She told him that she would think about it and call him that night.

"I'll be awaiting your call."

They hung up, and he called London. He knew his parents were having evening tea.

Jill was surprised by Raja's invitation.

He has come to Hattiesville each time we have seen each other. Is it time to go to Chapel Hill? Have we known each other long enough? It has only been three months. Where would I stay? What would we do?

Jill looked at the clock. She got up from her desk and went to the hospital to see Leah.

"Hello, Father. How are you this evening?"

"I am doing very well, son. And you?"

"Fine, sir. Are you having tea?"

His dad chuckled. "Yes. Are we predictable?"

"Yes, sir."

They both laughed.

Raja's father asked about his work, what he was reading, and they talked about sports.

"May I speak with Mother? I have a patient in a few minutes."

Raja could hear his father tell her he was on the phone.

"Manavendra, your cousin, tells me you are bringing a young lady here for the wedding," she said.

"Yes, Mother, I am. Do you remember Trey, my roommate?"

"Yes. He was very kind to you."

"Yes, ma'am. I am bringing his sister. Her name is Jillian."

"So you are bringing an American girl?"

"Yes. I live in America. I have American friends. I am a United States citizen, Mother."

"There are Indian girls who live in the United States. Why are you bringing a guest? I have someone to introduce you to."

Raja laughed. He had this same conversation with his mother each time he went home. He would talk with his father privately and tell him to call his mother off. Both his parents wanted him to come back to London and go through the traditional arranged marriage. But his father had made peace with Raja making the decision not to. His mother was blatantly ignoring the facts.

"Mother, I have to see a patient, so I'm going. I want you to make up your mind to be nice to Jill."

"Mana—"

Raja hung up and walked toward the elevator, thinking how many times he had had the same conversation with his parents, specifically his mother. It was good that his cousin had told his mother. Now he didn't have to fight with her. He hoped she knew when to stop. He hoped she knew not to disrespect Jill. He would warn Jill when he saw her that weekend, if she came. Raja smiled to himself. He had a fun weekend planned if he could talk her into coming.

Grant knew he shouldn't have answered a number he didn't recognize. It was Janis.

"Why are you calling me, Janis?"

"I want you to hear my side of the story because I know you have heard all the lies."

"Did you go to Leah's room?"

"Yes, but—"

"But nothing. You had no business at that hospital. None. Why don't you go back so you can go to jail?"

"Grant!"

"For the last time, Janis, don't call me again and stay away from the people I love."

"Grant, listen to me."

The line was dead.

Belinda couldn't imagine why Ben was standing outside the door to the lab. Her smile quickly disappeared when she saw the expression on Ben's face.

"What is it, Ben?"

"Hey, sweetie."

He took her by the elbow and took a few steps into the hall. "Brittani is in the hospital."

Ben still had his hand on her elbow, and that helped steady her. He went on to explain and then told her to get her things so they could go to the hospital.

Belinda spoke briefly to her professor and grabbed her things, and she and Ben headed out. She reached for his hand as they practically ran to his truck. Once inside, he recounted to her the events leading to him taking Brittani to the hospital.

"Thank you, Ben. Thank you so much. I am so glad they were able to reach you. I never turn my phone off. I just—"

"Whoa. Hold it. You didn't do anything. You don't need to explain."

"But she said this morning her leg hurt, and I gave her an ibuprofen and sent her to school. I should have called Trey."

"Belinda, stop it."

He reached for her hand. She was trembling. He started to pray. She closed her eyes and prayed too.

Jill walked into Leah's hospital room and was pleasantly surprised. Leah was sitting up in bed, talking to her nurse. She smiled at Jill, who winked at her and quietly took a seat. Leah looked rested, calm.

"I am going to ask Dr. Trey if we can put a different type of bandage on your head. That should relieve some of the pressure," Nurse Kim said.

The nurse talked with Leah for another couple of minutes and left. Jill sat down on the bed beside Leah and hugged her tight. Leah was glad to see her too. She was much better. They talked briefly about the night Janis came. Jill assured her that Janis would not be back.

"I talked to Grant, and he told me not to let her worry me. I have to get better so we can get married." Jill smiled and told her to keep that in mind.

As if reading Jill's mind, Leah asked about Raja.

"Actually, I want to talk to you about him."

Leah leaned back, tilted her head, and smiled. That was vintage Leah.

"Raja asked me to come to Chapel Hill for the weekend. I don't know if I should go."

"Chapel Hill?" Leah looked puzzled, and Jill didn't know if she should try to have this conversation with her.

"Chapel Hill is where he lives, about two hours from here."

"Trey went to school there." It was more a statement than a question.

"Right. Trey went to school there, and that's where he met Raja."

"And you met him because he's my doctor."

"Right again."

They continued to talk, and Jill patiently explained the things Leah didn't understand.

"Go. It's okay." Leah looked at Jill very seriously. "He's Trey's friend. He's a nice man."

The best friends hugged like old times. Jill knew in her heart that her friend was on her way back.

Ben dropped Belinda off at the door and went to park. She ran through the reception area down the hall and met Aunt Avis, who directed her to where the girls and Kirby were waiting. About the same time, Avis's phone rang. It was Grammy. She had called Enoch to pick her up, and they were on their way to the hospital.

Kirby and Ben had everything in order, which was a great relief to Belinda. Brianna was holding Kirby's hand, and Brittani sat in her lap. They waited for Trey to come in with further instruction.

As Ben parked, his phone rang. It was the bishop. Ben told him what he knew and where they were.

"I'll see you shortly. Ask Trey to allow me to see Brittani before he does any kind of surgery."

"I will, sir."

The bishop had gone to see Leah and found her in a serious conversation with Jill. She was much improved from a few days ago. He decided to let them visit and he would go back after he checked on Brittani.

Leah was concerned about Brittani. They explained what had happened. She told her dad that she wanted to see Belinda.

"I'll let her know."

Leah showed Jill the pictures that Clay had put in the album for her. They had a good visit on all fronts. Leah was definitely better, and Jill was going to Chapel Hill.

Jill wasn't going back to the office until she called and they told her the package from India had arrived—the dresses she ordered for the wedding. She would try them on, keep the ones she wanted, and return the others.

She picked up the package, went home, and laid all the dresses across the bed. All of them were gorgeous and very expensive. She only needed three, so she had to make a decision. She decided to try all five of them on, take pictures, and ask Leah to help her choose. Jill smiled. Leah was doing so much better.

"Thank you, God."

The bishop walked into the children's hospital waiting room and found Grammy and Aunt Avis there. After hugs all around, they updated him on Brittani's situation. He was a little puzzled as to why they were there, but he didn't ask.

They all walked down the hall toward the area where Brittani was waiting. One of the nurses started to stop them. There were going to be too many of them in the room.

Another nurse looked at her and shook his head. "It's okay," he mouthed.

Trey was examining Brittani. The room was extremely quiet. The trio stopped right inside the door. Brianna noticed them first and ran over to hug Bishop Robinson and then Grammy.

"We will do an MRI, but I feel sure that we're dealing with a clot," Trey said. "I can't give her enough medicine to dissolve it, so I'll have to surgically relieve the pressure. We should have the results in about an hour."

"Why can't you give me the medicine?" Brittani started to cry.

Brianna left Grammy and put her arms around her sister. Tears streamed down Belinda's face. She cried because her girls were crying. Ben put his arm around her.

Trey wanted to choose his words carefully. "Because you weigh less than eighty pounds, the medicine is too strong for you."

Interestingly, Brittani looked at Bishop Robinson. "Can you pray so the medicine won't be too strong for me?"

"Sure, baby. I can pray, but God gives Dr. Trey the information he needs. If he says the medicine is too strong, we need to trust that."

"I don't want to have surgery," Brittani said, folding her arms and looking from one of them to the other. The look of defiance on her face was actually kind of cute.

"Okay. I'll tell you what. Let's do the test, and then we'll decide."

Belinda was so glad Ben had spoken up.

The bishop laid hands on Brittani's leg, and he prayed. When the prayer ended, Trey asked everybody to leave except Belinda. Brianna and Ben were the last to leave the room. As they left, Trey and Belinda were having a doctor/nurse conversation. Ben was impressed with Belinda. He knew why the twins were so smart: their mother was brilliant. He and Brianna left the room hand in hand.

Bishop Robinson was in the waiting area, talking with the family. He told Kirby to ask Belinda to go see Leah. He noticed Ben and Brianna.

"Ben, let me speak with you for a minute."

They walked into the hall. Before he could say anything, Ben told the bishop, "I had planned to tell you in our meeting tomorrow."

The bishop laughed. "I know there's a lot going on here, but I really want to conference with you tomorrow. It's important."

"We'll know this evening what Trey's plan is. I can get Grammy to be here with Belinda. Unless something drastic happens, I should be able to keep the appointment."

Jill set up her tripod and camera. She looked at the clock. She had about an hour to try the dresses on, take the pictures, and e-mail them to Raja before he got off duty. She wanted to call him before he called her. She touched up her makeup and, one by one, tried on the five gorgeous dresses. It was hard to be the model and the photographer. She missed Miss Lola and Leah at times like this. Either one or both of them would have been there to help her in and out of the dresses and make the decisions.

Why can't I keep all of them? That isn't practical.

She knew that Miss Lola and Leah would say that. She managed to get the pictures taken and e-mailed to Raja and her mother within an hour and a half. Her room was a mess with the dresses and shoes. She called Raja and got his voice mail. She left a message for him to check his e-mail and call her. She called her mother and got her voice mail too, so she left her a message. She printed the pictures for Leah to see when she visited her the next day. As she straightened up her room, Jill thought about going to Chapel Hill.

Where will I stay? Should I offer to get my own hotel room?

According to Trey, Raja still lived in the townhouse they shared in med school. It had three bedrooms, but she thought that that would still be uncomfortable. Raja had done a good job with the reservations for London. She would just wait to see what he had done about that too.

The bishop went back to Leah's room after he and Ben talked. Ben would call him after they got the test results. He arrived there to find Ellen Strauss and Katherine. The bandage on Leah's head had been changed, and she had had dinner. He updated them on Brittani and told them that Ben and Belinda were an item. The three ladies seemed amused, but not as much as the bishop. Katherine knew that he was wondering how that news would affect his plan.

Raja was pleasantly surprised to get Jill's message. He had bought the tickets to the weekends UNC games but decided that he would give them away if she didn't come. The message said to check his e-mail and call. He laughed when he saw the pictures. A couple of the dresses he liked, but he would leave the choices to her.

"Hi, Raja."

"Hello, Miss Strauss. How are you today?"

"I'm good. Did you see the pictures?"

"I did, but I'll let you make the choices."

"You need to have at least one vote."

"Okay. But I'll vote when I see them in person."

"I can't drag all five of these dresses up there."

"Are you coming?"

"Yes, I'm coming."

Raja pumped his fist and mouthed, *Yes!* "You won't need to bring them. I'll see them when I come get you."

"You're coming to get me?"

"Yes. I'm coming to see Leah. Trey and I are going to consult with Dr. Strauss about moving her to rehab next week."

"So she'll be in rehab for Christmas?"

"I might let her family take her home for a few hours on Christmas Day."

Jill and Raja talked for almost an hour. He wouldn't tell her what he had planned, just that she only needed casual clothes and that they would be back for church on Sunday.

"You can stay here at my place and I'll stay at the hospital."

"The hospital?"

"Yes. I have quarters where I stay when I'm on call or have overnight surgery."

"How comfortable is it?"

Raja laughed. "It's okay. Really."

The test results came back just as Trey expected. Brittani had a blood clot at the point of the fracture in her leg. Trey decided to call Raja for a second opinion before he talked to Brittani and her family. By the time he got Raja on the phone, his dad had come in.

Trey uploaded the MRI so Raja could see it in his office in Chapel Hill. While Raja agreed that the medicine wouldn't work in its usual dosage, he asked Trey if he thought Belinda would agree to a longer term smaller dosage by IV. He wanted to see how she had progressed by Friday. He would examine her when he came to see Leah. Brittani would have to stay in the hospital, and it would be a slow process, but Raja agreed with Dr. Zack that if she had a bad attitude about the surgery, the healing wouldn't go as well.

"Trey, make it clear to them that if there's not some improvement by Friday, you will need to proceed with the original course of action."

"Thanks, Raja."

"No problem. See you on Friday."

Trey met with Belinda, Kirby, and Ben first. Belinda asked Ben to come and Enoch to stay with the girls. He explained the options, and they agreed that if the surgery was avoidable, that's what they would try. Belinda let out a big sigh.

"Talk to me," Ben said, turning to face her.

"I was thinking how I would have to take an 'I' in the two classes I still have exams in and Brittani will miss more school."

"Oh no. You have to take those exams. You'll lose your scholarship if you get incompletes," Kirby reminded her.

"But if Britt's going to be in the hospital all week, I'll have to miss school."

"Belinda, we'll work it out. You know Grammy and Auntie won't let you miss your classes. I can adjust my schedule too," Ben added.

Kirby liked the exchange between them. "I can make myself available too," Kirby told them both.

They walked back into Brittani's room to find her with the leading score in a game of tic-tac-toe. She appeared to have relaxed some.

"What did Dr. Trey say, Mommy?" Brianna asked.

"He will be here in a few minutes, but he might have a plan for you, Brittani."

Enoch and the twins fist-bumped each other. Kirby, Ben, and Belinda were left out of the celebration.

"We knew he would," Brianna announced, "'cause Uncle Enoch prayed!"

Enoch hit his chest and pointed to the ceiling. Brittani and Brianna giggled. Everybody laughed, and Ben asked Belinda if he could get Grammy and Auntie.

"Of course. Please do."

Everybody was there to hear Trey explain the plan. He told Brittani twice that it might not work, but they would try it. She said she understood.

"Can I go home and come back tomorrow?"

They all looked at her, puzzled.

"Why do you need to go home?" Belinda asked.

"I need to get my stuff if I have to stay here for four more days."

Kirby and Belinda said at the same time, "What stuff?"

"Mommy, I need my Bible and books and my…journal."

"Can't we bring it to you?"

Before she answered, Brianna whispered something in Brittani's ear. Brittani whispered something back.

"Uncle Enoch, will you take me home to get Brittani's stuff and bring me back so I can give it to her?"

Enoch knew that Belinda was going to protest, so he spoke up quickly. "Yeah, baby. We can do that."

Belinda just didn't understand why it was so serious.

With that settled, Trey went on to explain the process and procedure. When he finished, Ben asked Grammy and Auntie if they would be available to stay with Brittani during the day.

"Yes, Benji. We'll work it out. Avis will be at school to get Brianna, and I can be here."

She said it so matter of factly that all Belinda could say was thank you.

The girls laughed and repeated, "Benji."

Ben excused himself to call the bishop. He told him the plan for Brittani and assured him that they worked it out and that he would be there for their meeting. As he was driving to the church, it crossed his mind that Christmas was coming.

I need to decide on a gift for Belinda and the girls, for that matter. It has been so long since I bought a gift for a lady. Belinda isn't just any lady—she is very special. Jewelry is always in order. I will go to the jewelry store after the meeting.

Ben went to his office, put down his things, and checked his messages and e-mail. He prayed, picked up a notepad, and went upstairs to the bishop's office.

Ben knew that the conversation wasn't originally supposed to start like that, but the bishop asked about his relationship with Belinda. He was totally honest, telling him about their lunch date and the conversation that followed. He ended it by telling him that he wanted to marry Belinda.

"As you pray, please consider what I'm about to tell you and how the relationship figures into this."

"What is it, sir?"

"Ben, I want you to go to Atlanta to plant and pastor our first church."

He was looking directly into Ben's eyes. There was complete silence in the room for about five seconds. Ben shifted in his seat, looked at the bishop, and laid the notepad and pen on the table.

"My, my, my. I expected you wanted to meet with me about a new initiative, but I didn't know it would be three hundred miles away. Wow!" Ben got up and walked to the window. He turned around looked at Bishop Robinson. "Why me, sir? I'm sure there was another minister with more seniority than me."

"How long have you known me, Ben?"

"Many years, sir."

"Have you known me to make a decision without seeking God's direction?"

"No, sir. I'm just surprised, shocked actually."

"Ben, I don't expect you to give me an answer without seeking God about this. I know this will be a change for you and your grandmother and now you and Belinda Stewart. I know you will need to discuss this with them."

Ben exhaled loudly. "Sir, I will be prayerful about what you ask, but I know the answer. If God leads you to send me, I trust Him and I trust you. I don't want to leave Grammy or Belinda, but I'll go."

Bishop Robinson knew that the timing was interesting, but he knew that God's timing was perfect. They talked for almost two hours, more about the business part than the personal parts. Ben left the office and headed to the hospital, his mind racing.

How will I tell Belinda? What will she say? Our relationship hasn't really gotten started, and now I will be leaving. The move won't be permanent for about a year, but how can I nurture a relationship and build a ministry at the same time and do both in excellence? And what in the world will Grammy say? I know she will be happy for me, for the promotion, but I don't want to leave her again. I'll take her with me. She won't go. And Aunt Avis moved from her home in DC to be with Grammy. I can't ask her to move again. Then how can I ask Belinda to leave, uproot her girls, leave her sister, school, and the life she has finally embraced and move again? Ugh…

The more he thought, the worse it became. The new church plant was a great thing. Ben was humbled by the offer. He laughed out loud. "God, I know you have a sense of humor, but why me and why now?" He had completely forgotten about going to the jewelry store.

Ben had not mentioned meeting with the bishop to Belinda, and he knew now that he wouldn't until after the immediate situation with Brittani was over. Ben had really become protective of Belinda and her girls. He was falling in love with her. He knew it, but he couldn't verbalize it. And if he could, he couldn't tell her yet. He knew that she wasn't ready, especially not now, not with finishing exams and Brittani possibly facing surgery.

FORTY

Clay pulled into the parking lot at the gym as Delia was leaving. He blew his car horn. She waved but did not stop. He wasn't sure what to think.

When practice ended, Crystal and Delia were waiting with new hairdos. Clay thought to himself that they didn't stop because they were headed to the hairdresser.

"Hey, Crystal. I like your hair."

"Thank you."

"How are you, Delia?"

"Fine, Clay. How are you?"

"I'm good. Jeremy had a good practice."

"Good. We need to go."

"I promised Jeremy a sub sandwich."

"Actually, he lost a bet, Ma. I outran him, so he owes me," Jeremy gloated.

Delia's stern body language relaxed a bit. "Can he get a rain check? I've already cooked."

"That's cool. How about after practice on Wednesday, we'll all go out?"

"Please, Ma. I need to collect on my bet before he forgets," Jeremy said.

"Okay. That's fine."

Delia started walking toward her car and didn't look back. Clay walked Crystal and Jeremy to the car and watched them leave. Delia was really playing the "don't care" role.

I'll break her down on Wednesday. He laughed to himself. *This foolishness has gone on long enough. Now let's see if a nurse can give a brotha some time,* he thought, reaching for his phone.

Delia left Clay a message that she and Crystal would meet him and Jeremy at the sub shop. He thought that that was interesting but didn't respond. She was really playing hardball. Clay didn't intend to play that game with her. Her response to him that night would determine his next move.

Things went well at dinner. The four of them ate, talked, and played video games. It was like old times. At the end of the evening, the kids wanted Clay to go home with them, so they got in his car. Clay followed Delia home.

"Clay, can you come in and reconnect the cable?" Jeremy asked. "Ma paid the bill."

Clay reconnected the cable box while Delia helped the kids get settled for the night. Clay and Delia checked homework; the kids laid out clothes and took showers. All along, Delia and Clay said very little to each other.

"Glad you made good on losing the bet, Clay!" Jeremy said.

They both laughed.

"See you at the game on Saturday, and you need to put all that running to good use," Clay told him.

"Later, man," Jeremy said as he hugged his mom good night.

The kids went to their rooms, and Clay and Delia were left in the living room, alone.

"Look, girl, you can stay mad with me or we can work this out."

"There's nothing to work out, Clay. You are seeing somebody else, and I don't want to deal with you anymore."

"Dee, did I tell you I was in a relationship with her? You saw me getting a pizza with a friend and jumped to your own conclusion." He took her hands and led her to the sofa.

She took her hands out of his.

"Stop carrying on, Delia. You know you miss me, and I miss you too."

"I just don't understand where we are, Clay. How do you define our relationship?"

"Why do I have to define it? We do what we do. We are who we are to each other. We don't need labels and definitions."

"I want to know where we're going."

"How about we go in there?" He nodded toward her bedroom.

"We need to finish talking," Delia said as he kissed her hands.

"We can talk in the other room." Clay stood and led Delia to her room. He stayed until a couple hours before time for the children to get up.

FORTY-ONE

Campbell had tried to call Chloe to see if she wanted to come by the restaurant after he got off to have dessert. She liked coconut cake, and there was some left. She didn't answer, so he packed the cake up to take home. It was cold outside, but he decided to walk home rather than take the bus.

He was surprised to walk outside and see Chloe sitting there, waiting on him.

"I tried to call you."

"I know. I got your message and decided to surprise you."

"Wanna go back in and eat some coconut cake?"

"No. Why don't we go to my house, eat the cake, and watch a movie, and then I'll take you home?"

"Are you sure your parents won't mind?"

"No. My dad went to a Davis Town game, and my mom is there, chillin'. I'll call her and tell her we're coming."

"That works. Let me call my mom too."

When they got to Chloe's house, she and Campbell watched *The Great Debaters* and ate too much cake. Chloe made them hot tea and served it in mugs with her name on them.

"You have personalized coffee mugs?"

"They're for hot chocolate. I don't like coffee. My grandmother gave them to me a long time ago, before she passed. They are special to me, and I only use them on special occasions."

"So is this a special occasion?"

"Of course. It's the first time you have visited me in my home."

She was right. Campbell knew where she lived, but he hadn't ever been there. The house was huge, immaculately furnished. The picture on the fifty-inch television was the best he had ever seen, and the chocolate-brown leather sofa and loveseat were nicer than any furniture he had ever seen. Yet Chloe seemed to take it all in stride.

They talked about debating and how important it was to being a lawyer.

"How much debating are you going to do as a tax attorney?" Campbell asked.

Chloe laughed. "Who knows? I might have to debate the IRS to keep my client out of jail."

"If I go to law school, I want to be an agent with pro athletes and entertainers as my clients."

"That sounds great, Campbell. Where are you thinking of going to undergrad?"

"I don't know. Miss Robinson said I should go to a state school. It's less expensive. What about you?"

"I'm going to Spelman. That's where my mom went. It's a done deal."

"Did your dad go to Morehouse?"

"No. He went to Norfolk State and marched in the band. 'Behold the green and the gold!'" Chloe was standing at attention and broke into a marching step.

They both laughed so hard that they didn't hear her dad come in.

"If you're gonna do it, do it right."

Roderick Matthews joined his daughter, and they marched around the den. When Chloe couldn't march anymore because she was weak from laughing so hard, she fell on the sofa, and Roderick turned his attention to Campbell.

"How do you do, young man? I'm Roderick Matthews, Chloe's dad."

"Pleasure to meet you, sir. I'm Campbell Rice."

They shook hands.

"Nice to finally meet you, Campbell."

"Thank you, sir. Glad to meet you too."

At about that time, Sandra walked in, smiling and shaking her head. Chloe looked more like her dad, but she was built like her mother. Chloe had gained her composure and introduced Sandra and Campbell. Campbell was nervous. Being in their home was enough without having to confront both parents at once.

"I'm glad to meet you, Campbell." She had a beautiful smile, and her manner was engaging.

"Chloe, let me know when you are taking Campbell home and I'll ride with you."

"Okay, Ma."

Roderick put his arm around his wife, and they started out of the room.

"Daddy, who won the game?"

"We did."

"NSU wasn't playing!"

"Oh, you have jokes."

Campbell was intrigued by how easily Chloe and her parents got along. He made a remark to her about it. They talked a while longer about their plans for the future.

"Chloe, do you think we'll still be friends by the time we get to college and law school and all that?"

"We'll probably be married by then."

Before he could respond, she leaned over and kissed him.

Her answer surprised him, but not as much as the kiss. He didn't know what to say. She walked to the hall, pressed a button on the wall, and said into the intercom, "Ma, we're ready to go."

The ride home had been fine. Talking to Sandra had distracted Campbell for a few minutes. But now that he was home and things were quiet, he replayed Chloe's comment and the kiss over and over in his head. He had never considered that she would ever entertain marrying him. The truth was that he had thought about it but never considered that she had. Campbell didn't have a lot of experience with girls, but he knew that he would talk with her the next day.

Should I address it or act like it didn't happen or wait to see what she will say? He went to sleep pondering what to do next.

$\mathscr{F}$ORTY-TWO

Enoch and Kirby had finally gotten home and settled from the day's events. Enoch didn't say anything to her, but he noticed that she hadn't mentioned the in-vitro procedure all day, even when they stopped to eat. He wasn't going to bring it up. He doubted she was having second thoughts, but he knew how stressed out she had been by the whole thing.

"What do you think about Ben and Belinda?" Kirby asked, interrupting his thoughts.

"I don't think anything about it. Why?"

"You do so. I saw your face when they were together."

"I'm pretty amused with the whole thing, to be honest. Ben mentioned that they were going to lunch the night we were at Clay's house, and now he's making decisions and dealing with the girls like they are his."

"Are you jealous, Mr. Casebier?"

"No, I'm not jealous. Just protective of my nieces."

"You don't think Ben is sincere?"

"Yeah. He's one of the most for-real dudes I know. I don't doubt him. I just don't want them to get too attached to him if it's not gonna work out with him and their mom."

"Why wouldn't it work out?"

"I don't know, K. Stuff happens. Plus, she's not over Canady, and we both know that."

"You're right about that. But maybe Ben is good for her. I hope this does work out so she can finally let Canady go. She really needs to have some closure."

"Has Belinda talked to you about Ben?"

"She only told me they had gone to lunch and that it was a good lunch. He took her to Sheldon's. He bought her flowers. Just the regular stuff."

I wonder if Ben told her the whole story about Sheldon's, Enoch thought to himself as Kirby continued to talk.

"What did Ben tell you?" she asked.

"Same basic stuff."

"We just need to keep an eye on Ms. Stewart and Minister Coffey!" Kirby said, crossing her arms and smiling broadly.

Enoch laughed. "On another subject, it's my week to have the guys over."

"And you're telling me why?"

"'Cause I need you to work some magic in the kitchen."

"What's in it for me?"

"I'll pay your rent next month."

"Now you're my kind of man." Kirby put her arms around her husband and thought to herself that they were back on track.

The phone rang early, and Katherine thought that that couldn't be good news. She didn't look at the caller ID. She just answered.

"Hey, Mama."

"Leah. Hey, sweetie. How are you this morning?"

"Okay. I'm going to rehab today." Leah's speech was slow and deliberate, but she explained to her mom that they were moving her to the rehabilitation center and she needed her to come over.

"I'll be there as soon as I get dressed."

Katherine was overjoyed. That would be a great surprise for Lee when he got back. He was on a business trip. He had canceled several engagements since Leah had been sick, and Katherine was glad that he had decided to go this time. He needed a break.

Maybe I just won't mention it until he gets back tomorrow.

She called Grace to see if she could go to the hospital with her.

"Hi, Paul. You're up early. How are you?"

"I'm fine, Kat. And you?" Paul sounded particularly strong this morning. He still had more good days than bad, and everybody was glad about that.

"I just talked to Leah, and they are moving her to rehab today."

"All right! That's wonderful news. I'm glad to hear it."

"I wanted to see if Grace can go to the hospital with me. Is she around?"

"Right here. Just a moment."

When Grace got on the line, Katherine told her the news.

"Of course I can go," Grace said. "Paul will be fine. His attendant is here already, so he'll have some company for a few hours. He says that he'll try to get a hold of Grant while we're gone too."

Katherine and Grace arrived at the hospital just in time to see Dr. Trey and Dr. Strauss. They explained that they were moving Leah a few days ahead of Dr. Raja's schedule so if she didn't do well, she might have to go back to the hospital. But if she progressed as well as she had been, she could spend Christmas Day at home. They talked about the types of therapy she would have and the goals of the therapy. They stopped short of giving any timelines.

Packing Leah's things didn't take very long. She was moved by ambulance. Her room at the rehab center wasn't as nice as the one at the hospital, and she had a roommate. Katherine questioned her being able to have a private room. She was told that all rooms were semi-private. The patient interaction was a part of the therapy. Grace hung up Leah's clothes, and Katherine tried to make the small space as comfortable as possible, setting up pictures and putting her afghan on the bed.

The new physical therapist came in to get her started right away. As he started to roll her away, she reached for the album of pictures that Clay had given her. She told her mom that she wanted to look at Grant.

Lee called Katherine on his way back home. She told him about Leah. He was excited that Leah had been moved to rehab and even more excited that she might be able to come home, if just for one day. He let out a great sigh of relief. He had sought God seemingly endlessly on Leah's behalf, and it seemed like God wasn't listening.

Grant could hear his mother's smile when she answered. He was calling to check on Leah and was surprised with the good news.

"I am wonderful, sweetheart," she said. "How are you doing?"

They chatted briefly, and she told him as much as she knew, including the possibility of Leah being able to spend Christmas Day at home. Grace gave Katherine the phone. Grant and Katherine spoke for a few minutes, and she promised to have Leah call him when she came back to the room.

"Mama Kat, is she really better?"

"Yes, sugar. She is really better."

It had been a long week. Jill was glad that Friday had finally come. She was excited and yet somewhat apprehensive about the trip to Chapel Hill. Raja was already in town at the hospital, and they would be leaving in a couple of hours. Jill had packed as light as she could, but she always packed too much. She told Trey that she would be in Chapel Hill for the weekend and told her mother, explaining to them that Raja would be staying at the hospital.

Trey accompanied Raja to see Brittani first. He looked at her chart, the original MRI, and the repeat MRI. Only a slight change had occurred. Raja agreed to stay on that course until Sunday. He would reexamine her when he brought Jill back.

Leah had made substantial progress. Her lower body was stronger, but she wasn't ready to walk unassisted. Raja, Trey, and Dr. Strauss agreed that she could spend Christmas Day at home. Trey would have his office make the transportation arrangements.

Dr. Strauss made one disclaimer: "If there is any setback, any cause for concern, I will rescind the offer to let her go home. We can't, we won't, take any unnecessary risks."

They all said that they understood and agreed.

With that being done, Raja called Jill to let her know he was on his way. Jill hoped that she didn't look too casual.

When he got to her house, Raja was surprised to see Jill dressed down, but he thought she was still very beautiful. Jill was the first blonde woman he had dated, and the color of her hair intrigued him. Some of it was darker. One of the nurses at the hospital told him that it was called highlights. He knew that. He just liked to play dumb around them, and they got a kick out of it. He often remarked to them how American women spent too much time and money changing their appearances.

"We do it for men," one of his coworkers said, and he laughed.

They talked nonstop on the ride to Chapel Hill. The more time Raja spent with Jill, the more respect he had for her. She was very well read and learned, as Raja's father would say. She wasn't the princess he had thought she would be. He had prejudged her and their family based on what he saw from Trey. She was still very wealthy and could hold her own, but Raja was making peace with all that. If he was going to date an American business-woman, he would have to think like an American businessman.

Belinda had had a long week. She had been in school during the day and stayed at the hospital at night. Brianna had been with Grammy and Auntie all week. Kirby had offered to stay at the hospital with Brittani a couple of nights, but Belinda had said no until that night. She was deliriously tired. Kirby and Brianna were staying at the hospital that night. Enoch and Ben were playing Xbox. Belinda wanted a hot bath and a good night's sleep. Brittani was coming home in the morning. Ben said that he would be there early to pick her up to go to the hospital. Belinda smiled at the thought.

After a bowl of cereal and a bubble bath, Belinda crawled into bed and turned to the jazz station on the satellite television. She set the timer for twenty minutes. She didn't hear the television go off. She dreamed. It had been a while since she had.

She saw the fire, she saw Canady, and she saw Brittani and Brianna in their ballet clothes and in their white dresses, standing at Canady's grave. There were rows and rows of graves and white headstones. The sun was shining. Enoch was there; Kirby was holding the girls' hands. Ben was there. Trey was there.

She woke up, her heart beating fast and the images in her dreams running through her mind.

She thought about Canady almost every day, but she hadn't thought about the graveyard in a long time, Arlington National Cemetery, where those who die for their country are laid to rest. She had been there only once since the day he was buried, on the one-year anniversary. It was just too painful.

Belinda reached for her journal. She wrote what she could remember about the dreams. Before long she was dozing again. She dreamed again: the cemetery, Canady, Ben, Canady, Ben, the cemetery, over and over. Belinda knew she was dreaming and woke herself up. She got out of bed and got on her knees. Her prayer was for full clarity, wisdom, and understanding. When she finished, she went back to sleep and slept the rest of the night without dreaming.

Jill laughed out loud when Raja presented her with two tickets to UNC basketball games, one for a ladies' game that night versus NC State and the men's game on Saturday afternoon versus Duke.

"Do you know Trey would kill for these tickets?"

"Yes, I do know." Raja laughed.

"I can't wait to tell him. He won't be either of our friends."

Jill was excited about the games, and Raja was glad. He was surprised when he got back to pick her up and she was dressed in jeans and a long-sleeved Carolina Tar Heels T-shirt. He had not expected her to have the paraphernalia, but he knew not to underestimate her.

Their evening out began with veggie pizza and cherry lemonade, and they had ice cream sundaes after the game.

"Pizza and ice cream in the same day. I must be crazy." Jill laughed as she finished the pineapple sundae.

"No, not crazy, but I wouldn't recommend it every weekend."

"Why didn't you come to UNC?" Raja asked Jill.

"My mom and my grandmother went to Sarah Lawrence, so my grandfather thought that was a good place for me to go. It was kind of understood. As much money as he spent flying me back home, he probably wished he had let me stay in North Carolina. I missed Lola, Leah, and Trey, and I came home a lot."

"You didn't miss your parents?"

"Yes, but not like I missed Leah and Miss Lola. Leah was at UNC-Charlotte. After we graduated, I went to work at the foundation and she went to grad school at East Carolina. I drove to Greenville as much as I could, and Lola rode with me many days." Jill smiled at the memory.

She went on to explain to Raja who Lola was in her life and that she was not just the lady who the restaurant was named for.

"Miss Lola was our housekeeper and my and Trey's nanny, but she was more like a grandmother to us. She spoiled us, but she was firm. I could talk to her about anything. My friendship with Leah is more like we are sisters. I don't even have a female cousin."

"I can identify with that. I have only one female cousin and one male cousin and no brothers and sisters. I had imaginary friends when I was a little tyke."

"Most children do."

"Yeah, but my parents thought that it was a waste of time. They thought I should be reading or working a crossword puzzle. That was their idea of fun. My father taught me to play chess, but I didn't learn to play checkers until I went to college."

Raja couldn't believe he was being so transparent with Jill. He hardly ever talked about his family. His parents were difficult at best. While they wanted the best for him, their tactics were sometimes harsh.

"How did you convince your parents to let you come to the States for college?" she asked.

"They knew I would get a good education here, and the scholarship sealed the deal."

"Did you want to be a doctor?"

"Yeah. That was totally my decision. Because being a doctor is an admirable profession in our culture, my parents had no argument."

Raja and Jill continued to talk as they drove back to his townhouse. He stayed only a short while, picked up a book from his bedroom, and left. He would be back to get her for breakfast. The game was at 2:00 p.m. They needed to be in the parking lot by1:00 p.m.

Jill called Leah as soon as Raja left. She didn't know if she would get her or even if Leah would remember or understand. She walked around the townhouse. It was furnished very practically. He had hundreds of books on several bookshelves and beautiful art, sculptures, and paintings. There were only a few personal pictures. One she assumed was his parents, one of him with them at his college graduation, and one with a big group of people. She decided that it must be his family.

Leah answered, and Jill was pleasantly surprised at how strong she sounded.

"Hey, Leah. Did I wake you?"

"No. I'm not very sleepy. I'm glad you called."

"I'm in Chapel Hill with Raja."

"I remember."

"Great." Jill laughed.

She told Leah about the game, pizza, ice cream, and about the artwork in Raja's place. Leah listened intently, but she didn't say much. She told Jill that she was glad she had gone and glad she was having a good time.

"I'm glad I can tell you about it."

"Jillie, I am getting well. You don't have to worry. Tell me about anything."

They talked a few minutes more, and Leah told Jill that the physical therapist had put braces on both her legs to help her stand up.

Then the phone beeped in Leah's ear. She looked at the screen, and it was Grant. She and Jill hung up quickly so she wouldn't miss his call.

FORTY-THREE

Belinda woke up to the sound of the phone ringing. She looked at the clock and cleared her throat. She didn't want anybody to know she had overslept.

"Hey, sleepyhead."

"Hi, Ben. How are you?" She was trying to sound awake.

"I'm on my way, but I can kill some time. I know you aren't ready."

"Why do you say that?"

"This is the second time I've called."

Belinda started to say that she had been in the shower, but she didn't want to lie. "I can't believe I slept through the phone."

"I can. You have had a long, tough week. Do you want to rest and let me go get Brittani?"

"No, no. I want to go. Please give me thirty minutes and I'll be ready."

"Okay. It's pretty cold out here, so dress warmly."

"I will. Thanks. See you in a bit."

Belinda got up immediately. She was embarrassed that she had slept through the phone. What if the hospital had tried to call? She quickly went through the caller ID. There was only one call, from Ben. She smiled as she stood in the closet. Suddenly, the dreams came back to her mind.

"Not now. Not today," she said aloud.

Belinda decided that some music would keep her from thinking about it. She flipped on the television to some Motown music and quickly laid out her clothes, showered, and got dressed. She went to the kitchen and poured herself a glass of milk, but before she could drink it, the doorbell rang. It was Ben with a bag in his hand from the bakery. He was right. It was pretty brisk out there, but it should be. Christmas was only a few days away.

"Breakfast for the queen." He handed her the bag. Muffins and croissants. Her favorites.

"Thank you. You think of everything. Do I have time to eat it, or do I need to—?"

"We have time. Have a seat and eat your breakfast, and then we'll go."

"I poured myself a glass of milk. Do you want some?"

"Do you have any real milk and not that soy stuff you torture your kids with?"

Belinda laughed. "No, but I have some apple juice if you would rather have that."

"Yeah. That works."

Kirby had everything almost done when Belinda and Ben arrived at the hospital. As Belinda was getting the last of Brittani's things together, she dropped her journal. When she picked it up, it fell open to a page where Belinda saw the words "Mommy and Minister Coffey." She couldn't linger. She didn't want anybody to see her looking at it, but her curiosity was definitely piqued.

Trey came in and gave Brittani and Belinda the discharge instructions. She would need to come back the next day to see Dr. Raja. In the meantime, she was to put no pressure on her leg. The probability was that she would have to continue the oral medication that week.

"Be very careful not to get cut. No cross-stitching. You need to read for a few days." Dr. Trey was very serious.

Ben loaded Brittani and her things into the backseat of the SUV, and Brianna climbed in beside her. Kirby and Belinda were standing off from them, and Ben was curious what they were so intently discussing.

"Minister Coffey, we are supposed to call Grammy when we leave," Brittani said.

Ben gave her his phone and sat in the passenger side.

"Are you going to let Mommy drive?" Brianna asked, and they all laughed.

"You want me to?"

"Yeah!"

Belinda was telling Kirby about her dream the night before.

"Maybe you need to go to DC, go back to Arlington and see the grave. You need some closure, Belinda. And if you are going to have a real relationship with Ben, you have to let Canady go once and for all."

Belinda drove home, much to her chagrin and the twins' delight. Ben was amused that they thought it was so funny.

Once Brittani was in and settled, they ordered pizza. Ben went to pick it up and was gone much longer than Belinda expected. He came back with three boxes.

"What's all that?"

"All you ordered was veggie pizza!"

"Yes. So?"

"You might as well put that in a bowl and pour salad dressing on it!"

"So what did you get?"

"Barbeque chicken pizza and cinnamon sticks." He said it with a pout that Belinda thought was cute.

After they had eaten and the girls were settled upstairs, Belinda asked Ben if he could stay a few minutes. She wanted to discuss something with him. She told him about the dreams and Kirby's suggestion that she go back to DC. She repeated Kirby's comment about him.

Ben sat and listened intently. He wanted to say the right thing and not prejudice his response with his personal feelings.

"Babe, I don't know what dreams mean, and I won't try to address that. What I do know is that I agree with Kirby. Going back to Arlington will help you bring closure to Canady being gone. Whether for us, our future or not, you need to do that for you. Now let me tell you this and maybe the dreams about the fire will go away. The authorities know who started the fire."

"How do you know?"

"I've been in communication with the authorities since it happened. The bishop asked me to, and I was more than happy to oblige because Brittani was hurt."

"Why didn't you tell me?"

"You had enough to deal with."

Ben went on to explain what he knew and ended by telling her that all the boys were being punished.

"But how does that help Brittani?"

"I don't know that it does, but I hope it helps you to close that chapter too."

Belinda sat there, looking helpless.

"I also hope it helps you to let them go back to ballet."

"I don't know about that."

"Their being in ballet didn't have anything to do with the fire. There could have been a band concert in that auditorium that evening or a play, a dozen things. Somebody else's child could have been hurt."

"Is that supposed to make me feel better?"

Ben went on. "What if a child had been hurt who was not covered by a bishop and a church family who pray, or what if it happened to a child with no insurance? Belinda, God allowed it and you have dealt with it."

"I've dealt with it because you and Kirby and Enoch and Grammy and Auntie have been there to help me."

"And it's brought us closer," Ben replied.

She smiled.

He took both her hand in his. "How easy would it have been for you to tell me you were busy if I had asked you out?"

She didn't answer.

"We've seen each other almost every day and, in spite of the circumstances, enjoyed each other's company."

She nodded in agreement.

They talked a while longer, and Ben offered to go to Washington with her. She declined his offer and said that it was something she had to do on her own. She said that as soon as they knew what Brittani's prognosis was, she would make her plans. If it all worked out, they would be back in school and she would still have a week off. If Kirby and Enoch could keep the girls, she would make arrangements to go then.

"If Kirby and Enoch can't keep them, I know who will."

They laughed, but it was a comforting feeling to Belinda. Brittani and Brianna had a grandmother.

After the girls had gone to bed, Belinda went to their room and did something she had never done. She took Brittani's journal into her room. The words "Mommy and Minister Coffey" were still very curious to her. She vowed not to read any more than that page. She and Kirby had started to journal as teenagers. Their foster mother had encouraged them to write. And because Belinda wrote, the girls wanted to write too.

She eased the journal out of the stack of books on the night-stand between their beds. The entry was on one of the last pages written. The page started, "Dear God." The next-to-the-last sentence said, "Please bless Mommy and Minister Coffey to get married so that we can be a family." Belinda sat on the foot of her bed. She closed the journal and held it close to her heart.

"Oh, God, do they know something I don't know? Can they see what I don't see or refuse to see?"

Belinda put the journal back and started to get Brianna's but changed her mind. She knew that if Brittani had written that, Brianna had written more of the same.

She went back to her room and took out her own journal. She wrote about the dreams, about Ben, about what she had seen in Brittani's journal, and then wrote a prayer. She asked God once and for all to let her move past her hurt and her broken heart, to put her love for Canady and missing him in perspective so she could move forward into a real relationship with Ben. The tears rolled, and she let them. She prayed that they would be the last tears for Canady Stewart. The last paragraph for this entry said, "I will go back to Washington to visit his resting place one last time. I will say good-bye this time rather than farewell. I will let him go, knowing that he loved me enough to want me to move on. I know he is resting in Your arms, Jesus. He served You and this country and gave his life. Rest in peace, Canady."

Belinda put the journal down and looked at the clock. It was a little past eight o'clock on the West Coast. She called Lorraine. They hadn't talked in months, their lives having taken on different paths. But she needed to tell her what she was going to do.

After exchanging pleasantries and promising not to be so long talking again, Belinda told Lorraine the primary reason for her call. She told her about Ben, and Lorraine listened, smiling on the other end of the line.

Lorraine asked a couple of questions and then very matter of factly said, "Let me know when you're going and I will meet you there."

Belinda didn't know she even wanted Lorraine to go but was very relieved that she offered. Belinda thanked her and told her that she would call again in a few days with the details.

"Are you going to tell Brianna and Brittani where you're going and why?"

"I don't know. Maybe when I get back."

"It's your decision."

"Tell the general I said hello."

"Will do. He'll be glad to hear from you, and my love to the girls."

"Sure, and we'll talk in a few days."

Belinda went to sleep, slept all night, and didn't dream.

The Christmas celebration was in full swing. Ben gave all his ladies bracelets—silver charm bracelets for the twins, gold for Belinda. They each had a charm that represented an interest they had: ballet slippers for the girls, the letters RN with the nurses' symbol for Belinda, an angel, and the letter "B." But Belinda's also had a pearl surrounded by diamonds. He explained to them that for each occasion, he would add a charm. Grammy and Auntie's bracelets were gold with colorful stones, charms, and various other attachments. Grammy hugged Ben but, as always, said that he spent too much money.

The girls and Enoch had had their annual shopping spree online because Brittani couldn't move around too much. Enoch had taken pictures of them and had copies made, and the girls made frames and decorated them—one for Auntie K, one for Mommy, one for Auntie and Grammy, and one for Minister Coffey. Enoch felt a slight twinge of jealousy. The jealousy was all gone when they presented him with a drawing of him and them that they had had done at a carnival. He had forgotten about it. They had made a frame for that one too and decorated it with all the things he liked.

Ben and Belinda had gone back to Sheldon's for an early dinner on Christmas Eve. They sat in the window, and Fredric was their waiter. They exchanged their gifts there. She gave him a chess set made of soap stone.

$\mathscr{F}$ORTY-FOUR

Leah's day at home was the highlight of the holidays for her family, the Sturdivants, and the Strauss family. Katherine had had dinner catered by Lola's so that they could spend as much time with Leah as possible. Raja spent Christmas Day with them, and his being there took away the worry of Leah overdoing it. He did require her to have an hour of rest. Kathy set up the webcam so that they were able to talk with Grant.

Leah went back to the hospital that evening tired but very happy. She had had a good day. She remembered many significant things.

Kirby was anxious to get to her to-do list. Along with her long list of things to handle for Casebier Collection, she had two important calls to make: an appointment with the obstetrician and an appointment with a counselor. She knew that Enoch would want to know when the counseling appointment was first. That was his requirement, and she was going to make it happen to get what she wanted.

Kirby called the counseling ministry line and left a message. They promised to call back in eight hours but gave an alternate number for emergencies. As far as Kirby was concerned, it was an emergency, but she left a general message. The obstetrician's office gave her an appointment for one week from that day. She looked at the calendar. If she could have the procedure the next month, the baby or babies would be born in the fall. If it took a little longer, she could still be a mom by the end of the year. She would be pregnant during the hot summer months, but that was fine with her.

She would talk to Leah. She and Grant might not want a big pregnant hostess at their reception. But if she wasn't too big, she could find a really cute dress and still do it.

Her thoughts were interrupted by the telephone. It was a client. Let the workday begin.

Robin Brackett was surprised to hear the message from Kirby Casebier. She was concerned that it would be a longer conversation than she could have during her break. She would call right after school. Robin had been a certified counselor for a long time, and she knew better than to generalize or stereotype people, but Kirby Casebier would be one of the last people she expected to hear from.

Raja and Jill's weekend in Chapel Hill had gone well, and he had given her a gift on Sunday morning before they came back. He knew that she would be preoccupied on Christmas Day, so he wanted her to have it then. It was a stunningly beautiful white china tea set. The teapot had very intricate details, and the pot and cups had 14K gold trim. It was a replica of a set from the Taj Mahal. There was a book that accompanied it, which gave background on the set and the custom of evening tea.

Jill was thoroughly fascinated with the gift. She was impressed that Raja had even gotten her the gift. She read the book when she got home, and from all indication, he had to have had someone in India send the set to him.

She had actually bought Raja and Trey the same gift: a Kindle. But it hadn't occurred to her to bring it with her, so she gave it to him on Christmas Day. She had downloaded two books on his and three on Trey's. She knew Trey wouldn't take the time to do it.

Raja was surprised but delighted with the gift and the books she selected: *Dreams of My Father* by Barack Obama and *The Long Fall* by Walter Mosley. Raja was a big Mosley fan and was behind on his books. He had limited time for reading fiction. He had to decline Jill's invitation to come back for New Year's. He was on call, but he invited her to come back to Chapel Hill the following weekend.

"Only if we can go to another game," was her response.

"It's a date."

FORTY-FIVE

Raja and Trey were pleasantly surprised at how well Brittani had tolerated the intravenous anticoagulant. Raja was documenting her progress to share with his colleagues. They had finally ruled out any need for surgery. She was going back to school on Monday.

Things were basically back to normal, and Kirby encouraged Belinda to make plans to go to Washington. Interestingly, Belinda decided to talk to Grammy about it.

"Sweetheart, you need closure. If going back to the cemetery will give you that, then do it."

"What if it doesn't?"

"You won't know unless you go see, will you?"

"No, ma'am, I won't. Grammy, do you think Ben will be offended by me going?"

"No, I don't think so. And what I know is if he was offended, you would know. Benji is not scared to speak up."

Grammy offered to keep the girls before Belinda could ask.

Belinda made arrangements with the cemetery, made her travel arrangements and hotel arrangements, and called Lorraine. They would meet on Wednesday, go to the cemetery on Thursday, hang out on Friday, and come home on Saturday. Ben had to insist that she stay the extra day. He also offered to pay for the trip. She declined his offer, but he left it open if she needed anything extra. He made a mental note to give her his credit card before she left.

Ben wanted it to be a successful experience for Belinda. He wanted her to come back with a clear head. He needed to tell her about Atlanta, and he wanted to tell her about Sheldon's before she found out inadvertently.

Robin didn't come right out and ask Kirby what she wanted to talk about when Kirby told her that she didn't have to see her immediately. She did ask her if she wanted to meet at the church or if they could meet more informally. They decided to have dinner on Friday night. Kirby asked if they could meet somewhere more private than Lola's. They agreed to meet in Davis Town.

Robin asked Kirby what she should be praying about in advance of their meeting.

"I want to have a baby, and the doctor had advised me that to do that I will have to have the in-vitro process."

Robin was a little surprised but not shocked. "I will pray, Kirby, and I look forward to seeing you on Friday."

Robin knew that she needed to do some research too. She didn't know much about the procedure, but she had counseled women and couples before who were dealing with infertility. From past experience Robin knew that it was a fast-and-pray situation.

Kirby and Belinda decided that Brittani and Brianna didn't need to know where Belinda was going until she got back. Enoch told them that they wouldn't get away with that, and he was right. Belinda did not make a practice of lying to them, and she wouldn't start. When she told them that she was going away for a few days, they wanted to know where, when, and why. When she told them she was going to Washington, they remembered that their dad was buried there.

Belinda didn't know how much to tell them. She remembered her counselor telling her to answer their questions honestly but not to volunteer information.

"They will ask what they are ready to process," the counselor said.

She also didn't want to say too much about Ben and her. The journal entry crossed her mind. *Why wouldn't I? They were writing letters to God about me and Ben.*

"I am going back to Washington to visit your dad's grave. I am still sad about him passing, and I think if I go back, I can find some peace about it."

Brittani spoke up first. "Mommy, do you want us to go with you?"

"No. Ms. Lorraine is coming from California to meet me."

"Wow. We haven't seen her in a long time," Brianna commented.

"Mommy, did you tell Minister Coffey you're going?" Brittani asked, looking at Brianna.

Belinda felt a little uncomfortable talking to them about Ben. She hesitated, but they waited.

"Yes, I talked to him about it. He said he would pray too. If you all want to go to the cemetery one day, I'll take you, but this time I need to go alone."

They each said that they understood.

The rest of the conversation centered on Grammy staying with them and their responsibilities for the days she would be gone. They were delighted.

Grammy was surprised when Belinda's doorbell rang and even more surprised that it was Ben. She offered him some breakfast. He accepted, and he had a seat at the kitchen table. His silence spoke loudly.

"What is it, Benji?"

244

He let out a big sigh. "You know how you always say that God's timing is perfect?"

"Yes. Why?"

"I need you to remind me of that when I tell you this."

Grammy sat down at the table across from him. She took a sip of her coffee but didn't say anything.

"The Bishop asked me to go to Atlanta to plant and pastor our first church."

"My, my, my," was Grammy's response.

They were both quiet for a minute.

Grammy broke the silence. "What did you tell him?"

"I told him that I didn't want to leave you or Belinda but I would go."

She smiled, got up from the table, and kissed the top of his head. She put her arms around him. "God's timing is perfect, even now."

He closed his eyes and bowed his head.

"Have you told Belinda?"

"No. I wanted to talk to you first."

Ben told Grammy about his conversation with the bishop and his thoughts about leaving. Grammy chuckled, took another drink from her coffee, and looked at Ben. He didn't know what she thought was funny.

"I was thinking about your granddaddy. Do you know what he would say?"

"He would've asked me if I prayed and if I could take care of my family doing that."

"Exactly right! And if you said yes to both, he would tell you to pack up Belinda and those babies and go."

Ben laughed. He knew that his grandmother was right. His grandfather wouldn't have been going back and forth about it. But it was different. Belinda had a life, and so did her children.

"Grammy, Belinda and I haven't really established our relationship. How can I ask her to leave her sister and nursing school? She's been through enough. Plus, I don't want to leave you and Auntie."

"Oh, sugar, don't worry about us. We'll work that out. But do you know where Belinda is right now?"

"In DC, at the cemetery."

"Do you know why?"

"Yes. Because she needed to bring some closure to the situation and go on with her life."

"And so she can stop putting that between you and her. Benjamin Coffey, we are sitting in her kitchen. I am here with her daughters. She talked with me about the trip before she went. It seems to me that she has settled into a life that includes you."

They talked for a while longer. He asked Grammy if she would move to Atlanta with him. Her answer was that she didn't want to interfere with his and Belinda's life but that they had time to figure all that out.

"Don't tell Auntie or Enoch yet. I want to tell them myself."

"I won't. That's your story to tell."

FORTY-SIX

Snow was on the ground in Washington, and although the sun was shining, it was very cold. Belinda checked into the hotel, called Ben and the girls, and settled down with a magazine. Lorraine would be there in a couple of hours. Belinda was looking forward to seeing her. It had been too long, but Lorraine was a part of a past that Belinda had a hard time dealing with. She leaned back in the chair, closed her eyes, and allowed herself to replay that day in her mind. So many things had changed since then. Belinda thought that she would die that day too. But she didn't, and now she had a wonderful life, and Ben was a big part of it.

Belinda and Lorraine had dinner in the hotel restaurant and stayed up late, talking. When they finally turned off the lights, Belinda laid there, unable to sleep. She thought about Canady: the day she met him; the day she told him she was pregnant; the day they got married; the day the twins were born; the day he left for Iraq, the last time she saw him; and the cemetery, rows of white headstones and American flags. She prayed, asking God to really use the situation, the trip, to close that chapter in her life. She went to sleep praying.

Belinda had done a meticulous job of preparing for Brittani and Brianna while she was gone. Not knowing that Kirby was meeting with Robin Brackett for her counseling session, Belinda had asked her and Enoch to keep the girls on Friday night and let Grammy go home.

Kirby was so determined to get the counseling going that she forgot until she told Enoch about the appointment.

"No sweat. I'll keep 'em."

"Maybe you can get Ben to come over too."

"Maybe."

Kirby left the room, and Enoch had to check himself. Ben was his good friend. They had been friends for years, practically all their lives. He loved him like a brother. They had been through crushes, high school girlfriends, and adult situations.

Why has my attitude changed?

The answer was simple: he was jealous of Ben's relationship with his girls. Enoch loved Brittani and Brianna like they were his own. For four years he had been their father figure. If Uncle Enoch couldn't make it happen, it wasn't going to happen. When it was doughnuts for dad at their school, he went. When it was dads dancing with daughters at the ballet recital, he danced with both of them. Now Ben was cutting in on some of his time and attention with them. From all indication, he was serious about Belinda, and that meant he was serious about them too.

If the in-vitro process doesn't work and we never have any kids, I won't have them either.

Enoch allowed himself to think what he hadn't wanted to face. He had faith. He believed that God would bless them with children if that was His will. Enoch said that he was okay with that, and most days he was, but…adopting children was perfectly fine with him if that's what they needed to do. If that was God's plan for them, to be parents and orphaned children to have a family, so be it.

Enoch felt his phone vibrate. It was Ben.

"What's up, dude? I needed to talk to you anyway," Enoch said.

"That's good, 'cause I need to talk to you too." Ben sounded serious.

"You good?"

"Yeah, man. Just missin' Belinda." He knew that that would get a rise out of Enoch.

"Man, you know I don't want to hear that."

They both laughed.

"I do miss her, but I know that when she gets back, we'll get it together for real."

"Don't mean no harm, but even if you and her don't work out, she needed to do that."

"No doubt."

They talked about a few other things, and Ben finally asked Enoch if he could meet him for lunch the next day.

"That's what I wanted to holler at you about. I'll have the girls tomorrow night. Why don't you come over and hang out with us?"

"That sounds like a plan."

After they hung up, Enoch told Kirby not to tell the girls she wouldn't be there. He wanted to surprise them.

"Do you want me to cook?"

"No. We don't want healthy."

A military town car was waiting when they came out of the hotel to drive them to Arlington. Belinda didn't expect that, but Lorraine's husband had made that arrangement. Lorraine and Belinda checked in at the cemetery office. She was entitled to an official escort, who turned out to be a very young army soldier. Belinda silently prayed that his working at Arlington was all his family would ever know about it. The young man helped them onto a golf-cart-type vehicle and drove through the paths as close to Canady's grave as they could get. He helped them out, told them to take as much time as they needed, and stood beside the vehicle until they were a few feet away and then slowly walked behind them.

Lorraine took Belinda's hand. They were both wearing gloves, but Lorraine could tell that she was trembling. She put her arm around her, and they walked slowly through the snow to the foot of his grave. It was surreal to Belinda. It was so much like her dreams. She looked at his name on the headstone, but her eyes got stuck on the word *Iraq*. She had come to hate that word. If she heard a report on the news, a knot would develop in the pit of her stomach. Her knees buckled, but Lorraine caught her with the help of the young soldier. They didn't even realize that he was there. Then the tears came, like flood gates had been opened. She cried hard from her belly. Lorraine held on to her and let her cry like she did the day they informed her that he had been killed.

When she had become so overwhelmed with emotion that she could no longer stand, the young soldier led her to a bench a few rows over. She and Lorraine sat, and he stepped back. There were no words that could or would fix this moment. It had been almost five years, but there was still nothing to say. Whimpering, Belinda laid her head on Lorraine's shoulder, so glad she had come.

Belinda opened her eyes, and the warmth of the sun gave her strength. She sat up, wiped her face, took a deep breath, and stood. Lorraine's hand on her back steadied her, and she handed her another handkerchief. Another deep breath and she walked back to Canady's grave. Her voice trembled as she talked. She talked about the twins first and then herself and Ben.

"I know that you want me to be happy, and I know that he will make me happy," she said out loud.

She cried a few more tears, but her voice was firm.

"I want to make a life with him, so I came to say…good-bye." The words got stuck in her throat. She said it again. "Good-bye.

I will keep your memory fresh for the girls, and I'm sure they will want to come here for themselves one day."

Suddenly, clouds passed in front of the sun, and for about a minute it was dark, like it was going to storm. Then, just as suddenly, the sun came back out. Belinda looked toward heaven and smiled. She had gotten her release.

The ride back to the office seemed quick. As the young soldier opened the limo door for them, he said to Belinda, "On behalf of a grateful nation, it has been my pleasure to serve you today." That was the same thing they had said to her the day that they buried him.

Uncle Enoch came home with a grocery bag full of goodies: cherry soda, marshmallows, graham crackers, and all the stuff to make s'mores. Brianna and Brittani were ecstatic when they found out that they were spending the evening with him and Minister Coffey without Auntie K. There would be no rules that night. Ben showed up with food from Lola's: fried fish, french fries, hushpuppies. He made sure Kirby knew that he had salad so she wouldn't completely shut down the party.

They ate, made s'mores in the fireplace, and played horse and team Monopoly—Ben and Brianna versus Enoch and Brittani. The girls were so tired that they both fell asleep on the floor right in front of the fireplace. Enoch knew that Kirby was going to have a fit, but he put them to bed without a bath and in their clothes.

Enoch and Ben cleaned up, and when Enoch came back in from taking the trash out, Ben was sitting with his head in his hands.

"Man, she'll be back tomorrow," Enoch said.

They both laughed.

"I wish it was that simple," Ben said. "It's what I have to do when she gets back."

"Have you told her about your involvement in Sheldon's?"

"No, but that's minor to this. Bishop wants me to move to Atlanta to open the new church."

"Congratulations, man! That's awesome!" Enoch extended his hand to Ben, who shook it and kept talking.

"It's awesome except Belinda might not want to go." Ben shared with Enoch his concerns and his conversation with Bishop Robinson and Grammy. "I came back to Hattiesville to be here with Grammy, not to leave her again."

Enoch listened, but he didn't say much. What could he say? The ministry had to be the priority, but he could understand that Ben had no way to know what Belinda would say. "I know you're prayin', and I'll pray with you, but let me ask you this. Have you talked to Belinda about getting married? I promise you she's not movin' to Charlotte with you not married, and that's twenty miles away. So you know she won't go all the way to Atlanta."

Ben didn't know if Enoch was serious or trying to diffuse the tension, so he looked at him before he responded. Enoch had a very serious look on his face.

"Enoch, Belinda and I are a minute away from the altar, but that's certainly my plan. The issue is if she would even consider moving forward in a relationship with me knowing that I'm leaving."

Enoch relaxed a little, satisfied with Ben's answer. "Bro, all you can do is ask her, and better sooner than later. If she says no, you can move on with that information and she can move on too."

Ben didn't like the way that sounded, but it was true.

Kirby was glad that she and Robin had met at the small café. There wasn't anybody there that she knew. It didn't really matter. Anybody who saw them would just think they were having dinner, but even to her it didn't seem like formal counseling.

Robin's embrace was warm and genuine. She had been prayerful about Kirby's situation and had also done some research. They both ordered spinach salads with glazed pecans and dried cranberries and added grilled chicken. Kirby suggested that they have cucumber water. Robin agreed to try it.

"How in the world are your babies?" Kirby asked Robin.

"They aren't babies anymore. They are almost eight and ten."

"Wow! Where did the time go?"

They chatted a little more, and then Robin knew that she needed to deal with the real reason they were there. "Kirby, give me a little background on why you are going the in-vitro route."

Kirby told Robin the whole story very honestly. She was actually surprised at how open she was. She knew that counseling was Enoch's requirement, but she hadn't taken it very seriously until she started talking.

"You know that Belinda and I grew up in foster care?"

"No, I didn't."

"Yes. We're not biological sisters. And I feel like I need to make that right, fix it somehow. Enoch and I have talked about adoption, and maybe we will later, but I want us to have our own baby first."

"Did you live in one foster home your whole life?"

"Yep. Isn't that amazing? Belinda and I both did."

"Do you know why your foster parents never adopted you?"

"Sure we do. Back then the system didn't work like it does now. And in small-town North Carolina, you just didn't legally give black children to a white mother, even if her husband was black. Plus, in those days adoption meant that the checks and insurance benefits stopped. Our dad's theory was that as long as the checks came, Mom could stay home with us and not have to work outside the home. He worked and provided for us, and we lived well."

"Were the two of you their only foster children?"

"We were the only permanent ones. There were many others over the years."

"It's interesting that the state or somebody didn't press for adoption."

"We never talked about it, but Mom was friends with a lady who worked there, and we always called her our guardian angel. Belinda and I think she let us get lost in the system."

"Kirby, I read up on the in-vitro process. Did you research this on your own?"

"No. Actually, the doctor suggested it to me." Kirby went on to explain to Robin the events leading to where they are now. "We have an appointment on Tuesday for the first round of therapy."

Before Robin could ask, Kirby went on to tell her about Enoch's original reluctance and their eventual compromise.

"We agreed to a second procedure if it doesn't work the first time."

"So you acknowledge that it might not work."

Robin knew from Kirby's body language that she had hit the sore spot.

$\mathscr{F}$ORTY-SEVEN

Clay and Delia had worked their way back to their old routine. He was calling the shots. She protested, but nothing changed. Jeremy's basketball season was about to be over, so she decided that would limit the time she had to see Clay. Delia knew that the relationship with Clay wasn't what she wanted, but she didn't do anything about it. The truth was that they had never been on a real date. She had never been in his car without the kids, and she had never been to his house. He was great with Jeremy, and she was grateful for the improvement in his grades and behavior. Jeremy was more responsible, and she didn't want to mess that up, but she knew she should never have gotten involved with Clay. When she had attempted to talk with him about the relationship, he had sidestepped her questions. Clay was a charmer. Her grandmother would say that he could charm the birds out of the trees. Delia needed to make some decisions.

Clay looked at the calendar on his phone. If Jeremy's team won on Friday, they would play Saturday for the championship. He would be glad to have his Wednesdays and Saturdays free again. He hadn't been out of town on a weekend since the season started. He told Grant that he needed to check his traps.

"Dude, you ought to be tired of playin'."

"What I'm tired of is being with women who don't challenge me. I do what I can get away with. I like fine women and fine shoes, and I have plenty of both."

"What's up with Florence Nightingale?" Grant asked, laughing.

"Man, now I really do like her, but she works all the time. Most weeks she works seven days between the full-time and part-time jobs. She told me that she has a lot of student loan debt, but damn."

"Pay the loan off for her and she can be around," Grant said, laughing even harder.

"Oh, you have jokes. It ain't that kind of party."

"You know you got it."

"Yeah, I got it, but her name would have to be Mrs. Sturdivant before she gets it. Speaking of Mrs. Sturdivant, I checked on your bride-to-be today. She was real good. I can tell she's getting stronger."

"Yeah. We talked today. She sounded good. I'm trying to come home in April for her birthday."

"Can you do that and then come right back in June for the wedding?"

"Yeah. I got the time. It's just if I want to spend the money on the ticket just to be there four or five days."

"You short?"

"No, but I don't know what's up with Leah's finances. I don't know if she's gettin' paid or not. I didn't want to ask her, and I haven't had a chance to ask her parents. I might need to kick in on her mortgage or the wedding or something."

"Kathy's probably payin' the mortgage. She's livin' there, and you know the bishop has the wedding. But if you need anything, holler."

"I will, and I 'preciate it."

"As a matter of fact, if you want to come, I got the ticket."

Grant was right. Clay had plenty of money. He made a good salary, but he also had inherited a lot of money from his parents.

His maternal grandparents had owned acres of land that he sold to a developer at a premium. He had gone through undergrad and grad school and had plenty of money left. Uncle Paul had seen to that. Clay's father was Uncle Paul's younger brother who died young of cancer. His mother died a few years later, the family said of a broken heart. Uncle Paul made sure Clay lived practically, and Clay had gotten in the habit of doing just that. He had invested solidly and kept some rental property that his parents had owned and invested in a few other pieces.

Delia's thoughts had gotten the best of her. She got on the computer, went to the county property tax system, and put in "Clayton Sturdivant." His name came up six times on the registry: two condos, a set of duplexes, and two single-family homes. She clicked on the most expensive one. There was not a picture available. She wrote down the address. The duplexes and one of the houses had him listed as the owner with Millicent Sturdivant.

Who is Millicent Sturdivant? Is Clay married? No, he can't be. Maybe she's his sister.

Delia took the note with the address on it and looked up the directions on MapQuest. She was going to find the house on her lunch hour. The directions said that it was twenty-three minutes from her office.

Delia couldn't believe her eyes. If this was the house Clay lived in, he was better off than she ever expected. His five-year-old car told a different story. The house was in one of Hattiesville's older, more established neighborhoods. The homes had big yards and space between the houses, unlike the newer ones that were so close together. She pulled in front of the house across the street to get a good look at the house. The yard was immaculate. There were flowers on the porch in pots, and a hammock was tied between two trees in the back. One of the upstairs windows had lace curtains. A woman lived in this house. Delia's heart was beating fast. She cranked her car and pulled away. She didn't know what she was going to do or say to him, but Mr. Clay Sturdivant was more of a mystery than she realized.

"Robin, I don't think for one minute that the process won't work the first time. I agreed to a second procedure because Enoch was skeptical. The doctor didn't give me any indication that he didn't think it wouldn't work either."

"Kirby, have you gotten a second opinion?"

"Yes, and a third."

The waitress interrupted, pouring more water in the glasses and asking if she could get them anything.

"I'll have a little more dressing please," Kirby answered.

The two-minute break was welcomed. Robin could see that Kirby was a little annoyed.

"Did all three doctors suggest in-vitro?"

"No. The second one did, and the third one agreed. The doctor I'm going to for the procedure is the second one I went to, Dr. Jacobson."

"Have you and Enoch prayed together about this?"

"Robin, Enoch and I have been praying together and individually for over a year. We prayed for direction, and when I went to see Dr. Jacobson, he was the answer to our prayers."

"Apparently Enoch didn't feel that way if he was reluctant."

"Enoch didn't understand then how important it is to me to have a baby of my own, our baby. He was willing to give up and start adoption proceedings."

"Why don't you want to adopt? There are many children who could benefit from a loving home."

"I understand that, but why shouldn't I want my own flesh and blood? Why shouldn't I have the joy of feeling the baby grow and move inside of me? Why do you think I am any different from any other married woman who wants to give her husband his own child? You have your own children. Belinda has her own children. Am I not good enough to have what you have? Am I not worthy of the same blessings?" Kirby's voice had gone up an octave, and tears were in her eyes. "You don't get it either. I don't know why I'm here or why I even agreed to do this." She took a sip of water and looked Robin square in the eyes. "How dare you, Enoch, Belinda, or anybody else question my decision, my motive, or my direction on this! How dare my body fail me and not allow me to conceive in the first place! How dare my mother, who could obviously have a baby, throw me away!" By that time tears were rolling down Kirby's face. She picked up her pocketbook and slid out of the booth.

"Kirby, don't leave like this."

She walked toward the bathroom. Robin sat there and prayed, asking God what to do and what to say.

ORTY-EIGHT

Delia went back to her office more curious than ever about Clay. She logged back into the property tax system and typed "Millicent Sturdivant." The same two addresses came up. She went to whitepages.com but found no listing for Clayton or Millicent. She had to find out who Millicent was. If he was running a game on her and was married, she would definitely turn him in to the agency. The only way to find out was to ask him. He would be furious to know that she had looked up his personal information. She had to do a little more research before she could approach him, and she had to be very careful how she approached him.

When Gretchen walked into the shop and saw Janis Mitchell under the dryer, her first thought was to throw her out. But she didn't say anything, mainly because her mother was with her, but she let Janis know she saw her. Janis looked back down at the magazine she was reading. Gretchen put the cape around her mother and walked her to the shampoo bowl. Her mother hadn't seen Janis, and Gretchen decided not to draw any attention to her.

The stylist Janis was there to see came over to Gretchen and apologized. "I wasn't expecting you this early."

"It's okay. Really. No need to apologize."

Janis wanted to say something to Grace, but she knew that whatever she said would be taken the wrong way. If she made his mother angry, she knew that Grant would never speak to her again, not that he was speaking to her now. He had blocked her cell and home numbers and wouldn't answer her calls from work. She had left a dozen messages, but he had not called back. She had to find a way to get his attention. Maybe she would ask his mother to ask him to hear her out. But she had to try to talk to her without Gretchen's interference. Janis looked at her watch. She was about done and didn't really have time to stick around or get her nails done, but she had to have a few seconds alone with Mrs. Sturdivant.

"Jeremy, how far does Clay live from us?"

"I don't know how far it is, but he lives on the way to Grandma's job."

Delia was trying to figure out how the house she went to that day would be on the way to her mother's job. It wasn't. So Clay didn't live in that house after all. Delia was actually relieved, but she was still curious why it was in his name, unless he recently bought it. She couldn't ask Jeremy any more questions. She couldn't take a chance that he would mention it to Clay.

She got on the computer and once again looked up the addresses of the properties Clay owned.

I guess I'll just pay Mr. Sturdivant a visit, she thought to herself. *I can't see how any of these houses are in the direction of Mom's job. That doesn't make sense to me. But I can't say anything else to Jeremy about it. I'll just ask Clay. What do I have to lose? If he won't tell me, I'll know he's hiding something. I know. I'll ask him in front of Jeremy so he can't lie.*

Ben picked Belinda up from the airport and was surprised to see a very attractive older woman with her. She had the most beautiful salt-and-pepper hair. The girls had made a sign that said "Welcome home, Mommy" and were waiting at the bottom of the escalator. Belinda and Ben locked eyes for a few seconds before she noticed the sign. A huge smile came across her face. Ben introduced himself to Lorraine while Belinda hugged the girls. Then she hugged him, and it was a good hug. The girls vaguely remembered Lorraine, but they knew that she had been their neighbor when they lived in California. Brittani remembered her dog, but Brianna remembered that she had been with them when they were leaving to move to North Carolina.

"Lorraine has a short layover here. Can we stick around until time for her to board?" Belinda said.

"Absolutely," Ben said.

Brittani and Brianna had already engaged Lorraine in conversation, so Ben and Belinda had a minute to themselves.

"How are you?" he asked.

"I'm good—really good."

Her smile told him that she really was.

"I missed you."

"Missed you too."

"I know you want to spend some time with the girls, but can we talk later? I need to—" Ben paused and sighed. "I have to tell you some things."

He looked so serious that she was concerned.

"Sure. We'll work it out."

They joined the whirlwind conversation between Lorraine and the twins.

After about forty-five minutes, Lorraine told them that she needed to get to her gate. She shook hands with Ben, hugged Brianna and Brittani, and then hugged Belinda. They lingered. She whispered in Belinda's ear, "I like him."

Gretchen put a conditioner on her mother's hair and set her under the dryer. When she walked back into the other room, Janis walked over to Grace.

"Hello, Mrs. Sturdivant."

Grace looked up from the puzzle she was working on and was surprised to see Janis standing there. "Hello, Janis. How are you?"

"I'm glad to see you, Mrs. Sturdivant. I want to ask you a favor."

Grace didn't say anything. She kept her eyes on Janis.

"I really, really need to talk with Grant, but I've been unable to get in touch with him."

"Why are you telling me, Janis?"

"I'm hoping you will ask him to call me or you will call him and let me speak to him."

Grace smiled at Janis and shook her head. "Young lady, you will not play games with me, and you will not pull me into this nonsense you have created in your mind about you and Grant. My son is a grown man who decides who he wants to talk to, and I will not get involved with that."

Grace looked back down at her puzzle, and Janis just stood there for a few seconds. She could hear her stylist saying something from behind her. As she turned around to leave, Gretchen was walking toward her. Grace looked at Gretchen and put her hand up, so Gretchen walked past Janis without saying anything and got her mother from under the dryer.

Gretchen walked back into the other room and said to the other stylist, "Get her out of here. The first lady is on her way."

Janis walked out of the salon angry. *How dare Mrs. Sturdivant act that way toward me! All I asked her to do was call Grant on my behalf. What was so hard about that?* she thought.

Just then she noticed a car pull to the front of the salon. A man got out, came around, and opened the door for Katherine Robinson. Janis stopped right where she was and started back toward the salon. The gentleman noticed her and stepped in her way, preventing her from reaching Katherine. He opened the salon door and told the first lady to have a good day. Janis was so appalled that she couldn't move. He didn't say anything to Janis, just got back in the car and pulled away, leaving her standing there.

"I guess he was one of her bodyguards," Janis said, ranting to her friend on the phone. "They make me sick. I hate the whole family. Why can't she drive herself to the salon? Who do they think they are to have a chauffeur, like she's a celebrity or something? You should have seen how he blocked me from getting to the door."

"Janis, do you know how crazy you sound? Girl, you need to get a grip. If Grant finds out, or should I say *when* Grant finds out about this, he is going to hate you."

Janis got very quiet. "No, he won't, if he will listen to my side of the story."

"Janis, what is your side? You know you're wrong. You have really stepped in it now."

FORTY-NINE

A couple of souvenirs from Washington for the girls, including a charm for their bracelets, and a lively discussion about their time away from their mom over dinner was enough for them to run to their room when they got back home.

Belinda called Grammy to thank her again for staying with the girls and for the house being in such good shape. It amazed Belinda how clean her house was. She prided herself in being a good housekeeper, but Grammy took it to another level.

After she called Kirby to let her know she was home and thanked Uncle Enoch for the s'mores, she settled on the sofa to hear what Ben had to say. First, he wanted to know how things went for her. She told him everything. She told him how hard she cried and the things she said to Canady, including that she wanted to make a life with him, and she told him about the sun coming out.

"Ben, I left it there—the hurt, the pain, the grief. I've turned the corner. I am ready to move on with my life."

She was so beautiful, and he hoped she was still smiling five minutes from then.

"Sweetheart, I need to tell you a couple of things, and I don't know how to work up to it, so I'll just say it. First, I'm glad you really like Sheldon's because I own fifty percent of it."

"For real?"

He was amused at her body language.

"That's really cool, but what do you do there?"

"I don't really do anything. Sheldon and I have been friends all our lives. Mr. Eisner Sr. was my grandfather's employer, and his daughter was Sheldon's mother. She spent a lot of time away from home, and he was with his grandparents. My grandparents were raising me, so we had some things in common. As a matter of fact, both times I got in trouble with the law, Sheldon was with me."

Belinda was still smiling and was very interested in what he was saying. He went on to explain that Sheldon had had another partner initially and it didn't work out. He was about to lose the restaurant when he approached Ben.

"I still had all the money from my grandfather's estate, and Grammy agreed to let me invest it."

"Did you know why things didn't work with the first partner?"

"Uh, yeah. He was having an affair with Sheldon's fiancée. His wife found out and told Sheldon. It was a big mess."

"Oh my," Belinda said, folding her arms.

"I'll tell you the details later, but I did my homework and we have a contract. If worse came to worse, I could sell the building and get my initial investment back.

"Have you had to invest additionally?"

"No. Sheldon is a good businessman, and he hired great people. As a matter of fact, I have actually made some of my money back. He just wanted completely away from that other situation, and he gave some of the money back. Most of the people who work there never knew, and only a few other people know."

They talked about that only another minute.

"You said that you needed to tell me a couple of things."

Ben inhaled deeply and then exhaled. "Belinda, there's no easy way to say this."

She was looking directly at him.

"The bishop has asked me…is sending me…wants me to go…" He paused and took a deep breath. "To go to Atlanta to plant and pastor our first church."

"Wow, Ben! That's fantastic! Congratulations!" She sounded happier than she really felt.

"Thanks, but the timing stinks."

"Why do you say that?"

"Look, girl, I'm falling in love with you. I want to spend the rest of my life with you and the twins. You just made a very important step toward that, and now I add moving to the mix. I don't want to leave you, Belinda."

She was relieved to hear him say that. She was afraid that he was going to tell her that he was leaving to start his new life without her.

"Ben,"—she reached for his hand and motioned for him to sit beside her—"you said that God brought me to Hattiesville for you. If you really believe that, and I think you do, then we will just have to work it out. We'll have to make it work."

"What does that mean, Belinda, a long-distance relationship, or will you go with me?"

"In time, the girls and I will join you in Atlanta." She had been very careful how she stated that. She didn't want to say, "Marry me and we'll come with you."

Ben pulled her into his arms and held her tight. Neither of them said anything for a few minutes; they were lost in their own thoughts. She made it sound doable, almost easy. He knew there was a lot to work out, but he knew he could do it. He had her support.

Belinda was smiling to herself and thinking how perfect God's timing was. She had no idea what was around the corner when she told Canady good-bye. Atlanta. She had never thought she would leave Hattiesville unless it was just to move to Charlotte. Atlanta had big hospitals and great opportunities.

Ben interrupted her thoughts. "You fit good in my arms."

"I feel good in your arms."

She leaned up to look at him, and he kissed her forehead.

"Have you told Grammy and Auntie?"

"I told Grammy yesterday, but I told her not to tell Auntie until I talked to you. I told Enoch but asked him not to tell Kirby yet."

They talked a while longer, and he told her about his conversation with the bishop and that he had asked Grammy to go with him.

"Did she say she would go?"

"Not exactly. She said we have plenty of time to work that out. Would you be okay if she and Auntie come?"

"Absolutely. I can't imagine that Brittani and Brianna will go without them."

Ben was ecstatic. God had come through greater than he expected.

$\mathscr{F}$IFTY

The physical therapist was pleasantly surprised with Leah's
progress. She was working hard, and it showed. Her progress
in occupational therapy and speech therapy were not going as
well. It was okay, at best. Her daily talks with Grant were getting
easier. She understood more, remembered more, and didn't have
to concentrate as hard to hold a conversation. She and Kathy had
had one full conversation about the wedding.

Life was better for the whole family. Katherine was glad that
Lee had finally settled down, and she even thought he could see
Leah's progress. He had been so on edge. He admitted to her that
Leah's situation had shaken him to his core. The worst part was
that he felt like he couldn't tell anybody. He knew the congregation was praying for her, but he had had to put on a façade that he
was fine when he really wasn't. He knew the congregation wasn't
strong enough to see him weak. But now that Leah was better,
he would spend more time with Ben, working on the new ministry in the Atlanta area. Ben had let him know that he had spoken with his grandmother and Belinda, and the tone of his voice
told the bishop he was set to move forward without the strain of
his family and his future family not being on board. They could
get to work without distractions. But first, the bishop was going
away with his wife for a few days.

Leah had talked with Trey, Raja, and the physical therapist to
ask if she could take the braces off her legs and if she could go
home for another day. The physical therapist asked which one

she wanted most, and she said the braces off. He told her that if she had two more good sessions, he would take them off. If he didn't think she was ready, they were going back on.

She looked at him and laughed. "How many good sessions do I have to have to go home?"

"One thing at a time, Nurse Robinson."

Leah knew she was better. She hadn't had a headache since she came to rehab, her blood pressure had been good, and she felt stronger. She was reading some, even though she didn't always remember what she read. She wanted to go home and continue her therapy as an outpatient. She had to convince somebody to advocate for her. Her best options were Jill and her mother. She called Jill first.

"Can you come see me when you finish work today?"

"I can come right now if you need me to."

"No. Later is fine. I have to go back to therapy."

"Do we need to talk privately, or can I bring my mom?"

"That's good. Bring her." Leah thought that would be fine because she would work on Dr. Strauss.

After her talk with Jill, Leah called her mother.

"Hey, Leah, you okay?"

"Yes. Fine."

"I'm at the salon. Can I call you back?"

"Yes, but are you coming to see me later?"

"Yes. Do you need something?"

"No. I'll tell you when you get here."

"Are you sure?"

"Yes, I'm sure!"

The counseling session at the restaurant had ended so abruptly that Robin and Kirby didn't set another appointment. When Kirby came out of the bathroom, she told Robin that she needed to go. She didn't feel like talking anymore. Robin tried to get her to stay, but she wouldn't. She knew she had to call Kirby, and if Kirby wouldn't reschedule, her next call would be to Enoch. Robin took a deep breath and called Kirby.

Kirby looked at her phone and decided to let the call go to voice mail. She wasn't ready to talk to Robin Brackett. She knew she would have to eventually. Enoch was going to ask her about it, but not that day. Kirby had never felt so alone in her life. Nobody understood how she felt, nobody—not her wonderful husband, not her adorable sister. She picked up the phone and called Grammy. Auntie answered and told Kirby to come on out there. They were never too busy for company.

Robin debated whether to call Enoch right away or wait to see if she would hear from Kirby. She said their appointment was Tuesday. If she didn't see her at church the next day and Kirby hadn't called her back, she would call Enoch on Monday.

Kirby stopped to get two bouquets of fresh flowers to take with her. She loved visiting Grammy and Auntie. They always made her feel loved. She could tell them anything. They didn't judge anybody, and they were absolutely honest. She often wondered if somewhere her real grandmother had a sister, and she wondered where they were.

Why did they let my mother give me away? Was my mother some young kid who couldn't take care of me, or was she from a wealthy family who didn't want their daughter's life interrupted by a baby, or was I the product of rape?

All Kirby knew was she had to fix this. She had gotten an education and married well, and now she wanted a baby. She didn't care if it was a boy or girl, fat or skinny, light or dark. She just wanted a baby born out of her body that she and Enoch would keep, not give away, and raise in a real family.

Grammy and Auntie were cooking Sunday dinner. They still cooked on Saturday so dinner would be ready right after church on Sunday.

"She has something on her mind," Auntie told Grammy.

"Uh-huh. You're probably right, for her to be coming out here this time of day on Saturday."

"By herself," Auntie added.

"I wonder if Enoch had to work today."

Before Auntie could comment, the phone rang again. It was Brittani and Brianna. They were making sure dinner was still on for the next day after church. They talked to Auntie and then to Grammy.

"Where's your mama?"

"Downstairs, talking to Minister Coffey. Do you want to talk to her?"

"No. I'll see her tomorrow."

Grammy expected that Ben was telling Belinda the news and prayed that she was receiving it. She wouldn't break her promise and tell Avis, but she hoped Ben would tell her the next day so they could talk about it.

As soon as they hung up with the twins, Kirby was at the backdoor. There were hugs and kisses all around, and she gave them their flowers. They talked about Enoch. He was working. And they talked about Belinda's trip. Neither of them had heard any details. They guessed that she would tell them the next day at dinner. But she sounded good, they agreed. Grammy set a glass in front of Kirby—half tea, half lemonade.

Kirby didn't waste any time getting to the point of her visit. She told them she had been trying to get pregnant for over a year and about the in-vitro process. She admitted Enoch's original hesitation, and she told them about her counseling session with Robin Brackett and how it had ended.

Interestingly, it was Auntie who spoke up first. "Sugar, the first thing is you need to forgive your mother. You don't know what the circumstances were that caused her to make the decision she made, and you won't ever know. Have you ever considered that she could have had an abortion?"

Kirby didn't answer. She just dropped her eyes.

"Next, you have no control over how God designed your body. You can talk, walk, hear, and see. You are blessed, Kirby. Don't take that for granted."

"Think about Leah. She almost died. Do you think she's worried about whether she can have a baby or adopt a baby?" Grammy added.

Auntie continued. "Kirby, I'm glad that Enoch agreed to you having the procedure, but understand this: God will hold him responsible for this ultimately, so you have to be in agreement with your husband."

As if she was reading Kirby's mind, Grammy told her, "I know you didn't come out here to be lectured, but, Kirby Casebier, you are acting like you don't understand that God ordained before the world began whether or not you and Enoch would have a baby. Nothing is going to change that."

Auntie knew that Kirby was feeling beat up. "Darling, I do understand how you feel. It took me years to get pregnant, and then I lost two babies."

"Yeah, but you ended up with three."

"You're right. But I had long since given up, and back then we didn't know anything about in-vitro fertilization."

Grammy continued. "You are going to have to make up your mind to be content with what God gives you. Your situation could be totally different. What if you had a couple of kids and you had to work every day and Enoch was working somewhere rotating shifts? Instead you are able to have some flexibility. Enoch is making a good living so you can make a good home for an adopted child."

"I still say nobody understands how I feel. Everything you both are saying is right, and I don't mean to be selfish, but I just want a baby of my own, just one. I want to honor my husband with the fruit of *my* womb. Then we can adopt six more if he wants to."

"Kirby, I know you don't want to hear this," Auntie said.

"Then don't say it."

"Yes, I am too. If you have this first in-vitro procedure and it doesn't work, leave it alone." Auntie put her arms around Kirby as she said it. Kirby started to cry. She cried until she got it all out.

Jill and Ellen arrived at the hospital to find Leah working hard at rewriting a paragraph the occupational therapist had given her. She was grateful for the interruption. Ellen had brought flowers, and Jill brought a slice of carrot cake.

"Where's your roommate?" Jill asked.

"She got transferred to another unit."

Ellen noticed how clear Leah's words were and how obvious it was that she was stronger. She watched Leah and Jill. They were so much like they had been over the years. They talked about Raja and Grant like they had their first crushes. Jill was patient with Leah. She understood at a level none of the rest of them did.

"Leah, I think that's enough cake for now. I would hate for you to have to tell Zack that your blood sugar is high because of Jill."

"Mom!"

They all laughed.

"What did you call me for anyway?" Jill asked Leah.

"I was waiting for my mom, but I guess she's coming later. I want to go home, and I need you to help me..." She couldn't think of the word. "To help me...tell Raja and Trey."

"Did they say you're ready?"

"No. That's why I want you to help me."

"Okay. I'm confused. Do you want me to bust you out of here?"

Leah and Ellen laughed.

"You know I will. I just want to be sure!"

Katherine walked in and was pleasantly surprised. Leah and Jill were their old playful selves.

"Hey, Ma."

"Hello, all of you," Katherine said as she kissed Leah and hugged Ellen and Jill.

"Kat, your hair looks good. I like the cut," Ellen commented.

"Daddy is going to have a fit because you cut it," Leah said.

"It's just hair. It will grow back."

Jill and Leah looked at each other.

"She is so grown," Jill said as they laughed.

"Okay, Mama Kat. Leah wants me to bust her out of here!" Jill said.

"Leah Robinson, what in the world?" her mother asked, frowning.

"Ma, I want to go home, and I need the three of you to help me...help me convince...yes, that's the word...convince them to let me go."

"Leah, sweetheart, you can't stay...you're not ready to stay by yourself," Katherine said.

"Kathy will be there," Leah answered.

"Oh, please. We can't depend on her schedule. Plus, somebody would need to be there with you during the day," Katherine said seriously.

Ellen reminded Leah that she couldn't go up and down the stairs yet either.

"Well then, she'll just have to go to your house, Mama Kat, and the bishop will get somebody to stay with her when you all are not there," Jill said in support of Leah.

Leah was glad Jill was on her side. Ellen and Katherine looked at each other, both thinking the same thing. Leah and Jill could always talk Lee into what they wanted. He was putty in their hands. As far as they were concerned, he could and would move heaven and earth, and Zack Strauss would help him, and they were right. If it was in his power and one of the girls wanted it, he would make it happen.

"Mama Ellen, if you tell Dr. Zack, he'll agree with us," Leah said.

Ellen looked from one to the other. This was the same setup they used to ask if they could go to Alaska for spring break one year while they were in college. They talked Lee and Zack into it, and their mothers had to go along.

"Okay. Here's the plan. I'll talk to Trey first, and then I'll talk to Raja," Jill offered.

Leah smiled broadly when Jill said she would talk to Raja. Jill looked at her and rolled her eyes. All four of them laughed.

"I don't know if you should say anything to Trey. The two of you will end up fussing about it. He'll think you're telling him how to handle his patient," Ellen said to Jill.

"Mama, Trey will just have to get over it. You are always worried about how he feels."

"But I think your dad will be the easiest to get on my side."

"Well, let's just call him right now."

Katherine and Ellen just looked at each other.

She took her phone from her purse and called his cell phone.

"Hey, Dad. Are you in the hospital? Can you come to Leah's room? No, she's great. I just want to see you. Mom and I are over here." She hung up the phone and turned to the women in the room. "He'll be here in a few minutes. Oh! By the way, here are the pictures of the dresses."

The conversation moved to Jill's trip to London.

$\mathscr{F}$IFTY-ONE

Chloe and her parents were having dinner at Lola's. Nobody was surprised when she suggested it. Campbell was working when she got there, but he would be getting off in an hour. He was still nervous around her parents, and Roderick liked it that way. Campbell couldn't believe that Chloe just showed up with them without warning him.

It was Saturday night, and Chloe wanted to do something. So Campbell suggested they go skating.

"That's a good idea. Let me go home and get my car and I'll come get you."

"Okay, but give me time to change my clothes."

Campbell got a ride home with a coworker, and that saved him some time.

Campbell and Chloe didn't stay out late. When Chloe dropped Campbell off, it reminded him that he didn't have a driver's license or a car. It didn't seem to bother Chloe, though. Nothing ever seemed to bother her. To him she was always happy, bubbly. Everything seemed to come easy for her, but she didn't take any of it for granted. When they talked, she always seemed to get it, and she never judged him. It was amazing to Campbell that she liked him.

Since the night she first kissed him at her home, they would usually kiss good night, even when they talked on the phone. She would say she was sending him a kiss through the waves, and he would send one back. Campbell never wanted to disrespect

Chloe, but he figured it was okay if she initiated it. Two kisses and Campbell was getting out of the car.

"Call me when you get home."

"I will!"

He watched her drive away.

Kirby had finally made and kept another appointment with Robin. They had talked, but Robin wasn't really sure Kirby's reality about the situation was real. She had called Enoch, and they had talked too. Robin suggested that the three of them get together. He agreed, but Kirby was furious. She felt like Robin was causing her to prolong getting her hormone treatments started. But she knew that Enoch would not agree until he felt she had this under control. She had no choice but to go through with it.

Kirby smiled and went through the motions in the session with Enoch and Robin. The sooner she got it over with, the sooner she could get on with the procedure. The truth was that some of what Robin said and some of what Enoch said hurt her. Robin seemed to take a more assertive tone in Enoch's presence.

How dare she judge me! Kirby thought. *If Enoch challenges me on this as a result of something she says, I will deal with her directly.*

As they were leaving the church office, Enoch put his arm around Kirby, but he didn't say anything. The ride home was pretty quiet. They made small talk. Kirby knew that Enoch wasn't done with the conversation. Kirby decided not to mention the counseling session to Enoch unless he didn't mention it by the time she was to see the doctor. They had two days.

Enoch texted Ben to see where he was and if they could talk. Ben texted back that he was at home and for Enoch to come over.

"I'm going over to Ben's. I won't be long."

"I think I'll call Belinda and see what's going on with them anyway." She knew that his visit to Ben wasn't completely social. He wanted to talk to Ben about what was said in counseling before he said anything to her.

Kirby wasn't convinced that Belinda really understood either, but she didn't have anybody else to talk to.

"We came back from our session with Robin Brackett a little while ago, and Enoch went to talk to Ben. He hasn't said anything since we got home."

"How do you think it went?"

Kirby sighed loudly. "Belinda, I am so tired of talking about this. I'm not sure how it went. Robin said some stuff I didn't like, and Enoch agreed with some of what she said. She basically told him that psychologically I wasn't ready to do the in-vitro process because I am not realistic about the procedure not working. What's unrealistic about having faith?"

"Nothing is unrealistic about having faith, but you haven't admitted that there is even the possibility that it might not work." Belinda knew she had crossed the line, but there was no return.

Kirby didn't respond, so Belinda continued.

"The medical facts are that a percentage of these procedures do not work. I agree with you, I pray with you, and I just want you to be realistic too. I don't want you to be disappointed."

"I don't know how I can tell her no. I know she's not ready to accept it if the procedure doesn't work, but I also know that she will fall apart if I don't agree to the procedure. Man, she sat there and smiled and said all the things she thought I wanted her to say, and I saw right through it. I never thought my wife would try to fake me out."

Ben was listening intently as Enoch talked. His heart went out to his friend. He listened a while before he said anything.

"Belinda, I'm already disappointed that it's been a year and I have not been able to conceive a baby. I'm already disappointed that I even have to have in-vitro and not conceive naturally. Don't talk to me about disappointment. I read all the information my doctor gave me. I know all the statistics and percentages. I know all of that. But we won't know unless we try. Can you argue with that?"

"No, Kirby, I can't argue with that. You are exactly right. We won't know unless you try."

"This is not an easy decision, no matter what, and I know you've prayed. What do you feel in your spirit, in that space where you know only God is? What do you hear?"

Enoch looked at Ben and thought about the question he asked. "I think I hear God saying He has this. But I don't know what He wants me to do."

"Maybe He doesn't want you to do anything."

"Ben, I have to do something, say something to Kirby when I walk back in that house tonight."

"What do you want to say?"

"I want to tell her that I love her and it doesn't matter if we have a baby. We can adopt or not. It's still okay. But I've said that more than once, and she doesn't hear me."

"What will she hear?"

"She will hear me say, 'Let's go ahead with the procedure.'"

"And your fear is the procedure won't work and she'll be more distraught."

"Yep."

"You said that you think you hear God saying that He's got this. Is He saying, 'Go for it and I'll make it work'?"

"Perhaps."

"Then you won't know unless you try. You committed to the procedure. You can't break your promise to Kirby. If you go through with it and it doesn't work, then she will know it wasn't God's plan."

FIFTY-TWO

After Jeremy's game, Delia suggested they get something to eat as a victory celebration. Everybody wanted something different, so Clay suggested they go to Lola's. That was an interesting choice to Delia. Everybody in town ate there, and anybody could see them together. Maybe he wasn't trying to hide her. This would be her chance to ask him in front of Jeremy where he lived.

After they had all ordered and were talking about the game, Delia changed the subject. "Clay, do you live on this side of town?"

"No. I live off exit twenty-six, not too far from the church."

Delia couldn't figure out why Jeremy thought that that was on the way to her mother's job, and she couldn't remember any of those properties she looked up being up there. Something was definitely up, and she intended to get some answers.

"Do you have somebody good and dependable to keep your yard, or do you do it yourself?"

"I live in a community where that's all included."

"Must be nice. I need to find somebody. The man I had wasn't dependable, and I need to get that taken care of before it's time to starting cutting grass again."

"I'll ask around. There are a couple of guys at church who have landscaping companies, and one of them keeps my uncle's lawn. I'll let you know."

Delia really didn't find out what she wanted to know, so she would just ask him later. When they finished eating, she knew that Jeremy would ask Clay to come to their house, so she would find a few minutes alone with him.

"Can't do it today, man. I have something to do. Maybe we can hang out tomorrow after church. Call me when you get home."

Delia was angry, but she couldn't say anything.

The plan to convince Dr. Strauss to let Leah go home worked. He agreed that she could do some outpatient therapy and he would make arrangements for the therapist to come to the house on the alternate day. The stipulation was that somebody had to be there with her around the clock, at least for the first couple of weeks.

Trey was a little less enthusiastic than the others, but Raja convinced him that it might be for the best.

"The patient's attitude has a lot to do with recovery," he reminded Trey.

The terms of Trey's agreement were strict. The person there with Leah had to be CPR trained, and that included the bishop and first lady. He also suggested she have a hospital bed for a week or so, but Leah insisted that she didn't need it.

"I am a nurse. I know what I'm up against."

Leah decided not to tell Grant until she was home. Two days after the impromptu conference with her family and the doctors, she was waiting when her parents arrived to pick her up. Jill had packed her things the night before and told her to call when she was home and settled.

The guest room downstairs in the Robinsons' home was a small room, but Leah didn't care.

Enoch went home to talk to Kirby and intended to tell her to make the appointment for the procedure. He prayed that he was making the right decision. But he fully intended to be honest with her about her attempt to fake him out when they were talking with Robin.

He was smiling when he walked in. She was in the kitchen getting a glass of juice and asked if he wanted one. He said he did and asked her to bring it to him in the den.

"Have a seat, Mrs. Casebier. I have a bone to pick with you," Enoch said jokingly.

She sat down and folded her arms. "Pick away."

"I know you were trying to deceive me this afternoon when we were talking to Robin, but it didn't work. I saw right through your charade."

The smile on her face was gone.

"Kirby, I never thought you would try to fool me, not me!"

Kirby still didn't respond. Enoch's playful tone changed to very serious.

"Sweetheart, I love you. I love you so much, and beyond anything else I want you to be happy. I didn't ask you to go to counseling just to waste time. I wanted you to go to make sure you were prepared to make this decision. You played me, babe."

Kirby was looking at the floor.

"Look at me."

She lifted her eyes but not her head.

"This is the most serious, the most important, decision of our lives. I have prayed and struggled with this, and all I asked you to do was to prepare yourself emotionally."

"Enoch, I met with Robin, we talked—"

"Yeah, and you walked out when she asked the same question I asked: what are you going to do if the procedure doesn't work?"

"I didn't appreciate her telling you I wasn't ready. She's not God, and she doesn't know me. I am so sick of people with children telling me how I should feel and what I should do! The truth is, I don't know what I'll do, and I won't know until and unless we try. I love you too, and I apologize for this afternoon, but I am so over all this! I want to have a baby, our baby, and my chance to do that is with the in-vitro process. We are going to do it or we're not, but I have faith, Enoch. I do."

"I committed to a second procedure if the first one doesn't work. Will you commit to adoption if both fail?"

"I don't like that word *fail.*"

He repeated the question.

"If we do the procedure twice and it doesn't work, then I will know God said no and we can adopt. But sweetie, in my heart of hearts, I know it will work."

They both sat in silence for a minute or two.

Kirby broke the silence. "So may I move ahead with the appointment?" she asked very cheerfully.

"Sure, baby. Let's go for it."

FIFTY-THREE

One afternoon after school, Campbell was in Miss Robinson's classroom. They were talking as they often did, and he told her about Chloe. They had been friends since the year before, and he had asked her to go to the prom with him, even though the prom was five months away. Kathy knew her fairly well from school, and Chloe and her parents were members of Hattiesville Community Church. Her family was well respected in the community. Both her parents were attorneys and had a thriving practice. They were nice people, but their families didn't have much in common. But based on what he said, Chloe and Campbell were real friends.

The morning school announcements included that prom tickets would go on sale that day during the lunch periods. Campbell was excited and wanted to get his and Chloe's tickets right away. He would go to the bank after school and buy them the next day.

Today was his day off, so he and Chloe were going to hang out after school. It was raining, so their walk in the park would have to be rescheduled. They decided to go to the mall and look for prom attire. They couldn't decide on colors or style, but they had fun looking. They set a deadline to make those decisions.

"Do I get to pick the color?" she asked.

"If you want to."

"Campbell, you are so sweet and easy to get along with."

"What's the need to debate colors? You look good in every color."

Chloe was blushing.

They talked about who was having a party and where they would eat.

"Chloe, I'll have my license before prom time, so I'll be able to pick you up."

"That's cool, Campbell. But if it doesn't work out, don't worry about it. I don't care about all that. I don't mind driving."

He was thinking to himself that he cared. They ran into some friends from school and headed for the food court.

Jill was making a list of things that she would pack for the trip to London. She packed too much on every trip, and she knew that this would be no different. The dresses for the wedding festivities would take a lot of space. She listed the shoes and accessories. She considered a backpack or messenger bag for sightseeing and listed the perfumes and an extra pair of contact lenses. She would get a manicure and pedicure the day before they left but buy the polish in case she needed a touch-up. Leah would be so proud of her for being this organized. Now if she could just stick to the list.

Raja had had a very long, hard day. He wanted to get something to eat and go home. He checked his messages, and his parents had called. The other message was from his cousin Yash, whom he decided he should call first. He was glad he did. His mother had decided that Jill should not come for the wedding, and she had gone ahead with her plans to invite the young lady she wanted to officially introduce to Raja. His mother was starting the process for arranging a marriage for him.

He laughed as he listened to his cousin tell him the story. "My mother is a piece of work."

"What are you going to do?"

"Call her and put her in her place. I like Jill a lot, and she's coming to London with me. My mother had better get used to the idea and back off. Don't worry. I'm coming to your wedding, but I'm going to tell my mom I won't come if she doesn't back off. Who is this other woman anyway?"

Raja and Yash had a good laugh about the situation, but he knew his mother was serious and he had to handle it. He would be firm but respectful. He hoped his dad would answer. Maybe he could reason with her.

Raja waited until he got home to return his parents' call. His dad did answer, and after the customary pleasantries, Raja mentioned his cousin's wedding to see what his dad would say. His dad didn't bite, so he knew he would have to deal with his mother directly. She told him about a concert she had gone to, but he changed the subject.

"Jill is looking forward to the trip. She's decided on the dresses she wanted and sent the others back."

"Manavendra, I don't think it would be appropriate for you to bring her. Your father and I have sought the approval of the family of a young woman we want you to meet. We expect they will approve of the marriage after they meet you. Your friend's presence will present an awkward situation. We have invited the family to join us for a private dinner while you are here. The courtship doesn't have to be long, but it should be done properly."

Raja let her talk, and when she finished, he told her exactly what he thought. "Mother, you had no right to make any arrangements without my approval. I have no intention of meeting or courting this young woman and absolutely no intention of marrying her."

She started to protest.

"Mother, listen to me. I don't want there to be any misunderstanding about my position on this matter. I personally think an arranged marriage is an old custom that should be done away with. I want no part of it."

"That's our culture, son."

"It's a part of our culture that I don't choose to participate in. I will date whomever I please, fall in love with and marry whomever I please. All the arranging will be done by God, me, and her."

"Son, you are hurting your mother's heart."

"Mother, your heart will be fine. You just need to accept the facts, the reality of it. I fully intend to bring Jill Strauss to the wedding with me, and I fully expect you and our whole family to be kind and respectful to her. If not, I won't be back."

"She is not welcome!"

"If Jill can't come, I'm not coming either!"

Raja heard the phone fall and talking in the background. A few seconds later, his father was on the line.

"What in the world did you say to your mother? She practically collapsed."

"I told her I am not coming to the wedding if Jill cannot come. Now she can faint or whatever else she wants to be dramatic, but I mean what I said. You two need to undo this plan of yours, and I'm sure it's more her plan. There will be no arranged marriage."

"I must go and attend to your mother." His father hung up.

Raja was furious. His mother had gone too far, and pretending to faint was the icing on the cake. He sat and thought a minute if he should tell Jill. He called his cousin, Tara, for her advice. As always, she was glad to hear from him and laughed as he told her about the conversation with his mother.

"And you wonder why I don't care that they don't talk to me!"

She advised him to tell Jill the truth. "If you want to have a real relationship with her, be totally honest. If you two get married one day, she needs to know that you have a crazy family!"

He couldn't help but laugh.

"Manavendra, how is my brother? Is he excited about his marriage?"

"He's well. You should call him.

"Why? So we can fight about my choices and his?"

"No, so you can hear from him that he wants you to come."

"We've had the conversation. I will not go if Robert is not welcome."

"Tell him that and see what he says. Besides, it will give my parents and yours something to talk about: how defiant you and I are."

Raja appreciated having Tara to confide in. They talked a few more minutes, and he told her he needed to go.

Raja looked at the clock. It was after 10:00 p.m., and he and Jill had not talked all day. He called, and she answered on the first ring and sounded so pleasant. They talked about their days, and he told her about the conversation with his mother.

She wasn't sure if she should respond, so she just listened. She was glad he couldn't see the expressions on her face. One thing was for sure: Jill did not intend to bow out. She was looking forward to the trip, and his mother's attitude toward her wasn't going to change that. Mrs. Rajagopal didn't even know her. She decided to kill her with kindness, like Lola used to say. She would take her a gift.

"Raja, I'm sorry you're fighting with your parents, but I think everything will be just fine."

"Absolutely. Everything will be fine, and we're going to have a great time."

Leah's first few days at home were tough, but after that she seemed to flourish. The physical therapy was going as well as it had in the hospital, maybe better because Leah's attitude was better.

Lee had wanted her to stay in the hospital a little longer. He was going away for several days and didn't want Katherine and Leah to be there without him. His assistant assured him that she had covered all the bases. Chief Brackett knew that Leah was home, and he confirmed that the restraining order against Janis Mitchell extended to their home and an armor bearer would be available around the clock for anything they might need. The first lady's assistant had double-checked Leah's appointment schedule and confirmed transportation and the nursing attendant's schedule. Things were in order.

Grant was pretty amused with how Leah managed to get discharged. He knew that his old Leah was reemerging, and he loved it. He had asked Clay to keep an eye on things, and he knew that his mother and Gretchen would be around too.

Kathy and Jill spent most of the day Saturday with Leah. Gretchen joined them after she closed the shop. Jill mentioned the wedding, and they spent a lot time talking about it. There were some things Leah didn't remember, but a significant amount of the details she did.

They insisted that Leah rest before Gretchen came, and Kathy and Jill talked about Janis while they cleaned up and did laundry. Neither of them had seen her, and they didn't know if that was good or bad.

"We need to ask Gretchen if she's been in the shop," Jill said.

"And we need to ask her if Grant has heard from her crazy self," Kathy added.

The doorbell rang, and they looked at each other, puzzled. They weren't expecting anybody this early. It was Clay.

"We talked you up," Kathy said as she invited him in.

"What did y'all say about me?" Clay asked, laughing.

"We were talking about Grant, and basically you two are the same person," Kathy said.

Clay laughed and hugged them both. "Girl, you look so good I might turn in my player card!"

Jill rolled her eyes at him. She had always liked Clay, but she knew that he was a big flirt.

Through the course of the conversation, they asked if he had seen or heard from Janis.

"No, and I hope I don't. That nut is a piece of work."

"Is she still calling Grant?" Kathy asked.

"We don't know. GP blocked her number. She called one day from work, so now he just won't answer numbers he doesn't recognize." Clay spent about an hour with Jill and Kathy. He felt good that things were under control there. He left and headed home.

When Clay left the barbershop and decided to go see Leah, he didn't know that he was being followed. Delia had seen his car at the barbershop and decided to see if he was going home. She was pretty sure this wasn't his house. The name on the mailbox said "Robinson," and it was a huge house. She kept her distance. She had never followed anybody before, and she was nervous.

When Clay left the Robinsons, he went north on the interstate toward Davis Town. She didn't remember anything in this direction on the county listing she looked at. He pulled into a shopping center and went into the dry cleaners and the post office.

He has his mail sent to a post office box. That's interesting, she thought. Delia was afraid to go much farther. She decided to go home and explore that area another day.

She made sure he had left the shopping center, noticed the direction he went in, and then left. As she approached the interstate, she noticed a sign that read "Thank you for Visiting Windham Township." No wonder she didn't see that area on the listing. Windham was not in Mecklenburg County. It was in Iredell County. And Jeremy was right. It was in the vicinity of her mother's job.

FIFTY-FOUR

Sunday dinner at Grammy's was interesting. Ben and Belinda had decided not to tell the girls about his going to Atlanta yet. They had been concerned that Bishop Robinson would make an announcement and the girls would be caught off guard. But he said he wouldn't make any announcement until they were further along in the process. That bought them some time.

Enoch, Grammy, and Belinda got the girls involved in a game of Scrabble so Ben could talk to Kirby and Auntie. While they cleaned up, he told them about going to Atlanta. Their reactions were pretty much the same. Auntie wanted to know what Grammy said and how he was going to work out being away from her again. She was surprised when he said he wanted both of them to go with him.

Kirby wanted to know what Belinda said and if he intended to move her whole family four hours away. Ben felt a little guilty. He knew that she was only half joking. They did congratulate him, and Auntie told him how proud of him she knew his mother and grandfather would be. Ben had been so caught up that he hadn't even thought about his mother. She had been gone out of his life for so long. He didn't really remember her. He wondered if Brianna and Brittani really remembered their dad. One day he would ask them. Ben assured Kirby that he and Belinda were still in the discussion stage and at the moment they didn't want Brittani and Brianna to know, but he also made it clear to her that he wanted Belinda and the girls to go with him. And he promised she could visit as much as she wanted to.

Aunt Avis walked back into the dining room, wondering if this would be their last Christmas in that house.

Delia rushed home to get on the computer. She searched the Iredell County listings and found two listings for Clayton Sturdivant, one with Millicent Sturdivant. She still wanted to know who Millicent was, but she could deal with that later. Right then she wanted to find his house. She printed the directions from her house to the farthest point and from that one to the other one. The one listed with Millicent was the farthest away and had the higher tax value.

She knew this was crazy, but she couldn't stop herself. She got in her car and drove back to Windham. She followed the directions and found the first house. It was an older house on a huge lot. It looked really still, like nobody lived there. There wasn't a car in the driveway, so she kept going.

The second address was a few miles away in a new subdivision. There were apartments, townhouses, and single-family homes. Delia slowed down to look for the street and then to look for the number. The cul-de-sac had only six houses. They were all made pretty much the same: brick fronts and steps up to the decorative front doors. They looked expensive. She found the house. There was no car in the driveway, but there was a garage.

Delia walked up on the porch, took a deep breath, and just as she was about to ring the bell, she looked in. She could see straight through into the kitchen, and she could partially see the deck off the kitchen. There were two people on the deck, but she couldn't see who they were. She took a step aside to think what to do.

Do I get back in my car and go home, or do I confront Clay?

Before she could do anything, a car pulled in behind hers. How could she redeem herself now? The couple who got out had bags from the grocery store—one contained what was obviously a bottle of wine. Clay was having a party.

This was getting more complicated than she thought it would be. The truth was, if she had really thought this through, she wouldn't be here. As the couple approached, they were smiling at her and introduced themselves. The man rang the bell while Delia and the lady shook hands. Clay appeared in what seemed like one second. He was smiling until he realized that Delia was standing there. He greeted his friends and then Delia.

"Hey, Dee. What's up? Jeremy okay?"

"Yes, Jeremy is fine."

The female guest kept walking into the house, but the male guest lingered. Clay introduced Delia as Jeremy's mom, told the guy to check on the ladies, walked onto the porch, and closed the door behind him.

"What are you doing here unannounced and uninvited?"

She didn't like his tone at all. "I just decided since you hadn't ever invited me to your home, I would invite myself."

"Well, this isn't a good time. I'm busy."

"Obviously."

"I'll call you later…well, tomorrow."

"Clay, we need to talk."

"Not now we don't."

"Clay, we are sleeping together but we really don't have a relationship."

"Delia, that's your fault."

Before she could respond, the front door opened. It was the same woman she saw in his car at the pizza buffet.

Leah looked rested, and she felt good. Her therapy was going better than expected. She told Kathy that she wanted to get everybody together to talk about the wedding. She had made some notes and gone over them with Kathy before everybody arrived.

Katherine, Grace, Gretchen, Kathy, and the caterer sat around the dining room table. Jill was working. The caterer brought samples of four cakes and two types of chicken wings for them to sample and for Leah to consider for the reception. As the discussion proceeded, they were all surprised when Leah walked in on a cane and not her walker. She had been practicing when nobody was around.

Kathy took notes as they talked and was prepared to jump in if Leah forgot something, but interestingly, Leah was concentrating and staying on point. Many decisions were made, including serving all four types of cake and both types of wings at the reception.

The wedding plans were in full effect, and Leah was excited. She called Grant as soon as the ladies left.

He listened intently and asked a few questions but was more excited about her progress than the wedding plans.

"Leah, I'm not wearing a pink tie! You can kill that!"

She laughed. "I knew you were going to say that! Your shirt and tie are white. I had a pink rose...umm...corsage. I mean... uh..."

"Boutonniere."

"Yes, boutonniere, but I can change it if you want me to." That was the first word she had forgotten all day.

"I'll work with the boutonniere."

They talked a while longer, but Leah was getting tired. She knew that she needed to rest. If she was going to get back to 100 percent, she knew she had to rest. She didn't want to hang up, but she admitted to Grant that she was tired. He insisted that they talk later.

"I love you."

"I love you too, babe."

$\mathscr{F}$IFTY-FIVE

Kirby didn't realize how nervous she was until she dropped her earring because her hands were shaking. She had already dropped the toothpaste. The butterflies in her stomach were real. As much as she had prayed for this day, it was finally here, and she was nervous. Enoch had gone to work, but he would be back to pick her up. She took a deep breath and held on to the dresser.

"God, You did not give me a spirit of fear but of power and of love and of a sound mind. I love You, and I love my husband and this baby You have ordained for us."

Just then she heard the beep of the door. Enoch was there. It was time to go.

They made small talk on the thirty-minute ride. Enoch was noticeably quiet, but Kirby decided not to draw any attention to it. She wanted to just let it be.

Enoch recognized the tension too, but he decided that it was par for the course. They were in unchartered waters, and he prayed that they would swim, not sink.

They were there for almost two hours. After the procedure was done, Kirby laid there for a while, thinking. She rubbed her stomach and thought of the miracle of God that had happened inside her. She looked over at Enoch and smiled. He winked at her. She closed her eyes, and just as she did, the nurse came in. She checked Kirby's vital signs and told them that they could leave but she needed to rest for the remainder of the day and they needed to make an appointment to come back in three weeks. It was done. They had made a baby.

Kirby was still a little drowsy from the anesthesia, so Enoch helped her upstairs and into bed.

"Are you going back to work?"

He stepped out of his shoes and lay down beside her. "No, ma'am. I am at your service for the rest of the day. Need anything?"

"A hug."

Enoch put his arms around her and held her tight. She dozed off, and he watched her sleep. After a little while, he eased out of the bed. He needed a minute to himself. He went across the hall, into the room they had decided would be the nursery. The only furniture in the room was a rocking chair that had belonged to his mother. He agreed with Kirby that it was cool to rock their baby in the chair that his mother had rocked him in. He didn't want to be far away if she woke up and called him.

He leaned back in the chair and closed his eyes. They had done it, implanted a baby to grow in Kirby's womb. The truth was that he was a little disappointed. He had always imagined his excitement when Kirby told him she was pregnant and how he would react. Now they had to wait to see if the procedure worked. If it didn't, what was he going to say to Kirby?

As he rocked back and forth, his phone rang. It was Belinda checking on Kirby. He assured her that things had gone well, that Kirby had done fine.

"Are you okay, Enoch?" Belinda could hear in his voice that something was wrong.

"Belinda, I'll be fine when I know the procedure worked. 'Cause if it didn't, I don't know what state my wife will be in."

Belinda was concerned about what Enoch said. She hung up and called Ben.

When Enoch's phone rang again and he saw Ben's name on the ID, he wasn't surprised.

"What's up, man?" Enoch said.

"Just talked to Belinda. She thought I needed to check on you."

Enoch laughed. "I'm good. The reality of this whole thing just hit me I guess."

"Yeah. This is all real deep. I don't want to sound all philosophical, but you know that God's will won't take you where His grace won't keep you."

"I believe that, but I'm worried about Kirby. Once I know that things are good, I'll be good too."

"Clay, is everything okay?" the woman asked.

"Yeah, I'm good. Give me a minute." His voice was firm.

She looked at Delia and walked back into the house.

"What do you mean it's my fault?" Delia asked.

"Think about it while you're drivin' home."

Clay walked back in the house, and Delia realized that his guests had her blocked in the driveway. She turned toward the door, and just then Clay's friend came out to move the car.

She was embarrassed and humiliated. She knew that going there was a mistake, but it had turned out to be more of a mistake than she could have imagined. She still didn't know why Clay said them not having a relationship was her fault. What hadn't she done?

The ride home was quick, it seemed. Jeremy and Crystal were visiting her parents, and she was glad. She lay across the bed and thought through the time that she and Clay spent together and why he made that comment.

Was that Millicent who came to the door? she wondered.

Raja and his parents hadn't talked in a few days. He had heard from his cousin that his mother was fine. He braced himself and called. As usual, his father answered, and after speaking briefly, he told Raja that his mother was not well and was unable to come to the telephone.

"What seems to be the problem?" he asked his father.

"She is sad, I suspect depressed, about your defiance."

Well, at least he isn't beating around the bush, Raja thought. "I'm sorry to hear that. I hope she gets better before the wedding."

"Do you know your mother has been in bed since you last spoke?"

Raja knew that wasn't true. "Sir, I suspect mother is exaggerating, but if she isn't, she should see a doctor. I can call someone if you want me to."

"I don't think that's necessary. She is sick of a broken heart. If you would apologize and change your plans, I'm sure she will feel better."

"Father, if her illness is based on my plans, she will be too sick to attend the wedding. I have no intention of changing anything. Please give mother my best regards. And let me know if I need to get her a doctor."

Raja hung up and laughed to himself. He knew that his mother could and would be dramatic, but she was taking it too far. Raja had not been that happy in a long time, and he wasn't going to mess it up with Jill.

She had asked him for a suggestion of a gift to take his mother. Jill asked if she collected anything. Raja hadn't thought about it in a long time, but when he was younger, his mother collected teapots. She would purchase one anytime they traveled to a place she had never been. She particularly liked odd ones. Raja's favorite was the one that looked like a bear cub. His mother was very fond of one that looked like a sewing machine. Raja had given it to her as a gift.

Jill thought that it was a great idea. She knew the perfect place to buy a teapot that would impress Mrs. Rajagopal. She drove to Charlotte to a tea shop and bought a beautiful teapot that looked like a stack of gifts wrapped in pastel colors. The lavender bow at the top was the lid of the pot. It was the right gift for the occasion, and Jill was pleased with what she bought. The trip was one week away, and now she was ready.

Ben left Belinda a message simply saying that things had gone reasonably well and he would give her the details that night. He turned his phone off and leaned the seat back. The flight from Atlanta back to Charlotte was a little over an hour, time enough for a good nap.

He had been in Atlanta all week, working to get things started for the new church. He had seen half a dozen churches that were either for sale or lease. There was only one that he was particularly interested in. He had taken pictures to share with the bishop, and the Realtor had given him a packet with detailed information. She also offered to show him some residential properties in the areas. He told her that he hadn't decided what to do about that. He might move into a rental unit temporarily, "until I can move my family down here." He took great pride in saying that: Grammy and Auntie and Belinda, Brittani and Brianna. Belinda was the most incredible woman in the world. He so wanted her to be his wife, and the twins were a bonus. They had had in-depth conversations about being in Atlanta together. They had talked about living in the suburbs, the city, or the country. They had talked about hospitals where she could work and public or private schools for the girls. They had talked about Grammy and

Auntie living with them or on their own. They had talked about everything but actually getting married.

Ben knew that it was his move to make. He didn't understand why he couldn't or wouldn't bring it up. But he also knew for absolute sure that none of what they had discussed would ever happen until and unless they were married. Ben was so grateful that Belinda had embraced the idea of his grandmother and aunt living with them, but he knew the chance of getting them to move without the twins was not good. If he didn't get it together, he was going to Atlanta by himself. Ben dozed off, thinking that he was going to bite the bullet and look for a ring that weekend.

Katherine went downstairs, expecting Leah to be up, but she was still in bed.

"Hi, sweetie. Are you okay?"

"Hey, Ma. I'm okay. Just not ready to get up yet. Grant called in the middle of the night, and we talked a long time, and then I couldn't go back to sleep."

Katherine smiled at Leah. "Okay, but you know you have an appointment for therapy at ten."

"Ma, will you see if you can change it to a little later?"

"Yes. I'll see. But if not, you are going to have to get up, and you can take a nap later."

Leah didn't want her mother to know that she had a headache. It was true. She and Grant had talked, but the reason she couldn't go back to sleep was due to the headache.

Lee and Katherine took Leah to therapy. Friday was their date day, and he made every effort to make that happen. They were going to brunch while she was in therapy and to a movie later. Leah looked at her parents and hoped that she and Grant would be that happy and in love after thirty years of marriage.

The therapist questioned Leah about her lack of attention this morning, and she told him that she didn't sleep well. She simply was not making much progress, so he told her to rest for a minute. She asked for some water, and as he walked back toward her, he noticed that she was rubbing her head. He gave her the water and went to get the blood pressure cuff. She protested, but he took her pressure, and it was high—very high.

"Leah, I have to send you over to the hospital."

"Please don't."

"I have to."

The ambulance took her to the hospital, and Trey met her in the emergency room.

When the bishop and first lady arrived at the ER, Trey was able to give them an update.

"The bad news is her blood pressure is up. The good news is we can get it under control and that's all that's going on."

"Trey, is this normal?"

"It's not abnormal. From time to time, we see patients who have been through the type of surgery that Leah has who have periodic spikes in bp. What we have to do though is make sure Leah is forthcoming when she doesn't feel well."

"Can I take her home?" the bishop asked.

"No, sir. I want to keep her overnight, but I expect she can go home tomorrow."

"Trey, how much of a setback is this?" Katherine asked.

"Just a slight setback."

Leah was settled in her hospital room when her dad walked in. He had asked Katherine to give him a few minutes alone with her. Leah knew that he was going to scold her for not admitting she had a headache. She decided to go on offense.

"I'm sorry, Daddy. I know I should have told you, but I thought it was just a headache because I didn't sleep well."

"You know I expect more from you than this."

Leah dropped her eyes. She hated it when her dad got onto her. He didn't do it much, but she hated it just the same.

"I haven't said a lot throughout this whole ordeal. I just wanted you better. I didn't protest when you talked Trey and Zack Strauss into letting you leave the hospital on your schedule. You took things into your own hands, and now you're back in here. You have acted irresponsibly, Leah, and with no regard for the people who love you."

"Daddy, I was fine until today. This is just a temporary setback. I will be fine tomorrow. I am a nurse, and this kind of thing is normal."

"Yes, you are a nurse, so you should know how to be a better patient. You are not at one hundred percent, Leah, and you need to proceed with that in mind. Have you told Grant about any of this?"

"No, and I don't plan to."

"Oh, so now you're keeping the truth from the man you intend to marry?"

"Daddy! Why are you being so mean to me?" Leah started crying.

"Because I want you to think and understand how serious this is."

Leah didn't say anything. She just looked at her father.

Lee sat beside her, put his arms around her, and hugged her. "I love you, sweetheart. I want you well, and you have to take some responsibility for that."

"I will, Daddy. I promise." She laid her head on her dad's chest.

He laid his hand on her head and started to pray.

FIFTY-SIX

Jill and Raja had agreed to meet at the airport. It was the most time-efficient thing to do. When her mother dropped her off, Raja was waiting at the curb. Check-in was easy, and they had over an hour before time to board. As they sat and chatted, Raja reemphasized to Jill not to take offense to anything his mother said or did. She assured him that she wouldn't and he didn't need to worry. She laughed to herself, thinking about her conversation with Leah. She told Jill that she would pray for her.

When the pilot finally announced that they were on final approach to Heathrow Airport, Jill got a little nervous. They got their luggage, and Raja asked Jill if she had come to London to stay.

"Whatever do you mean?" she replied smiling.

"You have enough stuff to be here for a long time."

"You just never know."

He looked at her and smiled, hoping things would work out for them and his family.

"Manavendra!"

Raja looked around, slightly startled. He wasn't expecting anyone in the airport to call his name, and he was unused to being called by his given name. Jill didn't look around until she heard Raja laugh.

"What a surprise. I wasn't expecting anyone to meet us."

The two men embraced.

"It is good to see you."

"And you, Manavendra."

Raja turned to Jill and introduced her. "Jillian Strauss, this is my cousin, Yash Rajagopal, the groom."

Jill extended her hand. "It is a pleasure to meet you, Yash."

"It's nice to meet you, Miss Strauss."

"Please, call me Jill."

Yash knew why Raja was attracted to Jill. She was beautiful. Jill thought that Raja and his cousin had similar facial features, but she didn't think he was as handsome as Raja, and he was a little older.

"I wish I had known you were coming. I made arrangements for a car to pick us up."

Jill was impressed.

"Oh, I canceled the car"—his cousin laughed—"when you e-mailed me your itinerary. You should be greeted by family."

"Thank you," was all Raja said. He hoped that there were no strings attached.

As they were driving out of the airport, Yash announced that they would visit Raja's parents first.

"I prefer you take us to the hotel. I will call my parents from there."

Jill exhaled and hoped that Raja didn't hear her. She definitely didn't want to meet Raja's parents first thing. Raja didn't know if his parents had put his cousin up to it or if it was his idea, but Raja fully intended to control the situation.

They checked into their rooms, and before he could hang up all his clothes, the room phone rang.

"Dr. Rajagopal, you have a visitor in the lobby, and she insists on having your room number."

"I'll be right down." He couldn't believe his mother was in the lobby, creating a scene, but he would put a stop to her antics immediately.

He walked off the elevator and into the arms of his cousin, Tara.

"Surprise!"

Raja picked her up off the floor and spun her around. She squealed like she did when they were children. Although they talked regularly, they hadn't seen each other in over a year.

"Where did you come from?" he asked.

"I wanted to see you, so I bit the bullet and decided to come."

"You didn't have to come all the way to London to see me. You could have come to North Carolina. You didn't want to miss your brother's wedding."

"You are right, my dear cousin, but I couldn't do this without you."

They hugged again.

"Is Robert here too?" Raja asked.

"Yes. He went to our room. I wanted to let you know I was here."

"You know, I thought my mother was the one insisting on knowing my room number."

They both laughed loud.

"I knew you would think that. That's why I did it."

Jill had called her mother to let her know that they had arrived safely and asked her to call Leah. She put her things away and took a good look at her room. It was a gorgeous room complete with a sitting area and a beautiful view of the city. There was a silver tea service on the coffee table, along with a variety of tea bags. The bellman told her when he brought her luggage to inform housekeeping if she preferred lemon or cream in her tea.

"They will bring it to you straight away."

The knock at the door didn't surprise Jill, but the beautiful young lady standing there with Raja did surprise her. She was dark-eyed with a sassy, short haircut and long eyelashes. She was

307

average height but very slim, which made her look really short beside him.

"Hi, Jillie. This is my cousin, Tara Rajagopal. Tara, this is Jill Strauss."

"Tara, I am glad to meet you. I didn't think you were coming."

"I wasn't, but I didn't want to miss my brother's wedding because my parents are crazy."

"Do they know you're here?" Raja asked.

"No. I think I'll just show up at the restaurant tomorrow evening."

"Yash and your parents will have heart failure!"

The smirk on her face was priceless. "If I can face my parents, so can you." The expression on her face did not change. She just added rolling her eyes at him. She walked over to the phone and dialed. "Hey, babe. Can you come up here? We're in room one zero zero five." Tara hung up and changed the subject. "Jill, I hope we can see some sights and do some shopping together, without the guys."

"I'm sure we can work that out."

Tara and Jill chatted for another minute or two before Robert knocked on the door. Raja was glad that Jill and Tara had hit it off; Tara was like a sister to him. The trip was going to be even better than he expected.

Robert and Raja had only met once, but they felt like friends. They shook hands, and Robert introduced himself to Jill. He was very handsome. He reminded her of Idris Elba.

They agreed to meet for an early dinner and they would go to Tara's parents' home. If Raja's parents were not there, he was sure they would come.

Kirby was ecstatic. That day was her first check-up since finding out that the in-vitro process had been successful. It would still be a few weeks before she knew if there was more than one baby. She had passed up the chance to say, "I told you so," to Belinda, Enoch, and Robin Brackett. Grammy had advised her not to tell anybody until at least three months. Kirby thought that that was old-fashioned thinking, but Enoch agreed with Grammy, so she didn't tell anybody else. She had wanted to talk about baby names, but Enoch wanted to wait. He was meeting her at the doctor's office.

The truth was that Enoch was concerned because Kirby had not been sick or complained of any symptoms that he had always heard about. He talked with Belinda about it, and she reassured him that every pregnancy was different. Belinda also warned him not to share his concerns with Kirby.

"If something is wrong, you don't want to be accused of not being supportive," Belinda said.

Enoch knew she was right.

The doctor's visit went well. He had only good things to say, including that he thought that there was only one baby. They would be sure the next month, but he only saw one heartbeat.

"I hope it's a boy," Kirby told Enoch while walking to the car.

"Yeah. That would be cool. But a cute little girl would be cool too."

"Uh-huh, so you can spoil her."

"I spoiled you. What's your point?"

"Enoch Casebier, I am not spoiled."

"Kirby Casebier, you are spoiled, but it's all good. I love you anyway."

"Good. Will you buy me lunch?"

"See! That's what I'm talkin' about!"

Enoch was encouraged by the doctor's comments, and he had relaxed. God had answered their prayers. Everything was going to be all right.

"When do you plan to tell the girls about the baby?"

"I don't know. Belinda said that she wanted us to tell them. What do you think?"

"Let's do it for their birthday next month."

"Good idea. They are going to have a lot to deal with: the baby, Ben moving, and the possibility of them moving too."

"Kirby, are you really going to be okay with Belinda moving?"

"To be absolutely honest, no, particularly because Grammy and Auntie might go too. But I want Belinda to be happy, and if being in Atlanta with Ben makes her happy, then I'll adjust."

$\mathscr{F}$IFTY-SEVEN

Raja, Jill, Tara, and Robert arrived at Tara's parents' home in the midst of the first night of wedding activities. Everybody was surprised to see them, but Yash was glad to see his sister. Jill was a bit nervous, but she felt like she had an ally in Robert. She had decided to give Raja's mother her gift at her home.

The ceremony had just gotten started, so the foursome slipped into the back very quietly. The bride's parents were officially presenting her to Yash's parents and asking for permission for them to marry and presenting the dowry. It didn't take long to go through that part. Tara told Jill that they would need to wear traditional dress the next night.

Jill noticed that the bride had walked over but stood behind Yash until he invited her to join the group. He introduced Tara first and then Raja and then Robert and Jill. Yash and all the other men in the room were dressed in suits and neckties. The bride and all the other women were dressed in saris.

Raja's parents and Tara's parents totally ignored the fact that Raja and Tara were there with guests. Raja knew that he had to make a move before Tara did. She wouldn't be diplomatic at all.

Raja spoke to his father and uncle and then to his mother and aunt. He told them that he wanted them to meet Jill and Tara's friend, Robert. His mother refused and walked away. Tara approached her parents, smiled, and spoke. Her father smiled and thanked her for coming to support her brother. Her mother nodded. Raja introduced his father, uncle, and aunt to Jill and

Robert. They all nodded but did not speak. Tara took Robert by his hand, gave Raja the eye, and walked out. She was furious.

Leah was home, and things had gotten back to what Kathy called the "new normal," including the wedding plans. Leah had also called the hospital to see about coming back to work, but Trey said not yet. She had finally told Grant about her overnight stay in the hospital. He was none too pleased, and he told her. What he hadn't told her was that he had asked to be transferred back to the States, to Walter Reed Hospital in Washington. If he could get a transfer, he would be closer to Leah and his family. Leah could get a job at Walter Reed too if she wanted to work. He knew that Leah would be excited. Washington versus Germany was a no-brainer. Grant had told Clay but had sworn him to secrecy. If his parents, Gretchen, or Leah knew he had applied to transfer and it wasn't approved, they would be terribly disappointed. He would know in a few weeks, by Leah's birthday.

Since the scene at Clay's house, he and Delia had only seen each other in passing. His schedule with Jeremy had continued, and he had dismissed his concerns that Delia was going to tell the agency about their relationship. When Clay told Grant about the situation, Grant advised him to get it together.

"Dude, you need to correct that situation before it really gets out of hand."

"Man, I know. I never thought it would get here, but now I know that it can get crazy."

"What did Cicely say?"

"She didn't say anything, but I know she wasn't cool."

"Are you willing to mess up with her?"

"No, but we are not committed. If she wants to split, it's on her."

"I thought you were into her."

"I'm more into her than I have been with anybody else, but I have options."

"Dude, check yourself! You're too old for all that carryin' on."

"Just because you're turnin' in your player card doesn't mean I have to! And by the way, you heard from that crazy Janis?"

"No, and don't talk her up. I'm still gettin' calls from numbers I don't recognize and not answering them. It's probably her. Clay, what do you think Cicely would do if she found out about Delia?"

"The truth of the matter is, G, if Cicely found out I was dealin' with Delia or the couple of other people I holler at from time to time, she would walk away and not look back."

"So are you sayin' that she's just not that into you?"

They both laughed.

"No. What I'm sayin' is she is tough, no-nonsense, and very confident.

"She obviously has options too."

"I'm sure she does, but she hasn't said that."

"You sleepin' with her?"

"Naw! She has made it very clear to me that she will not have sex before marriage."

"Is she a virgin?"

"She didn't say that, but she shut me down. And the funny thing is, I'm okay with that."

"She sounds like a keeper to me. How 'bout you don't mess that up. Don't do something stupid like I did when I almost lost Leah."

FIFTY-EIGHT

The twins were going to a birthday party, so Belinda had a couple of hours free. It was too far to go back home and come back, so she brought Maya Angelou's new book to start reading. But she was hungry, so she called Ben to invite him to lunch. He was in his office at the church and asked her to come there. Just as she pulled into the area where Ben parked he was coming out of the building.

He put his things in his truck and walked over and got into the car with Belinda. She looked at him and laughed.

"Where to, Minister Coffey?"

"Let's go to the mall."

"The mall! I don't want to eat in the food court."

"Not the food court. Let's go to the seafood place across the parking lot."

When they arrived at the restaurant, the parking lot was full, but they didn't have to wait long for a table.

The waitress set their salads and a basket of cheese biscuits down. Ben loved the biscuits and ate one in two bites.

"Belinda, I had a particular reason for wanting to come out here. I want to go in the jewelry store and look at engagement rings," he said between bites.

She swallowed hard. "Engagement rings?"

"Are you surprised?"

"Well, yes."

"Why?" Ben leaned back, feeling very confident.

"I didn't know you were there yet."

"Belinda, I love you. I. Love. You." He leaned forward and folded his hands in front of him. "We have talked about everything having to do with my move to Atlanta except getting married, and I know you won't go unless we are."

Belinda smiled. "Okay. We can go look at rings after we eat."

Ben purposefully didn't talk about Atlanta during lunch. As they finished, he suggested that she call to let the birthday party host know that she would be a little late.

As they walked into the jewelry store, it occurred to Ben that most of the people who worked there knew him, and he was putting himself and Belinda on blast. He decided that that was okay. He couldn't back out now.

"Hello, Benjamin. How are you today, and who is this lovely lady?" The jeweler had known Ben all his life. His son and Ben had grown up together.

Ben made the introductions.

"Oh, so this is the special lady with the charm bracelet. Are we looking for another charm today?"

"No, sir. We want to look at some rings."

"Very good. Look here in these two cases and let me know if you want to try something on."

Belinda and Ben were grateful for the privacy. They both looked for a minute or two before he asked if she saw anything she liked.

"Show me what you like," she said to him.

He showed her a couple of really nice diamonds, big stones.

"You know what? I think I like something smaller."

"Smaller? Why?"

"I wouldn't want to take it off, and neither of those would fit with my surgical gloves. What about a band with a diamond or two?"

He started to ask her what she had when she was married to Canady, but he didn't. "I want you to have some bling!"

She laughed.

The jeweler walked over and asked if he could show them something. Belinda told him that she wanted something small, and Ben told him he wanted her to have something bigger and nicer.

"I have the perfect set." He showed them two band sets, one platinum with baguettes all the way around trimmed in round diamonds. The matching band was identical but half the width. The other set was gold with the same diamond band, but the matching wedding band was a thin ring of round diamonds.

"I like them both!" That was the first real excitement Belinda had shown.

Ben looked at both sets very closely. The jeweler handed him the jeweler's loupes for closer examination. While Ben looked at the diamonds, the jeweler sized Belinda's finger.

"Okay! I'm good. Let's bounce and get the girls," Ben said with a sly grin.

Belinda just looked at him. He looked at the jeweler and nodded, and they left.

The twins were quite amused but delighted that Ben was with Belinda when she got to the party to pick them up. When they got back to the church for him to pick up his truck, the girls got in his vehicle so that he would have to come to their house. After a couple of rounds of UNO, Belinda sent the girls upstairs to get ready for bed.

"I wasn't ready to stop playing!" Ben said, pouting.

"We'll play again another day, but I know you need some meditation time on Saturday night, so you need to be going soon." She was smiling at him.

Ben looked at Belinda very seriously. "Thank you for observing that."

They chatted for a couple more minutes, neither of them mentioning the rings.

When he got ready to go, Ben walked to the bottom of the stairs and said good night to the girls. They yelled good night in unison. Ben and Belinda walked to the door, holding hands. Just as he reached to open the door, Belinda reached for his other hand. She hoped he didn't hear her take the deep breath.

She looked into his eyes. "I love you."

"I love you too."

Tara was incensed at her family for just dismissing Robert and Jill. She told Raja that that was exactly what she expected and exactly why she didn't want to come to London.

"If that's what you expected, why are you so angry?" Raja asked.

"Because they are spoiling this for Yash."

"Well, I need you to adjust your attitude. We are going to my parents' tomorrow."

"Manavendra, I don't want to go. I'm done."

"Tara, I can't do this without you."

"If I hadn't come, you would be doing it without me."

"But you did come, so let's do this together." Raja put his arm around Tara's shoulder.

Robert and Jill just looked at each other. In a moment alone, he confided in Jill that if Tara wanted to go home, that was fine with him.

But Jill was determined that she and Raja were going to have a vacation and have a good time. They had a big day planned, and she wanted to get the meeting with his parents behind them.

They had breakfast on the sidewalk, did some sightseeing, and arrived at the Rajagopals' home right after lunch the next day. There was a lot going on. A few family members were staying with them while in town for the wedding festivities.

Raja knew that he would have to deal with his mother immediately. She was driving all the insanity. He walked in, spoke to everyone, and asked his mother if they could talk privately. She looked as if she wanted to protest, but she thought better of it.

A young lady who was there working in the kitchen asked the other three to have a seat and set a tea service before them. Tara thanked her and poured a cup for everybody. They chatted about nothing particular and laughed at Robert, who said he needed a mug because the teacup was too small for his big hands.

A few moments later, Raja came from the back of the house with a nondescript look on his face. Tara poured him a cup of tea, and by the time he took his second sip, his mother emerged. She approached the group with a half smile, and it was obvious that she had been crying. Robert and Raja stood, and Raja introduced him first. Mrs. Rajagopal extended her hand but did not look into his eyes.

"Mother, this is Jill Strauss. Jill, this is my mother."

Mrs. Rajagopal extended her hand and shook Jill's hand with a very limp handshake.

"It's a pleasure to meet you, ma'am. I brought you a gift." She handed the package to her.

Mrs. Rajagopal looked surprised. She opened the box, took the teapot out, and looked even more surprised.

"Raja told me that you collect teapots. I hope you can add this one to your collection."

"Thank you. It's very pretty. My son is right, but I haven't had a new one in a long time." A genuine smile crossed her face.

Checkmate, Jill thought to herself.

Mrs. Rajagopal set the tea pot on the coffee table and turned her attention to Tara. "How are you, Tara?"

"I am well, Auntie. Thank you for asking."

She sipped her tea and did not make eye contact. It was obvious that Mrs. Rajagopal felt uncomfortable. Raja made small talk with his mother, and eventually his father joined the group. He asked Raja about a book he had suggested Raja read.

"I haven't had time to read it yet."

"I've actually read that one myself," Jill interjected.

Mr. Rajagopal was caught a little off guard, and then, to add insult to injury, Tara said that she had read it too and began to engage Jill in conversation about the book, leaving her uncle out. When Tara was satisfied that she had annoyed her uncle, she suggested they leave, making it clear they had other things to do before that night's wedding festivities.

When they were all safely in the car, Raja started to laugh. "You are so bad," he said to Tara.

"Whatever, cousin! They are all so phony they make me sick!"

After a little more sightseeing, they went back to the hotel to get dressed for the evening.

Jill couldn't get over how absolutely gorgeous Tara looked in the traditional dress. Her dark hair and eyes made the light-blue-and-silver sari even prettier. She wore about a dozen silver bangles on each arm. She shared half with Jill. Jill liked the lavender-and-purple one she had chosen, but she didn't think she looked as good as Tara. Raja thought Jill looked great. It was an unusual sight to see blonde hair hanging on the back of the sari, but he liked it. Robert passed on the traditional wear, and that was fine with Tara. Raja chose to wear the traditional garb. They took lots of pictures. Jill couldn't wait to get back to her room and e-mail them to Leah and her mom.

The ballroom where the night's activity was being held was an amazing sight. There were so many flowers, many colors and types. All the guests were seated on pillows on the floor. From what Jill could understand, it was a beautiful ceremony. That night's part of the ceremony was a charge to the groom.

The bride participated in only one portion. She was dressed in a pink sequined gown with matching slippers, and a long pink scarf covered her head. She wore gold bracelets on each arm and long, gold, dangling earrings. She was beautiful. Jill had a passing thought. If she married Raja, she wanted an Indian wedding. She laughed to herself. She knew that her new friend, Tara, wouldn't think it was a good idea, and her best friend, practical Leah, wouldn't agree with spending that much money.

FIFTY-NINE

Kirby had been in the bathroom too long. Enoch went to the door to check on her. When he asked if she was okay, all she managed to say was, "Morning sickness."

"I'll get you some ginger ale."

Enoch went downstairs to get the drink, but he was actually glad that she was sick. Now he knew she was really pregnant. He hurried back upstairs. He knew she didn't need to get dehydrated. She was sitting at the foot of the bed.

"I know this baby is a boy. A girl wouldn't act like this." She took a couple of sips of the ginger ale.

"Can I get you something else?"

"No. I just need to rest a minute."

"Do I need to call anybody?"

"Yes. You can call my boss and tell him that I might be a little late for work this morning."

"You don't have to work today."

"Enoch, sweetie, relax. I'll be fine in a few minutes. You might as well get used to this. We have another few weeks of morning sickness to look forward to."

Enoch had bought her a gift and decided that it was a good time to give it to her. It was a brown bear wearing a navy baseball cap and a navy jersey. Printed on the back of the jersey were Casebier and the number 1. She loved it.

"I know you want a boy."

"All I want is a healthy baby. A girl can play baseball too."

"Yeah, if you let her out of the house."

"Oh, I'll be out there. You can bet on that."

They both laughed.

"What would you name a son, Enoch Jr?"

"Naw. I agree with my mom. She used to always say a child should have its own name."

"I understand that. When Belinda and I were growing up, we would talk about what we would name our children. We always named our sons for our imaginary fathers."

"You didn't want to name them after your foster father?"

"No. As much as we loved him, we still made up stories about our parents. Sometimes they were royalty. Sometimes they would be rock stars. Having lived in so much fantasy, that's why having a baby is so important to me."

"I understand, baby. I really do."

"You didn't answer my question."

"I don't know. Let me think about it."

Enoch made sure that she finished the ginger ale, and he got ready to leave.

She lay back in the bed and rubbed her stomach. "God bless you, little baby. Mommy loves you."

The food at the reception was incredible. There were so many choices.

"I am so off my diet," Jill said to no one specifically.

"We'll walk it off tomorrow," Tara answered.

Things had gone relatively well. Raja's parents had acknowledged all of them, and Tara's parents had thanked them for coming when they went through the receiving line.

The final ceremony was the following evening, and then they would have a couple of days to sightsee before returning to the States. Robert had asked the concierge at their hotel to see if they could go to Paris for a day on the train. He assured them that he would work it out. Tara agreed that the trip to Paris was a good idea, but the four of them had been together on every excursion, and she knew that Raja and Jill needed some time alone.

I can't believe Raja and Jill sleep in separate rooms, she thought. *How old-fashioned. Jill seems worldlier than that, more enlightened. But if that's what they want to do, hey, so be it.*

She had told Robert that they wouldn't spend the whole day in Paris with them.

After lunch, Raja and Robert wanted to go to a local gym to play basketball, so Jill and Tara went shopping. Jill asked a lot of questions about what to expect at the actual marriage ceremony.

"It will be a grand affair, I assure you. It's a matter of prestige and reputation for the bride's family. There will be lots of decorations, music, and dancing. Yash said that they are expecting almost five hundred people."

"You and your brother talked?"

"Yeah. He called me last night, and we talked for a long time. I'm glad I came, and he appreciates me being here. We agreed to disagree about lifestyles. I don't know when we'll visit again, but we're cool for now."

When they finally got to the ceremony, Jill was totally fascinated and in awe with what was going on around her. Again, there were thousands of flowers, and some even hung from the ceiling. The groom arrived at the ceremony on a white horse that was also adorned in flowers and jewels.

The bride entered, following the traditional drum cadence that signaled Yash, and his family had been seated for the ceremony. Her gown was stunning. She and the groom were adorned in matching flower garlands that accented her cream-and-gold dress and headpiece. The dress was a gift to her from the Rajagopal family.

The ceremony was a two-hour celebration that included walking around a holy fire. Then there was a lavish reception. When they left the festivities, it was 1:00 a.m.

Raja had watched Jill throughout the ceremony. He could see the fascination in her eyes. He was glad he had invited her to come and even more pleased she had accepted the invitation. He knew that they hadn't had much one-on-one time, but it had been a good vacation. His mother had backed off some after their talk. He had made it clear to her that he would pack his things and leave and not ever come back if she disrespected Jill, and Tara and Robert for that matter. He hated to have to threaten her, but he had to get her attention.

The next day they were all glad that Robert had made arrangements for them to spend a day in Paris. Jill and Raja had time to talk on the train. They walked hand in hand through the city, had lunch at a sidewalk café, and had their first kiss.

When their trip came to an end, as they sat on the tarmac, waiting for the plane to take off, they talked about the week, agreeing that it had been a great experience. They were glad that Tara had come and that she and Yash had made peace with each other. Jill liked Tara and hoped that they could be friends. They also talked about how they would nurture their relationship going forward. Jill dozed off with her head on Raja's shoulder.

Clay had set the alarm on his phone. He wanted to get home and shower. He was having breakfast with Cicely before he went to work. She had been working long hours for several days, and he hadn't seen her much.

The alarm awakened Delia too. She asked why he was leaving. He told her that he didn't want to take a chance on the kids knowing he was there. Delia accepted his explanation, but she wasn't satisfied with it. She walked him to the door and just stood there for a moment.

Why am I so gullible when it comes to Clay Sturdivant? She really liked Clay and wanted to have a real relationship with him, but she knew he didn't feel the same way. Yet she kept letting him come back. She thought about what he told her on his porch, that it was her fault that they didn't have a relationship. It was not her fault that they didn't have a relationship. She let him call the shots, so it was his fault. "I let him call the shots. I *let* him call the shots," she said aloud.

As she walked back to bed, she thought again that she let Clay determine when they spent time together and what they did. She lay in bed and thought about her situation with Clay. He was spending time with another woman. She was at his home. Delia had never been invited to his home. They had never been on a date. The only time they went out together was with Crystal and Jeremy. But she liked the way he made her feel. He didn't even introduce her to any of his family or friends. Even though they would have misunderstandings, he always came back. She always allowed him to come back. She always allowed him to come back to her bed. But he made her feel good, feel loved. He was so sweet to her when they were alone.

Who is he hiding me from? Maybe he is one of those guys who are afraid of commitment. I should just tell him to get out of my life and never come back. Her last thought as she went back to sleep was, *But I like the way he makes me feel, and I don't want to be alone.* She drifted off to sleep.

$\mathscr{S}$IXTY

The call came a day earlier than expected. Grant was getting his transfer back to the States. He would receive confirmation in ten days, but it was expected that he would be moving in approximately forty-five days to Walter Reed Military Medical Center, Bethesda, Maryland. He would be stateside again, close to his family and friends and his darling Leah. Under the circumstances, it would be good for her to be close to her family. The good news was he was going back to the States. The bad news was that he wouldn't get to go home for her birthday. He had to figure out how to turn the news into a gift for her. He would have to enlist the help of his posse: Clay and Gretchen.

Grant was surprised not to get Clay at that time of morning. He hoped he wasn't away from home. He had talked to Clay about his antics with those women. If he blew it with Cicely, he would be sorry, but he would be even sorrier if he ended up with an unplanned kid or some kind of disease.

When Clay called back, he told Grant that he was having breakfast with Cicely, but he didn't bother to tell him that he had been with Delia the night before. He knew that time was running out with Delia, and he had to make a move. He didn't want Cicely to find out, and he was also bored with Delia. Clay told Grant that he could hook them up by Skype. He would engage Gretchen's help, and they would work out all the details.

Campbell and Chloe's prom night was the greatest night of his life. They looked great, and they had had a great time. He had taken her to dinner at Sheldon's, and they had danced and danced, had enjoyed being with their friends, and had gone to an after party. Campbell had gotten his license, and Kathy had let him borrow her car. It had all come together nicely.

When Chloe invited Campbell to her home a few weeks after the prom, he expected to see a movie or play a rematch of Scrabble and eat something. Campbell couldn't believe his ears. He didn't want to believe what Chloe was telling him. She had missed her period and taken a home pregnancy test, and it was positive. He was absolutely speechless. He stood up and walked around the room.

"Chloe, I'm sorry. It's all my fault. I shouldn't have—"

"Campbell, you didn't make me have sex with you."

"That was the first time for both of us. I don't get it."

"Campbell, it happens. We should have used something."

He was pacing back and forth. She was just sitting there. Her parents were at work, so she knew that it was a good time for them to talk. He looked over at her, and she was crying.

"Please don't cry. I'll figure it out. Have you told anybody?"

"No, but I want to tell my mom."

"Not yet. Please give me some time to think. Chloe, please stop crying."

He hugged her, and they both sat quietly for a few minutes. Campbell was furious with himself. He was following in his father's footsteps, and he didn't like it. His mom had been in high school when she got pregnant with him. He wanted to go to college. Chloe wanted to go to college. He had to fix this. Abortion wasn't an option, so he would have to come up with another plan.

"Chloe, do you trust me?"

She thought that that was an interesting question. She sat up and looked at him. "Why did you ask me that?

"I need to know."

"Yes, I trust you."

"Let's go talk to Miss Robinson."

"Why Miss Robinson?"

"She'll help me figure out what to do."

"Campbell, you don't have to figure this out all by yourself."

"I am responsible for this situation, and God is going to hold me accountable."

Chloe actually felt a sense of relief.

Kathy had had the pregnancy conversation with students before, but she never thought it would be these two. Campbell was responsible, and so was Chloe. But life happens.

Kathy took a deep breath. "What were you two thinking? Oh, you weren't thinking because if you were, we wouldn't be having this conversation." She was angry and disappointed.

Chloe and Campbell just sat there. Kathy apologized and explained to them that she never thought she would be here with the two of them. They told her that they really needed her help.

Kathy was particularly attached to Campbell, and she was taking this situation very personally. He had to do well for himself but also for his family. Chloe would be fine, baby and all. Her parents had resources, and they would see to it.

"Does anybody else know?"

"No, ma'am."

"Okay. Let's keep it like that for a couple of days until we decide how to handle this."

Kathy felt guilty because she had let Campbell use her car to drive to the prom. She had done the math, and it probably happened then. The truth was her car had nothing to do with Campbell and Chloe having sex and now her being pregnant. They had not mentioned abortion, and she hoped that they wouldn't decide to do that. Kathy sent Campbell a text message first thing the next morning and told him that she wanted to see him and Chloe after school. He texted back that he had to go to work. She told him to call the restaurant and tell the manager that he might be a little late, and she would drive him so he wouldn't be too late.

Chloe got there first. She was in a good mood, not at all like the day before. They chatted briefly, and Campbell walked into the classroom. Kathy asked them to come into her office so nobody would see them in the classroom. She asked them if they had talked any more and if they had made any decisions.

"Miss Robinson, we talked almost all night. We made two decisions." Campbell looked at Chloe before he continued. "We definitely don't want to have an abortion."

Kathy silently thanked God.

"And Chloe wants to tell her mother. The only thing is she won't let me be with her."

"Why, Chloe?"

"My mama and I are close. We talk about everything. I just think it would be better if I tell her myself and then we talk to Campbell."

"But Miss Robinson, I don't want Mrs. Matthews to think I'm not taking my responsibility."

"Campbell, I will tell her. I will make her understand," Chloe said.

Campbell put his head in his hands.

Kathy spoke up. "What are you going to do about telling your mother, Campbell?"

His response was a big sigh.

"I suggest you tell her and Chloe tell her mom, and then we can talk again."

Campbell looked at Chloe, and she nodded her head yes. He exhaled loudly. His life was spinning out of control.

Chloe called her mother and asked if they could have dinner alone.

"Sure. I'll tell your dad to plan to feed himself."

Chloe laughed. "Okay. I'll cook for you."

"I wonder what else you're cooking up."

"Why, mother, whatever do you mean?"

"Uh-huh. I bet you don't know."

Chloe was glad her mother would be in a good mood when she got home.

After they ate and talked about some general things, Chloe had to bite the bullet.

"Ma, I need to tell you something, and you're not going to be happy."

Sandra folded her hands in front of her and looked directly at Chloe.

In one breath, she blurted it out. "I missed my period and took a home pregnancy test, and it was positive."

Sandra leaned against the back of the chair, folded her arms, and exhaled loudly. "Well…you're right. I'm not happy to hear that. But thank you for telling me and not making a hasty decision. Have you told Campbell?"

"Yes. I told him the day before yesterday, when I took the test. He's telling his mom now too. We talked to Miss Robinson yesterday and today, and she wants us and Campbell to come see her tomorrow."

"Why Miss Robinson?"

"She and Campbell are close, and he said that he knew she would know what to do." Chloe's voice cracked, and she started to cry.

Sandra put her arm around her. She wanted to cry too, but she couldn't, not now. When Chloe finally calmed down, Sandra walked her to the den and sat facing her on the sofa. Before she could say anything, Chloe spoke up.

"Ma, Campbell wanted to be here when I told you, but I told him that I wanted to tell you by myself. So please don't be mad at him. He's not running from his responsibility."

"I'm glad to know that, and I'm not angry with either one of you, but I hope you two understand that your life as you know it has changed forever."

Chloe was quiet.

Sandra continued. "What have you all discussed?" It was taking every ounce of God in her not to lose it. She knew that that would serve no purpose.

"The only thing we decided for sure is no abortion."

"I'm glad to hear you say that. So your options are to have a baby and raise it or put it up for adoption."

"Mommy, I don't know what to do."

Sandra didn't address that comment. In her heart she knew that she would support the decision they made, but Chloe Matthews needed to stew for a while.

"You know that I have to tell your dad and he is going to want to kill Campbell."

Chloe started to cry again. Between sobs, she managed to tell her mother, "He didn't force me or anything. He never disrespected me in the least. I kissed him first."

"Please don't tell your father that!"

"It was the first and only time for both of us."

Campbell knew his mother wouldn't be happy when he told her, but he wasn't expecting her to be so angry, and he was surprised that she had suggested abortion.

Chloe and Sandra talked a while longer while they cleaned up the kitchen. Sandra didn't want Roderick to see Chloe upset, so she told her to go to her room and she would tell him that she had gone to bed early.

"Mommy, please don't tell him tonight. Please wait until tomorrow."

Sandra promised her that she would wait.

Chloe hugged her mother. "Please forgive me, Mommy. I love you."

"I love you too, Chloe, and I forgive you. Don't worry. We'll work this out."

Chloe went to her room and called Campbell. She had felt her phone vibrate twice. She knew it was him. They shared the stories of their mothers' reactions.

"Campbell, if you apologize again, I am going to hang up."

"No. Please don't hang up. What do you *really* want to do?"

"I'm not sure. I hadn't given much thought to adoption until my mom brought it up. I was really trying to figure out how we can go to school and raise a baby."

"It will be hard, but we can do it if you want to," Campbell said.

"What do you really want to do?" Chloe asked him.

"I guess like you said, figure out how we can take care of our child."

The words got stuck in his throat. Chloe could hear her parents talking, and she wanted to pretend she was asleep if her father knocked on her door. She told Campbell that she would call him back. She could not face her father. She knew they would have to eventually, but not then, not yet.

Of all the things Sandra had imagined for Chloe, that sure wasn't it. She knew that Roderick was going to be incensed. She would tell him herself, and then they would talk with Chloe. But she couldn't and wouldn't break her promise. She would wait until the next day.

How could Chloe let this happen? As Sandra thought about it, she and Roderick were partly to blame for giving her so much freedom, but they thought that they could trust her. And they had been able to until that point. Chloe had straight A's and had never been in trouble. She had friends and was involved in extracurricular activities. And if anything was for sure, Chloe had a plan for her career, and a husband and babies were years down the road. She wasn't a bad kid; she just made a bad decision.

"She had the nerve to say she kissed him first. Rod would have heart failure," she said out loud to herself. *So now what?*

Sandra was more at peace about it than she was when Chloe told her. God was so amazing.

Before she went to bed, Kathy prayed for the baby, Campbell, Chloe, the situation, and herself. She wanted to be clear about her advice to them. She would do her best to convince them to give the baby up for adoption. And she would help them find a family to give their baby to. HCC had a resourceful congregation. She knew she could make that happen. Her spirit was settled about it, and God would do the rest.

"God, You do all things well, and You made this baby to bless somebody. Please show us this child's destiny."

It was obvious that Kathy was more prepared to meet them than they were to meet with her. Sandra was there too.

Campbell reached for Chloe's hand as soon as he saw her and didn't let it go until the conversation was over.

"Chloe and Campbell, did you all talk any more?"

"Yes, ma'am. But we haven't figured out how to make all this work, how we can stay in school and have a baby too," Campbell said, looking at Chloe, who was nodding her head in agreement.

"I want to offer what I think is a workable solution. I want you to prayerfully consider putting the baby up for adoption."

They all looked at each other and then back at Kathy.

"If you are amenable to that, I'll do some research."

"That's an option I suggested to Chloe, and I agree that it's a workable solution." Sandra tried not to sound demanding or like it was her final decision to make, but she had sense enough to know that the bulk of the responsibility of this situation was on her family. Emotionally and physically, Chloe would have the most to deal with, and certainly financially they would have to take care of things. But most of all she knew that Chloe and Campbell had too much future ahead of them to add a baby to the mix, not to mention that neither of them was mature enough to be parents.

$\mathscr{S}$IXTY-ONE

Jill had major jet lag, but she was excited and wanted to tell Leah about her trip. She had hundreds of pictures to show her.

Leah hadn't been out much, but Katherine had agreed to let her go out with Jill for a while. They picked up some food from Lola's and went to Leah's condo. She hadn't been there since the day she got sick. Kathy kept it neat and clean, but not as immaculate as Leah had.

Jill told Leah all about London, the wedding, Raja's parents, and Tara and Robert. She told her about their whirlwind day in Paris and their first kiss. Leah was totally engaged in the conversation and the pictures. She laughed about Raja's parents and gave Jill a high-five about the teapot. Jill told her that she wanted to do something special for him to say thank you. Leah suggested flowers, but they decided on a fruit bouquet and a card with a personal note.

Jill didn't want Leah to get tired, so she insisted that they go back to her parents' house.

"Can we please make one stop first, at Bella's shop?"

When they arrived, Bella was delighted to see Leah and to know that she was walking unassisted.

"I want to look at my dress."

"We need to schedule your final fitting too."

Janis couldn't believe her eyes. There were Leah and Jill, going into the bridal shop. Leah was walking. She was well.

What can I do to stop that wedding? she thought to herself. Grant had not been answering her calls. *Maybe I should call Leah. No. Her family will for sure have me arrested. I have to think of something. I might just have to wait and show up at the wedding and object.*

Looking at the dress seemed to give Leah energy. She went home and had her mom and Kathy go over the timeline with her. The wedding was eight weeks away.

When she talked with Grant later, she asked him if he had worked on the details of their honeymoon. He assured her that it was all taken care of. She had no idea where they were going. He only told her to find her passport and said she would need warm weather clothes. They talked over some other wedding details, and then she told Grant that she was planning to go back to work, at least part time. He hadn't seen her in a few months, so he didn't have a firsthand assessment of her progress. She sounded strong, but he wasn't sure. He asked her to just wait until after the honeymoon, careful not to give away the surprise that they would be moving to DC.

"By the way, how long will it be before I will be able to actually move out there?"

"I'm working on that right now." He needed to change the subject. "Did GG and my mom give you their part of the guest list?"

"Yes. And Jill put everything in the computer, so that's done. All we need to do is print the envelopes."

They talked for a good while, and Grant was ecstatic when they hung up. Leah was back. He had never admitted it to anyone, but at one point he didn't know if they were going to be able to get married. He loved her no matter what, but he knew that she wouldn't marry him if she had not gotten well. Leah was a very proud woman, and if she could not be a wife to him in every sense of the word, she would not marry him.

As Grant continued to think about their conversation, an e-mail popped up on the screen. It was from Leah with a pre-wedding schedule.

Kirby had been up almost an hour before Enoch realized that she was up.

"Babe, I'm so sorry you're sick. Please forgive us!"

"You and your son?"

"Yeah."

She wasn't as sick that morning as she had been. Belinda suggested that she eat a couple of saltine crackers and sip some peppermint tea as soon as she got up. That had helped a lot.

I have a lot to do today, and this little boy is going to have to cooperate, she thought. *But what if it's a little girl? That would be fine too. I'm just grateful I'm doing so well. It's going to be challenging without Belinda being here when the baby comes, and Grammy will be gone too. But I'm willing to make the sacrifice if it means that Belinda will be happy. I will just have to talk to Enoch about either hiring a part-time person to help at the office or getting a part-time housekeeper.*

Kirby's thoughts were interrupted by the phone. It was Belinda calling to talk about the twins' birthday celebration.

"Do you think we are springing too much on them all at once?" Kirby asked Belinda.

"No, because we don't want them to figure it out on their own and you are gaining weight so quickly that they are going to notice."

"Yeah, I am gaining quickly and early. I haven't told Enoch, but I am going to ask for an ultrasound to make sure there are not two babies."

"How would you feel about that?"

"I don't know now because he said that there was only one. I expected him to say twins, and when he didn't, I dismissed the thought."

They continued to plan the party. It would be at Enoch and Kirby's house on Sunday after church. Belinda had told the girls that they were going to do something different. They asked if they could invite one friend each. She told them no, that it would be a family birthday. They asked if family included Ben, Grammy, and Auntie. She assured them that it did. They reminded her that they needed to visit Leah. Her birthday was the day before theirs.

Gretchen and Clay had planned Leah's birthday celebration, Gretchen not knowing the whole story. She was preparing food and getting flowers. Clay was responsible for the technical parts. He also would have the official gift: the copy of Grant's transfer papers. Everything would be set up in a conference room at the church. The Robinsons, the Sturdivants, and the Strauss family, including Raja, were invited. Clay had also invited Cicely. Trey had invited Kim Horng.

SIXTY-TWO

Chloe was in her room. Sandra and Roderick were downstairs. Sandra knew that there was no way to do it easily, so she decided to jump in with both feet.

"I need to tell you something, but you can't comment until I finish."

"Well, make sure you include the cost so I won't have to ask."

She reached for both his hands. "Chloe missed her period and took a pregnancy test, and it's positive."

Roderick stared directly into her face. He was completely silent and completely still. After a full minute had passed, he took his hands out of Sandra's, stood, and kicked over the barstool he had been sitting on. He started toward the stairs, but Sandra managed to stop him.

"Talk to me before you talk to her. Please, Rod. Please."

He still hadn't said anything. Another minute passed before he finally spoke. "Chloe is smarter than that. She knows better. I don't know much about this Campbell, but he's obviously pretty irresponsible."

"Rod, they were both irresponsible."

"I'm sure that having premarital sex was not Chloe's idea."

"She said that he didn't force her, and I believe her. He wanted to be here when she told me, but she said no."

Roderick went on and on about the situation being Campbell's fault, and Sandra found herself defending him. Rod even implied that Chloe might have been raped, a comment that Sandra immediately shot down.

"Sandra, we have always told Chloe no sex before marriage. She's sixteen years old and can hardly take care of herself. How is she going to take care of a baby? And you know that Campbell won't be able to help. He works in a restaurant and has to help his family."

Sandra knew that the discussion was going to be tough, but she didn't expect Roderick to go down the "it's all Campbell's fault" road. He went on and on about Campbell messing up Chloe's plans for college and law school.

This is not all that young man's fault, and Roderick has to face that. "Rod, we had sex before we got married. We just didn't get caught."

"True, but we were not sixteen either."

"Campbell is not the fall guy. Your daughter…was a willing participant. Now you can have a rational conversation with her or alienate her by saying all the wrong things. Be grateful they didn't go somewhere and have an abortion."

Sandra went on to tell him about the meeting with Campbell and Kathy's suggestion of putting the baby up for adoption. She told him that she thought that that was a viable option and that she thought they should encourage Chloe to seriously consider it.

"There are a lot of decisions to make and some planning that has to happen, and we need to be supportive of both kids." Sandra put her arms around Roderick and held him tight. After a few minutes, she went upstairs to see Chloe.

Janis went back to her office determined to find out the date of Leah and Grant's wedding. She looked up the engagement announcements on the local newspaper website. The exact date wasn't in the announcement.

She went to the church website to view the calendar, but it wasn't there either. She took a chance and called the church. She wouldn't ask about Leah specifically. She had to make up a story.

What am I going to do if I get the information? Nobody is going to let me in that church. The restraining order will prevent it, but they probably have my picture posted on the wall like a wanted poster. I will figure that out later. Right now I need the date.

She called the church office and inquired about having a wedding in June. She asked about two dates. She was told that there was no available date in June. That wasn't what she wanted to know.

There has to be a way to find out. It isn't top secret information; it's not like they are celebrities or royalty.

If she could find out when Grant was coming home, she would figure out a way to detain him and convince him not to marry Leah. If he wouldn't listen, she would have to take matters to another level. She would do what she had to.

Leah does not deserve Grant. She doesn't need him, and she won't have him. I hope he's reasonable and doesn't make me use force.

Chloe gathered her strength and went downstairs to face her dad. Whatever he said, she would just have to deal with it. She didn't tell Campbell. He was at work, and that was just as well. He was hovering, and she wasn't up to that today. Campbell meant well, but she knew how to deal with her parents.

Sandra reminded Rod that he could make or break his relationship with Chloe based on what he said. He didn't know that Chloe was at home but wasn't surprised when she walked in and asked if they could talk. Chloe liked being on offense.

Rod told her how disappointed he was but that he was glad she didn't make another bad decision by having an abortion. He told her that he and Sandra would support the decision she made but agreed that adoption was the best option. She reminded him that it was not just her decision and that Campbell had input too. He reminded her that he needed to speak with Campbell.

Leah, Kathy, and their parents had dinner together, and Leah made two announcements: she was moving back into her condo and she was going back to work part time. Lee asked if she was really up to going back to work. Leah explained that she was. Her further explanation was interesting. She explained to her family that she felt strong and that her head was clear.

"You know how it feels when you get off a flight and your ears are stopped up? All of a sudden they pop and you can hear. Well, that's what happened, like my head just cleared."

"Why don't I just stay with you temporarily?" Kathy asked. "I can help you get packed to move!"

A look of relief crossed Lee's face.

"I think that's a good idea," Katherine said.

"Yeah, that will work. I don't know what I can move and what I can't, and Grant doesn't seem to be in a hurry to tell me."

The conversation moved to the wedding and Lee grumbling about the cost. The truth was he was grumbling because they expected him to. As long as Leah was happy, he wasn't really concerned about the cost. He would never admit to his wife or daughters that a month before, he didn't think there would be a wedding.

$\mathscr{S}$IXTY-THREE

Raja had been in surgery for most of the day. He had had a bagel and a cup of tea at six that morning and nothing since. He also had not checked his messages all day and decided he should. A message from his mother was not what he wanted to hear at that point in his day. The second message was from Jill, which brought a smile to his face. He returned her call. They talked about when they would see each other again. Jill also mentioned Leah and Grant's wedding. She wanted to confirm that he would be there Friday in time for the rehearsal dinner and the party.

"The whole weekend is on my calendar. I have no surgery scheduled, and I am not on call."

"Fantastic! Do you want me to book you a room, or do you want to stay with Trey?"

"Have you spoken with him about it?"

"No, but I will. I'm sure he won't mind."

After he talked with Jill, Raja headed to the cafeteria.

His phone rang before he could finish his salad. It was his mother. The wedding was almost a month before, but she was still angry with him for bringing Jill. She told him that he had embarrassed their family by bringing her when he knew that they had arranged for him to meet a young lady whom they wanted him to marry.

"Manavendra, you brought disgrace to your family, you and your cousin, Tara, bringing those people to a family occasion. My heart, Manavendra. My heart. I have been very ill—"

"Mother, stop it. Stop it now. You are not sick because I brought Jill to London. You are sick because you can't have what you want." Raja raised his voice. "Get over it, Mother, or you and I are going to be in the same situation as Tara and her parents."

"This family has disowned Tara. I know that's not what you want."

"What I want, Mother, is for you to let me make my own decisions. If you refuse to do that, then I refuse to communicate with you."

Before she could respond, he said good-bye and hung up.

Raja felt bad. He had never talked to his mother that way. He had never disrespected her. He had always done whatever his parents asked because they—particularly his mother—could make him feel guilty. But not that time. Jill was just that important to him. They could accept her and accept their relationship or not. He was not backing down. He picked up the phone to call Tara. She would understand.

Cicely was pleasantly surprised when the flowers arrived at the nurse's station. The card read "Miss you. See you soon? Clay." They hadn't seen each other in a week and had only talked briefly. She had been working an odd twelve-hour shift. She would call him, say thank you for the flowers, and tell him that she would be off Saturday and Sunday.

Clay really did miss Cicely. He had seen Delia once that week. He could have gone back. He didn't want to. He was tired of her, plain and simple. They had no depth to their conversations. She aroused him physically but not intellectually. Cicely was sassy, intelligent, and would never have let him get away with what Delia did. He would not renew his contract with the agency. That would get him out of his obligation with Jeremy. The decision was made. He just had to tell her.

Campbell's heart was racing. He was on his way to the Matthews' home. He knew that he had to man up. He was the responsible party, and like it or not, he had to act like it. He and Ms. Robinson had talked. She advised him to be honest and to trust Chloe. She was right. She knew her parents.

Chloe answered the door with a big smile that put Campbell at ease. She invited him into the den. Sandra came in with a pitcher of iced tea. Roderick was right behind her. From the looks of things, someone who didn't know the situation would think it was a social call.

The conversation went surprisingly well. Chloe took the lead. She explained to her parents that she and Campbell had decided to put the baby up for adoption and that Miss Robinson would help them find a good home. There was a collective sigh of relief.

"What can we do to help?" Roderick asked.

"I don't want to go back to Hattiesville High next year. I want to either go to private school or to DC to Aunt Natalie's."

The thought of her being gone brought tears to Sandra's eyes. Campbell had begged her not to go to DC. He wanted to be able to see her.

"We'll work it out," Sandra said.

Campbell needed to say something. He addressed his comment to Roderick. "Sir, I'll do whatever Chloe needs me to do to make the best of this situation. I don't want her to leave, but I'll support her decision."

"Campbell, I don't know you well, but Chloe has assured me that you are being supportive, so I believe you. But let me add that neither one of you were very responsible or we wouldn't be having this conversation."

"You're right, sir," Campbell said.

They talked for a few more minutes, and Campbell left. Putting the baby up for adoption was a good idea. Sandra just hoped that they wouldn't change their minds after the baby started kicking and moving. Right now it was not a real baby in their minds.

Campbell called Chloe as soon as he was home. He asked one important question: "Are we going to want to keep the baby when we see it?"

"We won't see it. I will tell the doctor to put me to sleep and take the baby away."

"So do you mean we won't know if it's a boy or girl?"

"No, Campbell. We won't know."

"Chloe, I don't like that."

She started to cry and admitted to him that she was afraid that if she saw the baby she would change her mind. He told her that he understood because he felt the same way. He went on to tell her about his conversation with Kathy. He told her about open and closed adoptions. After almost an hour on the phone, they decided to tell Kathy that they wanted an open adoption. They also decided not to tell their parents yet. As they were about to hang up, Campbell asked her not to leave and go to Washington.

"I don't want to deal with the gossip."

"I understand, but I don't want you to go."

$\mathscr{S}$IXTY-FOUR

Clay and Gretchen had everything in order for the party. Cicely suggested that Clay have the envelope gift-wrapped. He didn't see the significance, so she did it herself. Leah was excited. She loved the decorations. Her friends and family were there. It was a good party.

Clay dimmed the lights, and Grant appeared on the screen.

"Grant! Hey!" Leah said.

"Hey, babe. Happy birthday!"

"Thank you!"

The group greeted Grant. He was surprised but glad to see his dad.

Clay handed Leah the box. She opened it and looked puzzled when she saw the envelope. She slowly pulled the papers out. The room was completely quiet.

Leah read the top page, looked up at the screen, and read it again. She couldn't say anything, so Grant spoke up.

"So how do you like your gift?"

"I love it!" She looked at the rest of the group. "Grant is being transferred to Walter Reed!"

Everybody cheered, Gretchen louder than everybody else.

The party had a whole new energy. Leah was shocked. She didn't even know Grant wanted to transfer. She was looking forward to the experience of living in another country, but she liked the idea of being close to her family.

Grant and Leah talked later that night. He gave her details, and she told him that she would be going back to work part time. They prayed together before they hung up. Grant thanked God for their lives moving forward.

Paul had had several good days and decided that he was up to attending the midweek gathering at church. He asked Clay to accompany him. Clay was an irregular midweek attendee, but he said yes. He had planned to have dinner with Cicely and see Delia later to tell her things had to change. He called Cicely and asked if they could have an early dinner and go to church afterward. She said that she would but needed to meet him there. She had to be on duty at 10:00 p.m. He called Delia to cancel. He told her that he was going to church with his uncle. Delia didn't believe him and decided that she was going to HCC to see for herself.

The bishop had asked Ben to teach, and his message dealt with making godly decisions, doing what you know is the right thing to do, not what feels good or what's easy.

Clay was particularly convicted and took the message as his confirmation that he needed to end things with Delia. God was giving him a chance to do the right thing. He decided that he would call Delia after he got his uncle home and settled. He would go ahead and face the music.

Delia arrived a little late on purpose. She wanted to sit in the back so she could look for Clay. She knew that there was a special area for wheelchairs, so if Clay was being honest, his uncle should be easy to spot. Sure enough, there was Paul, so where was Clay? She didn't see him until the service was almost over. He was walking out with a female who was dressed in scrubs. It was the lady from the pizza parlor and from his house! Delia wanted to disappear. She couldn't walk out. She didn't want to run into him, but she was at the point of tears. Was he coming back in to take his uncle out? She had to get away without being seen. Her hands were shaking.

That's why he canceled. It had nothing to do with his uncle.

She decided that she would call him and tell him that she needed to see him that night, no matter what. It was over between them.

By the time Delia got out of the parking lot traffic, she had calmed down. By the time she got home, she had decided that she wouldn't tell Clay that they were through. There had to be an explanation.

Just as she walked in, the phone rang. It was Clay. He wanted to come over.

"Of course you can."

Ben was as excited about the twins' birthday party as they were. According to Belinda, he had bought too many gifts, including a three-piece luggage set for each of them. He would tell them to pack their things to move to Atlanta. The dilemma was what to tell them first—about Ben going to Atlanta or Enoch and Kirby having a baby.

Kirby had prepared the twins' favorite dishes, and Belinda brought the birthday cake. Ben, Grammy, and Aunt Avis came in with so many packages that it looked like Christmas. After dinner and ice cream and cake, Enoch asked Brittani and Brianna if they wanted his gift first or Ben's gift first. They giggled and looked at their mother. She shrugged her shoulders and smiled. After a few seconds of whispering between them, they decided that they wanted Uncle Enoch's gift first.

There were the usual books and clothes but then Enoch presented them with a doll each—not a Bratz doll or a Barbie doll, but a baby doll.

"I want you to practice changing diapers so you can help Auntie K and me with our new baby."

They screamed, jumped up and down, and hugged Enoch and Kirby. Brittani wanted to know if the baby would be a boy or a girl.

"We don't know. It's going to be a surprise," Kirby answered. "What do you want it to be?"

"A boy," they answered in unison. They knew that that was what Uncle Enoch would want.

A few more minutes of that conversation and Belinda was nervous. She didn't know how they were going to react to Ben's "gift." She spoke up.

"Okay. One more gift."

All eyes were on Ben. He gave them a charm for their bracelets, DVDs, tennis rackets and balls, and then the luggage.

They oohed and aahed over the luggage for a minute, and then Ben made his announcement.

"And I hope you will pack the bags and come to Atlanta."

The room was completely quiet. Everybody was looking at Ben, so nobody noticed that Brittani was crying.

Grammy finally looked at her. "Brittani, sugar, what is it?"

"What if my leg hurts again and I have to go back to the hospital? Minister Coffey will be far away."

"How far is Atlanta anyway?" Brianna asked, putting her arm around Brittani.

Brittani was crying, and Brianna was firing questions.

"Mommy, are you sad?"

This was going totally different from the way any of the adults had envisioned it. Belinda looked at Ben. Her eyes were asking for his help.

Ben opened his arms wide and motioned to both of them. With one on each knee, he explained that he wanted them and their mom to go to Atlanta to live with him. He was saying more than he intended to. As he talked, Brittani's tears dried and he got both of them to smile.

"Are we going?" Brianna asked her mother.

"I'm thinking about it. There is a lot of planning to do."

"Are you going, Grammy? Are you going, Auntie?"

"We'll see too," Auntie answered.

Ben noticed how quiet Grammy had been. He would be sure to talk to her about it.

$\mathscr{S}$IXTY-FIVE

Delia was a little antsy waiting for Clay. She wanted to tell him that she had been at church and seen him with his friend, but she didn't want to make him angry.

Clay had gotten his thoughts together. He would tell Delia that he didn't want to continue their relationship. He didn't want to hurt her, but if he had to, he would admit that it was only physical. And if he had to, he would tell her that his real relationship was with Cicely. She couldn't threaten him with the agency because he had already told them that he wasn't renewing his contract. It was over, plain and simple. He had to get back on track. He knew that God had given him grace, even winked at his sin for a season, but his time was up. And he knew that if he wanted Cicely in his life, he had to make some changes. She would not settle for anything less. She had standards, and he had to meet them or keep it moving.

Clay headed to Delia's house. He was ready to have the conversation. Delia seemed to be in a particularly good mood. They chatted briefly about Jeremy before she reached for his hand and turned off the lamp. Clay didn't get up from the sofa and asked her to turn the light back on. Delia was looking at Clay.

"Dee, this isn't working for me anymore."

She folded her arms.

"We don't have a real relationship, and that's not fair to you or me."

"I guess it's working for you and the lady at church tonight."

He looked surprised.

"Yes, I saw you. And I know she is the same person I saw you with getting the pizza and that day at your house."

"You're right."

"So you have been cutting out on both of us."

"Delia, I haven't cut out on you. You and I never had an established relationship."

"What do you consider established? We've been seeing each other for months." She had raised her voice.

"We've been having sex for months. That's not a relationship."

They went back and forth until Clay got tired of the debate. The bottom line was that he was not coming back, and she needed to understand that. The conversation was becoming an argument. He told her that she had no self-respect, and that made her furious. She told him that he didn't have any either.

"Touché! You are exactly right, and I need to fix that. Look, Delia, I'm done. I'll talk to Jeremy and square things with him, but this is it for us."

Delia had a big smile on her face. She held Clay's face in her hands and gently kissed him on the lips. "This is not it for us, Clay. I'm pregnant."

Clay didn't believe Delia, and he told her so. She shrugged her shoulders and smiled.

"Why are you just telling me?"

"I just found out."

Clay was acting cool, but he wasn't. Delia was acting like she was telling the truth, but she wasn't. He needed some time to think. He didn't want to do or say the wrong thing.

"Well, Delia, we'll just have to work it out, but I need to go."

"Are you going to tell your friend it's over?"

"I'm not going to tell her anything."

The wedding was exactly one month away. Everything was in place, thanks to Kathy and Gretchen. Leah was back at work but not doing the supervisor's duties. That way she could leave on time every day.

Grant would be home two days before the wedding. He would be in DC the ten days prior. She would move a month after they were married. He would only have a week at home after the honeymoon.

Leah had started to look for jobs in the area, but Grant convinced her to wait until she got there. There was no hurry, he told her.

Janis had found out the exact day of the wedding—a friend of hers who worked at the hospital told her—and she had a plan to detain Grant. She had become consumed with stopping the wedding. She knew that it was essential that the timing be perfect. There was no way she was going to let Grant marry Leah and humiliate her again. She had borne the embarrassment of the Hattiesville community once at the hands of Grant Sturdivant, and she had no intention of allowing it to happen again. She needed a weapon just in case.

"Man, I don't know what to believe. She might be lying, but she might not be."

"Clay, I thought you said you were using condoms."

"We usually did, but you know how once or twice you get caught up in the moment."

"No, I don't know. Damn, Clay. What's your plan?"

"I don't have one."

Clay knew that he couldn't tell anybody but Grant what Delia said. He knew that Grant would be angry but still help him figure out what to do. His advice was for Clay to make Delia prove she was pregnant. Clay knew that Delia would be angry, but Grant was right. She needed to prove it. If it was true, he would have to tell Cicely the truth and hope she cared enough to stick around. He absolutely would not marry Delia. They would just have to work things out with the baby.

Clay was scared. It was a first for him. He had always had an eye for the ladies and usually had more than one in his life at any given time. His lifestyle had caught up with him. The other point Grant made to Clay was that since he had gotten "caught up," he needed to be tested for HIV. That scared Clay more than the thought of a baby. Clay thought back to what Ben had said in his message the other night: "How do the decisions we make affect our relationship with God and the people we love?"

$\mathscr{S}$IXTY-SIX

Belinda and the girls prayed, and she tucked them in. It had been an interesting evening. She knew that Ben would call, so she decided to call him first. She wasn't sure what she was going to say. Her emotions were mixed. She loved Ben—that she knew for sure—and she knew that he loved her. Telling the girls that he wanted them to come to Atlanta with him was a commitment of sorts, but he had not asked her to marry him. As a matter of fact, he hadn't mentioned marriage or anything related to it since they looked at the rings weeks ago.

She took her journal and wrote for a while and, in the process, decided not to say anything to Ben about marriage. God had the situation, and she wouldn't get in front of Him. Her focus right now needed to be on her operating room training. She would take classes and work in the hospital. That would take a lot of discipline, and she couldn't get distracted.

When she finally called, she knew that something was bothering him. He had called his grandmother after they left Kirby and Enoch's house. She denied that she had been particularly quiet, but she admitted that she was a little overwhelmed by everything that was going on.

"Babe, I don't want her to be sad about this."

"I don't think she's sad. I think she is overwhelmed. You're moving. You want to take Brittani and Brianna with you. And Kirby's having a baby. If she goes to Atlanta, she won't be here to help Kirby. It's a lot. I actually understand how she feels."

"Are you overwhelmed?"

"Somewhat, but for some different reasons."

As they talked, she confided her feelings about school and Kirby but didn't mention getting married.

"It seems like the more things come together, the more opposition comes," he said.

"Oh no, Ben. It's not opposition. It's…it's…all so new. We are all trying to find our place in this new normal."

He was glad that Belinda was in his life. She had a way of making the impossible seem possible. She had offered to talk to Grammy to reassure her that everything was okay. The bishop had told Ben that Belinda would have to be his first disciple and if he was sure about that, then he was right about her. He was sure.

Kirby had gotten Kathy's message but had forgotten to call her back. She remembered as soon as she saw her name on the caller ID. Kirby assumed that Kathy was calling about the wedding. They did talk about that for a few minutes, but Kathy told her that she was calling for another reason. She had a couple of students who were expecting a baby and wanted to put it up for adoption. Kathy wanted to know if Enoch and Kirby were interested in adopting the baby.

Kirby was slightly stunned but interested. She listened attentively to what Kathy had to say.

Kathy did not initially share who the students were, but she did share that they said that they wanted an open adoption.

"I know you need to talk to Enoch, but what's your initial thought?"

"Kathy, you know that God has a sense of humor, right? The timing of this is so funny. Enoch and I found out a few weeks ago that we are having a baby. We decided to wait a bit before telling anybody."

"Congratulations! That's great. I know you all wanted a baby. Well, let me keep thinking."

"Hold on, Kathy. I didn't say no. Can you give me 'til tomorrow and let me talk with Enoch?"

Delia wondered what Clay was thinking. She hoped that he had believed her and was pondering his next step. If he didn't suggest getting married, she would threaten to have an abortion. She would have to fake a miscarriage anyway at some point. He had called earlier, but she didn't answer. She wanted him to stew. She really wanted him to be worried. Later in the day Clay sent Delia an e-mail that simply said, "Will be by tonight to talk."

Good, she thought. *I hope he told missy good-bye.*

Clay hadn't told Cicely anything. But he had talked to a friend at work and gave her the basics of the situation. She told him to buy a home pregnancy test and make Delia prove that she was pregnant. She offered to go get it for him. Clay bought her lunch, and she went with him to get the test. He would know that night for sure. If the test was negative, he would be committed to his relationship with Cicely. If it was positive, he would man up, tell Cicely the truth, ask her to forgive him, and hire an attorney to deal with Delia. Either way his life as he knew it was going to change.

"Lord, You know that Benji and Avis are all I have, but Enoch and Kirby are like my grandchildren too. I don't know what to do. I've lived in this house for over fifty years, and You have blessed me. I want to be close to Benji and his new family, but I don't know if I can really leave here. There's so much here, and I don't know if I want new. Lord, I need to hear from You. What would You have me do?"

Victoria Coffey found herself at a loss for what to do. She never imagined moving. She never considered that Ben would leave the area again, and she never thought that she and Avis might be apart again. She and Belinda had talked, and Belinda assured her that whatever decision she was led to make, Ben would be fine, she and the girls would be fine, and Enoch and Kirby would be fine. Belinda also told her that Ben had not asked her to marry him, so nothing was etched in stone. Grammy didn't tell her, but she was going to address that as soon as she got a chance.

"Lord, if I move, I'll have to sell this house and pack up all this stuff, and I could never drive in Atlanta. I can hardly drive in Charlotte." She laughed to herself. "I just don't know if I want that much change. The truth is seventy-seven is too old to start over."

Enoch was totally amused with what Kirby was telling him. She told him everything that Kathy had told her.

"We thought we were going to have twins anyway, so we'll just have two babies."

He couldn't believe she was asking him to adopt a baby in the midst of having a new baby. It all seemed a little too much. He had heard some guys in the barbershop talking about how expensive diapers were and one of them talking about his child having to have a special formula because of allergies. He had been grateful for not having twins, and now she presented him with that. As far as Enoch was concerned, God and Kirby had a sense of humor.

His really big concern, though, was the part about the open adoption. He didn't want to get involved and then have the kids change their minds or their families change their minds.

How can we raise the child in this small community with the biological family right here? This thing is very uncomfortable to me. Is there any guarantee that five years from now they won't want their baby back?

Enoch said exactly what Kirby expected him to say: "Tell Kathy we'll get back to her in a day or so. I need to give this some prayerful consideration."

SIXTY-SEVEN

Clay arrived at Delia's house, pregnancy test in hand. He had read the instructions, and he knew what he was looking for. Delia came to the door, looking good and smelling good. Jeremy and Crystal weren't there. She figured that they would talk, he would spend the night, and by morning all would be well. She did not expect what was coming.

She didn't waste any time inviting him into her bedroom. That was fine. There was a bathroom in there. She sat on the foot of the bed. He sat in the chair.

"You said that you wanted to talk," Delia said.

Clay and Delia had never been at odds. As a matter of fact, nothing emotional had ever happened between them. This was new. All their dealings had been physical or related to Jeremy.

"Have you been to the doctor?"

"No, not yet. I'll go next week."

"I want you to do something for me."

"Sure, Clay. What it is?"

"I want you to take this pregnancy test."

"Take that pregnancy test! Why? I've already taken one!" Her voice was loud and high-pitched.

"That's what you say, but I didn't see it."

"Why do you have to see it? Why can't you just take my word for it?"

"I want proof, Delia." Clay didn't raise his voice.

"My word, what I tell you, is the only proof you need!"

"I want to see for myself."

"Well, I'm not taking any test!" She slapped the box out of his hand.

He had his answer. She had totally overreacted. Clay had never seen Delia come unglued, but she had that night. She never admitted that she had lied about being pregnant, but her refusal to take the test was so blatant that it spoke volumes. She accused "that woman" of putting him up to it and told Clay that she was jealous because she wasn't having his baby.

Clay left Delia's house relieved. He had dodged a bullet, like his mom used to say. He missed his mom. If things went well between him and Cicely, maybe they would have a little girl one day and name her Millicent after his mother. One thing was for sure: he wouldn't get himself into that situation again.

Cicely was at work, but Clay needed to hear her voice. He called her cell and left a message for her to call him on her break. He had mentioned the wedding and party to her, and he wanted to be sure that she was going to be off. He wanted her with him. He knew that that would be a good time for him to tell her.

"Grammy, I am so hurt that you and Belinda don't think I'm on top of my game!"

"Don't play with me, Benjamin Coffey."

"I am really not playing with you, Ms. Victoria. I got this. I am going to ask Belinda to marry me. Just give me some time. I'll move in God's time." He knew that that would satisfy her.

They talked a while longer. But Grammy still didn't commit to the move to Atlanta.

Everybody expects Belinda to accept my proposal, but there is always a chance she will say no, Ben thought. *Not a big chance, but a chance just the same. She might want to stay in North Carolina to finish school or be here with Kirby. She might be satisfied with a long-distance relationship.*

Ben and Grammy ended their conversation so he could prepare for his appointment. He was meeting with Leah and Grant to talk about the wedding. Leah was coming into the office, and Grant would be on Skype. They had done most of their counseling that way. It would be the last session until the day before the wedding. That day's meeting would be about the ceremony.

"Leah, as it has turned out, I won't get home until the day before the wedding," Grant told her. "As a matter of fact, Clay will probably bring me straight to the church."

Ben observed their interaction, and he could easily see the love in their eyes. He could also see that Leah was still a little fragile. She seemed nervous. Maybe it was the wedding and all that went with it, but Ben wondered if Leah had fully recovered from the aneurysm and the surgery.

$\mathcal{S}$IXTY-EIGHT

The rehearsal was set to start at 5:00 p.m., the same hour as the wedding. There would not be a traditional rehearsal dinner. Leah and Grant had decided to have a party. There had been no bachelor party or bachelorette party—one big wedding party with their family and friends was what they wanted.

The staff from Lola's, including Campbell, had been there since early afternoon, decorating and preparing food. Campbell was grateful for the long day. He needed the distraction and the money. He and Chloe were going to meet the couple who was going to adopt their baby that night. They would be at the party, and Kathy thought that that would be less formal for their first meeting. Kathy had invited Chloe to the party. Neither of their parents had been invited.

Kathy, Jill, and Gretchen had things in order. They had done such a good job that they were afraid they had forgotten something. Gretchen had made arrangements for all of the ladies plus Katherine, Grace, Brittani, and Brianna, to have a spa day on Friday.

Raja would be arriving in time to see Jill before the rehearsal. Jill was looking forward to seeing him. Things were getting pretty serious between them. She was sad, though, that his parents were putting so much pressure on him. His mother was being totally unreasonable. She had gone so far as to tell him that he had to choose between Jill and his family. Tara told Jill to be patient and supportive. It was hard, but she knew that Raja would do the right thing. Jill hoped that his parents would back off. She wanted him to have her in his life and still have a relationship with his family.

As he drove into Hattiesville, Raja played over and over in his mind how he would tell Jill.

How can I blatantly disrespect my parents? The scripture says, "Honor your father and mother."

He knew that they had his best interests at heart. He just hoped he could make Jill understand. She was the most incredible woman he knew. His parents didn't give her a chance.

Kirby had been sick all morning, and Enoch didn't know if she was going to make the rehearsal and party. He thought that the morning sickness would have passed by then, but the doctor assured them that everything was fine. They were both a little nervous about meeting the young expectant couple. Enoch wasn't totally sold on the open adoption idea, but Kirby had been right about the in-vitro, so he trusted her on this.

There had been so much to do to get Brianna and Brittani ready for the wedding that Belinda hadn't spent much time with Ben.

He told her that he would pick her up for the rehearsal since the girls would arrive with the other attendants. Grammy and Auntie were not involved with the rehearsal, but Ben had gotten permission from Leah to invite them.

Grace wanted Paul to skip the rehearsal and the party so he wouldn't be too tired to enjoy the wedding and the reception, but he wouldn't hear it.

"My only son is getting married, and I intend to be there for the whole thing."

She gave up the fight. Gretchen had made all the arrangements, and things were in order, so Grace decided to relax and enjoy herself too. She had been so worried that Leah wasn't going to be well enough to get married. She was immensely grateful to God that the day had come. And Grant being back in the States was icing on the cake.

Katherine couldn't believe that Lee was working. He had a meeting that he said couldn't be scheduled for another day. His flight was due in at 2:00 p.m., which would give him plenty of time if the meeting didn't run over and there were no flight delays. She just wouldn't let herself think about that.

If he is late... She wasn't going to think about it. His armor-bearer would pick him up, and they would meet at the church.

Leah walked into the fellowship hall and literally jumped for joy. It was perfect. She and Kathy went over the last-minute arrangements, and the reception director told them what would be the same and what would be different for the reception. Leah stood there in awe. Tears rolled down her face.

"Don't cry, Leah! You are messing up your makeup!"

She rolled her eyes at her sister, who put her arms around her, and they hugged tightly for a long minute. Leah asked for a glass of water, but she didn't let Kathy see her take the pill. She had had a headache all day.

Janis had called in sick for the second day. Her plan was not coming together. She didn't know if Grant was in town or not.

But he's supposed to get married tomorrow, so he has to be. She laughed to herself. *There will be no marriage tomorrow—not if I have anything to do with it.*

She had not seen him or any evidence of him. She had checked the flight schedule from Frankfurt for the last two weeks and had spent a considerable amount of time in the airport, but to no avail. She had been by the barbershop twice that day and by Lola's and the church. She had to find Clay because she knew that if she found Clay, she would find Grant.

There was a lot going on at the church, but she had not spotted Grant, or Leah, for that matter. The only people she saw that she knew were the ladies from Lola's. It was going to be hard for her to hide in the parking lot, but she would have to figure it out.

Who can I switch with so they won't recognize my car?

Ben and the wedding director had talked prior to the rehearsal, and things were in order. Grant and Clay arrived at the church early enough for Grant to have a few minutes alone with Leah. Clay dropped Grant off at the door and went to park the car. Just as he got out, Delia approached him.

Where did she come from? he thought.

"Clay, may I speak to you for a minute?"

"I don't have much time, Delia." He looked at his watch for emphasis.

"I don't need but a couple of minutes."

They hadn't seen each other since the night he had asked her to take the pregnancy test. They had spoken only once when he called to get her permission to pick up Jeremy from baseball practice. He and Jeremy had talked, and he told Jeremy that he was going to be assigned to a new Big Brother. Jeremy was okay with it. He just asked Clay if he could still call him sometimes.

"Clay, I want to apologize for lying about being pregnant. I panicked when you said the relationship wasn't working for you. I needed a way to keep you around, keep you in my life."

"Dee…uh…Delia, we didn't have a relationship. We were not dating or courting, whatever you want to call it. We were having sex."

"But you had to have feelings for me, or do you just have sex with anybody?"

"My feelings for you were physical. You are beautiful. You have an amazing body, and the sex was great. It didn't go any further than that."

Tears were streaming down her face. She looked embarrassed by what Clay was saying.

"Do you remember me telling you that our lack of having a relationship was your fault?"

"Yes. Why?"

"But you never figured it out, did you? The reason I said that is because men are only as faithful as their options. You allowed me to have options. You didn't hold me accountable, and I took advantage of that. You were good with me spending the night and not even calling you back." He looked at his watch. "I gotta go, but hear me on this. You need to step up your game, have some pride, don't be so easy. Don't let anybody else do you like I did."

"So what about your friend? I guess she's not easy and she has pride. If I was like her, I guess you would like me." She was being sarcastic.

Clay chuckled and shook his head. "She's a class act, and we have a real relationship. We talk. We laugh. We eat together, things you and I never did. She made it clear to me that we would not have sex until and unless we are married. And you know what, Delia? I'm fine with that."

He walked away.

Ben had suggested to the wedding director that since Leah would be seated during the rehearsal, Belinda could be the one to stand in for the bride. She was a little surprised when the director asked her, but she accepted. She blushed when Ben gave her a single long-stemmed pink rose to use as the bridal bouquet. They hadn't been very public about their relationship, so it was a major statement.

The rehearsal went like clockwork. Grant clowned a bit, teasing Belinda about being the bride. When the wedding director asked at the end if anybody had any questions, Ben stepped up and said he had one.

He took Belinda by the hand and got down on one knee. Grant stepped out of the way. A collective gasp went through the group. The sanctuary was completely quiet.

"Belinda." His voice cracked. He cleared his throat. "Belinda, I love you very much, and I want to spend the rest of my life with you."

Belinda knew that everybody could hear her heart beating. She was looking down at Ben, and he was looking directly into her eyes.

"You are my best friend and my soul mate. I praise God every day for finding you. Will you bless me forever by being my wife?" He slipped the ring on her finger.

With a big smile, she said, "Yes."

The party was off to a great start. There was plenty of food and great music. Leah's headache had eased considerably, and she was having the time of her life. It was like a fairy tale come true. All the people she loved were there, and she was marrying Prince Charming. God had smiled on her, and she was eternally grateful.

Ben's proposal to Belinda exasperated the celebration. The twins had run to Belinda, screaming. Grammy and Auntie wiped tears, and everybody else was surprised. Belinda had been totally and genuinely shocked. Enoch wanted to know what Ben would have done if she had said no.

When Raja arrived at the church, the rehearsal had already started. Jill was standing in her place at the front of the church. He let his imagination run away with him for a minute. He imagined her standing there in a wedding gown.

With all the excitement, the party was going well. Raja hated to pull Jill away, but he was prolonging the inevitable. He finally asked her if they could go somewhere and talk for a few minutes. He looked so serious. Jill got up immediately, took his hand, and walked out of the fellowship hall. They went outside into the courtyard.

"Raja, are you okay?"

"Yeah, I'm okay. I apologize for pulling you away from the party, but I need to tell you something and I didn't want it to wait."

Jill's heart was beating fast. "What is it?"

She sat down on the bench, and he sat down beside her.

"You know that my parents and I have been at odds since we went to London for Yash's wedding. There is a lot more to it than I have shared with you. They have given me an ultimatum: to choose between you and my family. Jill, I love my parents, and I am their only child. I can't imagine life without them. Sure they, well, my mother, drives me crazy, but they're my parents. I know you understand because you love your family too and you understand how important family is."

Jill was getting angry, but she didn't say anything. She couldn't believe that he was letting them control him and his life.

He continued. "I had a long talk with Tara, and, of course, she told me to cut my ties with them and go on with my life. But how can I? Even the scriptures address how we are to treat our parents."

As he continued to talk, Jill was thinking to herself that she would not let him ruin the occasion for her. Leah had fought her way back, and she was getting married the next day. Raja could go back to Chapel Hill and out of her life. Tears were stinging the back of her eyes.

"Jill, you are so important to me, and I don't want you out of my life either."

She was thinking, *Okay. Here it comes. Can we still be friends?* She was going to say no.

As if Raja was reading her mind, he said, "And I don't want us to be just friends. I want more than that. So I have made a major decision, but I have to know that you are with me, that you want what I want. Once I tell my parents, you and Tara will be my family."

Jill took a deep breath.

"I don't want you to think I am a terrible person or an ungrateful child. Jill, I am committed to making our relationship work, and if that means that I have to cut my ties with my parents, so be it. For my whole life I have done everything my parents asked, but not this time. I want you, Jill, more than I want their approval."

Her heart was melting. She wanted Raja too, but how could she let him sever his ties with his parents? This was very serious. What if he resented her for that one day? *God, please tell me what to say*, she thought to herself.

"Raja, you are very important to me too, and I don't want to be out of your life. Yes, Raja, I am with you. I will be your family. I will be who you need me to be. Family is who loves you when you need them."

He stood and pulled her into his arms. They held each other without saying anything.

The door to the patio opened, and Jill looked up to see Clay and Cicely hand in hand. Clay winked at her. She smiled and realized that they had been gone for a while and needed to get back inside.

"Clay Sturdivant, why did you take me away from my shrimp, bring me out here, interrupt Jill and Dr. Raja, and you're just standing here, grinning?"

He put his arms around her, kissed her forehead, and stepped back. He looked into her eyes and said, "I love you, Cicely." Before she could say anything, he went on. "I have had a good run, but I'm done with the lying, the deception, and the games. I will tell you my story later, but I just want to say to you right here, right now, that I have asked God to forgive me for my foolishness, and I hope you will find me worthy of you and your heart."

Janis had switched cars with her brother and parked his truck in the back of the parking lot. A few people left, and she saw someone come out and put trash in the Dumpster, but she sat there for what seemed like hours. She had spotted Clay's car, and that's what she needed to keep an eye on. People started to come out, and eventually, she saw Clay walking a lady to her car, but no Grant. A few minutes later, Grant and Leah walked out arm in arm, her sister and a couple of other people behind them. Grant walked her to the car. They stood and held each other for a long while. Janis closed her eyes. She had to stay focused.

She reached in her pocketbook to make sure the gun was on top. She had never fired a gun before, and she hoped Grant would cooperate and she wouldn't have to. She also hoped that she wouldn't have to hurt Clay in the process. All she wanted Grant to do was call off the wedding and take the time to establish a relationship with her. She knew that if he just gave her a chance, she could make him happy and be a good wife to him. Once she and Grant were married, she would be well respected in the community and Leah would be the second-class citizen.

Clay walked over and said something to Grant. They laughed and shook hands. Clay got in the car with the lady, and Grant got in Clay's car on the driver's side. This was working better than she had planned.

Janis pulled out of the parking lot behind Grant but kept her distance. When he turned onto the interstate, she knew that it would be hard to keep up with him, but she had to.

Where is he going? This isn't the way to his parents' home or his sister's home. Does he know I'm following him and is trying to jerk me around?

When Grant got off the exit, Janis didn't know where she was. She looked for a couple of landmarks so she could get back to the interstate.

This has to be a new subdivision, she thought, *because there aren't many street lights.*

She slowed down to see what he was doing. He turned into a driveway, so she turned in behind him and blew the horn. Grant was puzzled about who was in the truck. Janis reached for her purse and put it on her shoulder, her hand on the gun.

He couldn't believe his eyes when he saw her standing there. "Janis, go home. I am not going to deal with you tonight." He reached for his phone.

She pulled out the gun. "Give me the phone, Grant."

"I'm not giving you anything. Janis, what do you want?"

"We need to talk, Grant. You are going to hear me out. You are going to call off the wedding, and you and I are going to get married."

Grant laughed, and that infuriated Janis.

"Are you going to say anything I haven't heard before?"

He started to dial the phone, and she made sure he knew she had the gun.

"Give me the phone, Grant."

"Give me the gun, Janis."

Grant knew that he could physically overpower her, but he had to figure out how to get the gun away from her without either of them getting hurt. Janis had cracked up. She had really lost it. Grant knew that Clay was on his way, but he couldn't wait. He had to manage the situation then.

"Janis, what do you want from me? I have told you over and over that I don't want you. I don't love you. I love Leah, and I am going to marry her tomorrow."

"You *will not* marry Leah Robinson, not tomorrow, not any day!" She was screaming. "Grant, I will kill you before I let you marry her!"

"Janis, if you kill me, then I can't marry you either."

She was standing close and waving the gun in his face. He had her attention with the word *marry*.

"Okay. Okay, Janis. I'll call her. I'll call Leah and tell her the wedding is off, but you have to give me the gun."

"Let me hear you tell her you love me and not her and you want me to be your wife. Do it, Grant!"

Grant dialed Clay's number.

"What's up, G?"

"Leah, this is Grant. I'm here with Janis, and I'm calling to tell you that the wedding is off. I am going to marry Janis."

"Oh, man. Is she at my house with you?"

"Yeah."

"I'm on my way, G. I'll call the police." Clay hung up.

"Let me speak to her."

"She hung up, Janis."

Clay called nine one one, and he and Cicely headed to his house. They were about twenty minutes away. The police should get there quickly. Clay sped up, and he dialed Grant's number. It went straight to voice mail.

"Call her back, Grant. I want to speak to her."

"Janis, you said if I called Leah you would give me the gun."

"Not yet. I won't give it to you yet."

"How can I marry you, Janis, if I can't trust you to keep your word?"

Janis was sweating and wide-eyed. Grant had to get the gun from her. He grabbed her, and they both fell.

"Nine one one. What is your emergency?"

"I heard what sounded like a gunshot at my next-door neighbor's house."

PILOGUE

Leah went to her room and took two more pills for her head-ache. She lay across the bed and recounted the events of the day. The sanctuary and reception hall were beautifully decorated. She looked across the room. Her wedding gown was absolutely gorgeous. She thought about Grant. He was the most wonderful man in the world, and he loved her. How cool was that? There could not be at that moment anybody in the world happier. She closed her eyes and prayed.

"…If I should die before I awake, I pray, dear Lord, my soul You'll take."

And He did.

Cheryl McCullough Writes
P O Box 410971
Charlotte, North Carolina 28241
www.cherylmcculloughwrites.com

Follow me on Twitter @cmwrites1
Like me on Facebook Cheryl McCullough Writes